9

THE MAN WHO NEVER CHANGED

Books by John Selby

SAM

ISLAND IN THE CORN

STARBUCK

ELEGANT JOURNEY

THE MAN WHO NEVER CHANGED

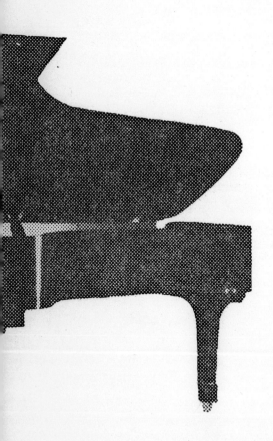

THE *Man*

WHO NEVER CHANGED

JOHN SELBY

RINEHART & COMPANY, INC., TORONTO : NEW YORK

C. 5

− BL

Published simultaneously in Canada by
Clarke, Irwin & Company, Ltd., Toronto
Copyright, 1954, by John Selby
Manufactured in the United States of America
Library of Congress Catalog Card Number: 54-9348

To E.I.N.

THE MAN WHO NEVER CHANGED

Denis Sandzen, the man who never changed, is one of the most dynamic characters of current fiction, a brilliant and disturbing personality.

At the age of twenty-two, precocious, handsome Denis promised himself he would be conductor of the New York Symphony by thirty-five. Over the intervening years he worked toward his goal, not conscious that he shattered the patterns of the lives of those about him.

1

The sparkling old Rolls swayed a little to the left as it turned into the Park at the Seventy-second Street crossover, swayed just enough to cause Denis to swing against Elisabeth, and Claire to nudge Denis. Claire instantly pulled back, little-girl fashion; Denis, in the middle, was briefly conscious of the answering pressure of Elisabeth's thigh before he, in his turn, straightened and looked hard at Stan's back. It seemed to Denis that Elisabeth and her daughter were at odds and that he was the cause. He envied the driver. Nothing seemed anything to Stan except the car he drove and Elisabeth McKee, whom he adored with a kind of monolithic devotion as substantial as Stan himself, which was considerable.

Elisabeth ignored whatever tension there was. "Wasn't that Gus Wagner and that secretary of his walking down the Avenue?" she asked. "It looked like him—like them."

"It was," said Denis, "headed south."

Elisabeth habitually gestured with her right hand; now she pushed back her blonde hair gently, and said, "Oh, Denis . . ." The hair was blonde from choice, not nature, and it was almost her only vanity.

Denis grinned. "It was my future, too," he added. "I guess there isn't a good conductor in America he doesn't have some sort of string on . . . is there, Elisabeth?"

She quite often made tangential remarks and these sometimes puzzled even herself. She said, "And on your birthday . . ."

"What?" Claire demanded. "What do you mean? I know it's Denis' birthday and I know he's twenty-two. . . ." She sud-

3

denly flushed, although neither of the others was paying the least attention. Claire was sixteen herself, and getting on with the change that was turning what had indubitably been a dark little monkey face into the kind of face people call piquant in a girl. She began again. "I mean, what I don't see is the connection between Mr. Wagner and Denis' birthday." And having said that, she stared straight ahead in the manner of one who expected neither to be understood, nor answered. But she saw her mother's right hand, the hand with the only ring she ever coveted, steal across and pat Denis' knee. The three huge diamonds snapped back what little light the gray dusk had left lying on the spring green of Central Park.

"Well—I suppose there isn't too much connection," Elisabeth said. "Only it's an occasion to make your debut on your birthday, don't you think so, Denis?"

"Um. Sure. It's an occasion to conduct a hundred men as good as mine tonight no matter if you're a hundred years old."

The huge Rolls was crossing the West Drive now. Elisabeth's hand reached for the telephone, and dropped. "Stan will never learn to stop, I mean really stop, for any sign," she said absently, "but I guess he's a very good driver."

"Um," said Denis again. He had put the others out of his mind entirely; he was thinking of the evening to come and nothing else. Turning in on himself was something he never had trouble doing. As the car emerged from the cross-drive and turned south on Central Park West he glanced perfunctorily at a girl and boy Stan missed by inches, grinned a little at Elisabeth's hand which again reached for the mouthpiece. Then he returned once more to his own thoughts, which were about himself.

The car was almost at Columbus Circle before anybody spoke, and then it was Elisabeth. "I couldn't be more excited if I were making my debut," she said, and nobody noticed the hard little lines that appeared around Claire's young mouth.

"Um," said Denis, and Elisabeth knew from experience that was all she was likely to get from him. She watched the brave young trees that lined the walk on the park side, their foliage a strange lavender-green in the late light, their branches some-

4

how more frail than they would have seemed earlier in the day. The car was turning into Fifty-sixth Street a block west of Carnegie Hall before she began gathering up the small things without which she could not have attended a concert—anybody's concert. There were her long white gloves, which she always carried but almost never wore; the gold mesh bag in which her opera glasses snuggled amongst a clutter of odds and ends; a small florist's box containing a spray of white orchids, and there also was a lorgnette without which she was lost, although nothing could have persuaded her to wear glasses.

"Yes, madam," Stan said as he opened the car door. "Pleasant evening, isn't it?"

Elisabeth smiled briefly. "Very. A quarter to eleven."

"Yes, madam."

The three seemed to be swept up the steps and into the tiny back lobby by Elisabeth's stiff white moiré opera cape. At the iron bar a whiskered little man in a derby held out his hand automatically for tickets, was given a slight frown instead, and at once subsided. The three climbed the iron stair to the conductor's room, where Denis flung his topcoat into a corner and sat down at the scaly little upright piano. He paid no attention to the others, but played the piano's first entrance in the first Beethoven concerto, and having done that, he smiled. "It'll be all right," he said, and in spite of herself, Claire smiled. "Yes, Denis," she agreed, "it will. You're too beautiful to fail."

This was a danger signal. "Now children . . ." Elisabeth broke in, but too late. Denis flung himself off the piano chair, caught Claire in his arms and quickly upended her. He yanked up her dress, white like her mother's, and slapped her behind hard a half dozen times.

"I'm tired of that old line," he panted. "Damn tired . . ." He stopped suddenly—Stan was in the door, tapping decorously although nobody had thought to close it. He was panting a little from the stairs.

"Excuse me, Mrs. . . . madam. Mr. Sandzen's extra shirt—you forgot it."

"Oh. Thanks, Stanley. You're very thoughtful."

"Yes, ma'am. Ten forty-five."

"Yes," Elisabeth turned to Denis. "I don't think——" she began, and got no further.

"I'm damn sick of that 'beautiful' business. I don't want any more of it." He glared at Claire, who glared back.

"You needn't think you can bullyrag me," she snapped. "And God knows you're beautiful."

Elisabeth had been a soprano of repute before she married Augustus McKee, and for that matter afterward. She had presence when she wanted to have it, and now she did. She snapped out the lenses of her lorgnette and looked at Denis and then Claire from what suddenly seemed a great height. "This is a very important occasion," she said firmly, "and I do not expect it to be violated by any such bickering as this. I hope you understand."

" 'Bickering!' " Claire's dark eyes snapped almost electrically. "Do you call being spanked bickering?"

"I do. Now stop." She looked at her diamond-paved watch. "We have thirty minutes. Do you want to see anybody, Denis?"

He seemed to have forgotten the spanking. "No, I don't"— and as an afterthought—"unless it's Gus Wagner."

Elisabeth nodded. "Go to your seat, Claire. I'll join you in fifteen minutes."

A little cowed, Claire did exactly that, even though the auditorium was empty except for the ushers and the two or three elderly people who seem always to arrive very early when there is no reason for it, and, thought Claire, doubtless late when there is.

Elisabeth smiled strangely at Denis after the door closed behind her daughter. She no longer seemed commanding; she seemed, indeed, a little frightened, as if it might be necessary for her to feel what the—what was he? boy? man?—opposite her was quite evidently not feeling. If I were making my debut as a conductor, as a real conductor, at twenty-two in the most important concert hall in America I could not sit relaxed like that, she was thinking. When I did make my debut it was at twenty-two, and I was frightened to the point of hysteria, and mother had to massage my shoulders and do her little trick with the back of my neck. But I was good, very good. Her right hand went to the side of her face and she held it there, as if she might be nursing a toothache.

"Even ugly old Berlin was lovely," she said aloud, and Denis looked startled.

"Berlin was what?" he asked wonderingly.

She smiled again. "I was thinking about something that happened twenty-six years ago. My own debut. It seems almost prehistoric."

Denis' hand touched hers for a moment. "I'll bet you were lovely," he said, and as always his voice reminded her of the lower tones of a clarinet, rich and reedy and controlled.

Unexpectedly, even to himself, he came out of his private affairs long enough really to see the woman before him: her carriage, which was superb, her figure which was hardly slender by the skinny standards of 1929 but yet was by no means heavy. For Elisabeth her true glory was her hair which she maintained as she wanted it at enormous expense; for most it was her skin, which was soft and fair but with a suggestion of a darker pigment which saved her from the blank blondeness of the Nordic. And her eyes, which were a sort of hazel-green, but a little darker than the usual hazel-green and very live indeed. They were innocent eyes which occasionally made men, even women, misjudge her. Elisabeth was all the more successful because at forty-eight she still looked like a young woman slightly afraid of the world—people forgot that for years she had kept well ahead of the ruck in one of the most difficult races of all. She was a concert soprano of stature and she had fought for every cubit of the stature. Even after she married Augustus McKee and his money, she still earned everything she received. It had been a good deal.

"Lovely?" She looked past Denis at the small mirror over a washstand in the corner and patted her hair unnecessarily. "Augustus thought so, I suppose." She looked again at her watch. "I'd better go. I ought to be in the box when Mr. and Mrs. Trilling arrive."

Denis laughed. "You'd never think Trilling made his mil-

lions out of washing machines, to look at that British getup."
His dark eyes narrowed. "Maybe he's part of my future?"

"Perhaps, if he's still around and on the Symphony Board."

Denis said flatly, "I've got a terrific lot to learn before I could
ever come back to Carnegie Hall. As conductor of the Symphony, I mean."

"Yes." Elisabeth again collected her belongings. "I'll leave
word nobody is to disturb you."

"Nobody wants to, except the gang from school—and I
told them no."

She hesitated. "Well . . . luck, Denis. And you'll have it."

As the door closed, he shut Elisabeth and everything else
from his mind. This he had learned as a boy, and this he would
never forget. He sat, his dark face closed and his mind set
against thought. There was no time, no thought, no worry, and
when the knocking began at the door, the fifteen minutes of
nothing might have been a few seconds or a few hours.

Denis rose quickly. "Come in," he called, and the door
snapped open. "Time, Mr. Sandzen," a bald young man said,
and Denis nodded. He walked briskly past the young man, ran
lightly down the stair, and in the wings tossed a smile at the
half-dozen men standing about, a kind of shy curiosity on
their faces. He took a deep breath, quickly crossed the stage to
the podium without glancing at the great, dim auditorium,
without seeming to hear the rattle of applause that greeted
him. Nor did he hear it: his bow was automatic and made
without the slightest feeling.

"Remember, I'll beat four, not two," he said, his low, firm
voice carrying quite clearly through the orchestra and into the
first rows of the audience. His arm went up, descended with a
snap, and the opening unison of Mozart's Haffner symphony
dealt the ears of the audience a sweet blow.

Elisabeth sat stiffly in her box. She had greeted Trilling perfunctorily, his gray-satin upholstered wife even more so. Now
Mrs. Trilling leaned toward Elisabeth. "Your hair looks adorable. I like it blonde."

Claire giggled tensely from the second row, where she sat in a curious state of suspension beside Trilling. If Elisabeth heard the quick little sound, she gave no sign. "I like it too," she replied. "I . . . I thought all three of us dark was a little too much."

Mrs. Trilling, whose vast bosom reminded people of Schumann-Heink, raised an eyebrow. "All three?" she asked with some innocence but more malice.

Elisabeth frowned at the slip. "Denis is practically a member of the family, you know. And Claire's certainly dark enough."

Exactly why she went to her mother's assistance Claire could not have said, but she did. She ignored whatever it may have been Trilling wanted to say and leaned forward. "Mother," she said coolly, "Denis *is* beautiful. I wish he didn't resent my saying so."

"Men don't think about beauty the way we do," said Elisabeth gratefully. The house lights were dimming. "Oh—I feel as if I were about to walk out on that stage." She looked unseeingly at Mrs. Trilling. "But he isn't the least nervous. I've never quite understood."

At that moment Denis entered. He doesn't even see the audience, Elisabeth thought a little wryly, for it had taken a great deal of work to fill Carnegie Hall, and some money as well. But if the audience weren't there, he'd notice that. Oh, dear, Claire's right about his looks, and the audience feels it. Ignored, it still set up an admiring, sibilant whisper, and its applause was more than perfunctory. The mystery that every audience always was to Elisabeth grew stronger now that the balconies and double row of boxes and the brownish walls were obscured and the orchestra floor was only a series of indefinite grayish rows and there were no individuals in the hall.

In a moment there was utter quiet, and through it she could hear Denis say a few words to the orchestra, see the baton go up, and for a moment, she seemed to choke up. She thought, I really can't bear it. Then the music, and in common with three thousand others, she forgot there was anything to bear.

But halfway through the first movement, with the orchestra sweeping along at, she knew instinctively, exactly the right speed, she forced her attention away from the stage. She slanted a glance at Mrs. Trilling, and was satisfied with her wrapt expression. She could not see Trilling himself, and she did not need to see Claire. Claire would be in that queer unthinking state that came over her when she was really interested in anything musical.

The whispering had died away in the box on Elisabeth's right, and on the left side Clara Boutell Meininger, her thin body wrapped as usual in something like a long strip of eyelet embroidery, was hanging half out of her box, conducting gently with her right hand and, thought Elisabeth, doubtless trying to imagine the glory of all that sound coming out of the Theramin. Clara was a character and played the Theramin because, it was said, its moaning horror gave her a wonderful opportunity to be graceful.

All the reviewers had been sent their usual seats, and all were in the house. One slept, which was orthodox. One sat lumpily with his chin on his chest, his small eyes darting about to gather whatever reaction they could. One, most noticeable of all because his bald head caught the little light left in the hall, was probably smiling as usual, although perhaps not quite so patronizingly as usual.

The *allegro* ended and the little rustle that rose from the audience died under Denis' upraised arm. It's the perfect speed, thought Elisabeth again as the *andante* began. She caught herself humming the tune and quickly left off, returning her mind to the stage. And it's the loveliest tune Mozart ever wrote, too, she insisted to herself. . . . Oh, the little grace notes don't sound like hiccoughs, thank God. And later, she thought, I wish the slow movement would never end. Later still she came to herself almost painfully when, just before the audience broke into a roar of applause, a deep and good-sounding bass voice shouted, "Bravo!" from the rear of the lower floor.

"That's Timmy Hoskins from the school," Claire said from behind. "I'd know that voice anywhere."

Elisabeth was confused. "I'm so glad he played the symphony with a reduced orchestra," she began. "And wasn't it lovely?"

Mrs. Trilling did not speak, but she nodded a firm yes. Her

10

husband's voice, warmer and less British than usual, said as usual the accepted thing: "A very gifted young man, that. Yes, indeed, a very gifted young man."

Denis walked off the stage as if nothing was tangible for him but Mozart. He was brought back three times, and he could have returned again, but instead he signaled for the piano to be pushed on and, quite disregarding the young woman who represented World Concerts, which organization had handled the debut for Elisabeth, ran up to his room and quickly poured a glass of water from the carafe on top of the piano. Then he returned to the wings and stood alone while the tangle of chairs and music stands onstage was straightened out, the piano chair was set in place, and the lid of the long black Steinway was propped up on the short stick, low enough so that he could see the second violins beyond, high enough not to confine the tone. It was done quickly, and the instant the men were re-seated, Denis entered. This time the applause was stronger—more demanding, Elisabeth thought as she turned toward the stage and settled herself.

I wonder, she asked herself fruitlessly, because of course it was now a fact, what they'll think of his playing as well as conducting? He thinks he should give 'a good sampling' of what he can do; with a little start, she realized that actually she had accepted unquestioningly Denis' decision to play and conduct the first Beethoven concerto, and that she almost always did just that when the matter had to do with Denis and his abilities.

Trilling touched her shoulder, and she half turned to him. "A very orthodox program," he whispered, "for so young a man. Doesn't he like modern music? Mozart and Beethoven, Brahms' First after intermission."

"Of course he does." The applause almost forced her to shout. "He says it's devil you do, devil you don't. If he did a modern program, the reviewers would say he was afraid to be judged on music everybody knew."

"So. He could be right, at that."

But Elisabeth had forgotten her guest. Denis had elected to stand at the keyboard to conduct the long introduction—one hundred and six bars, hadn't he said? She was barely aware of Trilling's voice as he said to Claire, "He didn't get that tailcoat at just any tailor's," and of Claire's whispered answer, "Stokowski's tailor made it." Denis raised his arms, this time without the baton. And the introduction did not seem long at all, perhaps because Elisabeth could not leave off wondering what impression the concerto would make. Would the audience consider it a stunt, or would they feel it was what she knew it to be: an honest effort to give his audience pleasure by using as many as possible of his gifts? Denis can play as well as he can conduct, she said fiercely to herself. Now, listen. . . .

The introduction had reached the cadence before Denis' entrance. Until the last possible second he held control; the closing notes got their values, no more and no less. In the two beats of silence Denis quickly seated himself, his dark hair tumbling down over his forehead, and his entrance seemed both spontaneous and simple, although it was neither. It was, Elisabeth thought, an example of iron control that very few would appreciate, but it was there. And his speed was precisely right, too. Denis said the movement was marked "fast with fire," and there was fire even though it merely smoldered at times. Oh, well—now she could relax. Only she did not; she remained fixed upon the slender, strong figure, watching as he watched the orchestra, quietly shaping its tone between his forays at the piano, seeing to it by sometimes very subtle means that it held a steady tempo and gave him firm support. Maybe, thought Elisabeth, as he began the cadenza, Hofmann was right when he said Denis ought to be a pianist and yet—there was the Mozart symphony, right as Tommy Beecham ever could make it.

Elisabeth was so far away with her thoughts that the first movement ended before she realized it, and the applause, like the sudden dropping of a great load of planks, seemed an affront. She watched Denis rise, smiling easily, bowing directly to her box, and without trying to prolong the moment, seat himself again and at once bring in the orchestra. The piano sounded now like another instrument—and Elisabeth corrected herself. Denis did so object when people said that—'There just isn't any reason why a piano always has to be brittle,' he insisted—and now it was anything but that. The boy could be improvising before a handful of friends, she thought, and certainly he is playing for friends, even tonight. You can always feel an audience more easily than see it, she said to herself, something she had learned through her own career.

Elisabeth always listened with her emotions. Now she was barely conscious when the last jocose movement began; it seemed right to her, and it raced along to the right ending, and there was Denis standing again, the orchestra standing with him and applauding almost as hard as the audience—not genteel tapping with the bow on the back of the fiddle, but the same good sound hand clapping that boiled over the apron of the wide stage.

Denis left the stage and returned, once, twice—how many times was it? Elisabeth suddenly rose and excused herself. She almost ran backstage, seeing no one and barely hearing Claire's, "Mother! He can change his own shirt." Of course he could—she only wanted to tell him quickly what she had felt coming from the audience, because that was something she understood as well as he—and he would understand.

When she tapped Denis called, "Come in," and she found him standing behind a screen swabbing himself with a wet towel, and laughing. "It's going, Elisabeth dear," he said. "Isn't it? You'll know."

"Yes. Perfectly. I can feel . . ."

"So can I. It hasn't happened to me as often as to you, but you can't be mistaken about it."

She laughed and nodded. "Oh, Denis, don't muss the shirt. Why didn't you put another set of studs in the fresh one?"

"Because, ma'am, I haven't got but one set. Here, you do it."

Denis handed her the shirt, and stood mechanically pushing back his hair while she inserted the studs and the links. "Queer I'm such a stupid with my hands, isn't it?" he asked. There was a knock; Elisabeth quickly handed him the shirt, and opened the door.

"It's Timmy Hoskins and some others," she reported unnecessarily, for the group was already in the room.

"Denis my boy," said Timmy, who was younger than Denis and fat, a figure most unlike a bass, Elisabeth thought. "Denis, it's grand and it's perfect, and we've probably got to run for our train the moment the Brahms is finished. So . . ."

Denis was stuffing in the tails of his shirt. "Thanks, all of you. First time I do the Beethoven Ninth I want you for my bass."

They laughed, and Timmy looked at his watch. "You'd better get going, laddie." For a moment he was serious. "God, I envy you," he said. "You lucky so-and-so." They trooped out and Elisabeth smiled distractedly after them.

"You're not, Denis," she said.

"Not what?" frowning a little.

"Stupid about your hands—look at your piano."

"Oh." He grinned. "Lady, I can see why you're so good in that office of yours. You just don't leave off until you finish, do you?"

She answered quietly. "No, I don't. We're alike there." And after a moment's flurried search, "Please, where did I put my lorgnette?"

He held the little flashing thing out. "I'll be ready in a minute," he said as she left. The woman from the concert bureau was standing outside, ready to tap on the door. Elisabeth looked at her through her glasses and shook her head.

"Give him three more minutes," she directed, and hurried past.

Exactly an hour later she was trying to force herself into the same room, through a twisting mob of her own friends, a few of Denis', and many more of those people who always attempt to stake out a claim on a new celebrity. Behind her she heard Trilling say, "This crush is not for me. We'll stop by your house." She nodded, and at last squeezed through the door, thinking grimly it was a blessing she had kept her figure.

At her left a young man with a calculating little mustache said with assurance, "The last movement is the test. Brahms must have meant that movement to fall apart." Behind her a woman panted. "But he's—well, he's gorgeous," and her companion snapped, "You should use the ears, not the eyes." Somebody in the far corner of the room laughed on a high pitch, and by now Elisabeth was close enough to see the desperate look on the hero's face. He caught her eyes, and drew down the corners of his mouth. "Claire'll meet us at the car," she said. "It was . . ."

But she got no further. A firm, apparently bored voice was saying mechanically, "Excuse me. I'm sorry," over and over. It was Gus Wagner, paying no more attention to the clot of people than if they had been little opossums in their mother's pouch. "Please, madam . . ."

Gus planted himself before Denis, and then Elisabeth noticed that close behind him was the secretary, a benign and slightly smug smile on her pink and cream Irish face. She could have been saying, "I told you so," to her boss, but being the perfect secretary, she was saying nothing at all.

"A very good show," Gus said, shaking Denis' hand in ritual fashion. "Come to lunch with me tomorrow."

His shadow grinned even more. "You've got a date," she said quietly, and Gus shrugged. "Change it, Moira," and again to Denis, "Twelve thirty at my office," and to Elisabeth, "Good evening, Mrs. McKee. Symphony Board next Tuesday."

"Yes." The room had quieted as if the crowd were watching a momentous meeting, which indeed it was. Elisabeth felt a little embarrassed, because there were at least six others in the room she might have asked. But she spoke only to Gus and Moira. "Won't the two of you stop by for a drink? There isn't any party—just a sandwich, perhaps."

Moira shook her head, because she knew Gus would refuse, and he did. "I can't. Always up at seven and . . ." The Irish in Moira finished for him, ". . . and he wants to walk home. I tell him, somebody's going to whack him a good one behind the ear. He even walks up through the Park sometimes."

"Don't be a clucking biddy," said Gus shortly. "Come on."

Stan had been waiting twenty minutes when at last Elisabeth and Denis appeared at the Fifty-sixth Street door. He was standing beside the car with a pleased expression on his face, and he had been with the McKees too long to keep its cause to himself. "I crashed the gate, madam," he said. "This guy there, he let me in."

"Stan—why? I gave you a ticket."

"More fun, Mrs. McKee. Besides, I gave my ticket to a woman."

They got in, and Claire roused herself. "It was grand, Denis, really grand."

"Forgive me?" he asked.

"I suppose so," reluctantly. "But it's lucky you weren't circulating at intermission. You'd have had a lot of fat ones to wallop."

"Now. . ."

"Mother, he would." She grinned impishly. "You'd have thought he was trying out for Mr. America of 1929, or something."

Denis laughed, a quiet laugh this time. "Is that all they talked about? I hope to God it wasn't."

Claire said no—she occasionally heard a remark about music. "They like you, Denis. A lot."

"Whew! It's over, and I guess I'm a little tired. Golly, Elisabeth. I'm glad you didn't have a party."

The car was wheeling north through the Park, and each of the three was quietly wrapped in his own cocoon, saying nothing. It was Denis who finally spoke, and characteristically it was a new sound, that of the tires sucking at the pavement, that roused him. "It's raining," he announced, and Elisabeth picked up the car phone.

"Stan, do stop and put up that leather thing."

But sudden showers were, Stan's shrug made it clear, one of the hazards attached to driving town cars. He neither stopped nor increased the Rolls' speed. And Elisabeth shrugged in her turn.

"I shall just have to put another body on the car," she said rather vaguely, and they were quiet until Stan drew up behind the Trilling's limousine and opened the car door. In his hand was an umbrella.

"The rain's not heavy enough to get me wet, madam," he said. "But thanks for thinking about me."

Elisabeth nodded. "Good night, Stanley. I'll go to the office at ten o'clock."

Claire and Denis ran up the steps to Elisabeth's door, and Elisabeth ascended more slowly under Stan's umbrella. Inside, peering through the glass curtains on the heavy door, she could see the tiny outline of Ellen, who was her housekeeper and personal maid and adviser and several things besides. Elisabeth frowned slightly, and said as Ellen opened the door, "Why didn't you let one of the maids wait up? You shouldn't have done it."

Ellen smiled, and took Elisabeth's long, shimmering cape. "They're very young and need their sleep, Mrs. McKee. I've made some sandwiches." She took Claire's coat, and Denis'. "I hope it went well, Mr. Denis."

"Splendidly, so they say," he answered. "And I don't want any sandwiches—just half a turkey."

Ellen's face was as small and as gnomish as Claire's, and cross-hatched with good-humored wrinkles. She smiled and said, "I'm very glad," and to Elisabeth, "Mr. and Mrs. Trilling are upstairs."

"You can give Mrs. Trilling the other half of the turkey," suggested Claire. "She'll eat anything. . . ."

Elisabeth's hand fluttered to her hair. "Now Claire! She'll hear you."

Claire wrinkled her nose and said nothing. They went up to the drawing room to receive the congratulations, carefully prepared. Elisabeth's house was wide, and the room's length was the width of the house. It had been done in the grand manner, with off-white damask valances and curtains at the three tall windows looking down on Fifth Avenue, dark paneling, a gray carpet over the floor and the right paintings and not too many of them—a Gainsborough over the white marble mantel, a Reynolds flanking it on each side—accents of blue and maroon in the lamps. But at some subtle point Elisabeth's love of comfort had taken over. The furniture was good, but it could be used without risking bruises. Two pairs of Italian side chairs

did not belong at all, and yet were right. And the fuel in the fireplace was combustible.

"Splendid," said Mr. Trilling in his brittle, high voice. "A great talent."

Denis did not always say the right things, but now he did. "A talent with a lot to learn, sir."

"Very commendable," put in Mrs. Trilling, who had installed her two hundred twenty-five pounds in the exact center of a sofa flanking the fireplace, and seemed likely to stay there forever. Her voice was dark and low and seemed odd coming from her round little baby mouth. "So many children think one robin makes the spring."

"Robin?" said Elisabeth, her mind on the concert and her hands busy with the champagne. "Oh, certainly. The spring." She handed the bottle to Mr. Trilling. "Pour for us, and let's drink to Denis."

It was done, and it was Claire who forestalled the speech Trilling could have made. When Ellen appeared with the sandwiches they were on their second glass of champagne, and Denis at last was himself—one of his selves, the relaxed one. And by the time the Trillings left he had had another glass, and felt a little tiddley—and more than a little sleepy.

He was standing in an old green and black plaid robe watching the lights in the houses on Madison Avenue, and trying to guess which house held the small dog barking noisily into the night, when there was a light tap at his door. It was Elisabeth.

"I just wanted to say how proud I was," she began. "I knew, of course, but it's nice to have three thousand people agree with one."

Denis crossed the room, and took her hands. "Maybe I knew too," he said. "But what you just said is the truest thing anybody has said tonight. What good would being capable do, if nobody cared?"

"I think not much." In her mind were a good many memories. "It was probably better for me to quit last year—but there is nothing to substitute for the feeling an enthusiastic audience gives you. Nothing at all."

Sometimes Denis resented Elisabeth's hovering over him, but

this was not hovering. "I've not had so much of it, I mean in the big time. But I know exactly what you mean."

Suddenly he leaned forward and kissed her. "Thanks, Elisabeth."

She returned the kiss, and backed quickly away. "Good night, Denis. Sleep well."

"Oh . . ." and the sound was lost in a yawn. "I always do," he said lightly as the door closed.

2

Gus Wagner worked standing at an old-fashioned bookkeeper's desk across one end of his large, rather impressive office. On the side opposite the windows there was a long table with a pair of telephones and a clutter of books; the only chairs were upholstered armchairs chosen more for comfort than looks. Gus always worked in his shirt sleeves; behind a tall gray screen at the end of the office next to Moira's quarters hung his coat where he could slip into it in the moment between Moira's announcement of a female caller and her entrance.

Now Moira was standing at the middle window, looking between two apartment buildings on Central Park South toward the sliver of green running brightly north into the thin gray April haze. Moira would have stuffed her own mouth with kitchen soap rather than refer to Gus by his first name before an outsider, but she never called him anything else when they were alone.

"Gus," she said, "you're a born lucky man, so you are."

It was just about the end of the concert season, and there were reports from all over, neatly stacked on the old desk. Gus dropped a paperweight on the pile and turned. "To pick up young Sandzen, you mean?"

"Of course not. To have me to force you to latch onto him."

"If you weren't overpaid already I'd raise you."

"Nuts. I'm serious—you'd have let that concert pass if I hadn't nagged you into going. You know damn well you would."

When Gus laughed the sound was rich and warming. "Moira Dillon, colleen, whatever you Irish call yourselves— don't you know Elisabeth McKee's been pestering me about that kid for at least two years? So now you've discovered him."

"Sure. And I know that three days back you said, and don't deny it, 'Just another snotnose with——' "

The telephone made a disconcerting sound, not remarkable when one knew that Gus had had the bells removed and a kind of wooden rattle substituted, because, he said, bells never were in tune and it didn't matter about castanets. Moira picked it up at once.

"It's Sandzen—and Mrs. McKee."

"Oh, good God." Gus scratched his prematurely white head. "Moira, you've got to get rid of her. Take her to lunch alone. Do anything."

"Damn. And you get that lovely boy, and I take out the mother hen. Or whatever." Moira scowled at Gus. "And why don't you play like very busy, and have lunch sent in? Then it won't look quite so obvious."

Gus was headed for his jacket. "Sure. I'll make the excuses and you do the rest."

The two went out into the reception room, Gus still scratching his head but now looking distrait, harried, hurried. In a couple of minutes he had Denis in his office, and Elisabeth, looking over her shoulder in mild wonder, was leaving with Moira. "Oh, the poor man," Moira was saying. "It's the end of the season and all that, and how he'll ever get everything done I don't know."

Moira would have been surprised to know that Elisabeth had herself done a good day's work in her office, selling stocks, putting the proceeds in safe places, fighting off droves of customers' men, each of whom had precisely the proper stock at prices Elisabeth's ready intuition and genuinely hard study told her were enormously above the level of reason. And Gus would not have been surprised, for he was doing exactly the same thing on a less grand scale.

Now he snatched off his coat, and ordered Denis to shed his as well. "I want to see you without your shirt," he added. "Take that off too." He grinned at Denis' puzzlement. "Look, son," he went on. "This isn't funny business. I put a good many thousands into young Kleinfeld a few seasons back, and he turned out to be half eaten up with tuberculosis. It takes a strong back as well as a good head to be a conductor."

Denis threw his shirt across the back of a chair; he wore no undershirt. There was a rather tentative grin on his dark face; his heavy eyebrows seemed to be tucked up in the middle, and his square jaw was relieved by sensuous lips now turned up at the ends.

"You're built like the proverbial brick you-know-what," Gus announced. "What's that deep scar on your belly?" He pointed to something that might have been a clumsy incision by a drunken surgeon, a deep scar that began in Denis' exact middle a few inches below the line of his nipples, and disappeared under his belt. The boy's lips straightened and his dark eyes cooled at once.

"I was thrown out of a window when I was a kid. It was a fire. I landed on a fence and——"

Gus backed away as adroitly as an insect whose antennae had touched danger. "But you're all right now, I can see."

Denis looked out at the Park a second. "Yes. I'm fine."

"Good. Pastrami sandwich and beer and some apple pie all right?" And when Denis nodded Gus picked up the telephone and gave the operator the order. "Now walk across the room."

Denis walked.

"Good carriage. How tall are you?"

"Five eleven."

"Fine. Just right. Above six feet's a dangerous height when

you're stuck on a box over everybody's head. Bad habits galore, I suppose. Smoke? Drink like a fish? Whore a lot?"

Denis was catching up with Gus in his fashion. He smiled. "Yes, I smoke. I don't drink much, and I don't have time to go around seducing girls."

"Hum," Gus grunted. "Plenty girls you don't have to seduce. Where'd you get that dark skin—put on your shirt—being a Swede?"

"My mother was from the south of France, from Nice."

Gus nodded. "I see where the Denis came from, too."

"Her name was Denise," soberly. "She was a pianist like my father. . . . Mr. Wagner, what's all this got to do with my job?"

Gus turned sharply; he was at the door admitting the girl with the food and not wondering at all at the miraculous speed with which it had come, thanks to Moira's having stopped at the delicatessen to order the standard Wagner luncheon. "Your job? That's the most sensible phrase I've heard from a kid your age in many a long moon. Denis, my boy, that's exactly what your kind of thing is. A goddam hard job, and one you'll never shake."

"I don't want to shake it. I'm going to like it."

"No accent, either. How come?"

"My people spoke English, mostly. And I was pretty young when they—died."

Gus did not push the inquiry—there would be other chances. "Here. Take a sandwich." He looked sharply into the box. "That Moira's been mixed up in this—I said two sandwiches and there are four." He glanced at Denis, who looked slightly puzzled. "She says it's boring to send back for more—and I guess I usually do."

"It's good," Denis remarked, but Gus paid no attention.

"Now," he began, "you listen to me. You think back over the conductors you've heard. Look at Bruno Walter's sort of shy beauty. And Stokowski's figure and hair and beautiful tail coats. And Pierre Monteux's sort of roly-poly cuteness—not a woman sees him but wants to push him over to see if he'll bounce back up.

"You've got the looks—and take my advice, don't ever let that dark brown hair of yours look really combed. Let it fall down like it does now. Where was I? Oh—and you've got distinctive looks. Women will love that sort of sulky look you've got."

He stopped short as Denis snapped, "The hell with them. I can't help——"

"No. Thank God." Gus threw the crusts of his first sandwich into the wastebasket, and picked up another. "Don't get touchy. This is kind of like buying a roast in a butcher's shop. And don't forget that I already know pretty well what you can do musically. I heard you last night, and it was goddam good. I thought you were a fool to be your own soloist, and I was wrong. It didn't sound like a stunt. Damn. . . ." He explored the box again. "Moira slipped."

He picked up the phone. "Sadie, get me two more bottles of beer. What they call beer, these days." Then he turned back to Denis.

"And I've talked lately with Hans Mayor—you couldn't have had a better teacher. And I guess you've been a damn good pupil, for that matter. What I mean is that I believe in your ability, and all I want to know is whether you can stand the gaff." He licked his fingers, finished the first installment of his beer. "You can, I think."

His guest was watching, his attention trapped by the curious combination of gifts paraded before him. Gus waited until Denis said slowly, "Yes. I can take whatever I have to take. I've worked pretty hard as it is."

Gus nodded. "Damn hard. You knew exactly what you were doing, last night. And you've got the flair—right speed, right balance—hell, you know what I mean. Come in." He took the beer and waved Sadie out. "Imagine having to bootleg beer. My God."

Denis grinned and reached out for his second bottle. "Mr. Wagner, what do I do next?"

"Hold your hat, boy. You're going South. You're going to conduct a brand-new orchestra. Maybe not even as good as the student orchestra over in Philadelphia." He smiled at Denis, his red face almost boyish. "You're going to learn routine in a town that's musical enough, but hasn't had any orchestra of its own for a godawful time, if ever. And you're going to work like a son-of-a-bitch, Denis. Believe me."

Denis stared hard at Gus, then shook his head dog-fashion. "Whew!" he said, and swallowed. "Will they take anybody as young as I am?"

"Yes, if I say so. And I will. Don't forget, sonny, I damn near have a corner on conductors in this fair land of ours. And likewise a good reputation. People may kick a little, but they believe me." His eyes narrowed slightly. "It'll cost you ten per cent of your first year's salary, maybe longer. Fifteen on guest jobs and twenty for radio and so on—if any. Don't count on much of that at first."

Things were whirling along, and Denis was a little shaken. "That's fine with me. Only—well—you see I had a little money and it took the last of it for the concert last night. So I don't——"

But that, too, Gus knew. His instinct kept him from adding that he knew the money had given out long before the concert. "Son, I don't want anything now, and if you need money to go down there with I'll give it to you. You're a kind of investment I think is a hell of a lot better than most of the crap they're selling on the Exchange these days. Which is another matter. Now listen to me."

Denis listened, and remembered. It was a lecture the like of which he had never heard, and never again would hear. It was just ending when the phone rattled, and Moira reported in. "Better come out," she said, and added, almost in a whisper, "Mrs. McKee isn't pleased."

"The hell she isn't," said Gus, and to Denis, "Come on."

Elisabeth was standing before Moira's desk, ruffled and ready for action. "Gus Wagner," she began, "you can't throw this innocent to the lions that way. Miss—Moira told me. I'll send him abroad myself. He doesn't need to slave——"

Gus broke in. "You know better than that. Where did you learn routine—in Carnegie Hall? Or the sticks?"

"That's different. If Koussevitzky could learn on a hired orchestra in Paris so can Denis."

"Nonsense. Koussevitzky didn't learn conducting in Paris. He learned taking a scratch orchestra down the Volga on a boat. Or some such river."

Denis and Moira were turning from Gus to Elisabeth and back again like people watching a table-tennis match. Suddenly Denis broke in. "Elisabeth, please. I think Mr. Wagner's right."

Gus shot him a quick glance. "Good. Now let's forget it. And call me Gus from here on out."

For a moment Elisabeth seemed to pout. Then she laughed a reasonably convincing laugh. "I'm outvoted, I see." Her eyes were a little misty as she looked at Denis. "I'd like to help, though. May I?"

"You're a really good egg, aren't you?" asked Gus, his hand going suddenly to his rumpled gray head. He scratched his head, and looked keenly at Elisabeth, and finally said, "I just had an idea for you, but it's too much to talk about now. Sure. You can help a lot."

Said Moira with a grin that included everybody, "Wonderful!" And to Denis, "You've got a lot to do if you're leaving in two days."

He grinned back. "You had it all planned first, didn't you?"

Moira shrugged. "And why not? Somebody's got to arrange things."

Gus was remarkably silent for him, still looking shrewdly at Elisabeth. Suddenly he spoke. "May I ask you to lunch after Denis leaves? I really do have an idea."

Elisabeth nodded. "If you promise not to try to exile me, too."

She and Denis had started down the long, dim echoing hall to the elevators when Gus' voice stopped them short. "Denis," he called, "don't dance so much when you conduct. It'll look like St. Vitus' dance when you get older."

Without waiting for an answer he turned back to Moira. "Good day's work. A new conductor, the best of the new crop. And"—wagging his finger at his assistant, who winked back at him—"the Elisabeth Scrivener McKee Foundation is about to be born. I'll give her a clutch of prodigies to support, so I will."

3

Stanley infuriated a long line of cabs at Pennsylvania Station by slowly, ponderously, getting out of his seat and opening the door of the town car for his mistress. Then, as if enjoying the business, he lifted Denis' huge brown leather bag out of the car and handed it to the waiting redcap.

"Good luck, Mr. Denis," he said, and Denis thanked him.

Elisabeth, Claire and Denis trailed the redcap through the lobby, Elisabeth issuing last minute instructions that even she knew were useless. As they reached the train gate, she dug nervously into her black handbag. She handed Denis a little fold of bills fastened with a wire paper clip.

"Remember what I said, my dear—be generous with everybody and wire me if you run short."

Denis caught his upper lip with his teeth, frowned slightly. "Elisabeth—I've got a little money left."

Elisabeth answered Denis, but she looked hard at Claire. "I know, but in this sort of thing money drips away terribly fast."

"Thanks." Then he grinned at Claire. "Kiss your uncle Denis good-by?"

She surprised him by doing just that, and not perfunctorily. "Well . . ." he said, and turned to Elisabeth. "Thanks for everything, Elisabeth. I'll write you."

"Phone me, don't write."

The redcap was impatient. "Y'all miss the train ain't my fault," he finally said, and Denis nodded.

"Good-by, both of you. Maybe I'm a little nervous. . . ."

"Silly. Good-by, my dear."

As he started down the stairs, Denis looked back a last time. He could not hear what was being said, but Elisabeth was looking at Claire with an expression as close to a scowl as she ever allowed herself. Then he lost sight of them.

His wrist watch said five twenty, and his stomach said an early dinner would be good. Besides, his compartment felt stuffy. Elisabeth had insisted on the compartment, and also that he not take along the bundle of pocket scores he was packing. "It's not exactly a musical trip," she said. "Give yourself a rest from music."

He smiled his dark, self-contained smile. "I'd be lost away from it," he answered, and stowed the bundle in a corner of the bag. Now he opened it and took out the thin score of the Franck Symphonic Variations; he never had played them, and he wanted to, someday before long.

He walked back through the train, quite unconscious of the looks he got from most of the women he passed. He stopped in the club car, and dropped into the one remaining place. Better drink a toast to me, he thought, and ordered a practically nonalcoholic beer, that being the best he could do. When the waiter brought it, Denis took out the Franck score and began reading through it slowly—it was the way he memorized most readily, away from the piano, able to hear in his mind everything on the page.

The train had left Newark and whipped through Elizabeth before the man next to him could attract his attention. Finally an extra-loud throat clearing managed it.

"Musician, I see," the man said. "Mean to say you can tell how it sounds just from looking at that stuff? Me, I can't tell one note from another—can't carry a tune in a basket, my wife says. . . ."

"That's unfortunate," Denis broke in, and tried to return to his score.

"I dunno." The man pulled at the dewlaps below his bumpy chin. "Hasn't cost me much so far, I figure."

"I make my living out of music," Denis said rather shortly. "And I enjoy it, too."

"Well, now." The man looked out briefly at the discouraging Jersey landscape, then returned to Denis. "Well—so what do you do? I mean——"

"I conduct. And play piano." Denis' distaste showed enough for the woman across the aisle to give him a small and secret smile. She was thinking her own thoughts about the contrast across from her: the scrawny man not old enough to be scrawny, and the dark and—yes, the word was sexy—boy. And he looked intelligent, too.

"Never could see how they did it," the stranger went on, "play piano that is. Me, I was raised on a farm with a parlor organ, and I couldn't even pick out a tune on that." Denis was closing the score. "That's the life. I've done pretty well in Chicago, but I guess you never get away from your roots. Squeaky windmill's still about as good music as you can get."

"Excuse me," Denis said rising. "I'll have to get along."

That he did, but he took with him the remark about roots. After dinner, after the train had slunk through Philadelphia and Baltimore and the porter had made up his bed, he remembered again. He was tired, and he would have liked very much to read himself to sleep quickly, and to waken next morning where? Tennessee? Georgia? But wherever it might be, fresh and ready.

He undressed and got into his bed naked, as he always did. He unfolded a copy of the *World*, read a headline which said that President Hoover was sure the economy of the country was soundly based, or perhaps the new, round-faced President was merely quoting somebody else. Then he gave up, turned out the reading light, raised the window blind a few inches. He stretched his legs under the sheet and burrowed his head into the pillows, watching the lights on the edge of Washington streak by—and thought. It felt good to be detached from the world in this flying box, unreachable for once, nothing in the offing more threatening than the bumpy man in the club car and him half forgotten—but not quite. Denis remembered his remark about roots.

Denis did have roots, and some of these were earlier and perhaps even deeper than those he knew and understood, those put down into the rolling middle of Kansas. Earlier tendrils that went back to Stockholm where his father had been born, and to Nice from which his mother had come. He remembered neither of these places although he had seen them both; his memories really began in a tiny hotel set on an alleyway called the Cité du Retiro in Paris. He could remember sitting quietly at the one window in the Sandzens' one room watching the girls sewing in the dressmaker's across the narrow alley, sometimes hearing words that made his mother flush, but which he did not understand. Or hearing his mother drudging at the piano, which, with the bed, almost filled the room; or watching her mend, endlessly mend things as she waited for Helge to come home.

Denis' small, plump, dark mother was a good pianist, and tall, blond Helge a very good one, and the two played wonderfully together. The difficulty was as simple as most really crushing evils are: nobody wanted to hear them, nobody would consider seriously their determination to be the best European two-piano team of the day. Denis could not remember that either of his parents ever had said a directly discouraging word before him, and yet he knew now that the air he breathed must have been miasmic with defeat, like the air over a swamp into which the three of them were slowly sinking.

It was that year, the year he was seven, that they left for America, because by some minor miracle a flamboyantly dishonest impresario had happened to hear the Sandzens while they were being endured for a week in some small Left Bank cabaret. Denis at twenty-two guessed the man must have been drunk that night—but what he offered was enough to cause his thrifty mother to dredge the very bottom of the barrel and come up with enough (another minor miracle, that!) for tourist passage to America.

Later Denis heard about Helge's first call on the impresario, and the irrefutable fact that there not only were no engagements—that there was no interest whatever. His father had gone in desperation to his consul, and a third miracle happened, this one because of something the man in the club car would have translated as proof that blood runs thicker than water, especially when it's Swedish blood.

Because the consul's brother was president of a small and very good college, Trinity College, set deep into the wholly Swedish town of Gutenborg, he knew that the college needed someone to head its piano faculty. Then Swedish blood called to Swedish blood, in spite of the fact that one of the Swedes was married to a Frenchwoman. The consul not only arranged a small concert for Helge and Denise; he and his brother paid for it. And got a brace of reviewers to attend, and write enough quotable material to convince the Trinity officials. Glad for a living, and bitterly disappointed at the death of a career, the Sandzens went West in a day coach, and—because it was cheap and had high ceilings—settled in a bare apartment over a grocery and bakery on the Main Street of Gutenborg.

Physically, then, Gutenborg in Kansas, and Trinity College in Gutenborg, formed the double taproot from which Denis drew nourishment. There was more, which were the warm and ever more beautiful memories Denise fell back upon. Always there were little stories to tell about the South of France, when things were difficult. They came to Denise most often in the bleak winters when the wind came from the north strong and solid and bitter cold, and the snow piled against fences, and sleighs slid clumsily over the drifts, sometimes to drag in cows and horses frozen stiff in remote pastures. Denise would remember a fisherman stripped to a breechclout and the color of old oak, methodically cutting off the tentacles of a little octopus hugging his bare leg; or the way she used to hide under the skirts of the huge papier-mâché figures borne down the Promenade des Anglais at carnival time; the brilliant yellow mimosa in the garden, which needed the wind for flowering, but which always blew over once a year at least. And about her mother.

Gutenborg was easier for Helge. Denise was "the Frenchwoman" in the town, and when Denis began his own small excursions his dark little face earned him "Frenchie" for a nick-name, though sometimes it was "Spig," and once or twice "sheenie." Denis had learned his English as a baby from both his parents, a little Swedish from his father, and good French from his mother, the soft French of the Riviera. Sometimes he spoke it without thinking and the Gutenborg people laughed.

He took to the piano because he liked it, and not to soften his aloneness, for when he was ten America entered the war and Sweden's neutrality, being not too popular, seemed to pull this little Kansas Sweden together and to draw in even the French—even, indeed, the half-dozen Norwegians who some-how managed to exist in Gutenborg. Denis played as naturally as he ate; he could not remember the time when he couldn't make sense at a piano. He was playing very young, but still good, Mozart at five—he always believed his songlike tone was due to the fact that his father could not afford an extension pedal for him until he was seven. As a child he could blot up anything he heard and reproduce it; he still read at sight with ease, and found it simple to pick up the basic facts of almost any instrument he could get his hands on, excepting a violin. In an orchestra or even a quartet, yes. Alone the fiddle had no attraction for him; actually the opposite, for the only time he ever had been spanked in earnest was when his father caught him with a box of kitchen matches trying to burn through the E-string of some visiting fiddler's instrument.

"It's out of tune," he explained firmly, and apologized only under duress.

There were seasons in Gutenborg, a real spring when roads sometimes were hub-deep in muck and what few motor cars there were paraded primly up and down the one paved street waiting for dry weather. The summer was hot and usually the spring winds carried over and dust grayed the lacy elms and stocky maples. One autumn night the frost would come, and next day the maples blazed. One night still later there would be a solid glaze of ice on the millpond, and the town wrapped itself up in preparation for its "Messiah" performances at Holy Week; the five hundred voices of the great chorus rehearsed weekly and there was a feeling, somehow, of dedication about the place. It impressed even the boy who, as a very special treat, was allowed to sit on a folding chair beside the organ console and watch his father.

Denis crumpled his empty cigarette pack, and fished a fresh one from his bag. The train was rocketing through a village that might almost have been Gutenborg except that the track curved, whereas all roads ran straight in that part of Kansas; the lonely lights he watched from his dark cell might have been those of Gutenborg's farmers. But the picture in Denis' mind was of a man and not a lamplit farmhouse. The man was Ernst Wetterstrom, who was tall and a little stooped and grave of manner—courtly too. He conducted the college orchestra and more importantly the great chorus, and headed the music faculty of Trinity so modestly that mostly it seemed to be held together by natural affinity.

Denis loved the man from the moment he first saw him quietly lead the chorus into its proper path. It seemed so easy, and it was not, for there was not one house in the square little town which lacked some connection with the chosen five hundred, and hardly one that did not also have opinions about the "Messiah" formed by some member of the family in the forty years or more since a pioneer handful had first sung the work. Wetterstrom seemed never to drive and always to persuade until rebellion came, and then he was like a man of iron.

"The composer says it should be sung slowly, devoutly," Wetterstrom would say. "Now, again, if you please."

The baton beat slowly, and the resonant old wooden auditorium filled with a great volume of tone which was shaped as Wetterstrom demanded. Then the man smiled and sometimes pulled his short spiky beard before he gravely returned to the business in hand.

There were lessons of another sort in the square brick schoolhouse exactly in the center of a bare, cinder-covered block. There were excursions in spring when half the town turned out to pick violets on the banks of the creek above the dam that made the millpond; and on summer nights there was Run-Sheep-Run under the arc lights; and winter nights an occasional party when even the young were given coffee with their Swedish pastries, coffee from the pot that always stood on the back of every kitchen range.

The smell of coffee and of fresh bread were always in Denis' nose, it seemed. Every morning at eleven men trooped from their stores to the bakery under the Sandzens' apartment for coffee and rusks, and Denis woke most mornings when the ovens opened below him and the bread sent up an odor that was so rich the boy almost could touch it.

A lovely odor until that night.

The Wetterstroms had called and the Stroms and the Pihlblads. Everyone played—Denis too—and with the coffee Denise served tarts made with the wild strawberries the boy himself had picked in the meadows past the mill. At ten Denis was sent to bed, early for a twelve-year-old, he thought. He went at once to sleep, and knew nothing until he heard his mother scream and felt the fierce heat and the suffocating smoke and knew in his daze that Engstrom the baker had been with the schnapps too long, and there was fire.

The train lurched around a sharper curve than usual, and began to slow. Denis forced himself to open his hands and let the sheet fall; he looked out and saw a lighted sign which read "Charlottesville," and for a moment he could watch the flurry around the station and postpone the rest of the scene. But not for long. The train started again and he was back in that same stifling room, his bare feet on the blistered floor. The floor was burning, he knew, but before he could stand his father burst into the room, and behind him crawled his mother on her knees; Denis could see her silhouetted against the light from the fire, he realized later. He heard her cough once, and then the rattle of the flames and his father's breath rasping in his ear were the only sounds in the world.

"Denise!" Helge tried to shout, but his voice was smothered by the smoke. He snatched up his son and without seeming to notice the smoking boards beneath his bare feet carried him to the window. As if the boy were a half-filled bag of unwanted grain, Helge forced him out.

"I'm coming," he shouted, ignoring the horrified calls

from the gesticulating group below, and turned back. But he was too late. The floor gave beneath him and a great puff of flame and sparks came out of the windows below. There was a thin, hard spurt of sound that might have been a scream. Or there may have been two. . . .

A buzzing that did not quite fit into memory aroused Denis. He quickly wiped the sweat from his face with the sheet and went to the door.

"Thought you was asleep," the porter said. " 'Bout to give up."

He handed in a telegram and went frowning back to his bunk in the smoking room, remembering the wild look on the young man's face and speculating on what bad news he might have been expecting.

Mechanically Denis ripped the end off the envelope. "Love and the best of luck," the message read, and of course it was signed Elisabeth. Who else, he thought, but gratefully, would risk wakening someone with such a gesture? And how welcome a gesture, just now.

Denis sat down on the edge of the berth, still shaken. Suddenly the tension snapped and he laughed until the tears came. He lay back comforted. How odd that the message should have arrived just when it did, a kind of harbinger in its way, since the rest of his life up to this moment had been good. Not quite all good—there were the awful first weeks under Hans Mayor in Philadelphia when Hans seemed to be trying to break him, to force him to admit that he did not know what he seemed to know, that he was a silly, callow boy with a flair rather than a gift. But even that had ended well.

The four years with Ernst Wetterstrom and his forthright wife seemed a little dreamlike now, thought Denis as he settled back, assured of sleep. He had worked hard at piano; he had conducted everything there was to conduct in Gutenborg in spite of the fact that he was very little more than a child. He played most of the instruments in the orchestra, always barring the violin, and on some of these he was very good indeed. While he was still in knickerbockers, he was the official

34

school accompanist, and the first concerto he ever played in public was the Mozart "Coronation," the spring after the Wetterstroms had taken him in.

There was even money. The one thing left to Denis was the insurance Helge had carried for his wife and his son—a vast sum it seemed to the boy, since it was twenty-five thousand dollars, an important amount to most Trinity College families. And one more thing—Mr. Edward Bear. When the men lifted his body from the fence and carried him to the little hospital, the nurse had been forced to pry the tiny furry little toy out of his right hand. Denis did not know how he happened to save Mr. Edward Bear—but he still had him. He lay now in the big brown bag under the berth.

The Wetterstroms had only laughed when Denis insisted on paying for his food and his room. "You," said Meta, "could make no difference at all. You buy your clothes and ice cream, but you eat and sleep as our boy."

That he did until the festival week when Elisabeth came to Gutenborg. She was not to sing in the "Messiah," but at an Easter Sunday recital, and when she arrived the Friday before she was flustered and angry. Her accompanist had been so drunk in Des Moines he barely knew which song he was playing, and in Kansas City she had sent him away. There had been dozens of telegrams and telephone calls and a good deal of hand-wringing, but there simply was no accompanist who could reach Gutenborg in time, and somebody in that God-forsaken village would have to do the job, or there would be no recital. This she told Ernst Wetterstrom in the bare, scrubbed lobby of the hotel, and when he smiled gently, she turned away rather than say what was in her mind.

"I shall have an accompanist for you in half an hour," he said quietly. "Will you come to the auditorium please, where the piano is best."

"Oh, God!" she sighed. "Yes, of course."

When Denis walked in she turned on him, and then said nothing. Later she told her friends she thought he looked like a dark angel—or perhaps devil, because she could not know what was smoldering behind his sixteen-year-old face. So she held her temper as she should have done, and merely asked quietly when Wetterstrom's accompanist would be there.

"I'm the accompanist," the boy said, and she laughed.

"Now really . . ."

"May I have the music, please?"

Whereupon Denis sat down at the piano without even a glance at her, looked at her program which he had clipped from the Gutenborg *Weekly Voice*, and said as if he were used to such doubt as hers, "Shall we start with 'Caro mio ben'? What key, please?"

Elisabeth replied automatically, and Denis began without bothering to find the music. She merely watched—and listened. When she did not come in, he began again, without a question. And she sang.

As she sang her excitement grew. Later she said, "We can change the Richard Strauss songs; they're tricky," and again he said nothing—only began "Morgen." When she came in she was flat, and he stopped.

"Would you like it lower?" he asked gently, and she flared.

"You uncanny little demon; of course not."

They finished and at the end she felt secure, more secure than at any time in the three weeks she had been on tour. She was also reluctant to let him go, and insisted he have supper with her at the hotel.

"The food is better at home," he said. "Let's go there."

That was the first act of the little play. The second was two days later, when she sang and Denis played and things went so well she begged the boy to play the last week of the tour with her. The third came that same night.

"You'll hear the chorus tonight?" Denis had asked perfunctorily. All Easter-afternoon-soloists always heard the chorus that night.

But Elisabeth said, " 'Messiah'? Not again. I've sung the soprano solos eighty-eight times, and I simply can't listen to it again."

"For me, would you?"

Later she explained that she "felt something" when he insisted so mildly, something compelling. Very reluctantly she agreed. "The first part, anyway."

She was seated in the "honor row," directly opposite the chorus in the first row of the balcony which ran around most of the white-painted, wooden hall. Denis was playing first trumpet tonight, and could look straight across the audience at her; he thought she was restless as the tenor had his opening and not too successful say. Then the chosen five hundred—women in white, men in black—rose, and Ernst's baton went up, and the first chorus struck the audience almost like a physical blow. "And the Glory of the Lord," they sang like four vast, incomparable voices, and it was truly like the glory of the Lord.

Denis could see Elisabeth reach for the balcony rail with both hands and half rise from her seat. She sank back, and shook her head as if to clear her mind and make sure she really heard what she seemed to hear. He thought tears came to her eyes even though he could not see well enough to be sure. But tears had come to his eyes the first time he felt the impact of that solid, incredible tone.

Afterward she came back and kissed Ernst, who was so embarrassed he dropped the handkerchief with which he was patting his perspiring face. Then she turned to Denis.

"I'll have to learn not to question you, I guess," she said and put her arm about him. "I didn't know a chorus could sound so. I honestly didn't."

Ernst looked quietly at her, calm again and deeply touched. "Madam," he said gently, "we believe."

That was the way it began. When Elisabeth offered to support him at Herkimer Institute in Philadelphia, Ernst explained about the money. "Then let me tell Mary Herkimer—I know her and she must have Denis. And Denis must have the Institute."

When Denis returned to Gutenborg after playing three more dates with Elisabeth things were arranged, with what pain to the Wetterstroms, Denis only guessed later. He had the summer before him and was impatient for it to end. In September he went East alone and was made welcome in the two somber, elegant old houses on Rittenhouse Square. For a while he thought Hans Mayor hated him, that Josef Gutmann went on tour so much with his specially made Steinways with their slightly narrower keys just to keep from giving him proper lessons. And he knew half the students—the instrumental half —thought he was a show-off because it was always he who could do what was wanted and do it better than the next one. At least until they realized that he did these things for the quite simple reason that it never occurred to him he could refuse.

The years whipped by as tonight the towns were whipping past his train. Once again he conducted everything there was to conduct, played piano whenever he possibly could, played other instruments as well. Once when Hans was conducting the Philadelphia Orchestra as a guest he even gave up thirty minutes of priceless rehearsal time to Denis, who was so happy he was almost drunk.

Now Denis asked himself whether all this had left him a dull jack. He had fumbled briefly at sex, but it somehow seemed not quite needful at the time. He had once got himself wonderfully drunk at Mary Herkimer's, but she had only laughed and herself walked him about the hemlock-bordered garden until she could send him home in the Rolls that everybody recognized because it had silk curtains in the back that were almost orange-red. He had seen a few plays and heard scores of concerts and had classes in the standard subjects at the University and carried spears at the Academy on Metropolitan Opera nights; even been pursued by one soprano and one tenor, but on different nights. He had seen a lot of New York, which meant Elisabeth.

If that made for a dull jack, then he was one, Denis thought, pulling down the curtain and driving his shoulder into the pillow as ready for sleep as if he had not lived his life over again in the hours just gone. Before he dropped off, he fumbled about and found Elisabeth's telegram and Mr. Edward Bear. These he pushed under his pillow.

4

Denis had thought the train unbearable, which it very nearly was. But leaving it was like breathing by mistake the steam from a tea kettle. The early evening was not only steaming; the heat was crawling so that it invaded the private crevices of his being, and from these it refused to be ejected.

Denis' light suit was beginning to droop before he reached the taxi rank; by the time he stood before the front desk at the Cleveland Hotel, he was running a handkerchief around his neck inside his collar in the irritated and irritating way of the overheated male, and his trousers were wet at the knee. "You've a reservation," he said to the thin clerk with the thin mustache who looked even more repulsive than he might because he also looked cool. "The name is Sandzen."

A slight woman with the largest eyes Denis could remember having seen suddenly appeared around the end of the key rack. "Mr. Sandzen—Mr. Wagner's office made the reservation?"

"Yes, it did," Denis answered, restoring his wet handkerchief to his coat pocket.

"I'm Mrs. Bogan. I know Gus Wagner well—please don't think I'm being—er—fresh—but I know why you're here, and I wish you luck."

Before Denis could answer, she had turned to the clerk, snapped, "Ten fifty-two," and disappeared. The clerk was impressed; he smiled ingratiatingly at Denis as he bonged the call bell. "You don't know Mrs. Bogan, but you will. The goddam joint'd fall apart without her." And to the boy, "Ten fifty-two for Mr. Sandzen."

The boy inquired for possible mail, and they waited a moment for the elevator. The room to which Denis was led was a corner room, very large, with two beds and enough white slip-covered chairs to give it the feeling of great, though impersonal, comfort that good hotels have. Just as they reached it, a maid slipped out, said, "Good evening Mr. Sandzen," and quietly slid out of sight.

"Jeez," remarked the boy, "you're getting the red-plush treatment all right, aren't you? Know Lamps—excuse me, it's her eyes—I mean Mrs. Bogan?"

"I just met her."

"She likes you—lookit that, windows open, fan on, damn' if I don't think the maid'd scrub your back if you wanted it."

Denis laughed. "I'll just stand under the cold water."

"Yes, sir. Anything more I can do?"

Elisabeth had said to be generous. Denis held out a dollar. "No, thanks. All I want is a shower."

"Good night. I'm Number Fifteen if you want me."

"Wait a minute." Denis usually did not care much whether he had a drink or not, but now he wanted one badly. "How about a quart of bourbon?" He could have a quiet drink, order up food, have a nightcap, go to bed under the lazy-seeming ceiling fan.

"Could be. Rotgut ten; bonded fourteen."

"Bonded."

Ten minutes later the boy was back with a small canvas bag Denis had never seen. "You forgot this," he said grinning, and took his money.

The whisky was good, and Denis poured himself a generous drink, the kind of drink Elisabeth was always pouring, sometimes with disastrous effect on old ladies who held the odd misconception that sherry, even taken by the tumblerful, was an innocuous drink. He filled the glass with ice water, shed his damp clothes, and forced himself to sit on the sill of one of the two large windows. As he did, he felt again the tightening in his belly that nearly all heights gave him. He was not even thinking about his work, but now he knew what disturbed him when he mounted the podium in Carnegie Hall, what always disturbed him. It was the feeling of nothing at his back, and he made up his mind what to do about it. There certainly was no law against having a railing behind him—and he would.

It was as if he were picking himself up and forcing himself to look out and down—but he looked, and there before him was his future. At least his next three or four years.

East, as far as the late dusk would allow him to see, there was flatness, splotched with green turning gray under the fading light—a few spires, a tall church protected by a very large cross, the railway station at which his train had left him.

But the view was different from the south window. Over the tops of two or three small buildings huddled close to the hotel was a wide street, Canal Street, down the center of which four busy trolley tracks ran, across which were business buildings, along which a band of street lights visible even now seemed to stretch into infinity. There was an almost constant *flong-flong* from the trolley bells, and occasionally the rasping screech of a car turning off Canal Street. Even though they were invisible, Denis knew that hundreds of people were strolling the street; he knew also that the men were every one in seersucker suits, or at least seersucker pants, and he made up his mind that tomorrow he would join them.

He picked up a blue and white magazine from the desk, and found a map. The Quarter, then, would also be on the other side of Canal Street, and off to the southeast somewhere would be the auditorium in which the orchestra, his orchestra, would probably play. He was finishing his drink when the telephone rang.

"This is Terence Metoyer," the warm voice said. "I'm from the *Pantagraph*."

"Oh?"

"And I'd like to talk with you." He must have heard the slight groan from Denis, for he laughed and added, "Not tonight. There's no hurry."

"You weren't supposed to hear that," Denis said. "I'm just in and hot and dirty. I'm sleepy, too."

There was another laugh. "I understand. You'll get used to the heat, you know."

"Maybe. Could you meet me for lunch tomorrow?"

"I'd love to. Twelve thirty all right?"

"Fine. I'll be here."

Denis liked the voice. It sounded friendly; even better, it sounded interested. For a moment he wondered how Metoyer knew he was in town when even Delphine St. Martin, whose baby the new orchestra was, had been told he would arrive next day. He thought of Mrs. Bogan—Lamps. That could be.

Next morning seemed almost cold by contrast, until he moved about. He ordered breakfast, shaved while he waited for it, and wondered the while where to go for seersucker suits in a hurry. I could ask Metoyer, he thought, only then I'd have to wear what I have for lunch. Mrs. Bogan? On impulse he picked up the telephone and asked for her.

"I'm Denis Sandzen," he said when she answered, "and I'll smother in the clothes I have with me. I wonder if you could tell me where to get a couple of seersucker suits in a hurry?"

He could hear a low laugh, and then she said, "But of course. Go up Canal Street to the Maison Blanche and ask for Mr. Leach in the men's department. I'll phone him for you, if you like."

By twelve Denis was back in his room with two suits in a big box. As he entered, the telephone rang. It's beginning, he thought, and he was right. He had a long conversation with Delphine St. Martin, or at least he listened to her almost masculine voice a long time, dripping as he tried to hold the phone in one hand and undress with the other. There was such a rush of information, wrapped loosely in so many words, that he could remember only a couple of things. He would see her that night at dinner, a matter confused a bit by her statement that he would get the invitation later because it would not be quite seemly for her to deliver it. And tomorrow there would be a meeting of the Symphony Board, which he would attend.

By the time she had finished, Denis was standing naked in a heap of his clothes, and it was twenty minutes after twelve. But halfway to the shower, he was stopped again by the phone.

This time it was Metoyer, who was downstairs.

"Come up," said Denis. "I'll unlock the door because I'm about to take a shower."

He made a third attempt, and the telephone rang the third time, only this ring seemed almost a snarl to Denis.

"Hold on a minute, please," the operator said. "New York calling."

The phone was between the beds, and Denis pulled up a pillow and sat against the headboard while he waited. A minute passed, he jiggled the phone. "Just a moment, please," the phone said. "They're trying to locate your party."

There was a knock, and Denis called "come in." It was a girl who entered.

"My God!" Denis almost shouted, dropping the phone and snatching at the counterpane, at first unsuccessfully. "Oh —I'm sorry."

He at last wrapped himself in the spread and half got to his feet. "I'm awfully sorry," he repeated somewhat unnecessarily, for his red face was apology enough. "I was expecting Mr. Metoyer."

"Oh?" said the girl, a rather tall girl with a very good figure capably revealed by a white piqué dress very low in the neck. She was cool-looking, and she was just as cool in her acceptance of the situation. Yet her dark eyes had gone over his body, all of his body, and they looked to be eyes that missed very little. "I guess I should apologize, not you. I called on the house phone and they said——"

She stopped when still another knock came at the door. Completely undone, Denis said weakly, "Please see who it is," something quite unnecessary, since the door was already opening.

"How nice to see you, Cécile," said Metoyer. "Coming—or going?"

"Shut up, Terry," Cécile said. "His phone was busy and I came up——"

"And he'd unlocked the door for me. I'm sure that's the explanation, although I could dream up better ones."

She gave him a look that would have singed a chicken. "I'm quite sure you could." Then suddenly she laughed, and they all followed suit. She sat down in the nearest chair weakly, her hands on her knees in a gesture oddly masculine for such an extremely handsome female.

"Oh, God!" she gasped. "Here I am in a strange man's room, and he's naked, and who should come in but the press. Oh. . . ." and she was off again.

When something like quiet was resumed, she returned to her cool manner as expertly as a ballerina finishes off a pirouette.

"I came to ask you to dinner tonight, at The Oaks," she said. "I'm Cécile de Knize, by the way, and my father's very much interested in your—the orchestra." She turned to Terry. "And you can come too, Mr. Terence Metoyer, if you can keep down your risibilities."

"Don't bow," Terry advised Denis. "That thing might slip." He bowed for both of them. "I'm delighted, and I imagine Mr. Sandzen will be, too."

Denis cleared his throat. "Of course. Is—I had a call from Mrs. St. Martin."

"She'll be there." Very sure of herself, Cécile picked up her white handbag and with a sharp look at Terry, took herself away. First she said, "The car will pick you up at five."

"My God!" said Denis, dropping the spread. "Lock that door for me, won't you? And bolt it!"

Terry smiled and did as he was asked. He looked at Denis, closed his eyes, and said, almost to himself, "Quite a picture," and pointing to the deep scar on Denis' belly, "What butcher did that?"

Denis' hand went automatically to the scar. "No butcher. It was an accident."

"Bother you?"

Denis shook his head. "There are a few adhesions, but they only tickle, sort of, once in a while."

"You were lucky. Well, have your shower—I guess that's what you started to do."

"It was. God, what a fool I felt. Look, there's a bottle in my bag. Why don't you make a couple of drinks while I dunk myself? We sort of deserve it, yes?"

"We sort of do . . . only don't give Cécile a second thought. She's seen worse, God knows." Terry watched Denis into the bathroom, a thoughtful, almost sad look on his face. Then he dug into the bag and produced the bottle.

The two had a pair of drinks apiece, and studied each other while they drank them. Terry was older than he, Denis decided, maybe ten years. But he was the sort with good bones and not too much flesh who would never look really old, and looked now a youngster. He was a little taller than Denis, perhaps half an inch. His eyes were blue-gray, his hair light, and he had a deep tan. He had, too, an easy manner and a casual way of putting things that minimized the fact that he knew much about music, which did not seem strange or even noticeable to Denis, but also much about things quite divorced from music.

They talked over the drinks, and although it was not Denis' first interview by a good deal, it was easily his least painful.

"Let's eat," he said finally. "Aren't there supposed to be a lot of good restaurants around?"

"Um . . . only we'd better eat in the hotel. Sort of a gesture."

"I see. It was Mrs. Bogan who called you?"

Terry nodded. "She's a damn good friend, and I think she even knows when God goes to bed."

"I see again. Let's go."

After lunch Terry left to write his story, and Denis remembered with a start that, hours before, New York had been calling. In his room the receiver was still hanging over the edge of the table; he picked it up and flashed, and the operator answered immediately.

"Your light's been on for hours, but orders were not to disturb you."

This time there was no doubt. "Thank Mrs. Bogan for me," he said, and asked about his call. This time, too, there was no delay at all. Denis could hear the little voice so far away say, "No, Mr. Wagner isn't in. No, he can't be reached." He almost called out to Moira but thought better of it. It was, he said to himself, his Southern attitude developing. But certainly tomorrow would do.

5

He and Terry were waiting on the hotel steps when the de Knize car pulled up. In the back seat sat a tall, thin woman, rather consciously aristocratic of carriage even though she was seated. Her face was thin and bony, her eyes gray but very sharp, and her arms and presumably her legs seemed to have been added to her torso as an afterthought. She was, Denis thought, as casually put together as a praying mantis. She was also, in spite of her masculinity, someone he knew he would like.

"Hello, Delphine," said Terry as the doorman opened the door and stood aside, and to the very light Negro driver, "Hello, Pete."

He took Denis' arm and eased him forward. "Delphine, this is Denis Sandzen."

"Good evening, Mr. Sandzen," she returned, although it was not evening, being only five o'clock. "It's so nice to see you at last."

The car started before Denis realized that, although the voice had sounded deep on the phone, it now seemed even deeper, so low in pitch it might actually have belonged to a baritone. He could barely hear Terry's chuckle; this was evidently a local phenomenon which was expected to surprise newcomers. She went on without pause. "Pete, please remember I don't like fast driving."

"Yes, Mis' St. Martin, I know."

And again to Denis. "I'm sorry Mr. St. Martin can't be with us. Business, you know."

This time Terry's chuckle was perfectly audible. "Oh come on, Delphine, you know perfectly well Rats is feuding with our respected host, and you know what about."

"Terence, how can you?" But the deep voice conveyed no hint of pleading; it sounded rather as if its owner were pleased. "Mr. Sandzen ought not——"

"Look, honey. Denis is very regular and let's not play-act. Rats—his name's Rathbone, by the way—doesn't like Huey and de Knize does, or anyway plays ball. It's that simple." And Denis felt a slight pressure of Terry's leg as if to say, "Shrug it off." Which he did.

"Perhaps," Denis said, "you and Mr. St. Martin would have luncheon with me tomorrow."

Delphine was indeed old Creole, and so was her husband. But she was also in business, being the proprietor of a decorating establishment rooted, with typical disregard for appearances, in the half basement of a building hard by Tulane University. The building had come to her from her family, and therefore should be used. It was also true that Rathbone insisted her business was not decoration, but rather rearranging heirlooms for the better people of the town.

Being in business had changed Delphine a little; she took the town's hysteria over the Mardi Gras cavortings of Rex and Comus with entire seriousness, such things having meaning which dated back to her own great day as Queen of Carnival. But on the other hand she had learned to like business, and even to manage quite well when salesmen for lighting fixtures called her Delphine after one meeting.

"How very sweet," she said to Denis. "Only the meeting is

tomorrow—well, let's see what Mr. de Knize has to say." She leaned forward a little, something not difficult since she was sitting bolt upright, and turned to Terry. "How is your lovely mother, Terence?" she asked. "And when will she come back to us?"

Terry had a low and engaging laugh which seemed all the more contagious because it was never loud. He laughed now, and Denis laughed in sympathy, and even Delphine smiled. "Honey," he said, "Mother would reverse that, and you know it. She doesn't live here and never did."

"Hmm. But when is she coming down?"

"I wish I knew—not until fall, anyway."

The conversation, which Denis had rather thought would brief him on the orchestra situation, never once got around to that point. The car tore north in spite of Delphine's occasional half-smothered cries, on a straight road between cane fields, jiggling gently every half mile or so when it crossed the narrow-gauge tracks on which ran the cane cars. In the distance were low buildings: two or three were the famous "country clubs" in which the stupid might leave their money in return for flesh —a rather sorry bargain as conducted there—or lose it at roulette, which was no bargain at all.

Quickly Pete whipped to the left onto a narrow black-top road that seemed to have a second paving of chickens and other barnyard creatures, few of which got themselves killed— either by Pete or by anybody else. Another quarter hour and the car swooped up the levee, and dropped sickeningly down the other side to a double gangway of warped planks which led to a wharf-boat floating on what appeared to be barely liquefied mud.

"Man jus' leavin' over there," Pete said, pointing to the flat ferry barely visible across three quarters of a mile of river drenched in the late sun. "Be jus' few minutes."

They waited while Pete left the car, dug a gnarled stogie, charred at one end, from his jacket pocket, and lighted up. Ten minutes later he reversed the process and crawled back into the car. "Jus' few minutes to home," he announced, and both Delphine and Terry made small sounds of agreement. Then Delphine turned to Denis, her deep voice surprisingly reduced so as not to reach the driver.

"You're about to see one of the loveliest houses in the state," she half whispered. "Paul has restored it perfectly—except for the pianos."

"And aren't you glad?" Terry added.

Delphine smiled, an exercise that softened her rather horsey face amazingly. "Of course. Only I do wish he had let me use just one piano of the period. Such a—a herd of big black Steinways I never saw."

They landed and turned north along just such another road as they had left, except that this one was clear of fowl, and this time the high levee was on its right. In hardly more time than Terry needed to finish his laugh over the herd of pianos, Pete had turned left into a long drive between board fences freshly painted white. Denis realized when he saw them that they provided the first evidence of fresh paint he had seen since leaving town. But he was tactful enough not to mention the fact.

Then the house, so lovely that the equally lovely grounds were for the moment eclipsed. Cécile and her father met the car in the graveled space behind the house—and how sensible to approach such a place from its least commanding side, Denis thought.

"It's still warm," Cécile said coolly, looking square into Denis' eyes without the faintest suggestion of what she had seen earlier that day. "You've got to have the full tour, so we'd as well start outside." She clapped her hands and a maid in a pale blue and white uniform appeared magically. "Tell Edgar we'll have drinks under the oaks."

The sharp little noise made by Cécile's hands startled Denis, or perhaps it was the assurance behind it. This girl was about his own age. She was slender and her face had strength for all its nearly classic regularity. Her dark brown hair was the sort that never would blow into tangles—but still it had softness; and her dark eyes which this morning had seemed brown and now in the dusk looked blue dark enough almost to be violet—they too were different. They looked at one directly, firmly. Yet they were not exactly hard eyes. As the group turned toward the house, Cécile walked ahead with Delphine and Terry. That left Denis with her father, but both men were conscious of her, as if she had left a little bit of herself with them.

Paul de Knize looked, Denis thought, about as unlike the owner of such a house as he well could. They walked around the place on the lower gallery; de Knize watched Denis a moment, and then said, "There are twenty-eight columns, and they do run all the way around the house."

Denis grinned self-consciously. "How did you know I was counting, Mr. de Knize?"

"I guessed. Look, Delphine," he went on without a pause, "the little stand of box there is growing."

"You're a very lucky man," she answered. "According to the rules it should have died last winter."

That was exactly what de Knize looked like to Denis—a very lucky man. He was short, at most not more than five feet four, and very round indeed. His hair was sandy-red, his eyes a pale gray but full of life, his face had the deceptively good-natured look of a she-bear. He was immaculate, even his seersucker suit looked fresh in a climate where most suits went limp within a half hour. When he walked he seemed to roll, but when he stood still a kind of rocklike solidity descended at once. He seemed intuitive, and at the same time adamant; he would, Denis thought, at first try leading a group, subtly, and failing that would drive it before him ruthlessly. Now that he had seen the man Denis was not so sure Huey was using him; it would be far more likely the other way about.

Then he forgot de Knize. They had arrived at the front of the house, and stood looking down the avenue of live oaks toward the road. De Knize leaned toward Denis, touched his arm lightly. "There are twenty-eight of them, too," he whispered and this time Denis laughed.

"They are the most beautiful trees I ever saw," he said, "and it's wonderful to have lawn under them instead of a drive."

Cécile looked sharply at Denis. "That was a very shrewd

remark," she said. "Most people would rather have the grand approach and all that goes with it."

At that moment a very tall thin Negro came swiftly around the house from the other side, moving with a curious half-dragging gait under a yard-square silver tray, carrying a folding stand in his other hand.

"There, Edgar," said Cécile, pointing to a group of chairs under the first pair of oaks. They sat down and Paul de Knize immediately took charge.

"You will not have a long drink," he said flatly. "There will be wine with dinner. A very dry Martini?"

Denis noticed that Edgar was already making the Martinis; along with the others, he took his. It was at least nine-tenths gin, and the coldest thing in the entire South.

"Make it last," said their host. "You'll have only one."

"Father may look like Puck," said Cécile, "but he really is carved out of granite."

There was a brief pause and then Delphine jumped at once into the middle of the orchestra situation. Denis could listen and still look about him—at the second-story gallery and its solid, yet delicate railing behind which another maid in pale blue seemed to float from window to window as she opened the tall green shutters; at the avenue of oaks locked overhead in the late light, dusky now at their bases; at the wide lawn which, he guessed, must keep three or four gardeners busy with mowers. And at Cécile, who indubitably looked as if she would be equally at home anywhere else. She looked very smart indeed, although even he knew her blouse and skirt, both white and very sheer, were not at all what the fashions of 1929 commanded for the ordinary female.

She caught his eyes, and it was as if something physical had touched him. He felt again as naked as he actually had been that morning, and as badly poised in the face of it. Then she looked back to her father, and Denis could listen again.

"Yes," de Knize was saying to Delphine, but with one eye on his other guests, "we have a good board. We have enough money pledged for two seasons at least. But we don't have it all collected, and that's bad."

Delphine frowned. "Paul, you know as well as I that one can't force people to pay up for two years all at once. Not even you could."

De Knize never frowned, but sometimes his smile could have the same effect. "Delphine, my dear, half our dear Creole brethren are counting on making next year's pledge in tomorrow's market. Only a few of them will."

"But——"

"No buts. The only thing is this. I personally want this orchestra, and I intend to have it." He rolled a little in his chair, but the movement was not at all a fat man's movement. "I hear you're as good a pianist as you are a conductor," he added to Denis.

"Well . . . that's a loaded question, Mr. de Knize. Any way I answer I pat myself on the back."

"That's a fact. Like to play after dinner?"

Cécile broke in. "Father, I wish that someday you'd learn not to ask musicians to——"

"Play for their supper. I know—but I don't think Mr. Sandzen will take it that way. Will you?"

"Of course not."

They ate very early, the candles in their crystal candelabra unneeded until the whole majestic parade of food had reached dessert. It was the kind of meal with the kinds of wine that could not possibly be hurried, but by eight o'clock the group had crossed the wide hall into the most magnificent drawing room Denis ever had seen. Even so, he could also see what Delphine had meant about the pianos. There were two concert grands locked tail into tail in the end of the room which looked out toward the alley of oaks, and their sleek blackness did force itself on one in a room with high white walls and curtains of grayish pink and a long beige and rose Aubusson carpet, and chairs and sofas mostly French and, as at Elisabeth's, mostly comfortable too.

"While Cécile pours the coffee, perhaps you boys will come with me?" their host said, and of course they did. The three went up the beautifully simple stair to de Knize's sitting room, and there again was a Steinway, this time the size under the concert grand. When Denis came out of the bath de Knize touched his arm. "Try the piano," he said and rather shyly at that.

Denis started the "Revolutionary" etude. . . . It was a magnificent piano, and he said so.

"But the action is stiff?"

"I rather like it." Denis was a little puzzled; this man would not, he thought, need to be told elementary facts about a piano. Then de Knize leaned over the piano.

"I wanted to ask whether you would play Mozart with me; one of the concertos."

Terry joined them. "You've been propositioned?" he asked Denis. And to de Knize, "I suppose I've lost my job for the evening."

"Yes. Or perhaps no. I'm a little timid when music is concerned."

Denis looked quickly at Terry. "I didn't know . . ."

"But of course I play. Not like you; not really well. But my mother thought once she'd make an artiste, spelled with a final 'e,' out of me. I started too late, or didn't work hard enough, or both."

De Knize was taking his turn in the bath. "Look, Denis—let me tell you something. This is a tough man and a hard man in business. In everything, I guess, except one. He really loves music and as long as he is behind you—well—you're safe."

"That wouldn't be a hint?"

"It would. Also, he adores Mozart. Also, there's still another Steinway in Cécile's sitting room. You're in an odd sort of nest, lad, but a pleasant one."

Neither of them had heard the little round man return. He had heard the last remark, and he seemed to like it, which was a relief to Denis if not to Terry. "Yes. It is an odd nest, and it is pleasant." He looked at his wrist. "I have a call due from New York at this moment. You run down and have your coffee and . . ."

There was something vaguely sinister, Denis thought, in the fact that just then the telephone did ring. And also in the instant transformation that came over de Knize. The man turned

53

without a spare word or gesture, putting the two younger men as completely out of mind as if they were two of the three legs of the piano. Quickly they left the room, closing the door as they went. "Not by a damn sight," was all they heard, and both of them were glad the phrase was not intended for them, although neither said a word until they were again in the drawing room.

It was exactly one o'clock when the car dropped Delphine at her uptown house. She remembered to ask them in for a nightcap, and was barely able to stifle a yawn as she did it. Denis and their host had played not one, but four concertos straight through, and de Knize had done a first-rate job playing second piano; what was more, he had loved every second of the evening. When he was putting the three into the car, Delphine, sleepy from sitting quiet for hours, and also from a good deal of first-rate brandy, had asked him whether he was not tired and he had laughed. "Not by a damn sight," he said, and shot an amused glance at Terry and Denis. But this time the tone was different.

"Look," Terry said after they had refused Delphine's nightcap, "it's still sort of early. Nobody goes to bed at one o'clock."

Denis should have been tired, but he wasn't. "What'll we do?"

Terry spoke to Pete. "Drop us at Canal and Bourbon," he said. "We'll take a walk." And to Denis, "We'll have a nightcap at Tony's and listen to Lulabelle for a while. Maybe her husband will be playing trumpet."

Canal looked like any wide street in any town at that hour, but a block down Bourbon into the Quarter it was different. Two blocks, and they were in a new world, or better, in a surviving corner of an older world. People were walking more slowly, as if they had no particular place to go and no particular time for arrival. The old houses flush with the narrow walk were sometimes shuttered, but not with the finality of shutters on the other side of Canal. Light was behind them, and movement too. Girls seemed to walk more easily, more naturally, and boys, all hatless as were Denis and Terry, made conversation entirely of hints, finishing few sentences. Four sailors in whites were drinking needled near-beer from paper cups on a corner, buying hot dogs from a cart in the gutter. Across the street a corner door was open under an elaborate iron balcony, and as they passed, the incredibly raucous voice of a woman split the night with a version of "Everybody's Doin' It" that could only have been printed on asbestos.

"I'm pretty sure you'll be living in town for a while," Terry said after a moment, "and all this won't seem so remarkable to you a year from now." They walked in the gutter past a group of tourists with faces still eager and still puzzled at half past one. "There's everything in the world in the Quarter," he went on. "I don't quite know how to say what I mean, but—well— the thing to do is to accept it and enjoy what you want of it."

A taxi zipped out of the side street, paying no attention at all to a stop sign three feet in diameter. "There, you see what I mean? Uptown he'd have stopped; here, nobody gives a damn."

In a moment Terry turned to the right. "Here's Tony's. And I can hear Lulabelle."

As rooms go in the Quarter, Tony's was large. It was supposed to be a restaurant, and running the depth of the room on the right there was a bar supporting a few sandwiches and dog-eared wedges of pie; three layers of customers, chiefly men, pressed against it and each other. No bottles were visible. Across from the bar was a platform for Lulabelle and her piano; in between were tables, mostly occupied. There was almost no light at all, and the room seemed packed with sound, not only from Lulabelle, whose voice had the authority and something of the tone of a trombone; everybody was talking and the highest voices did not always belong to the women.

Denis looked startled enough to please his guide. "Whee," he said, "prohibition doesn't mean a hell of a lot here, does it?"

"God no. Only that wasn't what I thought you were going to say. You . . ."

Denis grinned. "The boys?"

"Yes. Final word and I'll shut up. Nobody minds, and if you're thinking it's not exactly the right place for the new symphony's new conductor, forget it." He raised himself on his toes. "See that chap at the back of the bar—the one with the cigar? That's my boss, and the best editor in town I might add."

They forced a passage back through the crowd, and on the way Terry added, "There's another bar across the courtyard at the rear. We'll save it—it's a little gamey for right now."

"Hey, Terry."

Terry slipped his arm about Denis to keep him from being swept away in the crush. "Mr. Emmons," he said, "this is Denis Sandzen."

"Well thank God you look like a human being. Thought from what Delphine said you might arrive under a halo." He laughed a considerably alcoholic laugh. "Buy you a drink—hey, Tony."

The drinks were officially rye and water, better than most to be had but several degrees under the de Knize brandy. The amenities were observed; Terry bought and Denis bought, after which Emmons' eyes seemed to glaze, and he departed scratching under his right arm abstractedly.

"He's tight, but I'll bet he goes back to the office and writes the best editorial printed in any paper south of the Mason and Dixon line tomorrow." Behind them was sudden silence; Lulabelle had finished one more of her interminable parodies. The two turned, and Denis was all but paralyzed by what he saw standing beside Lulabelle—a Negro with nothing whatever remarkable about him except the fact that one side of his face was at least an inch higher than the other. He was holding a golden trumpet loosely in his right hand. Just then Lulabelle saw Terry, and quickly said something to her husband. Terry did not seem to realize that he had grasped Denis' arm and was slowly tightening his grip. "Listen, Denis," he said, "you'll hear something."

They did hear something other-worldly; a very long, very high note as golden as the bell of the man's trumpet, and then a cascade of tone that was more pure sound than melody, against which Lulabelle improvised a slow and gentle background that seemed to stroll along without destination, without thought. The room grew quiet the instant the first note sounded, and for a space there was not even the clink of a glass. When the spell broke, at the end, someone behind Terry shouted, "Make it hot, Spider," and the golden tone shattered like glass, and pieces fell about the people bewilderingly. Behind the piano was a little man with whisks on a snare drum, and in the very corner another short man on a stool, plucking a bull fiddle.

This was not jazz; it would be hard to name it exactly. It was, Denis thought, only the unabashed revelation of four musicians, a kind of giving in terms of themselves that made entire sense at just that time and in just that place. For a half hour neither Terry nor Denis moved more than was necessary to take an occasional sip from their drinks. At the end Tony himself leaned across the bar to Terry, pulling the ends of his drooping mustache. "Good for the business, sure," he said, "and bad alla same. Nobody he drinks when they play. Too goddam good."

Terry grinned at Tony, and pushed his guest through the crush to the platform. Denis congratulated the players of course, and they were glad to meet another musician—but there was no spell now. They were only four pleasant people on a platform, and Denis was another face out of the crowd.

"Tired, Lulabelle?" Terry asked, and she nodded.

"Up all day with the boy," she said. "He's no better."

All at once the bar and the people began pushing in on Denis. "Let's get some air," he suggested, and they left.

"Better yet, let's walk to my place and really have a nightcap," Terry offered, and Denis agreed. They angled through the Quarter and stopped on Orleans Street just before they reached the Cathedral. "This is it," said Terry, and opened a door leading into a hall out of which rose a bare and very clean stair which ran up one side of an inner court. "Fourth story, but it's worth it."

There had been a few drops of rain as they arrived and by the time they had climbed the stair, the rain was falling steadily. "This is luck," Terry added, "I want to show you something."

The apartment had a large living room and two bedrooms. Terry led Denis across the living room without turning on the light. They stood in a dormer, looking down into the dimly lighted garden behind the Cathedral, and over shining slate roofs touched with the night light of the city and, typical of New Orleans, the dilute light of a moon behind thin clouds. This time Denis felt none of his usual revulsion for windows opening out on heights, for there was no sensation of height— only intimacy. He thought of the word, and turned to Terry.

"That's it, intimacy." He laughed a little self-consciously. "I mean, it's the way the Quarter seemed to me. I don't know anybody, they don't know me, but nobody feels strange. I've never felt this way about a place before."

Terry chuckled. "It's got you too, then?"

"I guess it has. And how wonderful to live right where you do. You know, even if it only rains once a month, it's worth anything to be able to watch it from here."

"Yes. . . ." As quietly as he could, Terry made for the kitchen, and poured a couple of drinks. Denis was still standing in the window when he came back, and for a moment he hesitated to break the charm. But the moment had to be shattered for his own good. So he said as matter-of-factly as possible. "Here's your drink, Denis," and snapped on a lamp. "Funny —I just realized that I have been calling you by your first name from the moment I met you. No 'may I please?' or anything."

The view faded when the lamp was lighted. Denis crossed to a long, very low sofa and stretched out. "Same here," he finally said. "Why not?" He laughed. "I don't think I ever met a man and a woman when I was naked, before—after that being formal would seem kind of silly, don't you think?"

They talked for a few minutes, and then Terry went back to the window. "It's raining harder now; I could call a cab for you, but you might as well use the spare room. If you'd like to, that is."

"Do you read minds? I was just thinking that I hated to go back to a hotel after this—even Mrs. Bogan's hotel."

"Then it's settled. Tired?"

"Now that you mention it, yes. And you have to work to-morrow. Today, that is." Denis got to his feet. "In here?"

"Yes. I'll get you some towels and show you the bath. Also, there's a brand-new toothbrush in the cabinet."

In a few minutes Denis emerged, the surface scrubbed, himself yawning. " 'Night, Terry," and reaching out he patted his host's shoulder.

For an instant Terry tensed. Then he said quietly, "Good night, fellow," and turned off the lamp in the living room.

6

It was exactly eleven o'clock in New York when once again Gus Wagner put in his call for Denis. Or when Moira put the call in for him, since Gus both used the telephone constantly and hated its mysteries with passion.

"I hope that young squirt hasn't been drunk all night," Gus said amiably to Moira. "Ever been in that town?"

Moira cocked her head to the right. Sometimes she reminded Gus of a quail, and sometimes he insisted that he would not be surprised if she suddenly emitted a "Bob White." Now she merely said, "You know I haven't. It's you does the traveling, while I stay here with my knitting."

"Humbug. You make it sound as if a business trip were some kind of orgy."

"And who said it might not be—but you? And what I hope about Denis is something else again."

Gus infuriated Moira by keeping silent; Moira was easily moved to annoyance, but never more easily than by a dropped cue. At last she said, "So you don't want to know?"

"Know what?"

"What I hope happens to Denis down there. Well it's that something touches him," and she laid stress on the word "touches." "I hope some girl, or boy for that matter, gets to him. He's the biggest gift of the kind in America, and he could be too close to perfect."

Gus went through the routine of disgust. "Women. Too close to perfect. Balls!"

"It's true, Gus, and you know it. First you wouldn't have heard the lad without my pushing." Gus gave no sign of interrupting, but she hurried on as if to forestall interference. "Now you need a woman to tell you what more he needs. I'm right."

Absently, Gus said, "Sure you're right. As always."

The telephone rang, and Moira picked it up. "No? Well, Sadie, tell the operator to leave her number at the hotel and ask Mr. Sandzen to call her."

Up went Gus' shoulders. "On the town, probably."

Moira sniffed. "And why not? I should hope perhaps he was sleeping with that Delphine woman . . . St. Martin, or whatever——"

A huge laugh from the deep center of her employer interrupted Moira, who otherwise might have gone on with her picture of Denis and Delphine in a streaming sexual rapture. "Oh God," Gus said when he had calmed a little. "You should see Delphine. She has a voice like Tita Ruffo and looks like a very, very well-bred horse."

"Yes?"

"Yes, and she's old enough to be his mother." He computed briefly. "Could just about make it grandmother; Moira, my Irish lassie, give the boy a chance with someone not more than twenty years older. That's a good girl."

Defeated for the moment, Moira laughed. "Well anyway," she said slyly, "he's certainly not in his hotel. And that—that mare isn't the only female in the town."

"No. Now beat it; I want to read this stuff. And order lunch in for me. I don't leave this room until that call goes through."

"Isn't it lucky you've got that lavatory over there, now? Might be you'll be here all night." And she dodged out inches ahead of the slap Gus aimed at her rear.

It was one o'clock when finally the operator produced Denis' voice on the wire. He had wakened at eleven, and found a note propped on the bed table: "To the salt mines; grapefruit in the icebox, coffee on the stove. See you after the meeting."

He whipped out of bed, washed the cobwebs out of his eyes while the coffee was warming, and remembered all at once what he had not thought about for a dozen hours or more—Gus' call. Then the comfortable sensation of being unreachable overcame him, and he dug about and found bread for toast, and proceeded to have breakfast. Walking back to the hotel even seemed attractive, until he dressed. Then he found the telephone book, and a card attached to it with the number of the Quarter Taxi Service, and went downstairs to wait for the car.

Nevertheless, he was an hour behind New York and he put in the call the moment he reached his room, even before his shower. He heard Moira again at the other end, and then Gus' rumble.

" 'Bout time," Gus said, and Denis acknowledged it was. He even explained that he had dinner with the orchestra's chief backer, although he left the impression that The Oaks was much farther away than was actually true, and that he had not gotten back to town until close to the crack of dawn. And Gus was mollified, even congratulatory, although "Quick work," was all he allowed himself to say.

"Now listen to me," he went on as if Denis had threatened to hang up. "This meeting, it's merely a formality?"

"Well—I think so. Mr. de Knize and I played four Mozart concertos straight through, and I said his second piano was damn good."

Gus laughed. "Was it?"

"Matter of fact, it was. He's quite a character.

"Good. Now listen. After the meeting, when they send for you, demand twelve grand, and take half that if you must."

"Yes—only I'm going to the meeting. They asked me."

That seemed to stun Gus momentarily. "Well—that's the way they do it down there, I guess. Anyway, do what I said. And remember that you've got to use as many local men as you possibly can. Your host say anything about the size of the shebang?"

"He wants a hundred, and said he'd settle for sixty."

"Well—you won't. Seventy's the absolute minimum, and you stick out for it. Tell 'em otherwise you'll go abroad. I've already told them how lucky they are to have——" Gus suddenly stopped, it being no part of his policy to allow young squirts to know what he had done behind the scenes. "Anyway, try hard for seventy. Too many things you can't play with fewer men than that."

"I know. And hadn't I better stay here and audition the men right now before they all scatter for summer jobs?"

"Of course, and don't be too goddam strict, either. It's part of your job to make something good out of crap. If you've got to, that is." Gus was silent a few seconds. "Don't forget I'm sending Van Cleef."

"Sure?"

"Yeah. He's a genius at pulling fakes out of the line."

It was like offering to lend the prime minister of Britain to the Abyssinian Empire to manage a crisis. "My God," said Denis, "do you mean it?"

"Yes. Now listen—you call me after the meeting, and I'll arrange with Van. Set things up as soon as you can, but for God's sake leave time for the news to get around the union. Maybe you'd better just wire—I don't trust you with phone calls."

Denis laughed. "Boy, I wish I could have a trumpet I heard last night. What a man. . . ."

Gus pounced. "De Knize play trumpet, too?"

It was too late now. Denis confessed, and added, "The trumpet is a Negro."

"Then you can't have him. You'd start the Battle of Bull Run all over. Now don't forget. . . ."

When Denis put down the phone, he said to himself severely, "Sandzen, you've got to learn to keep your mouth shut. And be tough. You hear me. You don't want to be the dog that gets himself eaten."

He was not thinking of Gus, however; he was thinking of de

62

Knize, and the change in his voice when he dismissed Terry and himself, and became the businessman talking with—with whom? Deputy? Opponent? . . . With the outside, in any case. For there was always, Denis was beginning to realize and early, an outside for everyone, and it could assume control if one allowed it.

The meeting was both a romp and a lesson for the city's very young conductor. Its setting was perfect: an old club on Canal Street, a kind of gem between a men's clothing store and a jewelry shop which sold diamonds on time. The dozen or more men and Delphine also seemed perfect. All were sure of themselves for reasons, generally, of family, and none was quite sure of the project he was midwifing, none but de Knize and Delphine. Each of this pair knew precisely what he wanted and exactly how it was to be arranged; Denis wondered after the first half hour why there was a meeting at all, and guessed, correctly, that it was more a matter of properly introducing the orchestra than of gaining help for the launching.

The length of the season had been decided in advance, the number of concerts a week, which was one, the price of tickets, even the conductor. Denis was there only as an exhibit—if he had been scrofulous or lame, he probably would have been asked to stay in the hotel biting his nails. Delphine and de Knize even knew exactly what the association could afford to pay Denis. It was eight thousand for the season, and that would be perfectly satisfactory, Denis said with some embarrassment, for the first round. Later . . . who knew?

The meeting began at three, and was over and done with at half past four. Then de Knize disappeared and Rathbone St. Martin appeared unannounced, and Denis discovered that he was to be given a tour of the city by Delphine's tiny, goateed husband, a man with a thin and leathery face, a perpetual and almost childlike smile, and a will equal to his wife's and much more on display. Terry, who had stopped by for the already determined results, was asked to go along, and refused, Denis thought rather too quickly. But soon he knew why.

"I'll drive," said Delphine when they left the club. "Mr.

Sandzen wants to send a telegram, so we'll stop first at the Cleveland."

Rathbone looked coolly at his wife. "This happens to be my Model A. I shall drive."

And his wife looked coolly back at Rathbone. "Then Mr. Sandzen—Denis—must sit in the back seat. I shall not trust his life to your driving unless I am——"

"Delphine!" He was a tiny little man, and his beard made him look more like a marmoset than a human, but his voice was the equal of his wife's, though higher in pitch. "Delphine," he repeated, turning into the Canal Street traffic directly ahead of the largest truck in the South, "if you so much as move a hand toward the steering wheel, I shall drive directly over the curb, no matter what's there."

Delphine half turned in the seat; looked gloomily at Denis who hardly heard, for in defiance of all law and even good sense, Rats had crossed the four car tracks and made a U-turn which snarled traffic for a block and a half. She said, "Denis, the truth is that he would. Can you pray?"

"Lutheran prayers only."

"Even those might help. Oh, God . . ." Rats had turned left, slipping successfully, but that was through no fault of his, between two trolleys. "Rats, stop at the Cleveland, now."

Rats did just that, without even answering. "Now," he said, pointing toward the church across the street, "you can go into a huddle with the Virgin, my love, while our young friend sends his telegrams. I shall wait."

And wait he did, in spite of the no-parking sign, and some rather sprightly comment from a foreigner, meaning a man from out of state, who insisted on his right to enter the hotel even though this was the back door. Fortunately, Denis was back in a couple of minutes, and Delphine's communion with the Heavenly Powers had been from the car, and not in church.

"Now, son," Rats said, "we shall show you the part of town the tourists don't see." They headed out toward the City Park, stopping briefly at the University for a short lecture on philosophy and its justification. They drove as often on the left as

64

on the right of the street, but eventually they turned into the park, Rats still delivering a monologue. "Those scraggly trees yonder," he was saying, "are called the dueling oaks; people are horrified that men pistoled each other freely under them. Fiddlesticks! My only regret is that so many survived. The town——"

"Stop." Delphine reached toward the wheel, and thought better of it. "There's a breeze, and I want to arrange something with Denis."

Denis expected an explosion, or at least a lecture on the absurdity of business under a cluster of live oaks. Instead Rats left the car immediately, and headed off toward a pavilion which was gaily rotting away a hundred yards to the left. Delphine smiled, and it was a fond smile.

"He loves to play with the iron-claw machine," she explained. "One of those glass boxes with a lot of useless toys inside, and a kind of—I don't know what you'd call it. . . ."

"An iron claw?"

She laughed, and Denis was sure there was humor behind her stern front. "Yes, an iron claw."

Denis laughed, too. "I know what you want to arrange—auditions and so on. Yes?"

She nodded. "As soon as possible. You see, summer places open very early down here, and a lot of good men will be leaving by the end of the month."

Denis explained about Van Cleef, and Delphine said she already had a list of names; people had been suggesting people, and a few ("probably not the better ones") had offered their services. They decided that five days would give time enough, and that the papers, and particularly Terry, could help get the news into the right quarters. They arranged that the season would not begin until November, that the first season would run twenty weeks, that there would be six pop concerts in addition and probably, "provided that stupid man will agree, meaning the superintendent of schools," some concerts for the children as well. There were dozens, literally dozens of things to be worked out, and by no means all could be settled under a live oak late on an April afternoon. Without seeming to notice the change of pace, Delphine said, "I'm getting hungry. Would you mind a pickup supper?"

But Denis had another idea, which was to ask his hosts and Terry for dinner at Antoine's, luncheon having been out of the question. "Lovely," said Delphine. "It's not quite proper, but may I telephone Terry when I go for Rats?" She seemed a little embarrassed. "I'd send you, only Rats might be a little sensitive, sort of, if a newcomer caught him working that machine. But I shan't be calling you a newcomer long, I hope."

"So do I," Denis said sweetly. Then his expression changed. "Look, Delphine, let's get straight on one thing. I'm pretty young, but I know"—and he stressed the 'know' heavily— "what I'm doing. It's not going to be pie beating those men into shape, and there may be trouble."

Delphine looked sharply at him, her eyes narrowing slightly. "Yes?" was all she said.

"Yes. I—maybe I shouldn't put this into words, but I'm going to—I like being liked, but you may as well know that if I can't get what I want by being the sweet young man, I intend to get it by being a so-and-so. Anyway I can, and I will get it."

Delphine had slipped out of the car and was standing with her elbows on the rear window frame, looking in at her new conductor rather as if he were a young and most valuable animal. She left a space of silence just long enough, and then said, "I think I understand, Denis. Hold down as much as you can; we go easier here than in the North. I'll be frank, too.

"I think Gus Wagner would never have trusted his most valuable talent to us if he hadn't expected us to be the whetstone for sharpening him." She looked away briefly. "He threatened once to send you abroad. I know him quite well; I've managed as many concerts each winter as I could sell tickets for. He was using that for a whip, of course. But on the other hand, he could easily have arranged it, too. I'm sure Elisabeth Scrivener would——"

"You know Elisabeth?"

"Of course. She's sung for me several times. She admires you greatly; I know. She told me."

"Well. . . ."

"Let me finish. For some reason concealed in that handsome head of his, Gus prefers to let you battle your way through down here. Probably it's a very good reason, and God knows that if you survive—and you will—you'll learn more in a few years here than in twenty years of hired orchestras abroad and slick jobs as guest with orchestras like the Boston and Philadelphia. But it puts a kind of load on us, too, don't you see?"

"I do," said Denis, and rather to his astonishment Delphine turned toward the pavilion without a word, and came back in five minutes with Rats, who had a toy ladder, a soap-bubble pipe, a couple of bags filled with jelly beans and a dollar camera about the size and shape of a box of kitchen matches. He was very proud of the camera; before they picked up Terry for dinner, Rats insisted on stopping at a drugstore for film, and the pictures he snapped of his wife and Denis were remarkably good. But it was not until he saw the prints that Denis understood why they had driven down the wrong side of two miles of streets before Rats would take the pictures.

He and Delphine were posed before a billboard. Over their heads in enormous letters was this legend. "A Vote for Huey is a Vote for Dictatorship."

When Denis came back from the North the middle of October, it seemed to him there had been no summer at all, whereas the fact was that he had been too busy to notice it. He was just as unprepared for the Southern heat as he had been in the spring, too, and just as glad to return to the Cleveland and be given the red-carpet treatment all over again. But it was expensive, and after a couple of days Denis stopped on the mezzanine for a talk with Lamps. It was she who suggested the obvious—which was that Denis move in with Terry, install his own Steinway in place of Terry's less good piano, divide costs.

And of course it was the thing to do, although for his own reasons Terry would never have dared to suggest it. It even rained the night Denis moved his bags and the boxes of scores and Mr. Edward Bear into the apartment; they had a drink to the view out over the shining roofs, and considered it a good omen for the future.

Later Denis found that the months just ended had not evaporated after all; certain events formed a kind of bas-relief in his mind. He had stayed on three more weeks after his formal engagement, and they had been studded with parties. First Cécile's, which was almost, though not quite, too beautiful with white paper lanterns swaying gently among the old oaks, and small round tables with white wire soda-fountain chairs scattered about, and champagne punch—so much of the latter that Denis and everybody else but, of all people, Lulabelle from Tony's, had to stop trying to play piano.

Then several parties in town; it was Delphine's theory that anything could be settled at a party, and if she could not arrange to have someone else give it, she would gladly furnish it herself. Because her own house was small her party was in her half-basement decorating shop. What she called the commercial stuff was exiled to the back room, leaving only good pieces (heavily waxed against damp glasses) and three dozen undertakers' chairs distributed about the place—even on the walk in front, and on a concrete half-alley at the side.

Two things happened in the heat of that spring evening. It was then that Cécile took Denis' arm, firmly steered him through a half-dozen assorted members of the Petit Salon, the Creole version of the Hawthorne Reading Circle up North, and down the dim street into comparative quiet. There, and astonishingly, she said without a turned hair, "Denis, I want to say that I'm glad I walked into your room that first day."

He stumbled a bit, cleared his throat, said nothing. She went on, "I'm a little like Paul. I say right out what I want and don't hide behind a lace fan. It's you."

"But Cécile, dear. You don't——"

"There isn't time to do much this spring, not even to talk. . . . Next fall we'll have more time."

Feeling as much of a bumpkin as he was sure she thought him, he still managed to find a few words. "Cécile, please. You've got to understand something."

"Anything," but for a second she tensed, as if to prepare

against a declaration of—what? Incapacity? He suddenly wondered.

"Yes. It's that I'm sort of like your father, too. I'm coming down to learn my trade." He took a deep breath. "By God, that comes before anything else, absolutely."

"I like that," she said, and that was all she said until they returned to the party. There his second unique experience awaited him in the person of Delphine's mother. Emilie Roman Aimé was seventy that year. In her youth she had been small, and the years had pared her down to the thinness and the tension of a wire spring. She was sitting in a Chippendale side chair that should have been in a museum, and she suited it. Her dress was black, with a few sequins strategically distributed over it, and a little rose point lace. She rested her right hand on a silver-topped, slender ebony cane, and her eyes were as bright and malicious as a catbird's.

"Cécile," she said sharply, "release that young man this instant. I want him."

Cécile did what she had been told to do, and passed on at once. Out of the corner of his eye Denis could see Delphine edging toward her mother, whether to protect him or merely to hear what Madame Aimé might say he could not guess.

"I admire you," Madame said without preamble. "Any young man who can stake his future on this decadent civilization has what I believe the present generation calls guts."

"Thank you, Madame Aimé."

"That's good, too. Gentlemen should not run off at the mouth. Even"—and she looked up at him shrewdly—"if you couldn't think of anything graceful, it's still good."

Denis flushed and caught Delphine's look. She was half smiling, as if to say, "play up, but be careful." He tried.

"Madame," he said slowly, "I think it would be difficult for anyone as young as I to compete with you in knowledge. Or even manners," he added suddenly.

"Respect, too? *Incroyable!* Young man, I shall give you some advice. Beware of Paul de Knize, for he's *nouveau riche*, money mad." (Later, when Delphine heard, she said, "But that's ridiculous. He's from as old a family as Mother. It's that he has a

69

great deal of money.") She went on in a voice that carried like the ring of good crystal. "And the others, Lescaze the egg-headed one there by the door. He's wasted two sugar plantations and a small railroad in his time. And my esteemed son-in-law, who wastes what is more precious, time. Iron-claw machines, faugh!"

There was more, but there need not have been. The "faugh" was almost enough. Besides, Madame had another and carefully concealed side Denis knew about from Terry. She might slash down anybody, including herself on occasion. But the small income she still had from the family plantation, Felicity, went as readily to pay for the lyings-in of the Negroes around Vacherie and the neighboring villages as to herself. She would not have given Rats a dime, but she would bail out a black voodoo woman from Felicity, even if it took her last penny.

"Sons-in-law are not an obligation," she was quoted by Terry, "but retainers are. For my generation, at least."

And besides the parties there had been four unforgettable, long, grueling days of auditions, but well-managed days at that, thanks to Van Cleef. It was he who gently eliminated the superannuated clarinet players hardly able to hold their instruments, boyish trombonists whose service with a dance orchestra at high school was not enough, no fewer than three young lady harpists, all daughters of Petit Salon members who had taken up the instrument because they would look graceful sweeping its strings, and all of whom had a distressing habit of getting into unexpected keys by pushing the wrong pedal several times on a page—and giggling.

But worth-while days, too, because at the end only six men had to be imported, including a young concertmaster two years out of Herkimer Institute and two years in a training orchestra in New York. It was Van who arranged the importations with the union; who must have put several bugs in the ear of the local czar, too, inasmuch as that gentleman came in person to thank Denis for having been fair to his men.

And days of fun; nights, rather. The Quarter was new to Denis, and so for that matter was the idea of spending time with no return expected. He had not done it before, and he would not do much of it after the season opened, he suspected. So he and Terry drifted on their free nights from Tony's to Pat's to the "strip pits" to the drag shows to the sailor speaks to Glicks to the French Market to . . . wherever they wanted. It was fun and something more that Denis did not guess at the time he was doing it. It was the best possible preparation for an almost monastic summer at Elisabeth's house in Connecticut, a summer of study broken only by a pair of outdoor dates at the Stadium in New York and an occasional swim in the Sound.

Only Denis did not much like swimming in the tepid Sound.

7

Today was the first rehearsal, and last night he and Delphine had spent hours over the first program; it was Denis' theory that an audience should be told in advance all the programs they would receive for their money, only this season that was an evident impossibility—nobody, not even Denis himself, knew how the orchestra would work out, what it could manage to play. Nor did Delphine know what the subscribers could be persuaded to sit through, although she was quite sure that with Denis appearing as his own soloist, enough publicity could be whipped up to start the season with what she persisted in calling éclat.

So the program was all Beethoven; the first symphony, the first piano concerto, and the fifth symphony—God knows, Denis remarked, that's a middle-aged program for an orchestra in rompers. Delphine agreed. "Nice and short, too," she added, and Denis left her house and met Terry at Tony's for—but this time he refused to call it a nightcap, because the nightcaps were now reserved for the apartment, a logical arrangement, since that was where they were had anyway.

This morning Denis decided to walk through the Quarter to the Auditorium, a singularly ugly building full of needless angles, iced with mustard-brown stucco, and appointed more for the accommodation of patent medicine conventions and chicken shows than for music. It was a good morning for walking, cooler than usual in October and fresh-washed from an impetuous early morning rain. Denis wondered a good many things—whether section rehearsals would do any good, whether he could discipline his seventy men sufficiently to keep up with him when he played the concerto, what their attitude would be about taking orders from a conductor whose age was about half the average of the orchestra, whether the morning damp would bother the strings—a great many things that he decided he might as well worry about as they came up, instead of as he walked toward them.

"Good morning, Maestro," said his straw boss, whose name was Labate. "You're early."

Denis smiled. "Yes. But I wanted to see you." He looked speculatively at the round little Italian before him. "You may not like the first program; it's all Beethoven."

Then Labate smiled. "And why not? It's good music." He hesitated only a second. "Also, if I may say so, does it matter what I think?"

"I suppose not," Denis said, "only in this particular town, where there are so few Germans, it might seem odd."

Then he told Labate what music to put out, and sat down at the house piano in the wings. It was a concert grand, but it also was old and not quite in tune. Around him a few of the men were tootling and sawing as they warmed up, and it was a heady sound for Denis. Without thinking what he did, he began the last movement of the concerto, playing the first twenty bars solo, sinking deeper into the music as he went along. He was startled to hear Labate's oboe, a flute and a violin come in with the melody as he stopped, Labate's round face grinning and his round head nodding in time. The three gathered a half-dozen more instruments as they went along, so that at the end of the passage Denis came in again as naturally as if this were a performance and played along until spontaneously the music turned into laughter and the awkward moment of taking over was accomplished almost too easily. That's luck, thought Denis, and said to the men, "Thank you very much," and motioned them to rise and acknowledge imaginary applause with him.

"Very well," he went on. "Suppose we begin. 'Cellos on my right, then violas, second fiddles, first fiddles on my left." He suddenly changed his schedule. "And we'll push out the piano and try the concerto first."

The long black box was pushed out, and Denis motioned to Labate. "It's low," he said motioning toward the instrument. "Can they tune down to it?"

"Sure, Maestro." He struck an A, adjusted his oboe, sounded the A for the rest of the orchestra. "It's only a shade flat," he said between puffs. "Only everybody won't know the concerto as well as I and——"

Denis broke in. "I know. It's just a hunch; we had fun with it before." He turned to the two men pushing the podium under the tail of the piano. "Don't bother, I'll stand here at the keyboard when I'm not playing," and to Labate again, "by the way, I want a rail on that thing. Some kind of metal rail between me and the hall. I spoke to Mrs. St. Martin about it, but she may forget."

Labate nodded a little dubiously. "So you have a rail. But why?"

"I'll tell you later." The men were listening and even if they had not been, Denis realized it might be difficult to make this assured and really brilliant little roly-poly musician understand that he wanted a rail because, years before, he had been saved from death in fire by being thrown from a window. . . . His mouth closed rather too firmly; he spoke to the men firmly too.

"Gentlemen, you can see that I am a very young man to be conductor. Some of you have had more experience playing in an orchestra than I have; some less. I want you to know that I shall rely heavily on you, but also that we can't have a good orchestra if I don't get instant obedience from you. I promise you that I shall never come to you unprepared, and I want you to promise that you will give me the same courtesy." There was a flutter of applause. "Thanks. And one thing more. Every rehearsal will end by my telling you what we shall work through next time. If any of you has a difficult part, or even an unfamiliar one, please see Mr. Labate and take your part home for study. We're starting from scratch, you know."

Then he took a slow look around the stage, raised his baton, thought better of it and laid it in the piano. "Ready, now." Again his arms went up, and they began the long introduction. Or at least most of them did. After a few bars Denis stopped them. "It's early Beethoven, it's very suave even when it's dramatic. Try it again."

They made six starts, and never got beyond the first thirty measures. Denis could feel sweat running down inside his shirt. He snatched off his tie, understanding why in this climate an open shirt was invariable among the men before him. Then he sat down at the piano.

"Listen," he said. "Let me play the introduction."

He did, nodding toward the various instruments as their entrance came around. "I think you're straining too hard at it. It's very simple music indeed."

A few feet away the solo flute said under his breath, "Says you," and Denis laughed. He faced the man, who was as young as he and very good, but also very inexperienced. "Yes, I do. And while we're talking, your flute's a little sharp." Two or three men giggled nervously, and Denis frowned. The flutist frowned, too. "I can't get down to the piano. It's too low."

Quietly Denis got up and walked through the orchestra to the man. "Let me see." He ran scales for a moment. "It's in tune—you're overblowing a little."

He could feel rather than hear the little rustle that followed him back to his place. "Now again. Ready."

It was a little better, enough so that when his entrance came, he sat down and played his short, solo passage, nodding for the strings to come in, which they did after a ragged fashion; then the woodwinds and brass; then the brief stretch of passage-work. "Violas," he suddenly shouted. "I didn't hear you."

"We can't see you," someone replied from across the piano.

"Can't you count? Remember old Theodore Thomas? He said that he'd fire an orchestra if he had to indicate every entrance like a butler at a party."

There was a scattering of laughs, but the man who had spoken first said just loudly enough to be heard, "No I don't remember, and you don't either."

Denis' dark face colored as he rose in his place, and his temper rose with him. He was angry enough to have dismissed the man on the spot, something that might have been disastrous, inasmuch as viola players and hen's teeth were of approximately the same rarity in the town. Before he was calm enough to make a sound he could see Labate rising; he seemed rather to roll off his chair and to his feet.

"Maestro, please," he said in a voice unexpectedly strong. "It's time now for the break."

Still flushed, Denis turned toward the little man. Labate's face was as pale as his southern Italian skin would allow, but also there was a warning in it, and even a gentle plea. He shrugged. "It is hot, Maestro, and maybe a Coke and a cigarette will make us better."

Denis felt both cheated and relieved. After a second or two he nodded. "Very well. Take a break." And quickly walked off the stage.

They rehearsed a solid month, and while they rehearsed the world, or at least their country, fell to pieces around them. When, in November, the first concert came round there was a strange feeling in the town, and a stranger feeling within Denis. He had had a lesson at that first rehearsal; Labate had tried hard to tell him to go gently. And he had tried.

It simply did not work. Some days it seemed to him he was conducting a kindergarten orchestra, and that the men should be holding rattles instead of violins, tin drums instead of tympanies. At last and desperately he had said flatly and without

75

qualification that from that moment on, he would rule and would brook no dissent. The next day the market crashed, and within a few days from that time, he felt in his hand a whip which was fear, perhaps a small whip, but one that sufficed. He maintained his hold on the whip and the orchestra, and he did not compromise, because he felt he was nearly always right. He was, too.

"You are very hard, Maestro," Labate said one noon when Denis unexpectedly asked him to stop by the apartment for a talk. "Very hard for so young a man. And perhaps you are right to be."

"Yes?"

"Yes, Maestro." They were ascending the stair now, and the little round oboe player puffed in spite of his great chest and its capacity, of which he was proud in his quiet way. He stopped on the next-to-top landing. "The men are not like me. They do not all understand how very good you are, how fine a musician." They finished the climb as he spoke, and Denis sent him into the living room and stopped in the kitchen for a bottle of vermouth and, for himself, a bottle of the bourbon he got through de Knize. Labate went on as if there had been no interruption.

"They are in some ways children, Maestro. But they have children, some of them. And—forgive me if I do not understand it all—there is something wrong with the banks and with money. You are tired? Do I bore you?"

Denis was tired, but not bored. He said gently, "Go on Labate, please."

"So I do. A couple of banks close up. Dufour—you know that viola who, who made trouble—he was a little rich. Now he can get no money. He is afraid now, and others, too."

Denis put down his glass and crossed to the window, the only window he seemed not to fear. Now he almost wished it were raining, because rain on the slates seemed a sign of favor from above. Labate sat quietly in Terry's favorite chair, a big chair high enough that the little man's feet missed the floor by an inch. He was looking into his glass, perhaps putting together the explanation his superior was certain to ask. When Denis put the question, he did it gently. "Labate, please say right out what you mean." He touched the man lightly on the shoulder as he passed him, and settled into a corner of the long sofa.

"Yes. So I do. It is this. I do not ask you to be more soft, although perhaps earlier I might. We are better now, and I am glad. It is not a compliment to say it, but we are better because you are more, shall we say tough? And now the men do not know what all this closing of banks will do to the orchestra and how badly they will need the money you pay. So I say that you should go on as you are."

"A loose rein on a frightened horse breeds danger?"

Labate spoke almost perfect English; he betrayed his Neapolitan birth chiefly by the sound of his voice and his quick, gentle gestures. Still this was not a direct reply, and he thought a moment before his face lighted up and he nodded. "Yes, Maestro. Exactly that."

"Good. I accept your advice." Denis' eyebrows lifted at their middles quizzically. "You also would like to know how solid the orchestra is, moneywise, that is?"

Labate's small brown hand fluttered out and down like a piece of tissue. "I did not ask; it would be rude."

Denis abruptly leaned forward, his hands on his thighs. "Please let the men know we are safe at least for this season. Not as a message from me; just say you've heard it, anything you please. But it's true; I know from Mr. de Knize and Mrs. St. Martin. They have the money—he insisted, Mr. de Knize, that pledges be collected last summer, and he'll make up the rest."

The little man drank the last of his vermouth. "It is good." His soft dark eyes looked straight into Denis' eyes. "Maestro, you need badly someone you can trust." He rolled out of the chair, and crossed the room to Denis. "Me, you can trust." They shook hands.

It was true, and Denis knew it. He went back to the window and waited there until Labate appeared below him in the street. He whistled the first four bars of the Beethoven fifth and when the oboist looked up, he waved. Labate gaily lifted his entirely shapeless hat as he turned the corner.

Then Denis stripped and took a shower, and was at Galatoire's the necessary minute before Cécile arrived, cool, crisp, commanding as usual.

Fifteen minutes before the opening Denis said quietly that he would like to be alone. Cécile was there, and left without a word. So did Elisabeth, who had arrived from New York in a considerable clutter of luggage the night before. So did Terry, who attached himself to Delphine and managed to edge her outside before she could insist that there still were things to discuss. When the little dingy room was clear, Denis picked up Claire's telegram. "A great success to the Toscanini of the bayous," it read, and beyond it he could see the sender's small, dark face. Terry had thought it amusing; it somehow annoyed Denis.

He tossed the yellow paper back to the small table in the corner and stretched himself in the one decent chair. His eyes closed, and he forced himself to see in his mind the first page of each thing he was to conduct; when he could see clearly that much of any work he had studied, he was secure and knew it. As happened occasionally when he was under pressure, there was a faint tightness under the scar on his belly; it was not a pain and it meant nothing. He yawned, looked about as if he expected to see something new in the room, rose and walked aimlessly about, touching now-familiar things. If he thought at all, it was an unimportant thought as to whether his audience would expect him always to conduct without a score because he would do so tonight. He had no intention of committing to memory everything he planned to do—even everything that first season, when his programs did not include much that was new to him. Then there was a tap at the door, and he called "Coming!"

The last conscious thought he had before he walked briskly out and bowed before an audience that filled all the hall and a little more was whether he had crushed the tails of his coat. And that made him smile to himself, and perhaps softened the expression with which he faced his men. As the rustle behind him lessened he said firmly, "Gracefully now. And remember the rests!"

As he rode along with the symphony, he began to feel pride. It was not the best performance possible of the first Beethoven, but it was in its way a miracle considering the distance covered by the month's rehearsals. They were with him. The speed was just right, and even the rough corners were smoother than he had expected. His mind was freer too, free enough to sense movement behind him where there should have been quiet. Then he understood that ushers were still seating late-comers, and his too free movement on the podium, behind the rail he had demanded, tautened a little.

A seat came down with a creak, and his mouth tightened. Dead ahead he could see Labate, oboe silent a moment, glance toward the sound, and then quickly look at Denis and frown slightly. In spite of himself Denis relaxed, and sailed into the development section more himself. When the movement ended he was still angry, however, and because he would not give the ushers a chance to delay matters he kept his arms in the air, and began the *andante* almost at once. And when the symphony was finished he merely turned to the audience and slightly inclined his head before he stalked into the wings. Delphine was there, her long face radiant.

"It's wonderful," she exclaimed. "Simply wonderful—go back. Take a bow."

The applause was gaining, but Denis shook his head. "That racket," he said. "It was incredible."

Delphine bit her lip, swallowed. "It was my fault. Please take a bow and I'll explain." She pushed him gently, and because a corner of the audience could see, he yielded. He yielded three times, and the last bow he made directly to Elisabeth, who had compromised enough with habit to put on long white gloves, but had rolled the hands on her wrists; the rolls came undone as she applauded and it was as if four white birds were fluttering. Then he returned to Delphine in the wings while the piano, a perfect piano this time, was pushed out and the men rearranged.

"Delphine—I simply can't have that sort of thing. And I won't."

She looked hard at him; this was the rehearsal Denis, not the one she saw at parties, and not even the one who had worked hours with her over programs and the other details of the season. She knew when to yield.

"It really was my fault. The town is used to arriving when it pleases, and nobody has ever cared enough to make a fuss about it."

"But Delphine! Seats falling, programs rattling, people stalking down aisles in hobnailed boots. My God!"

"Please!" Her heavy, low voice was hardly more than a whisper. After all, there were people all about. "I should have told them not to seat people after you had begun. Although it would have been a long wait outside—a whole symphony."

Denis was already getting himself ready for his concerto. He could put things out of mind and he was doing just that at the moment. He did not mean to be cold, exactly, or even offhand. "Usually the first piece will be short. Let them wait."

Then he turned away and stood for a half minute forcing himself not to think at all. He was calm when he returned to the stage, even smiling a little as he stood before the piano to conduct the introduction, remembering how awful it had been that first day, and admitting now that it had been a mistake to begin his first rehearsal with it. How long ago? It seemed incredibly longer than a month.

Nobody in town would ever be able to say how much of the furore aroused by this first appearance of Denis as both conductor and pianist was due to his genuine ability, even virtuosity, how much to the fact that this was something the town had not seen, and how much to the picture he made as his dark head bent over the ivory and ebony of the keys, his hair tumbling down over his forehead. Not six women failed to feel inside themselves the magnetic attraction of this new, dark young animal who seemed to have forgotten audience, orchestra, time.

It was over too soon, for Denis as well as the audience. There were many bravos and a hail of applause. He rose, back to audience, and bowed first to the orchestra, more particularly to Labate whose round smile was childlike and beautiful. Then he signaled the men to their feet and turned to the audience. Bow and get off, Gus had advised more than once. He remembered and did just that; Terry and Delphine were waiting for him, Terry with a handkerchief in his hand. "Swab off, boy," he said, "and go back."

Denis grinned, the spell broken, and did what he had been told. He went back again and again, and finally signaled the stagehands to close the piano and move it off. He could hear, as he and the others crossed to his room, the excited roar that audiences make when they have been stirred—a happy roar punctuated by laughs and high-pitched phrases.

"I'm drenched," was all Denis could say. "Help me with my fresh shirt, Terry."

Elisabeth came back, and Cécile and her father, who patted Denis' bare back and said happily, "It could hardly have been better if it had been Mozart."

"Thanks. Whew—thank all of you." With no self-consciousness at all, he stuffed the tails of his clean shirt into his trousers and yanked up the suspenders. In the door stood Labate.

"Ai, Maestro," he called. "I am very proud."

"And so am I." Now he did not need to be alone. He reveled in Elisabeth's kiss and Delphine's baritone cluckings and Terry's quiet, "You can't lose now, boy." He took a deep breath and looked about him, suddenly a little shy. "Whew!" he repeated explosively. "Thanks, all of you."

His audience was so much with him that if he had played the old Fifth Symphony backward, it would only have thought it a mild eccentricity. Even though people in the town normally walked out calmly at the end of any concert, secure in the fact that it was The Town and a law unto itself, tonight they lingered to repeat the intermission scene all over, and dozens of them trooped backstage, so many that the well-wishers, the orchestra and Denis were for a time in a happy whirlpool, and might have stayed there indefinitely had not Cécile begun sorting the sheep from the goats with cool efficiency, readying things for departure. De Knize was giving a party at the Cleveland this time and not at the plantation, and she had no intention of waiting at the hotel for an hour while the guest of honor signed programs for old ladies and children, and was treated to the same congratulatory phrases over and over and over.

Denis drove to the hotel in the de Knize car, with Elisabeth, Delphine, the de Knizes and Terry. Rats and Emilie had preferred to slip away together—as a particular concession to Delphine both were going to the party, but neither would risk contact with Paul de Knize. It was different with an outsider like Elisabeth, who said flatly as soon as the car started how lucky Denis was that de Knize was a man of intelligence who obviously had not been taken in by the Coolidge-Hoover "prosperity." Denis was surprised by Paul's reply.

"Not luck, dear Mrs. McKee, as you very well know. I've been busy for many months selling stock and some bonds, and putting the proceeds away where they will be safe. Just as you have been doing."

A little jolted, Denis asked, "How do you know?" before he realized that it was certainly not his concern.

Elisabeth smiled fondly at Denis, who was sitting sidewise on a jump seat, his hand on the back. She patted the hand, and told the truth. "I'm a businesswoman as well as a singer," she said. "I've never met Mr. de Knize, but I know him well in a business way. Many people in New York do."

Terry looked from Denis to Elisabeth to de Knize. "Business reminds me of those prairie dog burrows that are so complicated," he remarked, and Cécile took the rest of what he wanted to say away from him.

"It is. There's an opening here in town, one in New York, one in Mexico and so forth. But what the underground connections are only Father knows—and Mrs. McKee."

Denis thought Elisabeth was rather preening herself, and why not? With businessmen flying out of windows like wastepaper, why should not a woman shrewd enough to have sensed what was coming feel proud? He was still trying to take hold of the ethical problem involved when the car stopped at the Cleveland, but by the time the party had reached the Snake Pit on the mezzanine, he had forgotten. The room was weirdly done with skeletons, witches and similar childish conceits, and was used as a kind of club for the owner and his political friends. But it was large and reasonably well ventilated, and now full of people who probably would not be seen with the owner unless "business" demanded it—and then not in public.

Elisabeth cornered Denis as soon as possible. She came directly to her point, too, quite oblivious of the fact that Emilie Roman Aimé was within earshot, and furthermore, was listening.

"It's wonderful, Denis. Gus Wagner was right, and I'm happy to admit it."

Denis' face was shining; he too was happy, almost but not quite too happy to talk. "Yes he was—but Elisabeth, you can't know how much work there is."

"But I can. Denis, dear, I want you to do something for me. I want to sing down here with your orchestra."

He could see Emilie now. He had a long way to go before he would understand Emilie's subtle side, but her face showed no sign of subtlety at the moment. Her imperious, still handsome mouth drew down a little at the sides and she deliberately looked past him at Elisabeth. And he did not know what to say, and stumbled.

"Look, Elisabeth. You know the programs are all made up. How—oh, damn, please don't ask me now." He was confused and resentful, but even so he understood a little the reason for her request. She, too, had some of his drive. He did not know why she would bother, but she wanted this thing and she went directly after it.

"Denis, we've been very dear friends," and he knew that, translated, this meant, "I've done a lot for you." But he only said, "Of course."

"And I don't ask for things unless I truly want them. I have a good reason."

He may not have been subtle, but he could be clairvoyant

at times. De Knize, he thought. Something happened there in the car—and there was no Mrs. de Knize. People said, according to Terry, that when she died Paul's energy went from adoring her into oil. But this was not extricating himself, maundering about a long-dead woman. He suddenly said, "Will you take the soprano parts in the Verdi Requiem? It's the last concert of the season."

Now he was watching Emilie, who stood with her thin hand on Rats' arm to keep him quiet, still listening. He thought Emilie smiled approval.

"I know," he said to Elisabeth, "it's not much, and it's not exactly your style. Only what can I do—we can't have more than twelve or fourteen soloists in twenty weeks, and we've got them already."

Elisabeth looked up, and saw Cécile bearing down. So did Emilie, who noticeably turned her head away. "Yes, I'll do it," Elisabeth capitulated, and she was fond enough of Denis to forgive the look of relief she surprised on his face. And to yield gracefully when Emilie, suddenly come to life, touched her arm and said, "My dear, you must not monopolize the hero. Talk to Rats and me." Madame bowed frostily to Cécile, and swept Elisabeth away.

"The harpy," Cécile said, but low enough not to be heard by Emilie. She pulled back a little when Denis snapped, "Don't say that. She's a grand old lady."

Cécile had not crossed the big room to quarrel. "Have it your own way. You're not rehearsing tomorrow?"

Denis shook his head. "I'm going to sleep until noon, thank the good Lord."

She laughed. "And at one o'clock you're going to take a boat ride. Father's boat's here, and he wants it brought up to The Oaks."

"Cécile, you know I can't possibly. Elisabeth's come all the way down here from New York, and I can't leave her stranded."

Cécile had been very circumspect through the long month of rehearsal, but even so, Denis felt a curious tingle every time she appeared. He could not forget her promise (or was it a threat?) last spring. He could not even be sure he wanted to forget; at times the urge to impress himself on Cécile mounted almost as high as the need for putting his stamp on the orchestra. They would be alone eventually. . . .

"Who suggested leaving her?" Cécile demanded. "I'd intended to ask her, only Madame la Duchesse snatched her away."

"Oh." He felt suddenly deflated. "Why—of course we'll go. I thought——"

"That I was kidnaping you? Don't be silly, although of course I will if I have to."

Entirely off guard, Denis fumbled again. "No, I didn't think you were kidnaping me. Only you said something, last spring."

She laughed, and his dark skin seemed to glow from the flush underneath. "If you weren't so beautiful, I sometimes think I wouldn't be able to bear you." He had been leaning against a sofa; now he jerked suddenly upright.

"You won't say that sort of thing again," he replied quietly, but in a voice as hard as the gray of Cécile's eyes. "I'm no parlor brigand, but I'm not a streetboy either."

Abruptly the tight moment shattered under the impact of half a dozen quite young and rather fluttery girls. "Oh, Mr. Sandzen," the most fluffy said in a voice as sweet and as colorless as corn syrup, "you just don't know what you did to all of us tonight. It was just wonderful."

What she and her friends themselves did not know was that Denis knew exactly what he had done to them. More, he reflected sardonically as he escaped and started tracking Madame down, he was learning rapidly exactly how he did it.

8

Cécile did ask Elisabeth next day, and several others, so there was no chance for a twosome with Denis. He was puzzled. He felt himself in a sort of vise; he knew Cécile meant what she had said in the spring, and he knew also that this was no cat and mouse business.

"Look, Terry," he said one night a couple of weeks later, "can I talk about Cécile with you?"

Elisabeth was gone; a routine was established, and now they were lazily drinking beer, good smuggled German beer, in the Orleans Street apartment; outside it was quiet with the deceptive quiet of the Quarter which somehow promised movement and life behind its shutters and usually provided it. It was late November, but the cold rains had not begun, and both were down to undershorts and still warm.

"Of course. Only perhaps you don't need to." Terry laughed but not very merrily. "I'm still seeing quite well."

Denis nodded slowly. "So is everybody else, I guess."

Terry said no—but not very convincingly. Of course everybody was watching, because of course everybody who mattered knew Cécile, and she bothered at no time to conceal either her thought or her action.

"I think they are watching—I mean people who know us. I feel it sometimes. Madame, for example."

"Madame is not a fair example. She's a benign witch and knows everything."

Denis laughed. "Sure, but being benign doesn't make that

look of hers any less sharp." He pulled himself a little closer to the vertical. "I feel like a little boy saying to himself, 'I won't, I won't, I won't,' and knowing all the time that I will."

"And you don't like it." Terry wondered how far he dared go, but, like Denis' hypothetical child, knew he would go on. "How much do you like girls? Girls in general, I mean."

There was no sound for a moment. Then Denis poured the last of his beer into his glass and faced Terry squarely. "It's not a business of liking. I'm afraid of them; I've never been around them much except Claire, and she doesn't count. She's sort of like a sister." He drank, and frowning, put down his glass. "Hell—when it's music I damn well know people aren't ahead of me, but with girls I always feel as if they knew everything I know—and more."

"Yes. The trouble is they do. You give it away."

"How?" Having plunged, Denis intended to swim or drown trying. But Terry did not answer directly.

"You ever have sexual experience at all? With a boy or a girl —anybody?"

Denis flushed, and Terry rushed on quickly. "That's exactly what I mean. You don't approach the thing right; it embarrasses you. Answer my question."

The answer came very slowly. "Yes. Both."

"And did you enjoy it?"

"Which?"

"Either." Terry was determined not to help, frightened now that he was close to an answer that might close a door he terribly wanted open, yet fond enough of this young genius to take whatever might come and still stand by. Then suddenly his self-imposed curtain of coolness split, and he quickly crossed to Denis and laid a hand on his shoulder where its light pressure finally seemed to force an answer.

"Both. And neither." He looked up at Terry. "I got a whale of a kick out of the end result. But I was scared before."

Terry took his hand away, now suddenly heavy. "Where was it, Denis? Or where were they?"

"Once with a boy in Gutenborg. He was a horn player," he

added irrelevantly. "He was scared, too. And with a girl in Philadelphia I met in Rittenhouse Square. She took me home with her. She made me pay her, too."

"Oh, God. Poor kid—were those the only times?" He sat down on the edge of the sofa, now almost as troubled as Denis. "Look, fellow; I'm not just being a curious fool. I want to be useful to you, and I'm damned if I know how."

"Tell me what in God's name to do about Cécile, then. That's what I want to know."

Terry was standing in the dormer now. "It's raining a little," he said almost to himself. Then to Denis, "I know what I'd do if I were you. It wouldn't be possible for me, because frankly I don't like girls that way."

He whirled around as he heard Denis say softly, "I know," but he said nothing, waiting and almost holding his breath. "What would you do?" he heard finally.

"I'd sleep with Cécile. And if it didn't work, I'd sleep with a man."

"And if that didn't work?"

"I'd shoot myself." He thought a moment. "Or I'd force myself to believe one or the other was worth while."

Denis got up and went into the kitchen. Terry heard the icebox door open and the rattle of bottles. "Here," Denis said, handing over a fresh, chill bottle. Then one of those rare moments when he was quite free of his burden of genius struck Denis. He was now only a very young man, twenty-two going on twenty-three and very unsure. He put his arm around Terry briefly and was sufficiently free to notice that Terry was shivering, and to understand why. He said simply, "I love you in my way, you know. And I'm not as stupid as I seem. Maybe I'm afraid for no reason, but I understand what you mean and I'll do what you say."

The other looked up with a smile. "It'll work," he said softly. "I think things will always work for you. And I'm glad."

As if a stone had been dropped through a glass table top, the moment shattered with the ring of the telephone. It was Gus calling from Chicago, and even if Terry had gone into his own room he still must have overheard, for Gus had one of those distressing telephone voices that, even when consciously held down, come roaring out of receivers.

"Denis? Gus Wagner." He did not wait for answers. "I'm just in from a little party at Fred Stock's, bless him. Sascha Fibich was there, and I heard something."

Denis interposed a weak "Yes," which Gus ignored.

"When do you have him?" he went on. "First January concert? I thought so. Yes. Well, he told Mollie Stutsman that he was damned if he was going to take anything from a young twerp like you. Yes. And you know what that means?"

Again Denis spoke, this time a "No." But Gus, furious, was racing on. "Well, the son-of-a-bitch is going to pick a fight and this is what the pitch is. Heifetz has got some free time around then, and let him pick his fight. I mean Fibich. At rehearsal. Heifetz will be laying over in Atlanta, and I could get him to you overnight. Goddam that bald-headed little squirt, I'll show him he can't do that to a client of mine. I'll pay the difference in fees myself."

By now Denis had slipped back into his shell as neatly as a safe door fits its many grooves. "I still don't see why Fibich should hate me that much."

"Oh, you don't?" Gus had his second wind. "I'll tell you; he hates all young musicians. Remember years ago when he made his debut? But of course you don't, you're too young. Anyway, he was cock of the walk for a while and then what the hell happens? Heifetz happens; younger, better, prettier, too. And the fool never forgave anybody, and he never will. How're things going? Fine? Money holding out? Hell, that's a stupid question. Elisabeth McKee told me all about that. So be good."

And the connection was broken. For the night it was broken between Denis and Terry as well, although after each was in his room, he thought of the other and not so very differently.

New Year's Eve was a night of glory in the town. The Quarter streamed with urchins and their elders making noise, and in City Park there were fireworks, and all over town there was a feeling that humanity was not bankrupt after all, and that life might be thinner in the 'thirties but people would go on even if banks didn't. It was pleasant to escape practical things for a time, and Denis was subtly grateful for Delphine's decision to forget her slackening business and give a party, a shop party.

Even Madame was a little gentler; she did not exactly embrace Cécile, but she did not ignore her and there was no need of snubbing de Knize, for he was in New York. Out of some dim resource champagne appeared in time for the New Year; they sang "Auld Lang Syne" with interlocked arms and everybody kissed everybody—and when Cécile kissed Denis she said softly, "We'll skip out in half an hour," and he was enough relaxed to say, "Fine."

It was nearer two hours before they left, but Denis' freedom held until they were in Cécile's car and driving past the University. Something like a cold hand took hold of his heart and squeezed it then, and he said to himself, this is it. Put up or shut up. A group of students were firing Roman candles into the air and shouting nonsense at passers-by; under a street light a boy held a girl tight against the lamppost, and she quite evidently did not mind at all. All the town seemed relaxed and uncaring, except Denis himself, in whom the glow of the champagne was rapidly being replaced by something chill. Goddam it, he thought to himself, I'm old enough, a male and . . .

"Denis," Cécile took her eyes from the street and smiled more gently than usual, "we're not going to Orleans Street for a while." They crossed St. Charles and drove slowly into the park until they reached the same great oak under which Denis and Delphine had waited while, a hundred years ago, Rats fished things out of the iron-claw machine. The car stopped and the quiet was almost tangible as Cécile cut the ignition. The car windows were down and the early morning air was as soft as it would have been in June up north. He felt Cécile's hand on his thigh, and more. He felt the combination of desire and—was it contempt?—in her.

"You're so beautiful, Denis, and you behave like a eunuch. Don't you have feeling, Denis? Not even a kind of brute truck-driver urge?"

This was wrong he felt, and he was angry, more angry than he ever had been, it seemed to him. He snatched at her hand and moved it. "Of course I do, you chilly little fool." He felt her tense, like a fiddle string tuned ruthlessly past its pitch. He felt her snap like a fiddle string, too, and lunged forward. Somehow, and just how he could never remember, they coupled like two cats in an alley and fought as they came together, tense and painful in the awkward seat, rearing against each other and for one short moment soaring above themselves to a brief and tearing satisfaction.

"Oh, God," she whispered then, and pulled him against her once more. They heard a step beside the car at the same instant, and Denis straightened.

"Y'all cain't neck here in the park," a cracker voice said at the window. "Y'oughta know better, this big car and all."

Perhaps it was the tone of the policeman's voice that restored Cécile's chill calm. She put out her hand and miraculously found her handbag. She pushed her hand about in it for a second, and handed something to the man. It was not money, but her card.

"I am Cécile de Knize," she said coldly, "and this is Mr. Sandzen, the orchestra conductor. We have some things to discuss privately."

The man put his flashlight on the card. "Well now, I guess y'are." Even Denis, stranger in the South, knew the fellow was fighting for a way to back out and at the same time save his face. "Well, now. Imagine that. Used t'know your pappy, miss. Used to work for him."

The flash was still on, and his face was visible in the edge of the light. It was a face thinned down to a razor edge by generations of semistarvation running back into the distant, pine-crusted hills. The mouth was working a little.

"Sure nice to see y'all, miss," it said slowly. "Nice night, ain't it?"

He turned slowly away, returning his flash to his pocket as he went. The two in the car said nothing until he shuffled off the asphalt of the drive and his steps faded out in the grass. Denis felt a little sick; he was wholly unprepared for Cécile's outburst. She turned on him. "It was vile, plain vile. Like a slut out of the five and ten and a soda jerk—oh!"

He could hear the snap of the key in the ignition; the motor coughed and roared. The car jumped into the black night, its rear tires screaming once. He thought she would forget to turn on her lights but before they were out of the park she did—and slowed to what was for her a sober speed. They turned toward the Quarter and as they passed under the first street light Denis could see tears sparkling on her cheeks; at the next light they were gone. He was sitting facing her, one leg doubled on the seat. Now her hand stole out again and tentatively touched his knee.

"I'm sorry for that outburst," she said softly. "It was terrible, but it wasn't like I said."

Gently Denis took the hand. "It's all right, Cécile." And a moment later, "Want a nightcap at the apartment?"

She seemed to be considering it, but she was not. "I'm sorry," she said again. "I was thinking about something. Nightcap?"

"At the apartment."

"No. I'm staying in Dad's rooms at the St. Thomas. You can drop me and take the car."

"Tony's?"

But she meant what she said; as usual, Denis thought. "I don't want the car, Cécile. I'll take you in and walk home."

At the hotel they turned the car over to the doorman, and Denis left Cécile at the elevators. They said nothing more until then, and all they could think of to say at last was "Good night."

A few minutes later Denis turned into Tony's, which was quite often bedlam at three in the morning, but now was worse if possible. Denis pushed through the swaying mob, his eyes squinted against the smoke fog. "Hi, baby," someone said, but he did not turn; he saw Terry and almost swam through the crowd toward him. Behind him he heard the same voice say, "Spoken for, huh?"

Terry was by no means sober, but Denis did not much notice. He had to shout to be heard. "Let's go home, boy."

Terry swayed a bit getting to his feet, then steadied. "Fine. And you don't need to tell me what happened."

9

The morning of Fibich's rehearsal Denis called Delphine before he left the apartment. "You've got to come, Delphine," he urged. "I don't care whose house you're working on."

Delphine's deep laugh heartened him. "I'm not working too hard, and I'm not getting paid for what I do. What's the trouble?"

"I don't know that there will be any." Then he told her about Gus' call. "We may need to do some quick thinking," he finished, and she laughed again.

"I wouldn't miss it for the world. I'll be a few minutes late though. I just might possibly sell those Chippendale chairs."

The rehearsal began badly, or rather it began late because for no reason at all Fibich was late. Fifteen valuable minutes had passed when there was a stir in the front of the auditorium and the great man entered; he was having nothing to do with the stage door, or perhaps he couldn't find it.

He was very short, and his velour hat sat on a head that sprouted very little hair indeed. His face was red and still should have looked young, only it never had looked that way. He stalked down the side aisle, followed by a harried and cadaverous-looking man who appeared to be a combination of accompanist (in which capacity he would not be needed) and servant. He bore a heavy music case, and over his arm he carried a mink-lined overcoat which seemed what it was, namely, the most useless object in all the town. And behind the accompanist came a round, tubby girl Denis recognized as one of the local violin prodigies, her mother in a beaded dress and a fruity hat on which cherries predominated, and another man, this one the teacher of the girl and nearly as thin as she was the opposite.

"Sit down here," Fibich ordered his entourage, pointing to the first row of seats. He turned his back, stalked to the edge of the proscenium, and ascended the short flight of steps to the stage. The orchestra looked at him, at the four people in the front row, and last at Denis; their heads moved in unison from one to the other almost as if they had been trained by a Y.M.C.A. gymnasium instructor. Visitors were prohibited. And Denis was taken unawares; he had not expected a break so soon. Oh, well, he thought, dropping his baton on the stand, Gus was right. Here goes. . . .

He said coolly, "How do you do, Mr. Fibich?" and he did not offer his hand. Then he turned to the visitors. "I'm sorry. We don't want to be rude, but we can't have visitors. You can meet Mr. Fibich later."

Fibich had yanked his violin from the case, and was nodding imperiously toward the concertmaster. He wanted to tune, something he forgot when he heard Denis' little speech. He turned on Denis in a manner that would have seemed imperious if he had not been so very short and so thin, except for a silly little round stomach; he merely looked ridiculous, Denis thought.

"I have asked them," Fibich said, and as if that settled matters, again began plucking his A string.

"I'm sorry," Denis was struggling for calm, and miraculously achieving it for the time. "This is a new orchestra and things do not always go smoothly. It is not good for us to have visitors."

Below him and behind him, he could hear the inoffensive four scrape to their feet. And at his side he almost could feel Fibich puffing up like a blowfish.

"Mr. Sandzen," he said, "if my friends go, I go."

At which Denis' calm became even more icy. He looked toward the wings, where stood Delphine by the grace of God and the circumstance of a lost sale. "Delphine! Would you be kind enough to put in a call for Gus Wagner? I think Heifetz can get here by tomorrow morning." He looked slant-wise at Fibich. "He's in Atlanta, I'm pretty sure."

"Certainly." In the stillness that followed everyone could hear Delphine's by no means light tread fade out as she reached the stage door. It creaked open, slammed shut. Still there was no sound. Denis pushed back his rebellious hair and smiled sweetly down at the little violinist. "I'm sorry, Mr. Fibich, if I seem severe. But with this orchestra it is I who say what shall be done. I say no visitors."

The magic word Heifetz had struck Fibich like a well-thrown dart. His mouth worked a little, and he turned slowly and a little pathetically to his friends. "Meet me at the hotel at noon," he ordered and turned his back on them. "Now Mr. Sandzen, an A please."

Denis felt his blood churn triumphantly. Over the sound of Labate's A, he called to a man at the last stand of the first violin: "Mr. Latour, please see if you can catch Mrs. St. Martin."

Grinning, the man rose. He guessed, and he was right, that Delphine had slammed the door with herself on the inside. The two stood laughing a few seconds, and Latour tiptoed back onstage. He nodded to Denis, who at once rapped for attention.

"Chausson 'Poeme,'" he said quietly. "Ready, Mr. Fibich?"

Later Delphine and Denis had lunch. "My dear," she said, "it was so wonderful. Wonderful!"

But Denis had forgotten the scene and was back with music. "He did do it well. A little oversweet, but good."

Long before the time was at hand, Delphine began worrying about Mardi Gras. This was the town's festival, a kind of social and moral safety valve which could have been necessary in a Southern town whose blood bubbled warmly through the year, whose inhibitions were few except in society, where they were numerous and to Denis, as to most outsiders, quite inexplicable. That young man had considered very little in life important but his music (Terry had mentioned Gauguin one day, and Denis spurred him to a small educational campaign by asking "Who's Gauguin?") and the question of who was to be Rex and who his Queen seemed even less than unimportant. It did not exist, except as a problem in scheduling the concerts. That was easily solved; there was no concert Mardi Gras week, so that the men might divide and subdivide and play at innumerable balls and on innumerable floats in the parade.

Delphine arrived at the bare little office in the Auditorium one day in a ferment. "Denis, dear," she said, her voice higher because of her delight, "I've an invitation to the Comus ball for you!"

She was considerably dashed when all he answered was, "Oh, my God!"

"Denis—you simply mustn't say that. Believe me, it's an honor a lot of people would pay a great deal for. It's not just an invitation, either. It's for the call-out section."

This too meant nothing, and he made the fact clear.

"My dear," she said, her heavy face downcast, "really. Don't you see that in your present position it's important, very, very important? It's even important to the orchestra that you go."

Like so many first-rate musicians, Denis could not dance. He could only march to the music, being constitutionally unable to release himself from it and embroider on the rhythm to achieve the small variations and distortions that help differentiate dancing from a military exercise. That, too, he explained.

"Oh dear, dear. What difference does it make? The floor's always so jammed you could stand on your head and nobody'd notice." A glance at Denis' slowly darkening face made her hurry on. "I'll tell you—ask Cécile. She knows."

"The hell with Cécile."

Desperately, "Then Terry. Paul. Anybody. Really Denis. . . ." This was a severe disappointment for Delphine and she showed it. She never could have gotten the invitation if she had not been a former Queen herself, if she and Rats had not had an unassailable background. And a man, a boy really, was putting all this aside because he could not dance—or said he couldn't. She could not conceive the real reason, which was that he cared nothing at all for such goings on.

"I'll think about it," was all he would say, and having nothing better, Delphine chose to take this as a good omen.

"That's a good boy—fellow," she hastily substituted, remembering at the last second that Denis was growing a little sensitive about his youth now that he had a man's success behind him.

It required a stormy scene with Cécile, whose usually cool dark eyes seemed to crackle from exasperation, to force Denis to yield. Even Terry, more gently, put in his oar. And when the Comus ball actually arrived, it was almost frighteningly innocuous.

Several hundred of the Best People were there, dressed to the conventional nines or costumed to the same degree. The costumes were in bearable bad taste, and the ritual itself was possible after a number of drinks, but still, Denis felt, rather funny. And the dancing was so crowded that when he and Cécile found Terry, and slipped away to the Quarter it would have been impossible for anyone to have missed them.

"Shall we mask?" Denis asked, and the others said, "Of course."

They bought masks on a corner, and then made for the Orleans Street apartment. There they methodically had a drink as prelude to methodical enjoyment of the tumble in the streets, and after the drink, changed into old slacks and old shirts and made for Tony's. There they had another drink, after a considerable battle to reach the bar. Then to Pat's, and then on indefinitely past mobs of males made up as females and females made up as males, with self-conscious oddity whenever possible. The streets were clogged, even Royal Street with its darkened antique shops, with minor parades and impromptu parades and just people, who for the most part were unable to move and too drunk to care.

But nothing happened until, around three o'clock, Cécile cried out sharply and quickly and efficiently kneed a boy who grinned at the three of them from behind huge, painted-on

97

freckles, and then as quickly changed the grin to a howl. "You bitch," he screamed, and lunged at her.

"Oh, God!" said Terry with surprising calm. "Let's be Galahads."

He and Denis caught the boy's arms and pulled him back. "Beat it, son," Terry commanded, something the boy could not do, since he suddenly crumpled on the curbing, holding himself and crying from pain. Then to Cécile, "Let's have an intermission. Coffee?"

They fought their way toward the river and the French Market, which surprised everyone but Cécile by being half empty.

"The sissies have come and gone," Cécile snapped, "and the others haven't got here yet."

Denis drew down the corners of his mouth. "Thank God."

Wearily the attendant juggled the pots and produced wonderful rich café au lait, and found crullers for them—just in time, for with miraculous suddenness the place was again full. Languidly the three stirred their coffee and watched the costumed mob fight for what they had achieved so easily. Terry yawned, and then spoke lazily.

"Let's get my car and drive out to the Lake. It's warm enough to swim."

Denis said, "But we haven't any swimming things," and Cécile looked at him with something too close to disgust for comfort.

"What difference does that make?" she finally asked.

Denis flushed. "None, I guess. I just happened to think . . ."

"You'd better confine your thinking to music," Cécile snapped, at which Terry turned on her, his eyes blazing.

"There are a few things you'd better do," he said, "such as minding your manners."

"Manners!" She put a world of venom in the word. "This is Mardi Gras, don't forget."

"Oh, for God's sake!" Denis shrugged.

"Oh, for . . . the hell with you both. I know when I'm not wanted."

Denis never had seen Terry angry at all, and he was stunned

by what followed. Terry quickly shot his hand across the table and grasped Cécile's wrist. He held it to the table, turning it just enough that any attempt to move it would produce bad pain.

"Now listen," he said coldly. "I've wanted to say something to you for a long time, and now you're going to hear it." She tried to pull away, but the pain was too much. "Stop it. Don't think I mind hurting you—it's a pleasure." His smile was about as fetching as a bloody razor blade. "You've presumed on your family and your father's money long enough. I'm sick to death of it, and I'm not the only one. Your father loves music and he buys an orchestra, which is fine. But you—what do you buy?"

"Terry! Stop it," Cécile bit her lip and swallowed; she looked at Denis and for the first time there was an edge of entreaty in her expression.

"I won't stop, and Denis won't help you." Terry looked at Denis and the flare in his eyes relented a second. "This is between us, and Denis knows it. What do you buy?" He paused a moment. "I'll tell you—tolerance. Who likes you? I'll tell you the answer to that—nobody. You get away with——"

But Denis did break in. "Terry—please. I—you really are hurting her."

Terry suddenly slumped. "I'm sorry," and to Cécile, "Just the same . . ."

But she had gone. Her evening bag and her mask were lying on the marble table top, but she was fighting her way blindly through the crowd, her sleek hair loosened and incongruous over Terry's blue shirt and old slacks. Denis pushed quickly to his feet, and Terry caught his arm.

"Don't follow her. She'll get to the hotel—and anyway we couldn't find her now."

Denis dropped back into his chair. "What in hell brought it on?" he asked, his young face puzzled.

Terry's hand shook so that he steadied his cup with the other as he drained it. "Liquor," he said at last. "Partly, in any case."

It was an evasion, and Denis knew it. But he could not force himself to press further. He put a hand over Terry's which still held the cup, and half rose. "Come on. Let's do drive out to the Lake."

Terry nodded, and together they pushed their way through an almost solid block of people and into the air. "We were all supposed to check in at the office tonight," he said. "Maybe I'd better call Emmons."

"What for?"

"Mardi Gras high lights—you know, man seen chewing a horse's tail on Bourbon Street, that sort of crap."

"Sure. It's just a step to the apartment. Call there."

"All right." Terry seemed tired out of all proportion to the hour and the events of the evening. His feet dragged, and there were tight lines in his face. They walked around the Cathedral to the apartment, and Terry's hand was on the street door when he suddenly said, "The hell with the office. . . . Let's get the car."

So they turned away and in a few minutes were skirting the Quarter gingerly, feeling their way toward the Lake through whatever street seemed to offer an opening. It was slow going, and before they reached anything like an open road the dash clock said four thirty. "Look, fellow," Terry said at last. "You drive."

Denis managed a little better, watching out of the corner of his eye as his companion first rested his head on his arm and the arm on the back of the seat, and then slid slowly down until he was resting against Denis' shoulder and sleeping soundly. By the time they had reached the White City and turned onto the shore road the scenic railway and Ferris wheel were gaunt and dead under their pale night lamps, and around the horizon there was the faintest smudge of gray light. Denis drove across a light wooden bridge, and in a moment turned off the road between two gaunt gnarled little pines. He cut the lights, and lay back, his head on the seat and his eyes closed; presently Terry pushed himself up and cleared his throat.

"Denis?"

"Here. Want to take a walk?"

"Sure. I must have been sleeping."

Denis laughed. "You certainly were. Feel better?"

"Um."

They crawled out of the car on opposite sides and when they had ploughed through to the beach they began undressing without a word. They left their clothes in two little heaps on the sand and sprinted for the water; they ran in and flung themselves forward together and both together shouted, "Whew!" as if in response to Denis' descending baton. Denis, skin so dark that in the morning dusk he was almost invisible in the water, flopped onto his back and floated lazily. "Seemed cold when we jumped in," he remarked, "but actually it's warm."

"Yes." Terry swam alongside. "I wish to God I could float like that. Too skinny, I guess."

The only reply he got was a grunt and a splash as Denis let down his legs and caught Terry amidships. He turned him over quickly, rested his hand under the small of his companion's back. "Relax," he said at last. "Anybody can float."

"Except me," and Terry slowly turned on his side as the hand was removed and, equally deliberately, sank until only his nose was visible.

"Try it again."

"No use." He suddenly put his feet against Denis' back and pushed off in a quick flutter of foam. "But I can swim to beat hell."

He could swim much better than Denis, who tried to catch up and failed. Presently Terry tired as well, and slowly they swam back to the beach and the disconsolate little heaps of clothes in its middle. There was more light now, and in it Terry's whiter body seemed to glow dully. Denis watched him drop to his knee and then abruptly stretch out, his head on his rolled-up slacks.

"I wish to God I could stay here all day, naked like this." He reached out a hand, touched Denis' thigh. "With you, preferably."

"Let's . . ."

Terry sighed, almost a little-boy sigh. "And go to jail, most likely. Not that I'd care so much"—he raised himself on one elbow and slowly looked Denis up and down—"if you'd go too."

Denis returned the stare just as frankly. He said, slowly, "I've never been in jail, but if I had to go, I'd rather I went with you."

Slowly Terry pulled himself up, and sat with his arms around his legs and his head resting on his knees. His shoulders jerked convulsively once, and in the increasing light Denis could see the muscles tense until they spoke as eloquently as words could have spoken. He touched Terry on the shoulder, and Terry drew back a little.

"Don't," he said. "It's just not going to work. I know it."

Denis turned face down on the sand, his head on his clasped hands. For a few minutes he said nothing, and then he spoke, his voice husky and low. "Maybe it sounds silly," he said, "but in my way I care more for you than for anybody I know." He hesitated, but only a second or two. "Terry—I'll do anything you want."

Terry did not raise his head. "No. If you felt as I do, you'd not offer; you'd just do it." Denis stirred and Terry's hand went out in a gesture curiously like Denis' when he was holding down a section of his orchestra. "No—I mean it. Let's go back to town."

The two pulled on shorts and slacks and shirts and wearily walked back to the car. "You drive," said Terry. "Maybe we'd better stop at Glick's for some breakfast. If we can kick our way through to the counter."

It was half light now. On the distant main road a heavy truck whined; on the lake behind them a fish rose for an early fly, and splashed back. The car started grudgingly, stalled twice in the sand before Denis could back it onto the lane. When at last they were headed for town Denis said, "Let's not go to Glick's. It'll be full of sweepings from the streets."

"All right." Terry yawned. "Oh, God, I wish I didn't have to work today."

"Tell 'em you're sick."

Terry merely groaned. "It's the one morning a year when that one won't work. Everybody's sick—including Emmons himself."

They drove slowly to Orleans Street. Once in the apartment

Denis pushed Terry toward the dining room. "I'll squeeze some oranges and scramble some eggs," he offered.

Terry dragged himself to the sofa, shedding clothes as he went. "Put some gin in the orange juice," he said. "Quite a lot."

From the street below came the rasping toot of a toy horn, followed in a second by the Rebel yell. It was the Death of Carnival; the belated beginning of Lent.

10

Gus Wagner had had his ear tight against the telephone for more than a quarter of an hour, and for once he was listening. It was the beginning of the fourth year of Hoover prosperity, full spring in the South and that chill mess that March invariably brings to New York visible just outside Gus' windows. The only thing that had gone right for him all morning was that the snowy drizzle had let up in time for him to walk to the office; it was now nearly noon, and the time between had been spent trying to hold together other people's businesses while the country around him trembled like a queasy stomach rebelling at last against too much rich food.

"That's the trouble with everybody," he ranted at Moira after a couple of hours spent substituting less expensive artists on concert courses already half bankrupt, bailing out minor impresarios who should have been selling ribbons. "Everybody still insists on eating high on the hog. Nobody's willing to come down to sow-belly and beans."

That was when Denis called. After a record stretch of listening, Gus stirred. "Sure," he said, "now let me get this straight. Huey wants the orchestra to help open the new Capitol. So does de Knize. Delphine's on the fence. And you said you wouldn't do it. Right?"

"Yes. I told them it was after the regular season, and I had engagements."

"What engagements?"

Denis fumbled at his end of the wire. "Well, Gus, I said I was conducting in Europe. But it was hell—Paul was cold about it and Cécile ('Damn Cécile,' Gus interpolated) got me out under the oaks and raised hell, and poor Delphine's running around like a crazy woman."

"Yes. I know what you did. But how did you do it? Confused small-boy act?"

"Look, Gus. This isn't funny; I've got a hunch they'll make things so unpleasant that——"

"That's exactly what I'm getting to. How did you act?"

After a moment Denis said slowly, "I was as arrogant as hell."

"Good boy. Go on."

"I told Paul that if after three years the orchestra association couldn't back me up when I was absolutely right, they could take the orchestra and——"

"And what?"

"And stick it."

Denis put down the telephone until Gus' roars had subsided a little. "Oh, Denis . . . sometimes I love you. Sometimes I honest to God love you. In those exact words?"

"Yes."

Gus went off into another series of gasps and shouts. At last he got control of himself. "All right, son. You've had it. Three good seasons in the heart of the live oak belt. Parties by the hundred. You've learned a lot—not everything, understand, but a hell of a lot. Mardi Gras. Family silver. Jalousies. Iron lace. Stacks of Creoles. Whew!"

In spite of his tension, or perhaps because of it, Denis laughed. "You make it sound like a comic strip," he said.

"It is one, son. Now hang up. I've got some things to do."

"But——"

"I know what you're asking. And the answer is, do nothing. Disappear. You'll hear from me in two or three days—before your last concert. I think," this almost gloatingly, "we'll give the lads and lassies something to chew over. Good-by."

Gus slammed down the phone, jabbed a button underneath the long table. "Moira!" he shouted. "Moira!"

Moira came in grinning. "Well—I guess we've got work to do."

Gus looked sharply at her. "Were you listening in?"

"I was not. The way you were yelling, they could hear you backstage at Carnegie Hall."

"Humph! Sure. Can you catch Elisabeth McKee before she leaves her office?"

"I can try."

"Sure. Get on the wire and line up three orchestra dates in Paris, one in London, one in Berlin, one in Vienna."

"What! Look Gus, you're getting beyond yourself."

"And call Aunt Clarissa out in Lakeland."

Moira nodded. "So Denis gets some European notices, and goes to Lakeland. Who gets his old job?"

"I've got a half-starved Italian for it—you know, Spontini."

"Where does Mednikov go from Lakeland?"

"He'll come here part time. You know as well as I that things are stinking in Lakeland."

"And Mrs. McKee pays the freight? Denis, I mean."

"Who else?"

Moira picked up Gus' phone. "I'd better call from here. It's noon already."

Moira arranged for Gus to stop by the McKee house on his way home that afternoon. Although she had not been told to do it, she also called Delphine. "Gus, you know you've got to let her in on it. You'd be as popular down there as General Butler if you didn't."

Grudgingly, he agreed. "Only I won't tell her a damn thing practical until it's all lined up. I'll just let her tell me what happened, old Creole version."

Moira smiled her most enchanting smile. "Good." The telephone rattled. "Yes," she said, "fine." And to Gus, "Clarissa Jane Garfield on the wire."

It was only the next day when Gus' call came through. Denis and Terry had just sent Cécile away with Delphine under her wing, and a few drinks went with them. Cécile had consented to have drinks at the apartment because it might give her one more lever to use against Denis—or might result in her staying the night, if Terry could be maneuvered out of the way. Only Delphine stayed on, and Terry stuck tight, and nothing of any importance happened. They had spent most of the time avoiding the subject that each of them was most interested in. It had been a strain.

"Whew!" Terry was picking up glasses and the remains of a Liederkranz cheese. "You're still the naughty boy, yes?"

"Here—let me take that." Denis lifted the cheese from its very precarious position on Terry's arm. "And the answer is 'Yes.' Listen—you know this place better than I ever will. Why? That's all I want to know. Why?"

Terry did not answer until he returned from the kitchen. "Sit down. Stop charging around like a baby hippo."

Denis did as he was told. "Now?"

"This is a lecture. You asked for it—and you really ought not to need it after three years. You wouldn't if you weren't the world's finest example of the one-track mind."

Denis flushed. "Oh, hell . . ." and then he reconsidered. "You're right as usual. I have got a one-track mind."

"Thank you, Mr. Sandzen. Notice I didn't say you had a dull mind. You don't—it's brilliant. But you think that because you're on the way to becoming the best living conductor that's enough. And that would never be enough for the South. Remember how they cheered and yelled after the Verdi Requiem at the end of your first season?"

"It was wonderful," Denis said simply. "I loved it."

"And who wouldn't. But if you thought that meant you were being accepted on your own terms, you were wrong. Sure, they know you're fine. But remember how many parties Delphine and I dragged you to? And how she forced you to put in an appearance at the Comus ball every Mardi Gras? And how frightened a lot of people were every time the Kingfish, or Share-the-Wealth, or city politics came up? And how even you had to compromise for the pop concerts the second season, with those two drippy female fiddlers? And—I could go on until midnight, Denis. But this is the truth——"

Denis broke in. "The truth is that I'm mixed up, I guess."

Terry shook his head. "The truth is that *we* are mixed up. You know what you can do—orchestra or piano or whatever. We don't."

"Look, Denis. We've been the stepchild of the rest of the country since the War between the States. The fact that much of the time we turn our back on the Negro question doesn't solve it. We're not bad; we're just scared."

"But how does that——"

"I said this would be a lecture. It's not finished. We are scared, Denis. We've abdicated a hell of a lot of our responsibilities, grudgingly, maybe, but with relief just the same. Along comes a tough bastard like Huey, and he plays our fears and our laziness and—even the climate, like an organ. So we get a few roads and bridges and a new capitol and a football team. So they all cost about ten times what they ought. I'm not proud to say it, but the truth is that most of us like it. Goddam it—it's the truth."

"Isn't that simplifying things pretty far?"

"Of course. There's more. Take—damn the phone—answer it won't you, audience?"

Denis grinned as he picked up the receiver. Terry saw him swallow, grinned in his turn when Denis explained it was Gus in New York. Terry could almost read the conversation from the ebb and flow of light in Denis' face. And he had plenty of time, too, for Gus was at his best, talking so fast that Denis had difficulty making a few notes and Terry got up and held the pad for him.

"My God," Denis said when the rush was over. "Gus—I can't say enough."

Apparently Gus said that he had said enough. At least he hung up, and Denis dropped the phone and flung his arms about Terry. "Oh, Terry," he said, holding him tight. "Oh, my God—you'd never guess."

Terry pushed Denis away, flushing. "Maybe not," he said in a suddenly shaky voice. "But I take it it's good."

Denis did not notice the change of atmosphere, which was as well, since it was back to normal in an instant. "I'm going abroad this summer, and I'm going to Lakeland this fall. The best second-string orchestra in the country. Oh, baby . . ."

They both turned sharply at the knock. "You go," Denis said, "I'm too excited."

"Sure." But they were both thrown off balance again when Delphine entered, this time with smiles and a general atmosphere of conspiracy.

"Boys," she began hurriedly. "I know; it took me half an hour to get rid of Cécile."

Terry shook his head wonderingly. "You know what, Delphine? Don't act like a little girl with a party invitation."

She was not to be thrown off the track. "I know—and of course I hate it. Only of course I knew, all the time, it was bound to happen."

"So you've talked to Gus," said Denis. "I'll be damned."

"Get me another drink, Terry," and Delphine seated herself in the exact center of the brown chintz sofa, bolt upright as usual. "Yes. He called me yesterday after he had talked with you and Clarissa Garfield."

Terry was making as little noise as possible in the kitchen, and Denis was in a state of mild shock. "Go on," Terry shouted. "I'm listening."

"Yes. And it's the best possible solution—provided it doesn't leak out." She looked about the room as if one of Huey's men might be concealed underneath the piano. "I know I can trust you boys—I think you're right, Denis. But I'm caught in the middle." She took her drink from Terry's slightly unsteady hand and nodded to Denis. "You see—you can go away, but I can only go on."

The last weeks were enough to prove to Denis how honest this deep-voiced woman was being, and also how frightened she may have been. Certainly there was nothing to conceal; if

Gus trusted her, what else could he do? He sat beside her on the sofa, and put a hand over hers. "I'm glad I don't have to hide anything from you. Tell me what to do."

It was Terry who spoke, however. "Keep absolutely mum for now. Absolutely. And let me break the story in the paper the afternoon of the last concert." His eyes went from one to the other, and there was pain in them. "I hate to say those words. . . ."

"Yes." Denis spoke slowly. "I hadn't stopped to think what I'll be leaving. I—I guess I just hadn't stopped to think."

This time it was Delphine who took Denis' hand. "At your age you shouldn't."

Terry nodded gently. "Mine too, I suppose," and before anyone could ask what he meant, he hurried on. "What's to be done first?"

"Gus says to sneak up to Lakeland at once, even if I have to miss a concert."

"Hold everything." Terry dove into his room and came back with the *United Railway Guide*. "My secret sin," he said, flipping the pages. "I put myself to sleep planning trips to places like Black Forks, North Dakota, and Ninety-six, South Carolina."

"He does, too," said Denis. "I suppose I could fly part of the way only—well—you know I hate heights."

"No need to." Terry was writing busily. "You can leave after the Friday concert this week, have two days or more in Lakeland, and be back for the Wednesday rehearsal. Can't Labate take the others?"

"Of course." Delphine had gone past transportation. "I wonder what we could tell people—you know, the orchestra men and Paul."

"And Cécile." Denis sounded just a little bitter. "Tell them I've been called to Gutenborg because Ernst is sick. If I can get away without somebody's seeing me, that is." He remembered, with a quick feeling of guilt, that it had been a year, at least, since he had written Ernst and Meta. But there was no time for remorse, not now.

Terry went back, briefly, to the *Railway Guide*. "I think," he said slowly, "I can drive you to Baton Rouge in time to pick up your train—it'll cut it close, but that late we can make all kinds of time. And I'll make the reservation in a phony name—you know, John Smithers or something."

"And I'll phone Clarissa." Delphine was enjoying this mild conspiracy. "I'll ask her to meet you at the station."

"Just one thing," said Denis. "How does Mrs. Garfield know she is even interested in me? It's one thing to read the guff in the music papers, but"—he looked at Delphine, who was behaving oddly—"and what're you laughing at?"

"You don't know Clarissa Jane Garfield, Denis. This will prove I can keep secrets, I guess, but she's been here twice already this year. She heard you play the Mozart 'Coronation' on the first program, and she heard another concert just before Mardi Gras. She was very, very impressed."

Denis pulled at his lower lip. "It's like trying to trace cat brier back to its roots. Everybody knows something but me."

The day was miserable. It was a usual day for Clarissa Jane Garfield, who had been born in Lakeland and as a child learned that the town had six or seven good days every year, and that these usually came in summer when she was in New England. She had driven herself down from her dark house on the Heights, hardly noticing the slush, the wet blustery wind, the soot from the distant factories. When she reached Mather Street ("the longest continuous street in the world"), she was forced to change her august pace because otherwise she would have skidded into a trolley; with that small interruption, her stately progress down Mather Street was interrupted only by an occasional traffic light, and frequent cluckings as she passed the former homes of the still great in Lakeland—a long succession of huge houses in horrifying taste that the Association of Commerce claimed had housed "more money than any comparable thirty blocks in the world."

This last was a circumstance Aunt Clarissa considered worthy of her attention, particularly since quite a lot of it was still being channeled toward the Lakeland Orchestra from the newer homes of the great on the Heights. The fact that the old houses now sheltered schools of chiropractice, Bible schools, nursing homes and used-car dealers could be overlooked. Symbols had been corrupted through the ages—there was the Roman forum, for example. It was characteristic of Clarissa Garfield that she could have combined although she did not, the glories of Rome and Lakeland in one thought, and found nothing incongruous about it.

At the Terminal she circled through mail trucks and parked out of the wet. She asked nobody's permission, and nobody thought to question her. Then she entered the empty too-huge central hall, consulted the arrival bulletin briefly, and walked calmly past the attendants at the stair leading to Denis' train. She had arrived precisely as the train arrived, whereas a more ordinary mortal might have been forced to wait from a few minutes to half the morning.

"Ma'am," called one of the attendants weakly, "you got a permit?"

But she was halfway down the stair, and did not even turn her head. At its foot she fixed an assistant stationmaster with her steel-blue eyes and asked quietly, "Where will Car 21-L be?"

"Location Four, ma'am," and he pointed.

"Thank you." Loosening her very good black Persian coat, she arrived at Location Four just as the porter finished handing out the bags. Without moving, she called to one of the redcaps who was helping, "Boy, I'll need you," and he meekly took up a position on her flank.

"Mr. Sandzen," she called, "I'm here."

The redcap took Denis' two bags. "Don't take them up the elevator," she commanded. "Follow us." And in the same breath, "Nice trip?"

"Horrible." Denis had shaved and snatched a cup of coffee as the train tooled through the endless suburbs of Lakeland. But he felt cindery and sticky, as if he had slept in the vestibule. He also felt a little daunted by this exceedingly smart-looking woman in the black Persian coat; somehow he knew that her short-cut hair the color of a—well, of what? he wondered and could only think of a dapple-gray Percheron—whatever it was would never be rumpled even if her smart little black hat were to be blown off in a tornado. The amber choker, the sensibly smart shoes, the firm tread all were a little oppressive at eight thirty of a vile morning.

Aunt Clarissa seemed amused. "Well, you're here now," she said as if arrival at Lakeland was compensation for anything. "We are going to my house for breakfast. This is the new terminal," she went on without a break as they emerged into the central hall. "It was finished a couple of years ago."

"It's enormous, isn't it?"

Aunt Clarissa began her indoctrination at once. "Not for Lakeland. The authorities left room in the Civic Center for expansion when the time comes."

The bags were stowed, the boy tipped, and the car neatly out of the taxi drive before she spoke again, and the long and careful lecture was something Denis instinctively knew he should remember and repeat to Terry and Delphine, and just as instinctively knew he could not. They drove out Mather Street, of course. Without seeming to concede much to the brief time at her disposal Aunt Clarissa was able to name the big stores they passed and sketch either the family or the financial position of the owner, whichever was more impressive. They passed the Slater Hotel, which being foreign received no attention at all—it was skipped for the Lakeland Club across the side street. There was a big jewelry store and then only a few colossal motion picture theaters standing, Denis learned, on land once owned by the Garfields. On down there was a decorating establishment. "Adolph Blitzstein," said Aunt Clarissa. "He's decorated almost every house in Lakeland that could afford him. He's very expensive."

Then the sooted relics. "I regret, sometimes," she continued, "that the better people ever gave up Mather Street. I can remember winters when they roped off the street and raced sleighs on Sunday afternoons—after church, of course. It was cold, but there were hot toddies afterward."

"It's still cold," Denis broke in desperately. "Mrs. Garfield, I can't blame people for giving up those things. They——"

"They aren't modern," said she, using the word modern as an

expletive. "Mr. Sandzen, do you realize I know practically every room in every one of those houses?"

"Oh," said Denis, and the travelogue continued. Without a pause it changed character as they left Mather Street and started up to the Heights. Like a well-designed motor car, the past changed into the present without a jar. This was the new Lakeland, the part in which people of importance lived; in which Clarissa Jane Garfield lived as well. She stopped briefly as she turned left across the car tracks, rounded a shiny new Gothic church, and smoothly slid into the drive of 6900 Scott Road. At the exact moment the car stopped under an overhanging glass canopy, the house door opened.

"Mrs. Garfield," the servant said, "I worried about you. It's slick."

"Everybody worries about me," said his mistress, "except me. Breakfast ready?"

"Yes ma'am. Soon as you are."

Denis felt a curious difference in the air. On the way out his hostess appeared almost mechanical, like a machine wound up and set to a certain degree of appreciation, even awe, for certain things that he could not even feel. But here there was quick warmth. The man had honestly worried; his greeting was not perfunctory. Nor had his casual suggestion that they hurry been impertinence. There were hidden depths in Clarissa, Denis was aware.

It was a good breakfast: sausages, eggs, little fritters with syrup, wonderful coffee. Until they had finished his hostess made small talk, but at the end the machine went into reverse, and she was again the perfect representative of Lakeland and the devoted servant of the orchestra. Her orchestra.

"Now," she said, tossing her napkin onto the table and rising, "we'll talk on the sun porch."

It seemed odd to speak of a sun porch on a day when there was nothing but thick drizzle peppered with soot outside, but the porch was a good idea, being the room with most light. The drawing room was huge and overladen with dark and heavy furniture and photographs of the favored in heavy silver frames. There was a Steinway concert grand, too; Denis sat down and started the E major Chopin etude while Aunt Clarissa read the orders of the day in the kitchen. It was a wonderful piano, and only slightly out of tune, and he enjoyed the feel of it so much he did not notice the audience of three standing in the dining room archway until he had finished and the three applauded.

"Jim Cleary you already know," said Clarissa. "This is Missouri, his wife. Her name really is Missouri," at which the woman giggled.

"How do you do?" said Denis, after which he was swept through the drawing room and onto the sun porch, and installed in a wicker armchair alongside a wicker chaise longue.

"They're such tiny people," Aunt Clarissa declared, almost as if she expected to be contradicted, "and they love me very much."

"Yes, they do." Denis spoke with conviction.

"Humh? So they do. Now, I've had Jim take your bags upstairs. You'll stay here. It's more——"

"No. I'm sorry, but I made a reservation at the Slater."

This was nothing. "I'll cancel it."

"No. I really am sorry, Mrs. Garfield, but I like to have my own place. I'm not being rude."

She looked hard at him. If she was annoyed, she concealed the fact. "I understand. Push that button, there beside you."

Denis pushed, and instantly Jim appeared. "Take Mr. Sandzen's bags back to the car; he'll be staying downtown." She smiled. "The food won't be as good, though."

Then she turned back to Denis. "I believe in being very honest, whenever possible. If you'll just listen, I can tell you in a few minutes all you need to know just now. The rest you can't help learning later."

Denis inclined his head slightly. He felt a little like a boy being told about sex by his father, although no father could have approached his subject so nervelessly. He listened.

"In the first place, Mednikov is finished, and I hate that. I found him and raised him on the bottle and perhaps that was a mistake. He's going and no use to worry about it now.

"Gus Wagner and I have been talking about you for three

114

years. I sneaked down twice to hear you, and you're good. You can be superb; that's why I've euchred the board into taking you. Some of them wanted Hans Mayor." At that Denis' eyebrows went up, but she whirled him along. "He's terribly difficult, as well as terribly good. However that may be, you'll be the next conductor of the Lakeland Orchestra, barring acts of God. And I won't make the mistake I made with Mednikov. He was tagged as my man; I'd have tried to make you stay here in the house if I hadn't thought it was just as well that you start differently."

Somewhere back in the house a telephone had rung; Jim appeared breathlessly. "Mrs. Gordon, and she says it's important, Mrs. Garfield."

"Drat. What ails Gloria?"

In three minutes she was back. "Just a slight act of God," she reported. "Harry Gordon's on a bat and his wife's trying to sober him for the meeting tomorrow. She says we'd better not stop by, and I'm delighted. He was next on my list anyway.

"He's a complete nobody. His father drove a one-horse wagon through the alleys and picked up bottles and such like. Now the son has a chain of yards all over the country, buying mostly metal scrap at depression prices and selling it abroad—Germany, Japan, Russia, when they can get the money to pay. It's about the only business that is actually better these days. Papa Gordon was a cultured man on a one-horse wagon; Harry's sometimes a boor in a limousine. Only he really likes music and Gloria—she's his wife—likes being the wife of the Orchestra-board president. It's convenient, these days." She looked hard at Denis. "You may find her a little—ah—inconvenient, with your looks."

"Oh, God!" said Denis. "Not that!"

"There's one in every town, my boy. You'll manage; you've got the same kind of drive I have."

That was exact truth; Denis shot his hostess a quick look, and relaxed again. The firm, slightly clipped voice went on.

"There are three others you need to know about in advance. John Dudley you'll like. He's younger than I, old Lakeland and money too, easygoing but by no means stupid. He looks a lot like a kewpie, but don't let that mislead you. He can be very tough, and all that. It's just that usually he saves it for business, which is steel." Without turning her head and in exactly the same tone, she added, "What is it, Jim?"

Jim was standing in the shadows of the drawing room, twisting his tiny hands. "It's Mrs. Gordon again. No—she's hung up. She says that if you want a meeting tomorrow you'll have to take charge. She's——"

"Going home to mother. Goddam that rattlebrain!" Clarissa Jane Garfield rose, and went into action. She turned briefly to Denis.

"Jim will drive you to your hotel. I'll pick you up about three, and show you the hall and whatever else you need to see." Denis was about to offer help. "Don't trouble. It's happened before. I picked him out of a whorehouse on Inferior Street last year." She pulled her shoulders still farther back. "Later you'll learn that I'll do anything, absolutely anything, for the Lakeland Orchestra."

And she swept out. As Denis followed the butler, he heard a car back out of the drive and slosh down the quiet street under the bare, lacy elms.

In the larger car the glass partition was down; Denis had a feeling that its owner talked with her driver a good deal. Tentatively, he said, as they started carefully down the boulevard toward Mather Street, "Mrs. Garfield seems efficient, doesn't she?"

Jim had been pumped before. "She is efficient, sir." And after a short hesitation during the course of which he apparently made up his mind that Denis was soon to be a member of the family and so was to be trusted, he added, "Excuse me, sir, but she's also sentimental. They don't call her Aunt Clarissa for nothing."

"I suppose not." Denis thought a minute. "I have the idea that she would do anything for the orchestra—absolutely anything."

This was exactly right. "Yes sir. That's it. She never had children or anything, just the orchestra. She was born right here and she's a cousin of everybody, everybody who amounts to anything. But when it's the orchestra—well, look at her now. She and Doctor Lieberman'll take over that house of the Gordon's, and when——" He broke off suddenly. "Excuse me, sir, I'm talking too much."

Denis laughed. "No you're not. You can trust me, Jim."

"Thanks." Even from the rear seat Denis could see the grin on the man's slender face. "I knew it, only sometimes I get carried away, me and Missouri. She's awful good to us both."

"And you to her?"

"I'd do anything for her." He said it without unction, flatly. "So'd Missouri."

"I knew it. But Jim, does she have to wet-nurse Mr. Gordon? Couldn't his wife——"

"She couldn't do nothing at all. She—well, you'll see, Mr. Sandzen. And—excuse me, sir—don't undervalue Mr. Gordon."

The rest of the long drive past the glories of the 'nineties was mostly made in silence, the slush having reached a depth where care was needed to keep the long car out of the gutter.

"I'll call for you at three," Jim promised as the doorman at the Slater took Denis' bags. Denis registered with a warmer feeling in his middle than he had had yet that day.

"And that," said Aunt Clarissa at half past three of the afternoon, "is Lister Hall."

All Denis could think of to say was, "Oh," not from lack of interest but because the hall was exactly what he did not expect: a monumental affair with columns, a flat dome, flights of steps which looked unused leading up to bronze doors, lawns surrounding it all, stretching down to a traffic circle, off to the left a glimpse of a long, low tomb bare of windows which turned out to be an art museum. Across a lake, a very small lake, Denis could see more smudged space which, come real spring, would be green, at least for a few weeks. And beyond this stretch stood a brand-new Gothic church with what appeared to be an exaggerated German helmet on top, and a comfortable-looking apartment hotel. I'd like to live there, Denis thought, and was a little astonished when Aunt Clarissa, who had pointed all this out item by item, said, "You'll probably want to live in the Hampton Park Manor. It's convenient and it's good."

"Uh—I was just thinking that," said Denis. "How do you get in—into Lister Hall, that is?"

He followed his leader around the building, and into a kind of tunnel. There was the practical entrance, complete with box office, stairs, elevators and, at this hour on Sunday, a watchman. As the elevator door closed Denis could hear the watchman telephoning someone; by the time he and Aunt Clarissa reached her long and very expensive-looking office, Denis felt sure that if there was anybody in the place besides the watchman, he knew the new conductor was aboard.

"What a nice office," he said. "I'm not used to such elegance, not since Herkimer Institute."

"Isn't Mary Herkimer a dear? You may as well know that I've talked with her about you, and also with Hans Mayor."

"I didn't know, but I could have guessed it." Denis was not too stunned by the surrounding opulence to miss his cues; today he was the very young lad being impressed, a part he could play well if he chose. "She was very good to me."

After the oppressively numerous photographs in their impressively heavy silver frames had been inspected, they made a quick whirlaround. The library was incredible with its immaculate steel cabinets instead of the pine shelves as down South. His own room looked like the robing room of a grand duke. Even the halls were less bleak than halls usually are.

"The auditorium!" Aunt Clarissa almost trumpeted as she suddenly opened a door and gently pushed him into the hall.

"My God!" said Denis softly. "Imagine!"

That was right, too. And deserved. Row after row of gray-upholstered seats set far enough apart that one's chin did not rest on one's knee. A single row of open boxes, the rails covered with grayish-rose material thick enough for a carpet. Walls in gray and the same soft rose of the boxes. A wide proscenium, and on the stage a box set that for once looked as if it might hold together for more than an hour. Terraces for the orchestra (they would come out the moment he took over, Denis made note). On the far side of the stage an organ console that caught Denis' eye.

"It's quite wonderful," he said simply. "Small—but perfect."

"It's small because Mr. Lister wanted it that way. And it got the final touch only last fall."

Her companion's puzzled look was as good as a question. She continued. "The lights—the architect made a mistake with his indirect lighting."

"But why? I should think that——"

"But you never wore jewels, my boy. When the hall was opened you could have worn the British crown jewels and nobody would have noticed. I had the chandeliers put in, and every woman in town loves me for it. Every woman with jewelry fit to wear, that is."

Denis had a hard time choking back a laugh. And yet it was almost frighteningly shrewd, that move. To cover himself he said, "Wonderful!" and pointed to the organ. "May I try it?"

"Of course."

Denis crossed the stage (there was an elevator to hoist pianos up from the basement) and turned on the organ. For fifteen minutes he put the huge instrument through its paces as if he were a groom and the organ a Kentucky filly. If he had not forgotten his guide, he would have seen that she was frankly astonished at what he could do; when at last he leaped into the D minor toccata and fugue of Bach she quietly sat down in the front row and rested her chin in her right hand. Denis stopped at the fugue.

"Finish it," she said quietly, and he went on.

"My boy," she said when he had finished, "there isn't a phony bone in your body. You know." And she emphasized the last word and pronounced it in such a voice that Denis felt a warm tingle run up his spine. She knew, too, and that meant everything to him.

The rest of the tour was somehow anticlimactic—the pillared lobby in brown-veined marble, the heavy doors, the gray-carpeted lounge, all seemed what they were, mere necessities, albeit glorified.

They were leaving when Aunt Clarissa said, again quietly.

"You handled that organ almost viciously at times. Don't you like organ?"

"No, I don't. But that's a good one, very good. A couple of stops are out of tune."

"Yes. They'll be all right this fall." She allowed Denis to help her into the car. "Would you like to look at apartments?"

It was a simple and innocent-seeming question, so much so that Denis almost missed its meaning. Not for long; she was telling him that he was engaged.

Denis looked sharply at Aunt Clarissa, his eyes narrowed a little. He was not surprised to see her own eyes narrow in response, and a pair of wrinkles appear at the corners of her generous mouth. They understood each other at once. He said, "If I don't have to make the final decision now, I'd like to look."

"Why not make the decision?"

"I don't quite know how much room I'll need."

"Expecting marriage, perhaps?"

The question stunned him for a second or two. "God no!" he finally said. "I haven't the time for that." He was silent while the car came to a stop in front of the Hampton Park Manor, and they got out, leaving Jim Cleary and the machine in the center of the No Parking zone. "I meant that I don't know yet how much room I need—how much entertaining I should do and, well, how much money I'll have."

She nodded, a small gesture that seemed a compound of acquiescence and understanding and knowledge, a wise little inclination of her handsome head. "I can answer those questions," she replied with a curious formality. "You'll need a good-sized living room, a kitchenette, two bedrooms, one for a study."

They were still standing under the entrance canopy. "Look," she said, "those corner suites are perfect. I'll get you one."

He hesitated, and after a pause she went on. "You'll get thirty thousand," and riding through his attempted interruption she continued, "I know Gus said to start higher. You'll not get it, and if I'm still in my right mind, he told you to take thirty."

Denis started to smile, but the smile became a laugh. After a moment his companion joined in.

"All right," she said at last. "One thing more. The hotel is half empty—depression and all that. They'll be glad to have a distinguished gentleman who happens to be solvent for a tenant. I'll get that suite for you on a three-year lease for a hundred and fifty a month. Watch me."

It was done in half an hour, even to the lease which appeared so quickly and so magically that Denis was sure it had been arranged in advance by Aunt Clarissa, which of course it had. But the apartment was very nearly perfect excepting the color, which was hotel green and which Denis insisted should be a brown so deep it was almost black. And the height—the suite was on the tenth floor. That he could force himself to endure, because he must.

Denis waited in Mrs. Garfield's sumptuous office while the meeting got under way next afternoon. He did not wait long. As he entered the board room there was a little flutter of applause, led by Clarissa, who sat at the right of the chairman. She rose, and presented him to each of the twelve members in turn. Only two of them made much impression: Harry Gordon and John Dudley, who really did look like a wise, middle-aged kewpie. It was Gordon who astonished him, however.

This was a man out of a magazine advertisement, the type of gray-haired, broad-shouldered, ruddy-skinned man that always appears in illustrations of exclusive men's clubs on the color pages of magazines. Denis had not expected exactly that, and he was perfectly aware that his astonishment showed, at least to the sharp Garfield eye. Gordon remained standing; when he looked directly at Denis the latter could see the bloodshot eyes, and when the light from the tall windows fell right, even the throbbing veins in his temples. But the over-all effect was superb, even distinguished.

"Mr. Sandzen," he began, and Denis was delighted to hear him pronounce his name as it should be pronounced, and not with the accent on the first syllable, "it's a pleasure to welcome you to Lakeland as our new conductor. If Mrs. Garfield will

121

read the resolution we have just ratified, and you approve, we shall all be pleased."

There was a rustling, and a few throats were cleared as Aunt Clarissa rose with majesty. The resolution merely said that it had been moved and carried that Denis Sandzen was to be offered the post of conductor of the Lakeland Orchestra for three years at an annual stipend of thirty thousand dollars; that with Denis' approval, it should be considered authority for the preparation of the usual contract. Denis arose in his turn from the chair which had been placed for him at the foot of the long table. He was a little nervous, and wondered what the men would have thought had they known his right hand was closed over Mr. Edward Bear, in his jacket pocket. He felt, indeed, as he had when he first raised a baton over his first orchestra, down South. Perhaps what he said was all the better for nervousness.

"I'm very flattered," he began, looking directly at Gordon. "I'm sure a good many of you must have questioned my age, which is twenty-five. I don't blame you. I"—he caught a hint of a smile on Aunt Clarissa's face and knew he was on the right track—"I only want to say that twenty of my twenty-five years have gone into preparation for this post. I hope I shall make you proud of the orchestra." And he sat down, with a rattle of gentlemanly applause sounding around him.

Said Aunt Clarissa, "Then I shall write the contract."

The group rose, happy that the meeting had been short and they could go back to their cherished worries without delay.

"Just a minute." Gordon was on his feet. "I think we should have a toast to Mr. Sandzen." He motioned to a table on one side of the huge, never-used fireplace, and a little hesitantly the group gathered around. "There are whisky and sherry." And he busied himself pouring. "For you?" he said to Denis.

"Whisky and a little water," said Denis, and took the glass from experienced hands. As he turned away he found John Dudley by his side.

"The only drink fit for a man," Dudley said. "I'm glad you know it."

"Thanks, Mr. Dudley." Denis looked about the group. "I'm

not good at names," he went on, "and I'm afraid I missed most of them this time."

His round little companion ran his hands through his bright white hair, which at once returned to a kind of kewpie point on his head. "Oh, well," he said, "you'll learn them soon enough." He motioned with his head, "John Lister, come here."

A heavy, almost ponderous, man slowly ambled toward them. "Sandzen says he can't remember names. I'm sure he's not as bad as you."

"Impossible," said Lister, obviously waiting for something.

"Very possible, sir," said Denis. "But I'd not be able to forget Lister Hall very soon. It's magnificent."

Lister cleared his throat. "I'm glad you like it," he said a little pompously. "Very glad. I'm told it has about everything the city needs."

"I'm sure that's true," Denis replied, "although I'm no expert on Lakeland as yet. I do know it has everything a conductor could hope for."

Denis was sure Dudley meant his sudden gesture as praise of a sort. "Let's drink to that," he said, "and the future. I've a good feeling about the future, you know."

The three raised their glasses, and Lister slowly retired from the scene, for Harry Gordon was approaching.

11

"And I shan't know any more about it all until we get back from Europe," Denis concluded.

"Until we get back?" Terry said. "Am I going?"

"Will you?"

"I—Denis, I can't. Unless the paper would send me, and I don't see why it should."

They were talking over their coffee the morning of Denis' return from Lakeland. Denis had reported the entire trip, even to the fact that dinner at the Gordons' had had to be postponed until fall because the host had once again drowned himself in a bottle of bourbon. Now he said, "Look, bring your cup with you and we can talk while I shower. I've got to hurry if I make the rehearsal."

Terry followed to the bath. "Denis," he said, "you know that Mother and I were pretty hard hit by the depression. I'm just not able to go along—although I'd rather do it than anything I can imagine. God—would I love it!"

"Then it's settled." Denis blew soap out of his mouth. "This is why. Elisabeth's foundation is paying my way, paying for the dates, everything. Gus thinks I ought to have someone along for—for kind of a protection. I haven't saved a lot, but there's plenty to take care of you. And I need you, Terry."

Denis staggered blindly out of the shower, and fumbled for a towel. When he had dried his face he looked around for Terry, and he was gone. Then his voice came from the living room, not loud enough for Denis to hear what was said. Finally there was a click, which was the phone going down, and Terry reappeared. He looked cheerful.

"I called Emmons," he said. "He'll buy a couple of pieces a week for enough to—sure, Denis, I'll go."

"Wonderful. We'll plot things later." Denis was hastily getting into his rehearsal slacks and open-necked shirt. "Walk to the Auditorium with me?"

When Denis stepped onto the stage he got a tutti from the orchestra, and it brought tears to his eyes. "We hope," said Labate, "that everything was all right in Gutenborg."

Denis could not be sure whether this was an honest inquiry or Labate's subtle way of letting him know that he, and perhaps the entire orchestra, guessed that something was afoot. If this was so, there was no further indication until Terry's story broke the afternoon before the final concert, and when that happened, Denis was quietly loafing beneath the de Knize oaks with Cécile and Delphine, whose idea the excursion had been. All through the afternoon the apartment telephone rang; it even rang at The Oaks, but there it caused no difficulty, although Cécile did.

She sat staring into the long dark tunnel of the oaks for a full minute after Denis told her he was leaving. She looked, he thought, more attractive in her plain white dress than he ever had seen her. She looked, for the moment at least, girlish and virginal, and sad, too. At last she turned her head and looked Denis straight in the eye.

"I think you or Father might have told me," she said. "What makes you think I couldn't keep a secret?"

Delphine's voice was low, and if possible deeper than usual. "That wasn't the question, Cécile, and you know it."

"Then what was the question?"

Denis broke in. "I didn't know I'd be leaving, for one thing. It was just a chance."

Cécile's smile was harder, more characteristic. "You know better. Those things don't get that far without one's knowing."

"And anyway," he went on, "I'd already—well—displeased Paul enough. He thought I was stiff-necked about not playing for Huey——"

"And you were," Cécile interrupted.

"As he saw it," admitted Denis. "The whole thing was embarrassing to him and me, too. But I'd have felt a fool to say what was up and dash off theatrically to Lakeland, and then come home with my tail between my legs."

Delphine started to speak, but Cécile silenced her by jumping quickly to her feet and turning her back on the two of them.

"Damn it, Denis," she said, and her voice broke a little, "I can't look at you and say what I mean. I wish to God I'd never let myself. . . ." She stopped and looked at Delphine. "You're a woman. You know what I mean."

Gently Delphine answered. "Yes. But Cécile, if you put it that way, aren't you admitting that what troubles you is—forgive me, dear—rather the personal side?"

"What other side is there? The orchestra? Nonsense! And you don't really think I give a hoot for Huey? And the new capitol? Of course it's personal."

For a moment there was silence. Cécile returned to her chair and reached for the planters' punch she had forgotten. She drank a good half of it and put the glass down with precision. She said coldly to Denis, "Probably you're hoping I'll ask Delphine what this Italian conductor looks like. So I will. Delphine, what does he look like?"

Delphine did not reply. She got up and motioned to Denis. "All I can say is that I'm glad Paul isn't in town. I'd not like him to hear that."

Cécile only motioned for them to go, and then sharply called after them, "Paul knows everything there is to know about me. Everything. And do you want to know what his first question will be?" They had stopped; Delphine shook her head. "Well, he'll ask, 'How about the new man's Mozart?' "

They walked around the lovely columned house, and Denis supposed it was for the last time. He looked back once at the oaks and saw the slight figure in white, her back toward them, pick up the glass once more. At that time Denis did not have the feeling of omnipotence he had standing erect before an orchestra. He understood that Cécile had offered him something good in the wrong way. But also he had taken the gift wrongly, and it was his own inadequacy that hurt. He ached, all at once, for his orchestra and what it could do for him. He wondered, too, whether a feeling of wholeness would ever come to him from anything but his music.

"One more concert," he said quietly to Delphine as they climbed into her battered little car, and when her great, coarse, kind face suddenly wrinkled and she cried, he felt lost and he felt alone.

Gus and Moira were beginning to feel as if they were members of some wartime propaganda unit, perhaps the heads of it. At six o'clock of a nasty spring morning in New York the two sat watching the drizzle obscure Central Park, seen distantly through the slot between the apartment buildings.

"I'm tired," Gus remarked. "In just three hours and a half it will begin, and I'm tired already."

Moira got up, and went into the outer office. When she came back she carried a pint bottle of Irish whisky, part of a present to her from one of the Dillon clan who, in his turn, had come by it through the police department. "I disapprove of drinking in offices," she said, "but 'twould be no sin to wish the boy luck."

Gus laughed. "Sure an' it would not. He's but a broth of a boy with the need of support."

"Your dialect is horrible." Moira went behind the screen, and was back in a moment with two glasses. "Here, and no more bad imitations of a race you're unfit to unlatch the shoes of."

Solemnly Gus took his glass and raised it. "Here's how!"

"An original remark if I ever heard one," Moira commented sarcastically. "Ah, Gus, it'll be all right, unless perhaps we've overplayed it. And 'tis possible, you know. Only—only I think not."

Gus looked again at his wrist. "Damn, still three hours and twenty minutes."

"And that's wrong, even. It would seem to me that a man who's traveled wide like yourself ought to know Denis is an hour slower than we here in New York."

"Yes. Finish your drink and we'll go home for dinner. I can't stand this goddam office any longer."

They did go home, and had a couple of drinks more, and a slow dinner, and still it was not quite time for Denis' concert to begin. Gus was standing before the window in his dining room fidgeting with a little glass of brandy and watching the cars slosh up and down Fifth Avenue. In his mind he was seeing the auditorium, sick-brown but good enough acoustically to please even him. He was seeing the goon squads that might be gathering under the seedy palms around the hall, seeing Delphine and Denis, and probably Terry, driving up. God, he thought, I guess I'm getting to be an old maid. But I'd personally kill a couple of them if they hurt the boy. I'd even risk my neck flying down to do it. He heard the rustle of Moira's skirt behind him, and felt her hand touch his.

127

"This isn't like you," she said quietly. "It's like me."

He nodded. "But this time it's me that stuck my neck out. I told the papers here about it. I got them to order special pieces. I got the *Times* to promise to interview the lad if there was trouble. And of course that's all got back to that slimy little cracker who runs the state now."

"Sure you did. But what has me puzzled is how Denis happened to make a stand in the first place."

Gus laughed for the first time in an hour. "You know, I wonder myself. And I think—mind you, I said think—he did it purely on musical grounds. That damn mousetrap of a new capitol does open after the season is closed, and Denis couldn't possibly get together a very good orchestra."

"And then Mrs. St. Martin's husband?"

"Led him on. Maybe, or maybe he got sore at de Knize for siding with Huey. That's more likely, because I don't think Denis sees much of St. Martin." He quickly reached down and picked up a telephone; there was a telephone in nearly every room of Gus' apartment. He put in a call for Delphine at the auditorium, insisting that it was an emergency and must go through at once. That it did—he could hear the operators haggle briefly, and then a man's voice, rather breathless, came on. "She's not here," it said. "She's around someplace. . . . No, ma'am, I can't; this is the box office. Hot dawg! Something's up." The line went dead.

Something was up. When Denis and Delphine arrived, there had been a little crowd around the stage entrance, not a friendly crowd, although it neither did nor said anything. Backstage there was a great moiling about, because after the Haffner symphony of Mozart, there was the Beethoven Ninth and the chorus was clotted in the wings, waiting to go on. Its members were excited. Every man and every woman watched Denis as he made his way through the tangle and into his room. Still nothing happened.

Delphine gave the house a glance through the proscenium peephole, and hurried after Denis. "The place is jammed to the rafters," she reported, "and there's a suspicious number standing."

Denis was oddly calm. "Let 'em stand," he said quietly. "I'll give 'em a reason."

"Fine!" Delphine was frightened, but saw nothing to gain by showing it. She looked at her watch. "It's time I was leaving."

Denis' smile was blended of gratitude that, on this last night, Delphine would remember his few minutes alone, and of thankfulness for her staunchness; not once since the chance of a demonstration arose had she wavered. He needed staunchness now, for the fact that this really was his last concert in The Town had unnerved him a little. He was self-sufficient, but he was not callous, and there were friends he did not want to leave—Madame, and Labate, and Terry, and of course Delphine. He quickly rose and kissed her on the mouth. "Thanks," he said. "Thanks an awful lot."

"I'll see you later, dear," she said and quickly slipped away.

Denis took Mr. Edward Bear from his pocket and sat him on the piano, where his beady black eyes caught the light, winking gaily. Outside the chorus was chattering; Denis wished now he had insisted on their being seated at the beginning, Mozart or no Mozart, intermission or no intermission. But it was too late to do anything. Slowly he succeeded in forcing everything from his mind, absolutely everything but his music. For a few minutes he sat in utter inner quiet; then there was a tap at the door, and a shaky voice saying, "Time, Mr. Sandzen."

The only thing he saw as he walked quickly through the aisle opened for him by the chorus was the first page of the "Haffner" score—but he could not help hearing the thunder that burst around him when he entered the stage. The noise seemed to fall upon him as if it had been held back by a dam, and at first he could distinguish no quality in it, only quantity. But by the time he had reached the podium and turned for his usual quick bow, baton in both hands, he knew quite well that mingled with the flood of cheers there were boos and catcalls and whistles; they'll stop, he thought, when I turn around.

But they did not stop; if anything they grew louder. He bowed again with the same result. He was not panicky nor was he frightened, but he was angry, more angry than he had been since the first night with Cécile in the park. He tried a third bow, and this time he caught a glimpse of Madame Aimé in Delphine's box, applauding like a man with heavy, slow strokes. He wondered where Terry was . . . probably standing at the back of the hall, possibly beset by one of Huey's thugs; there was no time to worry now. As he faced the orchestra the third time an idea struck him. He quickly bent down to the concertmaster, thanking his good luck as he did so that he had decided not to reduce the orchestra for the Mozart, after all.

"Pass the word," he shouted. " 'Star Spangled Banner' in B flat!"

The man nodded and turned. Denis repeated his message to the solo 'cellist on his right. Then he waited a half minute which seemed a half hour and brought the orchestra to its feet. The first phrase of the anthem seemed to beat against the roar from the hall with little more effect than a bird's wing fluttering against a pane of glass. He felt, rather than saw, someone run down the far aisle and jump to the stage, and thought, They can't mean to attack me. Then he understood; into the bedlam thundered the organ, opened as wide as possible. He smiled in spite of himself and looked quickly into the wings, where Terry, having coupled in every stop he could think of, was half standing on the pedal board as if his weight could make the bass still louder.

Then something else reached him: the audience was singing. He half turned, and barely could see the taut little figure of Madame standing stiffly in her daughter's box, singing like an ancient miniature Melba. His eyes filled; they were nearing the end and they were winning. Now there was more music than noise, but if there had not been, Madame would not have changed, he knew. She would have sung as loud if Huey's entire state "police" had surrounded her.

Denis held the last chord to the last possible second, then cut off the vast thunder clean, and turned once again to the audience. The quiet was not complete, but by contrast the dying sound that reached him was no more than a breeze sighing through cemetery cypresses. Now we'll know, he thought, and held up his arms.

"We will now play the Mozart," he said quietly into the yawning silence before him. There was applause, and he heard no catcalls. There were cheers when the symphony was done. Denis bowed first to the orchestra and clasped his hands prize-fighter fashion in congratulation. Then he brought them to their feet and turned to the audience. He bowed, and stood quietly as the applause rolled on. Always he had detested conductors who talked to their audience, but not tonight, for he had something to say and a full heart from which to say it. At last the hall was quiet.

"I want to thank you for what you have done for me to-night," he said. "I have already forgotten what went before, and you must." His voice caught for a moment, and he swallowed before he went on, "In a few minutes I shall say good-by to you with the greatest symphony ever written. It is the most beautiful thing I can give you."

As he left the stage, his dark face glowing, he could feel the hands of his men reach gently out to touch him. He could only smile as he passed them. Alone in his room he saluted Mr. Edward Bear, who still watched with beady eyes from the piano.

12

The venerable *Times*, Gus noted with delight next morning, carried a headline which read, ANTHEM CALMS HOWL-ING MOB, and a long story, as was its custom, on what happened. "They ought to change that line to read: 'Too much of the news that's fit to print,'" Gus growled to Moira. But he was delighted, especially because the other papers were following suit, more concisely. Now it would be necessary to bring Denis into New York before the memory of his last Southern concert had died, and that should be easy enough.

It was not quite as easy as Gus thought, however. Denis was ready enough to leave everything except a handful of friends and the apartment in Orleans Street. But he refused to go directly to New York because he insisted that Lakeland had a right to know what its programs would be, and in any case he was needed in that city for the formal announcement of his choice—or so Aunt Clarissa said.

So the edge was taken off things in the East, and a considerable fillip added in Lakeland, where Aunt Clarissa was leaving no stone in place which she could upend. Up to the moment Huey's goon squad made their unlucky attempt, Denis had merely been the best available young conductor in America. He was still the best available conductor, but he also was the most recent hero in the arts. "Damn it," he reported when Terry joined him in Lakeland for the trip abroad, "you'd think I had thrown Huey into hot lead."

"You did worse," said Terry. "You made a fool of him."

The two were a week longer in Lakeland, working almost around the clock and glad to have an excuse to remain indoors, free of the weather, which as usual was dreadful. They heard the last two concerts of the deposed Lavrenti Mednikov, and they were good. As a matter of policy, insisted upon by Aunt Clarissa, they heard the concerts from her own box and Denis led the applause and later was interviewed. INCOMING CONDUCTOR PRAISES PREDECESSOR, the headline read, thus lifting the review of the concert off the amusement page and onto the front page.

The same morning Aunt Clarissa made an early descent on the Hampton Park Manor. Denis' piano had arrived, and already was covered inches deep in scores and notes for programs and curiosa of whatever sort; in the midst of it all was a tray with coffee and a couple of stained cups.

"Come in," said Denis. "I'll send for some more coffee."

"Thanks." Aunt Clarissa brushed aside the morning paper and took her position on the sofa, one of those luxurious hotel sofas made for everything but sitting. "You'll probably want to replace this thing," she went on. "It's far from comfortable."

Terry laughed. "I don't think Denis would have noticed," he said, "but I did."

"Good." She surveyed the two of them, the apartment, the papers (which she stroked lovingly) and then asked innocently, "What about the orchestra men? How many shall you want to replace?"

Tieless and barefoot, Denis was sitting on the floor beside the sofa. He looked up at his manager and grinned. "None. Next season perhaps three or four, but not now."

Clarissa patted his shoulder. "That's perfect, Denis. It'll get you off to a good start—the men are all atremble."

"They won't get the idea I'm easy?"

Clarissa laughed. "Does it matter if they do? From what I've heard, you'll take care of that at the first rehearsal."

The coffee arrived, and Terry busied himself with pot and cups. "Why don't you make capital of that?" he asked over his shoulder, and before the sentence was done Clarissa was on the way to the telephone.

She called the paper, the one that mattered, and reported immediately that a man was on his way out.

"Oh, God." Denis looked about him despairingly. "I guess I'll have to clean up this mess—and I know where everything is."

"If you touch it," Clarissa said in her most magisterial tone, "I'll rough it up again myself." She shook her head sadly. "Mr. Metoyer, didn't you teach this lad anything about publicity down South?"

"Not much," Terry answered. "Everybody was too busy making an orchestra grow where there was none before. He learns fast, Mrs. Garfield. Don't worry."

"You mean I'm supposed to be one of those scatterbrained Bohemians?" Denis demanded. "I'm damned if I will."

It was a small division, but Terry could see and Denis could sense that Clarissa welcomed a chance to establish with it what she considered the right relationship. So she said, quite evenly, "Yes, Denis. We'll leave it as it is. I shan't interfere with your side of the orchestra, but you've got to allow me to use my judgment in other ways. Agreed?"

Denis was still sitting on the floor, a position in which haughtiness was practically impossible. For a moment she thought he was about to sulk; his dark face clouded and his brows drew together ominously. But then he smiled.

"Agreed—but I'll hold you tight to your half of the bargain."

"Good boy," Terry said. "If you'll pardon a thought from the outside——"

"We will," Clarissa broke in.

"——this is the beginning of the big time for you, Denis. It's not New York, yet. But it's next door."

Presently the reporter arrived, a stringy young man whose acquaintance with the wide world of art was limited to what he saw on billboards. Both the men wondered at Clarissa's unlimited patience, at her care to spell out everything, point out the evidence of hard work in the room, almost write out the story she wanted. But Terry at least knew what the result would be—an almost sob-sister piece about the new and handsome young conductor and his incredible industry, undertaken so that Lakeland might know what programs it would pay its money for next season. Clarissa even drove the reporter back to his office, although this was largely because Denis insisted that he had been away from a piano too long, and would not eat lunch until he had worked at least a couple of hours. She had spent too much time over a keyboard herself, in days past, to enjoy listening to the sort of drudgery she knew she would hear.

And then New York, and much the same sort of thing all over, plus a mountain of detail about Europe and what was to happen. The mountain was so high Terry eventually took it all over, leaving Denis free to be exhibited in the proper places by Gus and by Elisabeth. Although he was not always alone, because there was Claire.

The morning after their arrival at Elisabeth's, Terry was running downstairs from his room, when Claire whistled. She was standing in the door of the dining room, dressed in a cherry-red robe that darkened her skin and her hair, but at the same time enlivened them. She was an attractive nineteen-year-old, even striking in her far from classic way, especially when she was laughing—which she was doing at the moment—so hard she had trouble with the whistle.

"Come here," she said in a low voice, and led the way through the large, dark dining room to the breakfast room at one end. "Have some more coffee, and be comfortable."

Terry said he would, but there was question on his face.

"The drawing room's off limits," she explained. "Old Bumblebee Bowles is putting Denis through the hoops. Nobody ever"—she pounded the table—"ever disturbs him when he condescends to talk with a musician."

Terry laughed. "As a newspaperman of five years' experience, I can tell you the result—if Denis is lucky. One of those interminable Sunday pieces in which Denis is supposed to have said whatever Mr. Bowles wanted him to say. Heigh-ho!"

"Well said, Southerner. The girls at Miss Spencer's have given him a degree—D.T."

"Meaning?"

"Doctor of Turgidity."

"I know what they mean," Terry agreed. "But his paper is powerful. . . ."

Claire was too busy pouring herself another cup of coffee to say anything for a moment. At last she nodded. "You know, I've often wondered what would happen to somebody like Denis if he'd just refuse to talk to all the people he's supposed to talk to—or be talked at by, if you can figure out that sentence."

"It'd probably be too terrible to contemplate." Terry was suddenly serious. "It's not the fault of the Bumblebee Bowleses, either. They're just the instruments."

"Even at the risk of getting philosophical, you might explain," Claire suggested.

"I'm not trying to be funny. You don't live in Huey's state, although you've probably got people around New York who are almost as bad. What I mean is that people have been so conditioned to having their thinking done for them that they're frightened when a politician, or a paper, or a preacher isn't handy. They don't want to know facts. They just want to be given something to say."

"Very profound—and very true."

"Sure. Why else would they stand for these think pieces—you know: 'Berlioz was, in the opinion of many, the greatest master of orchestration who ever lived. And yet, on the other hand, there are those who feel that Rimsky-Korsakoff may perhaps have been his equal, perhaps even his superior.' You know—junk like that."

"The word is crap, Terry." And they both laughed.

"Anyway," she went on, "Denis is in for several days of it, poor lad. What are you going to do?"

"Go see Gus Wagner. He wants to brief me: who the real boss of the Conservatoire orchestra is, what to pay the Paris reviewers, what to say in Berlin to keep out of trouble. He's got the thing plotted like a murder mystery, and it's up to me to take over because Denis simply won't."

"He's lucky to have you."

Nor was Claire the only one to think so. Terry spent almost the entire afternoon in Gus' big office going minutely over the vast file Moira had prepared. There was a folder for each city, a sheet for every person, a schedule of arrivals, reservations, dates to be kept, even the amounts to be paid the Parisian reviewers Terry had mentioned. "And don't try to pay anybody in Berlin or London," Gus interpolated as they ran through the list. "They don't do business that way."

Everything that could be bought or arranged in advance had been arranged; there were even the first names of people casually involved and oftener than one might think, the first names of their wives as well.

"This is superb," Terry said when at last they had finished.

"You're damn right," said Gus. "Nobody in town can do this sort of thing as well as Moira. Now . . ." But he did not go on, and after a minute Terry said, "Now what?"

Gus did not answer until he had taken a turn around the office and come to a halt before the north windows. His shirt had pulled out, Terry noticed, although Gus did not. At last he turned to face the younger man.

"It's Elisabeth McKee," he said bluntly. "She—her foundation rather—is paying for the whole thing, and that's tied my hands a little."

Terry said nothing, but there was a question in his face.

"You see—she wanted to go along."

"Oh, Lord, no."

"Oh, Lord, yes. And I had hell's own time getting out of that." Gus cupped his chin in his right hand and seemed about to twist it off. "Fact is, I didn't quite get out of it. She'll be in London when you are."

"The house party?"

"Yes. She cooked that one up."

"Does it matter? Everything will be finished then."

Moira slipped quietly into the room, ostensibly to bring the day's letters for Gus' signature. But she had no intention of taking them away again. Instead she leaned against the old book-keeper's desk at the end of the room and waited. Gus finished scratching his name a half-dozen times and put down the pen.

"Well," she said at last. "Tell mother. What's disturbing you boys?"

"You're in the family now," Gus said to Terry. "When she gets familiar with me in front of somebody new, it means they've been voted in."

Terry laughed. "Thanks, both of you."

"And, Miss Busybody, we were talking about Elisabeth and England."

Moira pursed her lips. "And it is too bad, at least a little. Only I think you're making too much of it." She looked wisely at Terry. "I suppose he hasn't told you what's in his mind. It's that Elisabeth sang many seasons at Covent Garden and was very popular and the English never forget, whereas the Irish always do. Except me."

Gus' hand came down on the arm of his chair. "I just don't want to dilute the impression Denis is going to make. And there's Claire—she's been crazy about the lad since before he made his New York debut."

137

At that Moira gave up and laughed. "Oh and aren't you stupid? It would be the best thing in the world if she did seduce him, so it would."

Terry was not quite sure, afterward, why he said what he did. Perhaps he was thinking out loud. But he spoke with such firmness that both took his statement with entire seriousness.

Slowly he said, "No. It wouldn't. It's been tried before, and all it did was frustrate both of them. I don't know Claire very well, but I think she would understand. He'll never really accept any woman until he goes to her—and that won't happen until he's got what he wants in music."

It was Moira who broke the silence after half a minute. "Then he's not the sort to work all day and cat around all the night?"

"Not now," Terry answered. "He's more likely to work all night too."

The invasion began, actually, with dinner at Elisabeth's the night before Denis and Terry sailed on the *Ile de France*. It was not a policy dinner, all the needful entertaining having been done before. Only Elisabeth, Claire, Gus, Moira and the two travelers were there. It was a long, quiet meal, punctuated now and again by Gus' gusts of laughter; and when afterward the group gathered in the drawing room, there was even less boisterousness; up to this night Denis had not realized quite the importance of the trip, perhaps because he had had no time to think of that side. It was Elisabeth, unexpectedly, who clothed the matter in words.

"It's all so painfully familiar," she said as the coffee tray went out and another loaded with good liquor replaced it. "I remember how my mother and I bravely refused sleeping capsules the night before we sailed—it was on the *Nord-Deutscher Lloyd*. And how we finally had to take them, because neither of us could sleep. And I was up at seven although we didn't sail until noon, and there was nothing, not even last minute packing, to do. All the way over we worried; one day I wrapped up like an Indian papoose to avoid a cold, and the next I decided to toughen myself and wore as little as a young woman could wear in those days. They told me champagne would keep me from being seasick, and I made myself drunk on it before Mother found out. . . . I hope you're not going to be miserable all the way, Denis."

"I'm not," he said positively, and remembered the remark the second day out when, alone in his deck chair, the whole venture began to seem quixotic. Just one man, a very young man of twenty-five, against the Continent. His good sense told him that only a few thousand on the Continent would care in the least what happened, but at this moment they seemed like hordes, and even France, where he had been born, seemed alien. It was alien, he thought, because there was just one person in the entire country who might be expected to have a personal interest: his grandmother in Nice. When the tour was finished he would look her up, Marie-Louise Levasseur, who must now be in her eighties. He hoped the old lady would know her grandson. But he had not written for years.

The crossing was better after the third day, when Terry came out of his sickness and began to eat. Except that he forced Denis to play at the ship's concert, which meant a curious horde about him for a day or so, a mostly female horde which circled around as if waiting for a chance to stick him with pins.

There was no trouble with customs, but the ride to Paris from Le Havre did not do what Denis had hoped, which was to restore the feeling of belonging that he must have had as a child. The Norman cottages looked as picturesque to him as if he had been born in Gutenborg and not in this very land; the meadows and the cows and the two-wheeled carts and the storks standing one-legged on ridgepoles merely seemed different. And so did Paris and certainly so did the Meurice, where his suite was full of roses and minor officials of the hotel hierarchy, so full that within an hour he and Terry escaped, and walked slowly along the Seine in the early dusk hoping to find a place to eat—and failing.

They finally turned back and into the Rue Royale and behind the Madeleine found a very bourgeois restaurant indeed called Bernard's, where they had the best lobster bisque in Paris and a good deal more. When dinner could not be stretched

139

out longer, they walked through to the Opéra, still lonely and still alien, and stumbled into Sam's. By some miracle a genuine American soda fountain stood before them, and instead of the brandy they had felt obligated to take, they had a chocolate ice-cream soda apiece, and felt very touristy, but also less forlorn.

Three days later they had made their duty calls and likewise certain payments, and Denis stood ready to walk out on the stage of the Salle Pleyel where a hundred and ten Frenchmen waited to rehearse. When he did walk out his spirits hit bottom almost audibly; not a man even looked up. They continued sawing and tootling and talking, and until the exact stroke of ten they ignored him. In that instant, however, the noise stopped and the men faced their racks, neither interested nor uninterested, but merely ready for a job.

Denis did not realize that he had snapped the baton in his hand until Terry brought him another, and as he handed it over, he whispered, "Our friend the manager says to make them work hard; they're used to doing this sort of job with one rehearsal and three makes it seem too easy."

Denis nodded. He rapped for order, something he already had done, and turned to the concertmaster, a very un-French-looking man wrapped to the chin in a soiled gray sweater. "Monsieur," he said coldly and in French, "will you ask the third chair to tune his violin, the outside man?"

The concertmaster frowned, spoke rapidly to his colleague, who flushed and plucked his A string in the suddenly tense silence. He was a shade flat.

Denis nodded to the first oboe. "Your A, please. Will you all tune carefully?"

"Monsieur?" The concertmaster, looking more than ever like a wrestler from the Far North, peered nearsightedly up at Denis. "We rehearse 'Le Sacre du Printemps'?"

Denis nodded.

"Then such extreme precision, is it necessary? No one can be sure."

"I can be sure," Denis said, still cold, as he tapped again for attention. "Gentlemen, I shall give you an exact beat at all times. Rubatos you will take within the beat."

He nodded to the first bassoon. "Ready!" The rehearsal began.

When it ended he smiled suddenly, and his warmth thawed the ice around him in a second. The one hundred and ten men before him fumbled a moment with their instruments, smiled back and then applauded. The applause was sincere— far more meaningful to Denis than that at the first concert, and there was enough then to satisfy anyone.

The audience (Where did it come from? Denis wondered) was wonderful. It seemed to him that nearly every American in Paris was in the house, and a good many French as well. The American Ambassador was represented by his first secretary; at the second concert the Ambassador and his family were there in person. And the reviews; Terry collected them almost reverently.

"I think we wasted some money," he remarked after sorting through them at the hotel. "They couldn't have said anything bad; what we got is most likely more space."

"What we've got is an invitation to an embassy garden party tonight, and the same thing all over in Berlin and Vienna and London," Denis replied lazily. "Right now I'll settle for our week on a Swiss mountain."

The telephone rang, and a Paul Vinay was announced. He and his congratulations quite filled the sitting room when he arrived and nervously balanced his slender self on the edge of a sofa. But what he wanted was something neither of the visitors had expected. After everything proper had been said twice, and sincerely too, he explained.

"There is still some of the season in Monte Carlo, M. Sandzen. It is my orchestra, not so good as you are accustomed to perhaps, but good enough. And you play piano superbly, I am told, even though you chose not to play here. So—perhaps you might arrange a concert with us, an all Mozart program perhaps? I hope?"

This was the one situation not covered by Moira's exhaustive folders. Denis hesitated, caught Terry's slight nod.

"Is it the fee?" asked M. Vinay directly. "It is small, but it will pay expenses for you and your friend. A little more, perhaps."

"It's not the fee," Denis said. "It's a matter of time. Can we, Terry?"

"We have ten days before we're due in Berlin. Let's."

Denis remembered his stranger-grandmother. The work would be worth his while if only it proved that her daughter had had a success, even if the success were once removed. So it was arranged, and there was no week in Switzerland. Instead, there was Grandmère.

After the last rehearsal Denis and Terry rented a car and drove over from Monte Carlo, a little timidly. They lost their way in Villefranche, but in midafternoon they arrived and rang the gate bell. They were admitted by a very young and very shy little servant who seemed astonished when they explained who they were, and ran shouting for Madame.

Madame was eighty-seven, and the word for her was spry. She was tiny, as was her little pink stucco cottage in the Cimiez district of Nice, high on the hillside and buried under small pines and mimosas and huge begonias, except for a tunnel-like path leading to the front door, and thence around the house to the kitchen, outside which was a succession of tubs filled from an icy spring that made a tinkling sound all day and all night.

Madame met them at the door, and for a moment Denis felt his eyes were wrong. Madame was older than Emilie Roman Aimé by a good ten years and her ears were a trifle dull, but her tiny body was as straight inside its Edwardian laces as that of a girl. She looked very like Emilie, and she seemed to find it incredible that her grandson stood before her. Yet there was his mother's face to prove it.

She kissed him, and they went in. The little sitting room was so French it was almost painful: the sideboard that down South on Royal Street would be called French provincial, the stiff chairs upholstered in tapestry from Madame's needle which were designed in a day when all women and many men sat straight and needed little or no support, the big roses in the wallpaper—even the single bulb hung from the center of the room and draped with a thin silk scarf.

They talked; rather Marie-Louise Levasseur asked questions and Denis answered as well as he could. His mother? Had she been happy in that crude little town? His father—a good man but ineffectual—he was a hero, no? M. Wetterstrom and his wife—did he see them now? And so on for a long time that slowly came to have the effect of a dream for Terry, the sort of dream in which a whole life is conjured out of sleep, and reviewed in detail.

At last Madame's thin hand began searching her pockets and came out with a tiny watch on a long black cord. "It's late," she said, "and we eat about this time." She clapped her hands; the little maid appeared, still nervous.

"The soup—there is enough?"

There was, and they had their early dinner under an arbor on the gravel terrace behind the house. The soup, which was thick and heavy and almost as Italian as it was French; a salad; some unbelievably good Brie cheese and fruit. And coffee, which Madame insisted on measuring into the filtre herself; perfect coffee.

They left when the sun was very low, and drove slowly back into the usual world, talking. They had learned a lot, and Denis was relieved of one worry at least. Madame had subtly made it quite clear that she had enough to manage with, although she stopped short of the whole truth, which was that she had saved it franc by franc from the rents paid by roomers in the large house which was literally all her husband had left her when he had given up his struggle nearly thirty years before.

"I've learned a good deal about you," said Terry as they turned over their car to the gold-braided admiral at the door of the Hôtel de Paris.

"There's not much you didn't know already," said Denis.

Terry smiled. "But now I understand a little more what makes you tick. Grandmère provides the drive."

"It just skipped a generation?"

"Precisely."

Next afternoon they sent a car for Grandmère and her companion, and seats were saved for them in the third row, so the old lady might miss as little as possible. Denis played Mozart for her instead of for M. Vinay; the "Coronation" concerto had never gone as well, had never been so crisp and yet so flexible and moving.

When it was over she was escorted backstage, and there she kissed him good-by, but not sadly. "You have, dear boy, what your mother could never have. She had feeling, yes. But not what you have here," and she struck him lightly on the belly, on the scar which now was almost his only connection with his rapidly receding boyhood. For a moment he wanted desperately to put his head down on her thin shoulder and weep.

All this and much more Denis tried to tell Elisabeth and Claire a month later on another terrace, this one grass-covered and in Sussex. The time was early afternoon, and they were resting in the shadow of a very old though not very large house that presumably, but not provably, dated from the time of Elizabeth. The three were alone; the others were in their rooms, the others being Lord and Lady Brackenhurst and their gloriously horse-faced daughter Laura. Laura was, Denis felt, the only female he ever had seen who actually neighed, a vocal exercise which she performed at mechanically determined intervals just as an American quail calls, when in the calling mood, every fourteen seconds.

Free of Laura, Denis had reviewed Paris and Monte Carlo, had gone through Berlin which he remembered chiefly because he had almost come a cropper in the cadenza of the Fourth Beethoven concerto, through Vienna, whose memory was of stinging poverty. London both Claire and her mother knew about, for of course they had been present and enormously proud. Even allowing for the unnatural determination of most British reviewers to be patronizing toward visiting American musicians, the result of London was another stack of notices which, judiciously managed, could last even a young conductor his lifetime—and, in other cases, had.

They were nearly perfect reviews, the only fault mentioned being Denis' "athleticism" on the podium. And this was a red flag in Denis' face. "I can't," he snapped, "conduct as if I were in a strait jacket, damn them."

"It's not important," Elisabeth said, but Claire shook her head.

"You could try to be more calm," she advised. "You know you could."

It was the concerts and the reviews that interested Elisabeth, but it was Grandmère who interested Claire.

"Could Mother and I go see her someday?" she asked.

"Of course, only you'll have to speak French. She has no English at all."

Claire frowned. "Do you suppose Miss Spencer's French would do? It's all I have, and Mother's is just for singing, *'l'amour'* and *'à toi'* and so on."

Denis laughed, and so did Elisabeth, albeit a little less heartily. "You'll manage." He looked hard at the girl. "It just came over me like that, something did."

"What? My stunning beauty?"

"Oh, hush—only you are a lot less repulsive than you used to be. No—I meant it just occurred to me that you'll manage most things. Right?"

"Dears. Please." Elisabeth from long habit was warding off a clash, only this time there was no clash impending. But Denis turned toward her nevertheless.

"Elisabeth," he said, "what did Gus mean about—well—about your being here at the same time? He said you were very popular, and you might draw too much attention. Or at least I think that's what he meant."

Elisabeth smiled. "That's what he did mean. He finally told me. He's a very single-minded man, you know."

"So that's why you were so late getting to London. I see."

"Yes. Only of course he was quite wrong. They may remember me, but after ten years or so they certainly wouldn't make much of me."

Denis looked out over the terrace to where a small and stolid sheep grazed quietly on the lower lawn. Beyond the sheep was a willow-fringed brook, and beyond the brook was a lane, along which a high, square Daimler was approaching solemnly. "That's Terry. I guess he got his stories off all right."

Terry reached the group just as Laura, dressed in a white sports dress starched stiff as armor plate, strode across the terrace, racket in hand.

"Anyone for tennis? Hna, hna, hna!" she demanded, and in spite of everything he could do, Denis laughed.

When he had quieted he apologized. "I'm so sorry. It was just that I thought that 'anyone for tennis' line was something reserved for English parlor comedies."

Laura frowned, in a well-mannered way. "But I don't understand. I only meant anyone for tennis."

"Yes." Denis glanced helplessly toward Claire. "Go play tennis," he ordered. "I see Lord and Lady Brackenhurst on their way to the court."

"Spell me, Terry? Denis is too clumsy."

Terry nodded. "I'll go change."

Their host and hostess may have started for the court, but now they went into the other tack and veered toward the terrace. They looked like older editions of Laura, which of course they were. Said Lord Brackenhurst, whose mildly obscure nickname at Cambridge had been "the Cob," "Really, my boy, Bess and I have been looking at the *Times* ('and the *Manchester Guardian*,' interpolated Lady Brackenhurst), the *Times* I said. You had a stunning success, didn't you? Perfectly splendid!"

"Perfectly splendid," echoed Laura, her distinctly upper-class voice even more raucous than usual.

"Per——yes," Denis caught himself just in time, "very fine."

Lord Brackenhurst cleared his throat. "I understand Sir Tommy Pritchard went backstage to congratulate you. Isn't that right, Elisabeth?"

This could have been confusing, since there were two Elisabeths present, but Lady Brackenhurst's kindly face, very like that of a good Morgan mare, was turning toward Elisabeth McKee, and it was she who answered.

"Yes, Henry. He liked Denis very much." She laughed.

146

"The only thing he wasn't really enthusiastic about was what he called Denis' dancing. And that's odd."

"Dancing?" Lady Brackenhurst was confused.

"He thought Denis' movements were too, shall we say, free?"

"Oh? And why odd, may I ask?"

"Because I distinctly remember," Elisabeth replied, "one occasion in America when Sir Tommy danced himself right out of his trousers."

"Really! How dreadfully embarrassing," said Lady Brackenhurst. And her husband said, "Ha! Faulty braces I take it."

This was all too much for Laura, whose only experience of music after early childhood was with the horn used in fox hunting. "That's all well and good," she interrupted sturdily, "but I mean, anyone for tennis?"

And now there was, because Terry had changed in miraculous time, and stood ready.

At tea later, having lost two sets to Laura, who then took two more from Claire without working up even a faint dew of perspiration, Terry felt entitled to some rest and quiet talk.

"I never realized how difficult it is to describe seven or eight tremendously successful concerts," he said. "You know what I mean. . . ."

"But I don't," his host countered.

"Perhaps not; I hadn't thought. What I mean is that it's the failures that are easy to write about. One success is very like another."

"Hna, hna, hna!" said Laura. "Perhaps in the musical world but not in tennis."

Her father looked speculatively at her, and at Denis, who was waiting patiently for another cup of tea. "You might take Mr. Sandzen's cup," he said at last and rather shortly. And to Terry, "I do see what she means, even though she hadn't quite the words to say it. She really meant that to the player, each success is not like the last."

"True enough." Terry now was waving his own cup at Laura, who finally saw it. "But you see, I've been forced to write a set of stories for my paper, and it's hard to interest the average reader in a clutch of stories—cool reception, warm applause at intermission, cheers at the end, six or eight times in succession."

Lady Brackenhurst had been silently watching, her pale blue eyes, Laura's eyes, shaded by her hair, which was gathered in a twist atop her head and then squashed out as if with a sandbag. Her one out-of-doors interest was gardening, her one indoor interest was politics, although she had so far managed to get her husband no further than an under-secretaryship. "Like my delphiniums," she blurted suddenly. "To me each one is different—sometimes I name them, even. Only I couldn't describe each in turn satisfactorily."

The discussion had pretty well exhausted Claire by this time, and Elisabeth and Denis were fidgeting. It was Claire who seized the subject in both hands, and jettisoned it.

"What shall you do now?" she asked Denis. "Play a while?"

Denis shook his head. "Can't. Not possibly."

"Why? You've arrived now. Why can't you play a while?"

"Denis knows what he wants to do, Claire," Elisabeth interposed gently. "Don't badger him."

"I'm not badgering him. But he has done a terribly good job and he can relax a little."

"Look, Claire." Denis was very serious. "Why do you say I've arrived? I haven't—all I have is the best possible start, thanks to Elisabeth and Terry and Gus and a lot of people." He put down his cup and turned to Terry with an almost adolescent appeal. "You know what I mean, don't you?"

"Yes. If you don't mind my putting it into words I shall. You're just starting the second step. You don't like Lakeland very much, the place, that is. You'll have to stay there quite a while. And you want to take over in New York——"

"Before I'm thirty-five. That gives me ten years."

"Well I'm dashed," said milord, bringing his hand down on the empty teacup he had carefully balanced on the arm of his chair. "I wish more young Englishmen had as firm a program as that."

Claire felt almost as shattered as the teacup lying disregarded in the grass. Obscurely, and especially to Denis, in that moment she felt alien. "I didn't mean to imply that I hate industry. Perhaps I know what I want as definitely as Denis, and perhaps one day I shall get it."

"I think you will," Terry agreed quietly, and no one asked what he meant.

But Denis compromised. He did work through the summer but not in America as he had expected. For this Claire may have been a little responsible, although it may have been even more the Brackenhursts and their talk about the Tyrol. This district, whether on the Austrian or the German side, represented something to the Brackenhursts that even they could not have explained—perhaps it was only that it was the direct opposite of Sussex, a place too foreign for Lady Brackenhurst's feverish gardening, too un-English for Laura's tennis, entirely away from her father's business. He did have a business in addition to his under-secretaryship, and a very good one, importing and otherwise manipulating tin, although a casual acquaintance might have been with him a very long time without knowing it; it was Elisabeth's shares in Bolivian tin which had brought her and the Brackenhursts together, and not her singing.

Denis wanted a place not too far from music, but quiet. He chose Salzburg, and since Terry still had a month's freedom the two arrived in Salzburg one night about eight and tilted wildly about the streets in a taxicab almost as tall as the Brackenhursts' Daimler, looking for a pension recommended by the American Express in Paris, a pension "of the better class, moderately expensive." They found it at last, sitting in rather dignified, stolid fashion a rod or so back from the street in a graveled garden shaded by three great plane trees.

They were shown in by a maid whose astonishment was plain, not, they realized later, because two young men had arrived, but because they had arrived with a great deal of luggage. Frau Lehmann was delighted to see them; she took them at once to the second floor and showed them a huge corner room with two beds and room for a brace of pianos if a brace were needed. She even asked them if a bottle of

Pilsner might not relieve their travel fatigue, and sent the blonde little maid for it when they agreed it might. The door was open into the hall, and just before the maid returned light dawned on the travelers. Terry glanced up, and standing in the doorway were two girls, both young and blonde like the maid, and both mildly tipsy.

"For me," said one, pointing to Denis.

The other pouted prettily. "You always choose and you shouldn't," she said in perfect English. "The gentleman should choose."

"Girls!" Frau Lehmann snapped, but in German. "You have come too early."

They were not afraid of her. Both came farther into the room, and the shorter one seated herself on the foot of the nearest bed. "Why too early?" she asked. "The gentlemen can send us away—if they want."

The gentlemen looked at each other; Terry was the first to laugh. Denis joined him, and for a minute or two they roared helplessly, tears streaking down their faces through the dust of the train. "Oh, God!" Denis choked presently, "it's a whorehouse. I'm supposed to work all summer in a whorehouse!" And they were off again.

But Frau Lehmann was not amused, although she was good enough to pour the beer when it arrived, and to hand each of her prospective guests a glass. "None for you," she said severely to the two girls. And to Denis, "There may have been some mistake, but it is not mine. Believe me, gentlemen, many have stayed with me, knowing that my businesses are kept separate. These girls should have stayed on the ground floor. This floor is for——"

She was never allowed to finish. Terry's shoulders were still shaking at intervals, and he was afraid to try to drink his beer for fear of blowing it over the room, something he was sure Frau Lehmann would not like. But he explained, "Frau Lehmann, this is a young symphony conductor from America——"

"For the Festival?" she broke in.

"No. For a summer's hard work. For study. This is not the place for hard work and study."

She did not agree, but also she did not argue. "I am sorry," she said. "Very sorry. Get out, girls; there has been a misunderstanding. But I wonder"—and for a few seconds she thought and her dignified, middle-aged, rather motherly face showed the effect in an added wrinkle or two—"I wonder if perhaps the carriage house might serve."

"I doubt——" Denis began, but she paid no attention.

"It is completely separate," she said, "and there is an entrance from the next street. You would be alone, and Liesl could serve your meals from our kitchen. It is, gentlemen, a very good kitchen. You would have no connection with this establishment; you would not even see it unless you wished."

Both Denis and Terry were tired, and in any case a separate cottage of their own had great appeal. "There is room for a piano?" Denis asked, and Frau Lehmann nodded.

"Let's look," Terry said, and they trooped downstairs leaving the giggling girls sitting on the bed. Frau Lehmann led them with great dignity and no humor at all through a side entrance and up a cobbled drive into a stone carriage house of considerable size, and up a short stair to the apartment, almost fantastically clean and more than large enough. There was a sitting room, two small bedrooms and a bath, plus a bellpull which, when yanked sturdily, made a distant jangle and brought Liesl on the run.

"You see," Frau Lehmann said quietly, "it is perfect for two young men."

It was, and they engaged it on the spot. After their bags had been carried in and still more beer poured, Frau Lermann left them alone. They could hear her firm step leave the stair and crunch down the drive, and knew that they already liked her more than a little. The liking grew as the days passed and they came to understand that she was neither a good woman nor a bad one, but a person dedicated to the comfort of the male in whatever department, and one capable of knowing which department was suited to which male.

When, in September, Denis stopped off for a long talk with Gus, full of Salzburg's "Everyman," and "Magic Flute" and miscellaneous music not all of which was too well prepared, he told the story. Gus called in Moira, and Denis told it all over again.

"It's good," said Gus. "Very. But it's not the first time a set of programs has been prepared in a whorehouse, my boy."

"Were the girls nice?" Moira asked innocently.

"It's information you want?" Denis inquired. "And it's information you don't get."

Denis rather wanted to tell Claire the story too, but she had suddenly gone off to visit friends in Maine. She left the day before Denis' ship docked.

13

Familiarity with one particular height seemed—and this was fortunate—to release that nagging fear that never, Denis knew, would disappear entirely. He stood now in his living room window alone, which was something he did not much mind, but lonely too. And that he did mind.

By forcing himself to bend forward and peer straight down, he could see the car he just had bought, shining in the blistering late afternoon Lakeland sun. It was a convertible, deep maroon with a light tan top, and since it represented the first substantial luxury he ever had allowed himself, it seemed important beyond its station, and also a kind of symbol of success. It had cost three thousand dollars, a sum that in his past might have seemed stupendous. But it represented only a tenth of what his winter's work would bring him and, the Swedish half of him recalled, it would last for years because it was a sound car.

When he looked straight out, he could see, ten stories down, the lake coppered by the hot sun, and its border of singed grass and rattling, dry trees and on benches and the ground a sprinkling of people thinned and tired by the summer; discouraged too, because one day not too far off the season would change in an hour and the rawness and damp of a Lakeland winter would descend darkly. And would stay on and on unshakably until these same people would long desperately for a break in the sooty smog, even for the heat that was now such a burden.

Denis struck a sort of balance with himself. This was a city he would never like, no matter how good it might be to him. In it were people like none he had known before, people whose conception of graciousness, if it existed at all, grew out of nothing rooted in the city, but from roots planted elsewhere. There would be none of the relaxed warmth he had loved in the South, and none of the clear simplicity of his boyhood in Gutenborg, where weather was either good or bad and people the same. This was a place to be endured for the sake of a fine orchestra which he would make finer, and an opportunity which he felt was unique, the intermediate step between his apprenticeship and his maturity. Again the Swedish half spoke. Here he would be paid for producing something that would always be alien except to the very few, to people like Aunt Clarissa, perhaps Harry Gordon and John Dudley, perhaps a few others who would present themselves through the years. But he would be alone; once Terry had said that the only profession more lonely than music was writing, and this was quite likely true. Terry—there would be no Terry, and he would be the most missed of all. Terry, who had forced him to read Hemingway when he could be pried away from study; who also tried stubbornly to interest him in painting, and succeeded only in a meagre degree.

The telephone rang. It was Clarissa—who else?—to say that she would send Jim for him at seven; he hadn't forgotten dinner at the Gordons, had he?

He had not, but neither would Jim pick him up. "I'll stop for you," he said. "I want to take my new car."

She hesitated a little, and he knew why. She would be in control with her own car. But she yielded gracefully, and furthermore, she was ready when he pulled into the drive at 6900 Scott Road. Nor did she offer advice about the driving, possibly because none was needed—like most men of his age, Denis drove instinctively, having grown up with motor cars, none of which, up to now, had been his own.

"The Gordons' place is Italian," she said, "and do say something about it."

"Of course, if I can think of anything."

They parked in a graveled space beside the house, and climbed stone steps to a flagstone terrace. "They brought the balustrade and the Cupid from Italy," Clarissa said, and added a little waspishly, "the stucco is Lakeland and the vines just grew."

Denis laughed. "Who did the inside?"

"Blitzstein. Everybody has Blitzstein in Lakeland."

Then Gloria admitted them; she evidently had been waiting to do just that.

"Come in," she said. "I thought I heard a car drive in."

Denis was a little surprised at the change in Clarissa. Her strong voice lowered a little, and there was a tinge of pomposity about her manner, just a tinge.

"You did, my dear," she said. "And may I present Denis Sandzen?"

Gloria looked like a quite handsome rabbit, except that her ears were small enough. She moved more or less like a rabbit, too—a rapid spurt, followed by a short pause. She was younger than Denis had expected, not more than thirty, which would make her at least fifteen years younger than her husband. And she was not the beauty-parlor type, or if she was, the parlor had worked more modestly than usual; her short hair was brown with red glints which might have been added through artifice, but which looked as if they belonged. She was small and her figure was girlish though not immature. Even her white satin gown was modest, perhaps consciously so, but its effect was right just the same.

"Do come in," she said, and Denis realized that if anything gave away her origin (some said a five and ten, some said an institution equally public but considerably less inhibited) it would be her voice. She seemed to watch it, as if she feared it might escape her and tell stories of its own.

She led on into the drawing room, the typical Blitzstein room Denis came to realize later, after experience of a dozen or more, each like the other in their scale, which was invariably large, and the arrangement of the furniture, which was always in groups designed to make conversation easy, but so inelastic that the individual pieces seemed to have been nailed to the floor. One did not drag chairs about a Blitzstein room.

There was a marble mantel and over it a painting, certainly a master if not an old one, turned out in appropriate colors by a good friend of old Adolph Blitzstein, who would just as readily provide something more expensive by a foreigner if urged sufficiently. Two sofas with a large, rectangular coffee table between, flanked the fireplace, and there was a profusion of rather heavy Italian sidechairs and a scattering of small tables supporting lamps with beige silk shades. In one end there was a large Steinway looking sheepish in its coat of gilt; beyond, an archway led to the dining room. A small portable bar had been pushed flush up to the tail of the piano, and it was at this that Harry Gordon worked.

"'Lo," he said, putting down the pitcher in which he was making a Martini, "Glad to see you." He shook hands and took orders, and turned back to his labor.

"The Dudleys phoned to say they might be a minute late," Gloria said, her hazel eyes running up and down Denis like mice. "They'll be along."

"They're at the Listers for cocktails," Aunt Clarissa said, for once without thinking, and it was obvious from Gloria's quick glance that this was not the story they had told her. But she nodded.

"It doesn't make any difference," she said. "Dinner's not until eight. Hurry up, Harry. I'm dying for a drink."

Harry approached, the silver tray in his hands tilted just short of disaster. Exactly why Gloria should beat the bushes for a substitute for this extraordinarily handsome man was certainly not clear to Denis; forty-five years of a strenuous life and nearly thirty years of drinking to match had left him just what he had seemed months before—the most distinguished man, in appearance, one might find in a long, long search. He was a little drunk, but not dangerously so; except for a barely noticeable carelessness of movement there was no evidence at all.

"Let's relax," he said. "Let me tell you a story."

"Harry! No stories." Gloria was firm.

"All right. Let's play anagrams."

"Oh, Harry. . . ."

"Well, we can't just sit, can we? Or can we? I never know."

The evening began to slip a little at just this point, but only a little. Clarissa sat up straight and spoke directly to her host. "I think we shall have something very fine at our opening concert," she said. "It's sort of a tradition with Denis to play a concerto on his first program."

Harry grinned. "Who'll conduct for him? Old Dingbat?"

"It's Harry's pet name for Mr. Dattner," Gloria contributed. "He's the assistant conductor."

"So I've heard," said Denis a little more dryly than normal.

Aunt Clarissa sorted this out. "Mr. Dattner is still in the sanitarium, and I'm sure he won't be back in time. Denis will conduct for himself."

This pleased Harry, who said so and got up to mix more drinks. "That'll be a neat trick," he added over his shoulder, "kind of like drinking a bourbon and water while you keep three balls in the air."

"It's not that difficult," Denis said. "Actually it's simpler in some ways. At least with a really good orchestra."

"Gee, I can't wait," said Gloria, her eyes again traveling up and down Denis so obviously that he was not quite sure what she meant. Perhaps her husband felt the same way about it.

"Here," he snapped, "drink this."

Gloria flushed and Clarissa stiffened and Denis got up and walked as unself-consciously as he could to the piano. He played the piano's opening five measures of the Fourth Beethoven concerto, and then rose and beat time with his left hand while he played the orchestra's entrance with his right. He began to feel a little foolish and stopped after a few seconds.

"You see—it's really no trick at all."

"No I don't," Harry answered truthfully, "but I like it. I like the way you go at the piano. Kind of friendly, I guess."

The Dudleys had slipped into the room, having been admitted by the most overpaid houseman in Lakeland. Said John Dudley, "Before we say hello, I want to remark that that's the best piece of musical criticism I've heard for a very long time." At which Harry bowed a little unsteadily, and said, "Thank you, John."

Dinner was served almost immediately, since both the Dudleys refused a drink, something that relieved Aunt Clarissa almost as much as it did Gloria, because it also denied Harry another. It was a good dinner and it went along without untoward incident until the wine did what the drinks before dinner had not quite accomplished: released all the brakes for Harry Gordon, which happened while the dessert was being served. He turned to Clarissa, and said, "You knew my father, didn't you?"

"Of course, Harry. Everybody did. He was a very cultivated man."

Now Harry's chin almost struck his chest when he nodded, which he did frequently. "Not happy, though." He looked down the table at Gloria, who now saw nothing but embarrassment approaching with airplane speed. He said, "Hadn't been for him, I'd be beating the tail off a skinny horse up and down every alley in this town. And you"—his glance at Gloria might have meant frustration or merely dislike—"you'd still be in the basement——"

John Dudley suddenly laughed, very loud, nodding to Clarissa. "That's very good, Clarissa," he said in a voice to match. "Let me tell the others."

Harry Gordon laughed. "That's also a very old dodge," he said. "Been worked before. Anything to stop old Harry."

There was a flutter of conversation which nobody bothered to make logical. But Harry ploughed on.

"I'm wrong," he said stubbornly. "Wasn't my father made the dough. Mother did it; she used to threaten to sell the old man's books if he didn't show up with so much every night." His head again nodded ponderously. "She'd have done it, too, poor guy."

Denis sat frozen, looking about at the Blitzstein dining room with its refectory table (genuine Italian), its high-backed Italian chairs (from a cardinal's palace), its six seven-branched iron candlestands (from heaven knew where). He at least accepted the fact that there was nothing he could do except share the general embarrassment. Abruptly his host rose.

"Let's get out of here," he insisted. "I've got the impression of a six-hundred-dollar chair on my backside, and I don't like it. Gloria!"

"Yes, Harry, I know you want a cushion."

"Damn right I do. I won't eat another meal in this second-hand store without it." And he marched ahead of the others into the drawing room, where coffee and brandy waited on a silver tray the size and approximate shape of Lake Erie.

Their host relapsed into a moody silence like that of a semi-active volcano, and while he was quiet, coffee was served and Gloria offered brandy to the others. Harry roused himself enough to demand some for himself, and then resumed his inspection of nothing. The conversation, if it was such, was skittery until John Dudley caught Denis' eye and motioned him toward the piano. Dudley followed, and underneath a babyish smile said, sotto voce, "For God's sake play something loud. Somebody's got to do something."

Denis smiled rather wanly, and flung himself into the "Revolutionary" etude, and when that was ended—louder than he could remember ever having played it—he began the "Winter Wind." He had not finished when Harry pushed himself out of his chair and succeeded in making the piano in a series of crablike, sidewise staggers.

"Don't blame you, Denis," he said. "John here made you. You'd never hammer a piano like that on your own." Then he faced the room, approximately. "See you in church, Episcopal of course," he half shouted, and left the room.

"Sorry," said Dudley. "I guess it was a little obvious. But what do you do?"

If Denis expected any reference to be made to his host's departure, he was disappointed. Now Aunt Clarissa took over, after Denis halfheartedly finished the "Winter Wind" etude.

"I know you won't mind," she said to the pianist. "Please do something for me. Play a Beethoven sonata—and then we'll talk."

"Which one?" Denis laughed. "It sounds as if I was up on all thirty-two—I'm not. I'll do this one. . . ."

He began the twelfth in E flat, mostly because it was one of his own favorites, and in a couple of minutes he was lost in his own world and quite unaware of his audience. When he had finished Clarissa said, "That's the best performance of the last movement I ever heard; everybody plays it as if they were ashamed of the rhythm."

Dudley agreed. "I gather you've got all the programs in shape," he added. "I'm glad; they've been a little scattering in the past."

"It's pretty simple," said Denis. "I can't see that we've much right to ask people to pay in advance for something they know very little about."

There was a good deal of shop talk, but Clarissa rose early. "I've a hard day before me," she said, "and I'm going home. I can call a cab if you're not ready, Denis."

But he was, and so were the Dudleys. At the door Gloria squeezed Denis' hand, and said, "I loved hearing you play. Maybe you'll come back and play some more."

"Of course," he said, and as he and Aunt Clarissa crossed the terrace he could feel a tingling at the base of his spine; he could not see Gloria's eyes this time, but he knew they were again running over his body. He said nothing until he had put Clarissa in the car, and was opening the door on his own side. "Damn!" he exploded. He jabbed at the starter pedal. "I wish she'd——"

"I know. Don't talk about it; we'll manage."

Nor was the "we" lost on Denis.

Denis saw nothing unusual in the fact that his opening was again a very fine success. He would, indeed, have been very much surprised if it had not been. He was prepared, he could have played his Beethoven concerto backward if he had been so minded, and the orchestra was really first-rate. It was good enough that two weeks' rehearsal were more than enough for him to feel he had made the hundred men his own. And they seemed to have accepted him, with the usual exceptions. There would always be a man or two in every group who would have to be forced into line, he was beginning to understand; who would go so far as to make mistakes deliberately to see whether they would be caught.

This time it was his solo 'cello, a small man with a thin, gangsterlike mustache and hard eyes, who appraised the new and young and completely assured conductor coolly, and then absented himself from the second rehearsal without excuse. He was late for the third, and when he arrived he found his chair occupied by the second man, and the only vacancy at the end of the row. Denis was going through the Fourth Beethoven concerto. He did not give ground by so much as a glance until the end of the movement, which went extraordinarily well. Then he looked at the man, who was about to oust his confrere and reclaim his usual seat.

"Take the chair at the back," Denis said, and when the man stood his ground, he added, "Also, don't fail to telephone next time you're ill. Or were you ill?"

"Uh—yes I was." A slow flush was spreading over his face.

"Your face is still flushed. Perhaps you aren't well?"

"I'm okay. I just want my seat back."

"I told you where to sit." Denis rose, slapped the keyboard so viciously the man jumped. "Take that chair or get out. I don't give a damn which."

For perhaps ten seconds the 'cellist hovered between obedience and rebellion, with Denis staring coldly at him. Then he shrugged and slowly walked down the line to the last stand. Denis waited until he was seated, then turned to the orchestra.

"The first movement was splendid," he said. "Let's go on." But to himself he added, "There's the first man to go."

It was all forgotten at the opening. The Haydn symphony had been close to perfect; the concerto brought the audience up standing. When Denis finished the recalls he hurried into his

160

room and through it to the bath, leaving word with the stagehand on guard to keep visitors out. He quickly stripped and climbed singing into the shower. He just had turned off the water when Clarissa entered the room. "Watch it!" he called. "I stole a shower."

"Here." She handed in his underwear. "Now come on out. I was married twenty years to an athlete. I'm used to it."

Denis laughed. "Remind me to tell you about Cécile de Knize and our first meeting," he said. "How do they like it?"

"Wonderfully. It couldn't be better."

He laughed again. "I see what you meant by the new lights. The women looked like Christmas trees, they sparkled so."

"It's a wonderful audience. Even the Dornmans are here, and they never go anyplace. Nell Dornman's wearing her coronet!"

"You don't say?"

Clarissa was too impressed to recognize sarcasm. "She really is—I haven't seen it since last spring when the Metropolitan Opera was here. It was her wedding present from Henry; they say it cost more than a hundred thousand."

"Whew! It would take me three years and four months to pay for one."

"And Harry is stone sober—at least he looks stone sober. And John Dudley didn't fall asleep. And Nathan Snedeker has his score as usual; he brings scores for window dressing, I think. I doubt he can read music even if he is a critic."

"I hope," said Denis, deftly tying his white tie, "he can write English. And also, who is the old lady in the front row?"

Aunt Clarissa's voice dropped several tones, from awe, he thought. "That's Hetty Stoneman, sister of *the* Stoneman. Copper, you know."

"I wish she'd get a more modern ear trumpet," was all Denis could think of to say. "If I didn't have the rail behind me, I'd be afraid of falling into the thing."

She looked quizzically at him. "My boy, if Hetty Stoneman wanted to bring a Great Dane to these concerts she could, and the rest of the audience would show up with dog biscuit in their pockets."

"I see. Not just millions—hundreds of millions."

"Hundreds." She looked him over. "Perfect. Ready?"

He nodded. "See you afterward. The Listers' party, isn't it?"

Something in his tone told Clarissa that one day he might get out of hand and refuse to be exhibited about town. She resolved that by the time such a day arrived, if it did, she would have him so well established that even his refusal would be an honor. This was material with which she could work, and she would work.

But she might have been a little less sure of the result if she could have heard the telephone call Denis made after he got back to the Hampton Park Manor from the Listers' Blitzstein house, a house even more ponderously Blitzstein than the Gordons', as was suitable, since the Listers were heavy of mind as well as body. The call was to Terry, and it went through almost instantly.

"I thought you might call," Terry said. "Anyway, I stayed home on the chance."

"Good boy. Terry, you remember what you said at the Brackenhursts' last summer? About how hard it is to describe one big success after another?"

"Was it that good, Denis? That's wonderful. God—I wish I could have been there."

"So do I. *Everyone* else was. The Dornmans were, and Nellie wore her tiara. It cost over a hundred thousand. And Harry Gordon was sober, or at least he looked so. And Hetty Stoneman was there with her ear trumpet, the old-fashioned kind. And . . ."

"You sound like Aunt Clarissa. Right?"

Denis was still keyed up. He went through the evening, even through the party, and at the end he said, "Oh, I forgot. Have you got Roosevelt elected yet?"

Terry's reply was a firm "Yes."

"Well," said Denis, "when you come up Christmas don't say a word about it. The people that pay me don't like him. He's a radical."

This time Terry merely repeated a blunt four-letter word. "I'll

162

bet they're not saying too much, just the same," he added. "Oh, well—Denis, do me a favor. Write me now and then."

"Of course."

"No, I mean it. It's sort of—well—grim without you."

Denis did mean to write when he hung up. But two chains of events began almost at once, and for a while at least there seemed to be very little time for writing.

14

Gloria called four times before she found Denis in; then it was at his office in Lister Hall, and Clarissa was seated beside his desk. She would not have succeeded that time if the first bad November storm had not struck without warning just at five o'clock so that it seemed sensible to wait for Clarissa and let her drive him the short distance home. When he recognized the voice he drew a memorandum pad closer and started to write her name. Then he realized what that meant: that he, at twenty-five and a half years, was unable to handle a simple situation, and he began doodling. Aunt Clarissa began smiling.

"Yes," said Denis, and after a few seconds, "Oh, no, not on an afternoon like this. Have you looked out in the last half hour?"

There was another pause. "Well, anyway I couldn't. I've got a date." Still another pause. "Tomorrow? Why—sure, if we're not all snowed in. Yes . . . all right." And he hung up.

"If it hadn't worked out tomorrow, she would have made it day after tomorrow, or the day after that," Clarissa said, her smile broadening. "Believe me, I know."

"How did you know?"

"Don't be naïve. You don't think I haven't gone through this before?"

Denis shrugged. "I suppose so. But Mednikov was married."

She looked very hard at Denis, and after a few seconds he grinned. "I'm naïve again?" he asked.

She nodded. "And before him it was Blum. His mustache must have charmed her." She hesitated. "How are you getting along with dear Mr. Blum, by the way?"

Denis' brows knotted a bit as they always did when he was annoyed—or puzzled.

"Frankly, I don't know. I haven't caught him at anything more, if that's what you mean."

"Watch him. He's a snake in the grass, and a pretty subtle one." She walked across to the window. "It's letting up a little; let's get along."

In the car she added, "Why don't you fire him? I can fix it with the union."

Denis thought a moment, while Clarissa drove calmly between two clanging trolley cars and into the quiet side street leading to the Hampton Park Manor. He already had learned that something protected his manager in traffic, and he no longer rode with his hand on the door handle, ready to jump. "I guess because he's really very good, Aunt Clarissa," he answered at last, and added slowly, "also, I think that's what he would like—I don't know why, but I've got a hunch."

What a curious boy, Clarissa thought. Just let music enter, and he gets wise all at once. "I hadn't thought of that," she admitted, drawing up at the hotel canopy. "He's not exactly popular with the men, but he's got some influence. Well—we'll see."

But nothing happened at rehearsal next morning, and he did not see Clarissa all day. She was beating the suburban bushes for contributions to the orchestra endowment fund, and she was still having tea out on the Heights when Denis locked his office door and sent the doorman for his car. "Lousy day, Mr. Sandzen," the man remarked unnecessarily when he returned. "They're all lousy in this burg."

"You weren't born here, then?"

The man was scornful. "Me? Hell no. Kansas City."

Denis grinned at him. "That was better, yes?"

"God's country, Mr. Sandzen. See you tomorrow."

Denis nodded and drove off to Gloria. He was a good half hour making the fifteen-minute drive, too, thanks to a smash on the hill which reduced traffic to a snarling mass for blocks, and when he finally turned into the Gordons' drive between two gateposts which bore bas-reliefs of puffy mythological characters (real Italian) it was with relief. Gloria couldn't, he reflected, eat him in one evening, and he could use warmth and, for that matter, a drink.

"Hi," she said as she let him in, "I thought I heard a car in the drive."

"Hello. I'm late—I got caught in traffic."

"Poor lamb. Come on in."

Empty, the drawing room looked less Blitzstein and more comfortable, and why he could not have said, unless it was the snapping fire and the very low lights. A Dalmatian wandered in from the dining room, presented his head for a scratching, and settled with a sigh on the hearth. A maid entered the dining room singing "Old Black Joe," and suddenly stopped as she heard voices. The little noises of a home sounded good to Denis; he suddenly relaxed in the corner of one of the vast sofas and lazily watched Gloria expertly putting together a Martini for herself, bourbon and water for him, chattering as she worked.

"Harry'll be along later," she said, "although how much later God only knows. He's working too hard, these days. He's in politics, kind of. I tell him he's got enough to do with the business, and he oughtn't mess around outside. But you know Harry. . . ."

She handed him his drink, and rather surprisingly to Denis, sat on the opposite sofa. She was not delicate, nor was she beautiful. Her movements still reminded him of a rabbit—a flurry of movement, a dead stop. But the fire caught the gold lights in her hair and painted a high light on the gilt buckle that fastened her long, ivory gown at the waist, and oddly her eyes were quiet now, not avid and not demanding.

"Here's how," she said, raising her glass.

"To you," Denis responded. "Gosh—it's comfortable here."

She smiled. "It's lots better than the basement of the five and ten," she said quietly, and Denis blinked. She went on. "I guess you thought that when Harry got started that night I shushed him because I didn't want people to know where I come from." She shook her head slowly from side to side, like a child making a firm denial. "It's not that. I just didn't want him to lay himself open in front of Aunt Clarissa and the Dudleys. You know —they're old Lakeland and all that. They wouldn't understand."

"I think it's a compliment for you to think I would understand."

"It is," she said quietly. "Denis, make me another Martini."

He got up and busied himself with the bottles.

"Oh, no. That's too much vermouth."

He stood, pitcher in one hand and bottle in the other, looking helpless. "What shall I do? Throw it out?"

Gloria laughed. "Of course not, silly. Put more gin in it. You don't like gin?"

"No. It gives me a rash. Or it used to, anyway."

"It makes me rash too, sometimes," Gloria said abruptly, and Denis thought this might be the signal for the entrance of the Gloria he had expected to find in the first place. But she only said, "Denis, does it bother you when people ask you to play? If it doesn't . . ."

"Of course not." He took his glass with him to the piano. "I don't think pianists ever mind playing much; it's playing for people who don't listen that's annoying."

He put his glass in an ash tray, and began the A major Mozart sonata, the one with the variations. He stopped after the first movement and glanced at her; she had turned and was watching him over the back of the sofa. "Go on," she said softly, "finish it."

He did, and at the end she said, "Now—oh, damn it." He could hear a door opening, the thud of a damp coat being tossed on a chair, and he knew that Mozart had been the prelude to something, and the something was not going to happen.

166

"Well, where's your orchestra?" Harry stood laughing in the doorway, his handsome face a little red from the cold.

"It's after hours," Denis said. "They wouldn't come."

Harry kissed his wife, and at once bent over the coffee table. "How's your drink?" he called to Denis, who held up his untouched glass. "Don't let me stop the music," he went on. "Play something else."

Gloria broke in. "Let him rest; he's played quite a while."

"Sure." He laughed. "Let's talk politics. I'm really in the middle this time."

Gloria looked across at Denis. "Don't say a word, or you'll get a lecture a yard long."

Harry was in high humor. "He could do worse. This thing is fantastic, Denis. Absolutely fantastic."

Denis thought Gloria sighed as she burrowed down into her corner, but her husband paid no attention. He went on:

"This is a Republican state, except around here and some other industrial towns. Everybody who has anything—and plenty do even yet—is Republican. They all dumped dough into the Republican campaign like mad, and they lost. I had lunch today at the Union Club with old Conrad Mann. Know what he said?"

"Cue him in," said Gloria.

Denis glanced inquiringly at her, and said, "No, I don't. I don't even know who he is."

"I keep forgetting. Of course you don't." Harry took a long drink, and laughed again. "Said he'd made back every nickel he put into Hoover's campaign betting on Roosevelt. Said, 'Hell, you can't elect a man who can't smile.' Lot in it, too."

"Well," said Denis, "I couldn't vote because I haven't lived here long enough. But if I had I'd have voted for Roosevelt."

"Good boy." Harry's voice lowered a little. "Don't breathe it, but I did too. The powers that be are scared, plain scared. And Roosevelt isn't. That's enough for me."

"Denis," Gloria broke in, a slight edge of desperation in her voice, "can't you stay for dinner? We'd love to have you."

A little desperate on his own side, Denis fumbled. "No. I can't. I've got work to do."

"There's hot borscht," Harry urged, "made from my mother's recipe. I know, because I ordered it myself."

"Well . . ." Denis could think of no lie that sounded strong enough. "If I can leave right after?"

He could, of course, and he did. He also was glad he stayed. The borscht was perfect, the roast the same. And he was able to plant an idea and squelch one of Clarissa's.

The first idea was his feeling that Lakeland had no right to confine its audience to the faithful eighteen hundred who could go to Lister Hall for concerts. Denis wanted—not this season because there was no time for arrangement—to tour his men through the state, since there was no other group to take on that responsibility. And Aunt Clarissa wanted the orchestra to go to New York in the spring, while the news of Denis' appointment and the foreign tour was reasonably fresh.

"Why don't you want to go to New York?" Harry asked directly.

"Because we're not ready." They were back in the drawing room; he put down his coffee cup, and leaned forward. "It's this way: I'm not afraid for myself. They'll say I'm too free with my movements on the podium all right, but I'll get good enough notices. I did before, and I'm much better now. Believe me.

"Only my orchestra needs another two years with me. They're good, except two or three. But a new conductor is like putting on a new pair of gloves. They may fit the first time, but they haven't set to your hand."

Denis refused the drink his host offered. "I don't like to say this now," he added, "because it looks as if I were campaigning behind Clarissa's back. But I've said all that to her. She knows how I feel."

"Don't worry about her. She's talked to me. About Blum too." Harry was a little mellow now, but far from drunk. "I know what Blum's up to. If I have to, I'll tell you what it is—and I hope I don't have to."

Denis left in a few minutes, and it was Harry and not Gloria who saw him to the door. "You're all right, boy," his host shouted as he ran through the sleety, cold rain to his car, and when he drove past the door on his way down the drive Harry was still standing there, a tall figure in a frame of warm light, his right arm up in a good-night salute.

But, Denis thought, would I have had this good feeling if he had come home fifteen minutes later? His instinct, if that was what it was, told him he would not.

During the holidays there was a reunion. Elisabeth came to hear the orchestra, and so did Terry. Claire stayed home. And the day Elisabeth left, Denis asked the Gordons, the Dudleys, the Listers and of course Aunt Clarissa for cocktails. It was a small party, the more decorous, perhaps, because Harry was not in town and Elisabeth would have to leave early to catch a seven-o'clock train. The talk was musical for the most part, relaxed and good. Finally the Dudleys and the Listers left, taking Clarissa with them; then Terry looked at his watch and Elisabeth, and said they must hurry, and could he borrow Denis' car so Elisabeth would not have to bother with a taxi.

"I'll help you straighten up," Gloria said quietly. "Perhaps you and Terry might take me to dinner later?"

Elisabeth looked sharply at Gloria, but now there was nothing she could do. She kissed Denis. "I love your orchestra," she said. "You too."

Denis remembered to send his love to Claire, and in a few seconds the door closed, and he was alone with Gloria. At least she's different each time, he thought, as she walked straight to him and put her arms around his neck. There was nothing demure about her now, in fact there was nothing at all but her complete confidence that she had her man cornered.

"Kiss me," she commanded, and when he did what she asked, her lips opened and he knew that whatever the implications for the future the time was now, not then, and that he would do what she wanted.

For a long time they stood where they were, lips together and their bodies almost fused in a quickly mounting flame. It was she who spoke, and all she said was, "Terry can't get back for an hour. Oh, Denis—I want you so much."

He picked her up in his arms, and carried her into his bedroom. This has happened before, he thought. She doesn't really want me. She wants—it. And yet she did want him and him only at that time, and that was enough for him. Sardonically, his inner monitor added, it's enough any time if somebody else makes the advances. Denis suddenly pulled her to him and roughly; he heard a little sound from her, but it was not a sound of dismay, rather of happiness. Then the buzzer at the living room door sounded.

"Damn!" Gloria said. "What is it this time?"

"Pay no attention. They'll go away."

But that was no good. Any one of the people who had just left might have forgotten anything—and nobody could have overlooked the fact that Gloria had stayed on. "Oh, hell," Denis said after a moment, "I'd better answer."

It was Harry, half-seas under and full of news—so full he seemed not to think it odd that the two should be alone.

"Harry!" Gloria darted across the room, "I thought you had to go away."

Harry kissed her perfunctorily and turned at once to Denis, who could think of nothing to do but pour a drink, which he did at once.

"Thanks," Harry said briefly. "Sit down, both of you."

His voice was cool and a little hard in spite of liquor; maybe this is it after all, Denis thought. He's come in twice this way. But he sat down.

"Look, Denis," Harry began. "I was supposed to go to Pittsburgh this afternoon, but something came up. So I put it off. I want to warn you."

"About what? I haven't done——"

"Of course not, at least nothing that bothers me." Did his eyes slip knowingly from him to Gloria, and back? If they did, he was making nothing of that situation, for he went on. "But your friend Blum has."

"Blum?" said Gloria. "Blum?" No ship captain, Denis noted, could be more wholly secure in his command than Gloria was of herself.

"The 'cellist. And it hits me on a tender spot, goddam it."

Me too, probably, Denis thought. He frowned, but before he could speak Harry said, "I'm damned if they'll get away with it, either. There's too much of that kind of thing going on for anybody's good." He looked directly at Denis. "You have any Jewish blood?"

"What? God, I never thought about it. I don't think so—what makes you ask?"

Harry poured down the last of his drink, and held out his glass. "It's—oh—sort of anti-Semitism in reverse, I guess you'd call it. You sure you've got no Jewish blood at all?"

"Look, Harry, I honestly don't know. Why should I? My father was a Swedish Lutheran, and my mother was a French Protestant. But I don't know a damn thing beyond that, only I saw my mother's mother last summer, and well, she . . ." He was floundering, and Harry came to his rescue.

"She looked a little Jewish, you mean. A lot of old French women do, and it doesn't prove anything."

It was Gloria who pinned the situation down. If she was not to be allowed to go to bed with Denis, she at least deserved a little excitement. "Harry, for God's sake get to the point. I'm getting hungry," she said sharply. "Please."

"Okay. Blum's been telling the right people, I mean the wrong people, that after that blowup at rehearsal you called him into your room and said something about 'No goddam Jew 'cellist was going to run your orchestra.' I know you didn't say that, but what did you say?"

"I don't believe it," said Gloria.

"I don't either." Harry turned back to Denis. "But what was it?"

Something burst in Denis' brain, rocketlike. "The lying son-of-a-bitch," he burst out. "I'll kill him. I—listen Harry—I said exactly what he claims with one change. I said 'No damn 'cellist is going to run my orchestra.' And I damn well meant it, too."

"Good for you. Fire him." But then Harry shook his head. "That's liquor talking. No, don't fire him. We can do better than that."

More to calm himself than otherwise, Denis poured another drink for Gloria and himself, sloshing around in the silver ice bucket for the last pieces. "What?" he finally asked.

"Let it ride. Let it build up, if it does. And don't worry. We can handle it." He got up and walked slowly around the room, burning with slow anger inside. "You know, Denis—or maybe you don't—that there are always professional Jews, and Englishmen and Catholics (Gloria was born a Catholic, you know). That kind of thing. Sometimes they even form associations and the officers collect salaries for snooping around looking for insults. It burns the beJesus out of me. Sure, I know there are anti-Semites and anti-Catholics and anti-Swedes and all that. I could be wrong, only I don't think so—I think it's exactly what that bastard Mussolini, and Hitler too, have in mind. I think a Jew ought to have the right to say what he thinks. And how the hell can he if he objects to Catholics saying what they think? It's when somebody actually does somebody dirt that it counts. And you see, that's what that 'cellist bastard is doing. He's using imaginary prejudice to knife you."

Denis looked at Harry with admiration which was no less sincere because it was a little adulterated with astonishment. "Well," he said, "that's a damn fine speech. If it keeps growing, what shall we do?"

Harry further astonished Denis by refusing another drink. "I've had enough for now," he said. "And we won't worry about what to do. I've been making last-minute decisions all my life, and they've been all right, for the most part." He looked sharply at Denis. "This isn't my business, maybe—but did you ever notice how tough Aunt Clarissa is? All that business of her being the mother of the orchestra is plain hogwash, you know. In one sense she is, but she's more just a woman doing a damn good job, and she'd cut the ears off you, or me either, if she thought it would help the orchestra."

Denis looked shrewdly at Harry, his brows knotted. "You're trying to tell me something. What is it?"

"Something else that's not my proper business, I guess. Only —well, are you absolutely comfortable about this orchestra?"

"I think I see." He glanced briefly at Gloria, whom he had

almost forgotten. "You mean that perhaps I'm still not tough enough."

"One way of saying it."

"Yes." For the first time since the opening in October, Denis felt the tension beneath the jagged scar on his abdomen, as he always did when he was really disturbed. "I'll tell you the truth. This orchestra is so much better than the one down South that I haven't wanted to disturb things too much, right at first. And the men do play for me."

"Sure. You'll have to excuse it if I'm wrong, Denis, but I don't think this Blum thing would have happened if you'd been a bigger son-of-a-bitch than he is, right from the start. Think it over." Harry got up. "Come on, Gloria. Time for the feed bag."

Denis stood in his doorway until the elevator stopped. He waved to the Gordons and said hello to Terry who got out. Then he reported the entire exchange, almost word for word. Terry listened silently, and at the end surprised Denis by laughing.

"I thought you told me that Gordon was a lush," he said at last. "He's a damn smart lush, Denis lad. I'd say that he is the one person in Lakeland you'd better not be a son-of-a-bitch toward."

Denis agreed, and a little mellowed by a slight overdose of bourbon, he went farther. "He put the fear of God in me when he arrived. We—I——"

Terry laughed again, and harder. "You don't have to tell me any more. I heard Gloria say he was out of town, and I saw her lag behind the others. You're a marked young man, and she'll get you in spite of hell and coincidence, too."

Denis' grin sat a little uncomfortably on his dark face. "You know, Terry, she's got depths you don't suspect, too. At least I think she has."

"I'm hungry." Terry was finished with the Gordons and especially Gloria. "Let's go downtown and eat." But he did have a final word on Harry's advice.

"I'd be tough, all right. But I think I'd try making your friend Blum uncomfortable. I wouldn't ride him, and I'd be absolutely fair in a professional sense. He may expect you to ignore him, so

173

I'd be absolutely sure he gets exactly the same treatment as everybody else. No more, no less."

After dinner the two of them went to a movie, and left the theater after half an hour because Denis refused to listen longer to the squawks from the screen. Home again they talked a long while over the inevitable nightcap, and when Terry went to bed Denis sat on in the living room, head resting on the sofa back.

There was a lot Denis did not understand in his relationship with Terry. He wondered, sometimes, whether he too were not —odd—since he could not feel the way so many would feel if they knew everything about this Southerner—or at least, the way many would insist they felt. I honestly feel a little ashamed that I can't be physically closer to him, Denis thought, and the idea of being that way isn't distasteful. It's just that I can't, quite. And the whole thing does not change the way I feel toward him.

I wonder, he thought, whether he could be a finer person if he were like the majority, and he felt silly to have asked even himself that kind of question. He did not think that among all the people he knew there was one more honest, more honestly decent, than Terry. If that side of him has warped him, Denis said to himself, perhaps more should be warped the same way. Impulsively, he filled two jiggers with bourbon and carried them into Terry's room.

"Asleep?" he said softly, and Terry smiled.

"Then let's drink to the best friendship I have."

Terry raised himself on one elbow and they drank. Denis took the glasses, patted his guest's shoulder, and said, "Good night, boy."

He could feel Terry's eyes on him as he left the room.

15

When it came, Gloria's triumph was ridiculously simple. It was the beginning of March, perhaps the dreariest of all the months of the Lakeland year. Lister Hall was surrounded, almost concealed, by a dirty snowfall which had begun the night before and which might continue for a couple of days. At some point the snow had been white, but long before it reached the surface of Lakeland it had turned a dirty brown-gray. It was a little too cold for melting, so the streets had filled except for a few that had been ploughed, and the snow was further fouled by the passing cars and occasional horses. Rehearsal had begun a little late, and Denis was sharp about it; in this he was wrong and knew it, but weeks in which there literally had been no sun at all had left his nerves as jagged as anyone's, and he could not help himself.

And Blum had been crowding Denis' beat all morning, just a shade. An outsider, even a musical one, might have thought he was merely being extremely efficient, but Denis and the orchestra knew better. He was carrying the war of nerves one step further, and when his rebuke came it was bitter as well as deserved. And his entire campaign was the more infuriating because at concerts he played like an angel, if such a word could be used about a man with a useless little black mustache.

Denis held such a tight rein on his hundred men that he was never quite able to know how the whole thing affected them. Technically the orchestra played superbly; he forced it to. But it seemed to him there was no heart in its performance, or not enough.

At the end he said, as usual, "Thank you gentlemen," and

left the stage with the feeling that for once he was even more delighted than the orchestra at the end of work for the day. And also that there was more whispering in corners than was strictly necessary. He hurried back to the hotel and changed; he had promised Clarissa to go with her to a Women's City Club luncheon and "say a few words," and there was no time to think about 'cellists.

Clarissa drove through the snow with disdain, as if she dared it to force her to call on Jim and the larger car. The Slater was too hot, in the first place, and the luncheon ran too long in the second. Also the chicken à la king was oversalted, and Denis' favorite dodge in such situations betrayed him. He usually said that he was a musician and not a speaker, and since there was a piano on the stage, he would play for them. Only this time middle C on the piano was completely out of tune, as if some mischievous creature had deliberately lowered one string, and the effect was barely endurable.

And then Aunt Clarissa chose that of all afternoons to begin worrying about soloists for the next season, and he spent the rest of the afternoon in her office trying to find sufficiently big names who also would satisfy him musically, and still be within the budget, that sacred and supposedly inviolable thing which never, no matter how hard everyone tried, quite balanced.

Denis left the Hall at four and stumbled to the hotel through snow almost deep enough to cover his galoshes. There were drifts on the walk skirting the frozen little park, and the copper helmet on the church looked almost gay, its pale green patina flat against the chill gray of the sky. His apartment was pleasant enough any day, but more now than usual it seemed a refuge against a sullen world; even a Roy Harris score was not quite so bleak in a warm room. He should write Terry, too, although writing letters was never a pleasure for him. The way a pen inched across a white sheet of paper, always well behind his thought, made him impatient.

Later it occurred to him that there was something very close to a leer on the elevator man's pinched little face when he said "Nice day, Mr. Sandzen," although at the time it seemed merely one more repetition of a standard Lakeland pleasantry.

"Not fit for a dog," Denis replied, and the man laughed as if the remark had been funny. Then Denis let himself into his living room.

Gloria looked up from the sofa. She had the score of the Harris symphony on her lap, which indicated a certain desperation for reading matter, inasmuch as a full score was as far beyond her as ballet dancing would have been beyond Denis.

"Gloria! What in God's name?"

She closed the score and wrinkled her face in disgust. "How you read those things beats me," she said, and in the same breath, "I got the elevator man to let me in. I didn't think you'd mind."

"Look, Gloria. These things get about, especially when you're well known. We can't afford——"

"I can't afford to stay away. Don't you understand? I had to come."

Slowly Denis took off his overcoat and galoshes and shook the melted snow out of his hair. "But Gloria . . . just to sort of defy everybody. Don't you see?"

"Stop 'but Gloriaing' me. And I don't see. If you're worried about Harry, why don't be. I talked to him in New York not over an hour ago. He can't even fly home before tomorrow."

Denis gave up. But even so, he wondered exactly what there was about him that had drawn two dissimilar persons like Cécile and Gloria to him in exactly the same way—his looks, which he hated? His reluctance? Perhaps the fact that he spent no time whatever in pursuit?

"All right," he said quietly. "You're here and even if I think you oughtn't to be, I can't throw you out. Let's have a drink."

"That's better. Let's have two."

He laughed, and disappeared into the small kitchen. When he came out he brought a Martini for her and whisky and water for himself. She looked up. "This is lots better. Now go put on a robe or something. You look all damp and mussed up."

"All right." He took his drink with him, and when he came back in a dark blue robe and slippers, she motioned him to the sofa and took his free hand.

"I don't know what you think of me," she said suddenly.

177

"I'm years older than you even if I don't look it. The funny thing is I simply don't care."

"I think you're nice, Gloria, honestly I do." She looked as if 'nice' were an unconvincing word. "What do you think of me, anyway?"

"That's you're the best-looking man in Lakeland. And even if you don't know it, the sexiest."

He could not keep a blush off his face. "I don't act that way, do I? I—I'm too busy I suppose."

"I suppose." She finished her drink and handed him the glass. When he brought another, she went on as if there had been no interruption. "I don't care much. I know perfectly well you don't love me, and I won't let myself love you. It wouldn't work that way. But that still leaves something."

One part of Denis' mind, his monitor, was sitting coolly aloof, watching and listening. You have your ambition, it seemed to say. You want what you want, and it's costing the kind of relationship that most young men of your age have. But the other part of his mind was slowly giving way. The warmth of the room under its low lights, the light odor of very good perfume, the liquor—and the unashamed sexuality of the woman beside him seemed to combine for a moment into a force that . . . He made himself stop before he finished the thought. He had been about to compare this slowly building-up climax to something in music. And even he knew that not everything could be expressed in those terms.

Later he thought that their coming together was as if they had been jerked into a bundle by a giant rubber band. One moment they had been talking, not even touching hands. The next they were enfolded in each other, mouths sealed together, each as if drowning in a stormy sea. For a little time they lay together, taut. Then without a word they rose and went together into Denis' room, dark now and smelling faintly of masculine things —leather and spicy toilet water and tobacco. Their clothes fell in two heaps beside the wide bed.

Later Denis sat cross-legged on the bed, wrapped in his robe, watching her dress. "I'll call down and have dinner sent up," he said, and the words put a definition to their relationship. It had gone as far as it could go; it was that of two animals who, having satisfied one primary desire, were now ready for food and the usual things until pressure once again built up and the cycle could begin again. And oddly it was not the woman who sensed the inadequacy of the situation, perhaps because she knew what to expect, and Denis knew almost nothing.

"Don't," she said, stepping into her shoes, smiling softly. "I'd better not stay; the servants'll wonder about me."

Denis laughed softly. "You're amazing, Gloria, truly amazing."

She was bent toward the mirror, replacing her lips. "Why?" she asked out of the corner of her twisted mouth.

"You came here and bribed the elevator boy to get in, and didn't think a thing of it. But now you're here, you're afraid the servants will talk if you don't get home to dinner. It seems pretty inconsistent to me."

She was ready now. She ran her hands down over her slender hips and turned to face him. "I don't see why," she said. "I know what I mean."

"And?"

She smiled. "The servants live in the same house with Harry. The elevator boy doesn't. It's that simple."

"Have it your way." He followed her back to the living room. "One for the road?" he asked.

"Sure." She sat down on the sofa and picked up the Harris score again. "Oh, Denis," she said, "I've made a blot on it."

"You know, Gloria, if they play the blot instead of what was there, it won't make any difference to anybody. Here . . ." He handed her a glass.

"Thanks. You're sweet, Denis. Brutal in bed . . . oh! Don't be offended. I loved it."

"I'm not offended." He had something important to say, and he had not the words. He stumbled on, "It was wonderful . . . and terrible. I've got . . . well, I've got a lot to learn." And he wished he had said nothing, because something went out of the room with her next words.

"Gloria's the one to teach you," she said a shade coyly. "When shall teacher come back?"

The explosion came with the end of the season, and the detonator was a small item in the only paper that mattered, one that quite obviously the music editor knew nothing about, even if Snedeker ever had deigned to be a reporter as well as a reviewer. The item merely said that "a prominent Jewish man" had written a letter to the Orchestra Board complaining about the "alleged discrimination" of the orchestra's conductor. It was evident that the city editor was walking softly, ready to jump in any required direction, even straight up.

The night before the item appeared Denis and Clarissa had been trapped at the Gordons' while Harry demonstrated the lengths to which steady, all-day drinking could lead one. They left early, and behind them they left Harry prostrate in his own drawing room.

"Go on. Don't worry," Gloria said. "He can sleep it off here as well as anyplace. 'Night."

Denis read the item at breakfast, and picked up the telephone. Harry would be feeling ghastly, but perhaps if he caught him before he had had more than an eye-opener, something might be done.

Gloria was five minutes getting Harry to the telephone. Denis heard a sound between a grumble and a roar, and then a tired "H'lo." He explained; actually he explained twice.

"The bastard," Harry groaned. "This morning of all mornings."

"Look, Harry," said Denis. "Maybe we'd better wait awhile."

Harry was still a little confused. Distinctly, Denis heard, "Gloria, get me a shot," and then softly, "Wait hell. We'll move in right now." He laughed. "You hear what I said?"

"Yes, I did. What should I do?"

There was silence for a moment while Harry gulped his bourbon. "Brr-r-r," he shuddered. "Nothing, Denis, only be in the board room at eleven. Don't talk to anybody except me and Clarissa. Call her right now and tell her I'll round things up."

"Right. Hell, Harry—I hate this. I really hate it."

"Sure. What was it the President said? 'We have nothing to fear but fear itself'? Maybe I'm glad to have it come to a head. Maybe I'll get to say something I've wanted to say for a hell of a time."

"You're a good egg. Thanks a lot."

"Okay, boy," and the phone clicked off.

The two hours until eleven o'clock were enormously long, and Denis spent most of them locked in his office at the Hall, reading the Harris score automatically and seeing nothing, not even the blot left there a month or so before by Gloria. Then Clarissa tapped, and called that it was time to go. He was trembling a little, and the tightness was in his belly, although he looked cool enough; he forced himself to look cool enough.

But his astonishment at what he found in the board room was evident. He had expected two or three members of the board, and he saw nearly all of them. Blum was there, his thin mustache making a little black streak on his thin white face. So were half a dozen members of the orchestra; Rabbi Glazer of the Congregation Beth David; the head of the musicians' union, as round as John Dudley and more than merely puzzled; Howard Dietz, editor of the paper; two strangers—and of course Clarissa, more dignified for the occasion than dignity itself. Harry was standing at the end of the long table.

"Come in, Denis," he said, his face grave. He turned immediately to the group in front of him. "I want to read this item from the morning paper for the benefit of those who may not have seen it."

As he read Denis looked at him and marveled. His skin was clear, his carriage erect, his grooming without any fault. And he seemed perfectly sure of himself and his position. As he finished there was a wordless movement from all but one. Blum rose and said, "I want to make——"

"Keep still," Harry commanded. "You'll get your turn."

Blum sat down, and Denis saw a look almost of repugnance touch Rabbi Glazer's face, and fade away. Harry went on,

"There are seven of us in this room who are Jews. I don't include Blum, because I don't know what to call him. When a man indicts himself and his own people to gain a point, and a wrong point, he deserves a name I couldn't use in front of Mrs. Garfield."

Clarissa stirred involuntarily, and Harry smiled at her. "Maybe I'm wrong about that," he said. "Mrs. Garfield has been with us a long time, longer than any one of us. But"— and his face clouded again—"we're not here for name-calling. I want you to know what actually has happened, all of you. Denis, this began when Blum was absent from rehearsal without permission and you disciplined him when he returned. You made him sit for the morning at the last stand. Right?"

"Yes."

"And later you called him into your office and told him off. Exactly what did you say?"

"I said no goddam 'cellist was going to run my orchestra."

"Did you say, 'No goddam Jewish 'cellist is going to run my orchestra?"

"I did not."

Blum again rose, and Harry again forced him to sit down.

"Now Mr. Mayer—Mr. Mayer is our assistant solo 'cellist —will you tell me how Blum first reported this exchange to you?"

Mayer was young, thin, with dark Oriental-looking eyes. He was also nervous. "As nearly as I can remember, Mr. Gordon, he said just what Mr. Sandzen reported."

"Thanks. For everybody's benefit," Harry continued, "the gentlemen from the orchestra I have asked to come may or may not know directly from Blum what was said. They were chosen at random. Oh, and Mr. Mayer, did you ever hear from Blum that 'no goddam Jewish 'cellist' and so on? And if so, when?"

Mayer rubbed the back of his neck with a slender, almost womanish hand. "Yes," he said slowly, "only I can't tell you exactly when. A few days later."

"Yes." Harry gestured toward the concertmaster, also young but chunky and more self-assured. "Mr. Reiner, the same questions to you."

"And the same answers exactly." He grinned, the first sign of a break in the grimness around him. "The reason I know—should I say?"

"Certainly."

"The reason I know is that I told Blum I didn't blame Mr. Sandzen, and I wouldn't have said it if he'd used that word."

"Thanks." Harry went the rounds of the orchestra group. All knew the situation, and one or two went into some detail about the growth of feeling. Two had heard nothing from Blum directly.

"Now, is there anybody in the room who has not heard this rumor? Anybody at all?" There was not a sound. "You see," Harry went on, "what has happened. Unrest, suspicion, all based on a lie. Isn't it based on a lie, Blum?"

There were two spots of red, almost like tubercular spots, in Blum's cheeks as he rose. His hands were clenched, and his mouth was one-sided, as if he were about to snarl. "This meeting is rigged," he said bitterly. "I——"

The Rabbi turned on him sharply. "This meeting is not rigged," he snapped. "And who are you to talk about rigging? You are a member of my congregation. Do not lie to me. Did you insert that word or did you not?"

"What chance have I got?" Blum demanded. "I'm just the hired help."

"You haven't answered me," Rabbi Glazer said quietly. "And don't play for pity; you're a very good and valuable 'cellist, and there have been times when I wished I were that instead of what I am." His dignity was the very real kind, not dependent on appearance or rank, but on simplicity. "I shall have to assume if you do not answer me directly, that you cannot."

Blum hesitated; the cords on the backs of his hands tautened. "It's the way I remember what he said. That's what I thought he said."

"Thank you, sir," said Harry to the Rabbi. He turned to the two strangers, who seemed uncomfortable or worse. "Now gentlemen," he continued, "do you see what you have done? I hope you do."

The taller of the two replied. "It is my duty to act on complaints of discrimination."

"Without investigation?" snapped Harry.

"They're usually true. It's too bad if Mr. Blum was—mistaken."

"Mr. Blum was more than mistaken. He was a deliberate liar. Weren't you, Blum?"

There was no answer; the only movement in the room was the slow, sad shaking of Rabbi Glazer's dark head. The Rabbi looked at Denis, and said in the tense silence, "It is not because I believe you are the most gifted young musician I have ever heard that I say this. It is because these others"—and there was a delicate flick of scorn on his tongue—"keep silent. I am sorry this has happened. I know that we can never quite overtake this" —and now there was pain in the soft voice—"this lie. I have heard more than once that you were anti-Semitic. I should have done more than refuse to believe. I should have come to you, and for my neglect I apologize."

Howard Dietz had said nothing throughout the session. Now he smiled at Rabbi Glazer. "Spoken like a man," he said. "Like a great man." He looked around the room. "This is almost as bad as a meeting of the Oxford Group," he went on, "but I feel bound to say that my city editor has his share of blame. He should have gone to headquarters, too. But I shall do all I can, which is to report this meeting. I know they usually claim that it's better to let things like this die away. They don't die so easily, though."

"It's all you can do." Harry was again standing, his face a little paler. "My point was not to deny that we do mistreat each other. Lakeland does bad things to her Negroes, and her Poles and many others. But it can work the other way—and I wanted you to see. Thank you, gentlemen."

Denis could not help noticing that not one member of the board had spoken, excepting its chairman. He stood with Clarissa as the men filed out, impulsively putting out his hand to touch Rabbi Glazer as he passed. The union president stopped a moment, noticeably affected but determined that no one should know. He said slyly to Denis, "And who'll the new solo 'cellist be?"

Denis could sense Clarissa's tensing. "Is there to be a new

one?" he asked, and the president winked and passed on into the hall.

Lister was just behind. He waited until the man was out of range and said firmly, "Of course there will. You can't take this lying down."

"We'll manage it, Douglas," Clarissa said. "Thanks for coming."

Harry Gordon was just behind. He looked weary, as if the hour had drained him.

"You were magnificent," Denis said. "Terrific."

"Yeah?" he replied. "What I need's a magnificent, terrific drink."

16

Gloria asked a clutch of twenty or twenty-five orchestra people for a buffet supper the night before they were to leave for their first tour of the state. The time was the second year of Roosevelt, and already the frightened men who had a year before grasped the President's coattails and oriented themselves after four years of floundering were talking in corners, worrying about that man in the White House, and when there was the slightest excuse, berating him in absentia for having deserted his class. This was happening in one corner of the Gordons' drawing room, and the two men involved were Douglas Lister and the only Stoneman on the Orchestra Board, a very minor Stoneman, whose copper holdings were a scant five million.

Denis was in the group, and so was John Dudley. Dudley looked at Denis, whose political knowledge was nil but whose political sympathies he knew would be liberal, and said quietly,

"These gentlemen are good for a half hour of this," at which point Douglas Lister looked at him pompously, through a frown. Dudley ignored him. "Show me something at the piano," he added to Denis.

"Of course." Denis was a good deal happier at the piano.

"What is it—or was that just a dodge?" he added when he was seated before the gilded Steinway.

"No. Anyway, not altogether a dodge." Dudley grinned, looking more than usual like a kind of adult, sardonic kewpie. "I used to play piano a little, and I worked nearly a year on the A flat Polonaise . . ."

"And you always had trouble here, where the left hand takes over the 'ta-de-da-da—ta-de-da-da.' Right?"

"Yes. It never came off smooth."

Denis laughed, watching Gloria edge through the room toward them. "I wish there were a trick, John. There isn't, except not to start it so fast when you have both hands that you can't play the octaves when the left takes over. Listen. . . ."

Gloria was leaning on the piano, pouting a little as Denis played a few measures before the bad spot, and then played through at a terrific pace. "Could you have told where I changed?" he asked.

"No. You sounded like Horowitz."

"Nobody sounds like Horowitz but Horowitz," Denis said flatly. "He's the finest living technician, and the rest of us can only listen and hope."

Gloria had said nothing, nor did she seem much interested. Finally Dudley asked her whether she played.

"No," she answered. "I wish I did, like that, I mean. Then I could go on tour with the orchestra and be soloist."

Both men laughed, but she held her ground. "I mean it. It'll be fun gypsying around the state in buses."

"Why don't you go anyway?" Dudley asked only because he wanted something to say, and then knew from Denis' impatient jab at the keyboard that he had said the wrong thing. "It would be a good thing if you and Harry made part of the tour," he finished lamely.

But Gloria shook her head. "We'd just be in the way."

"Oh, nonsense!" Denis did not look at Gloria. "You'd be bored to tears after two days." He watched John Dudley's retreating back, and said softly, "Besides, that's not what you want to go along for and you know it."

Like a child, she agreed. "Two whole weeks," she said with a dramatic sigh. "It's a long time, Denis—isn't it?"

"Don't be silly; the summer is ten times longer."

"And I think you're looking forward to it. Honestly I do."

This was closer to a whine than he ever had had from her, and her mood filled him with a feeling very near to disgust. His reasoning was direct: she has known from the first, he thought, exactly what the score is. She is getting as much as I can give her. She ought to take it and let me alone. None of which he put into words, and all of which was evident in his manner.

She looked resentful now. "Oh—I know what you're thinking. And it's just like a man." A maid had appeared. "The food's ready. I guess we might as well eat."

None of which was lost on Aunt Clarissa, either.

She and Denis were making the trip in Denis' car. The start in Lakeland had been in a morning haze which might have produced anything from a drizzle to a thunderstorm, but a few miles south the sky was a wonderful April gray-blue with here and there a few puffs of cloud like carelessly dropped gobbets of whipped cream on a pastel dessert. The country was rolling and very green, and the houses seemed to be better tended the farther they went, as if the flaking paint of Lakeland were due to some blight in the air which, Denis thought grimly, it probably was.

"Let's put down the top," his passenger said unexpectedly.

"Most women don't want their hair blown about," Denis answered, and Clarissa laughed.

"Mine is only about two inches long and the wave is natural."

"It's beautiful too," said he, and Clarissa smiled.

They stopped briefly, and Denis lowered and stowed the light tan top. He stood by the car and stretched, and said,

"There used to be an old man in Gutenborg who always said, 'Bless me this is pleasant' every time the sun shone. I feel like him."

"So do I." But her mind could not stay off her baby long. Presently, as they ran swiftly through a little village, Clarissa remarked tangentially, "A cousin of mine lives in that old brown wreck," and almost without pause, "Denis, I've been so busy I doubt that I've mentioned it. But I think the orchestra has been close to perfect this season; it's better with Blum out, isn't it?"

Denis was enormously pleased. "Thanks, Clarissa," he said. "And the other answer is 'yes.' Lisburger is splendid and he's a damn nice chap."

"Also"—she was not to be distracted—"is Gloria bothering you too much?"

It brought Denis up short. "I'll manage Gloria," he answered stiffly. "She's, well . . ."

"Please. I don't mean that quite the way you took it. It's none of my business except as it affects the orchestra. You should know by now that the orchestra is an obsession with me; I've got a one-track mind, Denis, and I admit it."

"So has she," he said before he thought, and Clarissa laughed heartily.

"Yes," she answered after a moment, "she has indeed. I probably wouldn't have said anything, only I couldn't help but see that she was pouting about something—when you and John Dudley were at the piano, I mean."

Denis had been following a truck over the crest of a low hill; he passed now and shot on between freshly ploughed fields in which birds were still excavating for grubs. "You miss very little," he said finally. "But don't worry—she won't say I'm anti-Semitic, anyway."

Clarissa let it pass. The events of a year ago had not been forgotten, nor had their lessons. Denis as well as she and Gloria had a one-track mind, she thought, but Denis, like herself, could learn.

He continued to learn in Columbia, which was not only the capital but also geographically the center of the state and a good-sized city. They pulled up in front of the O'Neill House across from the old capitol itself, with its flattish dome surmounted by a small cupola which made the building look as if it wore a tonsure. They were in time for a quick luncheon, before the afternoon rehearsal.

When the boy checked for messages there were several for Denis. There was the expected note from the leading piano teacher suggesting that if Denis could find time, it would be splendid if he would hear the leading piano prodigy of Columbia. There was another from the woman who ranked second, with a list of half a dozen alleged prodigies who certainly must be heard. There was a note from the leading Columbia hostess-to-the-notable, a Mrs. Ehrenberger, which said that transportation would be waiting for Denis and his party after the concert in the University Auditorium that night; going to her party would be painless, indeed almost automatic. And finally, there was a message asking Denis to call Room 1143 at once, signed Gus Wagner.

Clarissa, he noticed, seemed quite unsurprised to hear that Gus was on deck. "You can never tell where he'll be," she declared, "and I, for one, have given up trying. Call him as soon as you get to your room."

Denis did, and while he was getting into a fresh shirt, Gus arrived.

"Hello, son," he said when Denis came to the door.

"Hello, Gus. I take it you're in your paternal mood today."

"Sure. Go ahead and tie your tie, and then we'll eat."

They met Clarissa in the dining room, but only briefly. She had in tow a youngish and wispy chap with an almost invisible jaw who seemed entirely colorless, but managed to exude the aroma of hard cash even through his Brooks Brothers single-breasted, buttoned to the chin suit. His name was Decker, and he and Clarissa established themselves in a corner of the room and appeared to be interested in each other.

Gus called the headwaiter over as soon as they were seated. "Who is that man with the lady who just came in?" he asked.

"That's the young Mr. Decker, sir."

"And what does he do?"

"Nothing. He just inherited half the real estate in town from his father, Mr. Henry Decker."

Gus turned to Denis. "That, my boy is one way to succeed."

"Meaning to inherit?"

"Hell no. Meaning to latch onto semi-imbeciles with money."

Denis laughed. "At least there won't be any sex involved."

They ordered, and then Gus picked up where they had left off. "What put sex into your mind?" he innocently asked.

"I don't know—nothing I guess."

Gus veered away from the subject. "I had dinner with Elisabeth the night before I left New York," he remarked. "She's still as crazy about you as ever, in a nice way, of course."

"How's Claire?"

The waiter was already returning, bearing two large plates on which were two club sandwiches, cut into odd shapes with the individual sections impaled on heavy red toothpicks. "They never made up those sandwiches fresh," Gus said. "Claire's fine. She's the most attractive girl I know in many ways. Not exactly beautiful, but handsome. Bright, too. Why don't you marry her?"

It may have been an idle remark, but it touched off something in Denis. He snapped, "Because I don't want to," and picked up a section of sandwich, which at once fell into pieces in his plate. "Damn!"

"Don't be so vehement, Denis. A good conductor with millions is still a good conductor."

"No! That family's done enough for me."

They silently picked at the sandwiches for a few minutes. Denis was a little ashamed of his outburst, nor could he understand it entirely. He was fond of Claire and it was not entirely a platonic fondness either. She had a curiously mixed appeal for him, when he could remember the fact that in a day or so he would be twenty-seven and that she was now twenty-one, and not the dark little brat he had known first. He had not often tried to analyze his feeling; the appeal came partly because he admired her shrewdness, but it was physical too. Oh, hell, he thought, I'd better forget it. He turned to Gus.

"I didn't exactly mean to be snappy," he said, "even though I did mean what I said."

"Okay. Have it your way. These damn sandwiches were a mistake. Waiter!"

Gus ordered the dessert that, of the entire menu, might have seemed least likely to attract—a banana split. Denis listened with horror, and ordered melon for himself. "We'd better hurry," he added. "I make a terrific fuss when the men are late, and I don't like to keep them waiting."

"Hmm. The kindly young father?"

"You'd be surprised to know that I've heard I have the reputation of being the toughest conductor in the country."

"No I wouldn't, but I'd be glad. Even if you are anti-Semitic."

"You're sort of riding me today, aren't you? That thing left some scars, you know. I still get echoes of it."

"I know." Gus was scooping great spoonfuls of his banana split into his mouth. "Every so often I have to have a gooey dessert." He added without stopping for breath, "You'll keep on getting them. That's one reason why I hope you'll never try to be the charming young man as long as you're on the podium."

They were on time for rehearsal, only a few minutes of which had anything to do with the night's concert. Next day the caravan would go to what Clarissa called "a little gem of a town" to be the principal attraction of a festival honoring the little gem of a town's only composer, whose improbable name was Bulwer Hillman O'Hara, and whose product seemed to run largely to cantatas. Half of the program would be a cantata called "Gulliver's Travels," and the other half would be orchestral, and there had been no time to rehearse the orchestra's share of the cantata up to now.

Gus and Clarissa were whispering in the rear of the auditorium as Denis opened the huge, hand-written score. It was so large that it more than covered his music stand; it was also full of mistakes. The librarian had spent hours checking from the full score to the parts, and had caught errors by the handful, but Denis had no hope that the parts were really accurate.

And since Bulwer Hillman O'Hara was elderly and unused to leading an orchestra, he dared not let him take over without doing the best he could to have things ready.

"Ready?" He tapped the stand vigorously. "One, two . . ." and they were off, but only for about ten bars.

Denis held up his hand. "Mr. Wright, weren't you playing a C natural?"

"Yes, sir," the first horn said. "It is a C natural here."

"Correct it, please." And they continued for another page. This time it was the first trumpet. And then half the 'cellos were found to be playing one note, and half another. It was a nerve-racking business, and both the conductor and his men were gradually working themselves into a temper. But the break came before the explosion and Denis, cigarette pointed belligerently upward, joined Gus and Clarissa, who still were whispering in the back of the room.

"Why didn't you have your assistant conductor do that job?" Gus asked. "It's slavery."

"And why don't you two stop whispering while I'm rehearsing?" Denis returned.

Gus looked startled. "Well, the truth is we should have known better. Now you answer my question."

Denis smiled, for the first time in an hour. "Because Dattner's ear isn't good enough. He refused to check from the score to the parts, to be honest. I gave him hell, too."

They talked quietly for a few minutes. Just before the break ended the youngish Mr. Decker arrived looking as insignificant as at lunchtime. About the only distinguishing feature Denis could discover was that he had a slight lisp which he attempted to conceal by an intermittent, apologetic cough. Then Denis returned to the stage, and the labor of the hour.

If possible, the work went worse than before. Denis found four mistakes in as many pages, and his voice took on an edge; the men also were being rubbed raw—and even faster. Finally they stopped for at least the thirtieth time in the midst of a huge climax, and not a very well-prepared one either. "The high drum should be D and not C," Denis shouted. "Goddam it, your ear should have told you that."

The perspiring tympany man bit his lip, then burst out, "And whoever checked these parts should be nutted."

From the back of the hall came a half-smothered laugh. It was the last straw. Denis whirled around, snapped the long baton in two, and flung the pieces toward the three in the back row.

"Will you shut your goddam mouths?" he bellowed, his face like a dark flame. "I want the hall cleared—right now."

The laugh froze in mid-air. The thunderstruck men on the stage stopped breathing, and for a few seconds the only sound was the distant throb of a distant airplane. Then Gus snorted. But that was all. Clarissa put her hand on his arm.

"I think we had it coming to us," she said quietly. "Let's go."

If Denis had needed any proof of the fact that nothing whatever would ever be allowed to stand against the well-being of her orchestra, Clarissa had given it. For an instant he thought of calling out a thank you, but instead he turned back, wearily, to the job in hand.

It was done at last, and the quicker, Denis felt, for his outburst. This at least had had the clearing effect of a thundershower; it had still another effect which he did not realize until that night at the inevitable party with the inevitable table piled high with indigestibles, and the equally ubiquitous punch bowl which nine tenths of the men present avoided in favor of drinks produced from the butler's pantry by the host. Gus was catching a very late train for St. Louis, and before he left the party he cornered Denis in the hostess' very expensive sunroom for a last word.

"You were right about that blowup this afternoon," he confessed, "but I think there was some kind of a subconscious business at work."

"Yes?" Denis was not being haughty, merely puzzled.

"Yes. I told you to be a son-of-a-bitch, you know. But it didn't do any harm for your men to see that everybody gets the same treatment when they're bad boys—or girls."

The younger man laughed. "You're still fairly subtle, aren't you Gus?"

Gus grinned. "My taxi ought to be here," he said. "Have a happy time with Bulwer Hillman O'Hara."

The two weeks of bucketing around the state were successful. They were also tiring—and when the orchestra returned to Lakeland, there was the inevitable series of long, long sessions at which the next season's programs and soloists would be chosen, and a couple of new players as well, and the usual struggle over budgetary limitations and delayed pledges of support, which were of course Clarissa's problems in the main. But only in the main. Denis was beginning to see that everything affecting the orchestra affected him sooner or later.

The group arrived from a town called Alsace about two o'clock of a rainy morning. Denis and Clarissa were ahead of the buses, which was of no importance. The last hour of the drive they made in almost complete silence, with the steady slush-slush of the windshield wipers, the slurping of the tires and the dull thumping of the rain on the convertible's roof the only sounds. Finally the lonely lights began to slip past more frequently, and at last they were on the longest street in the world, still silent and so tired they almost could have drawn up at the curb and slept.

Wearily they climbed the hill to the Heights and turned into Scott Road. Under the porte-cochere Clarissa gave Denis an avuncular good-night kiss while Jim Cleary, who had waited up for her, extracted her bags from the trunk.

"Nightcap?" Clarissa offered.

"Lord no. I'd fall asleep with my glass halfway to my mouth."

She chuckled and said good night, and he backed out into the rain and drove as fast as he could through the downpour to the Hampton Park Manor garage, which was underneath the hotel, a grateful circumstance for a weary motorist, Denis thought.

He left his bags for the attendant to take upstairs, and picked up a thick bundle of letters at the desk as he passed. Even ten floors on a fast elevator seemed a chore, and the walk down the long hall another. As he put his key in the lock his nose

194

twitched involuntarily—someone was making coffee, and it smelled incredibly good.

Someone was, and it was Gloria.

"How's my hero?" she asked more gaily than necessary, to cover the fact that she knew quite well she should not be where she was. She came toward him, arms out.

It was, Denis thought, the last straw. The very last.

"Oh, my God!" he shouted, his normally low, rather reedy voice as strident as the upper octave of a clarinet. "What in hell are you doing here?"

Before she could reply there was a knock at the door. "Get out of sight," Denis ordered sharply, and she scooted into the bedroom and closed the door.

The boy came in with two bags, banging each of them on the door as he entered. He too sniffed. "That's the quickest coffee-making I ever heard of," he remarked. "Smells good."

"Doesn't it?" Denis replied coldly. "Thanks very much."

He all but pushed the boy into the hall, and then yanked open the bedroom door. Gloria was standing in the middle of the room, her round, pretty face looking as if she might scream or weep in the next half-second, and also as if she did not much care which it was.

"That's not a very nice way to act," she snapped, "especially when I waited for you, and—and all."

He was still furious, and his voice still out of control. "You come here too goddam often, and I certainly don't want you here tonight."

Her instinct told her a smile would infuriate him still more. "But, Denis dear," she said, "nobody knows. I've got a key, and you gave it to me."

"I don't care if I gave you a hundred keys," he shouted. He still carried his raincoat; now he flung it at her, and missed, and brought down the heavy lamp on his bed table. The porcelain base struck the wall and shattered; the crash sounded unbelievably loud in the early-morning hush.

The fury left Denis, dissolved by the noise. But now there was another sound from the apartment next door, a steady tapping.

"See?" said Gloria. "You're waking people up."

"The hell with people—it's only that old harridan next door."

"Listen, Denis." She looked down at him as he picked up the debris. "Harry's in New Orleans; I talked to him just after dinner. He couldn't get back unless he was a magician."

Denis grunted, flat on his stomach retrieving a shard which had fallen under the bed. "I thought you were so nervous about the servants. Remember?"

"Oh, let the pieces go; it won't matter." She smiled again, rather smugly. "The two sisters are away. Their mother's sick. And the man—well, I think he's being naughty. He asked for the night away."

"And he won't think it odd if he comes in and finds your car gone."

Gloria was pleased with herself. She almost purred. "He won't find it gone. I called a cab. Oh . . ." She darted toward the kitchen, and in spite of himself Denis, carrying the broken lamp, laughed as he followed her. She was a rabbit again.

"Denis! This coffee's perked for simply hours."

He shrugged. "It won't matter. I'm so tired it probably won't even raise a hair."

They had reached a compromise or a stalemate; Denis could not have said which. When Gloria scrambled eggs and made toast, he found he was hungry and was glad to have food. And when later they went almost silently to bed, he was glad she was there and curled up against her with enough of passion and even more of relief. He had felt alone all the two weeks, and tomorrow he would be a solitary once more. Tonight was a time between, perhaps false because there was no love, but— the word, Denis thought sleepily an hour later, was "comfortable."

They slept late next morning, and the only difference between their supper and their breakfast was orange juice. When Gloria left at eleven she might have been any kind of caller, dressed as she was in a very trim gray suit and a hat of scarlet; he kissed her and opened the door, and barely noticed that the old woman next door left her apartment and followed Gloria to the elevator. She too wore a suit, but it looked as much like a box as it did like clothing, and the round, bumpy hat she wore was crushed down over a scraggly black bob which could have served a burlesque comedian as a frightwig.

Denis closed the door and yawned. When he reached home light pains had been flickering under the scar, which meant utter weariness, and the quarrel had not helped. Now he felt buoyant, so much so that when he strolled across the room to the window of which he was no longer afraid he was sure the day would be lovely. But in that he was wrong.

17

When he left at noon to meet Farrell Clisby, who was Clarissa's new assistant, for lunch he remembered nothing much of the quarrel, nor did he have any particular thing on his mind. In the lobby he stopped at the desk, but when he was handed the one piece of mail so far that day he tossed it back to the clerk. "The Literary Guild ought to know I don't have time to read," he remarked as the man dropped the envelope into a waste basket.

"Sure waste a lot of money on advertising these days," he replied, and then added with rather elaborate casualness, "Old lady Lodge complained about you."

Denis frowned. "Who's old lady Lodge, and what in God's name did she complain about?"

"Oh—you know, Mrs. Rutherford Lodge."

"Never heard of her."

The clerk took little stock in the complaint. "She's in ten-o'-

three, next to your apartment. Said you and some dame were quarreling and throwing things. Last night, it was."

"She's crazy. Looks it, too."

"Crazy like a fox—she's a lawyer."

"She's just plain crazy this time. I live alone, remember?" But as Denis turned away he remembered that the old lady had ridden down with Gloria and, for all he knew, had pointed her out to the clerk as one half of the guilty pair. And then he dismissed the matter.

He walked to the Hall, and from there Clisby drove him across to Middle Street and about halfway downtown. When the car stopped, it was in front of a raddled store building which might have been a relic of early Lakeland, or merely a building left to decay by an absent-minded, and absentee, landlord. Painted on what had been a display window at some time was a small legend: "Larrabee House," it read. In the window was a miscellany. Denis saw a wide silver bracelet hand-chased in a Greek key design, a wooden figurine of a boy bending over in the attitude of a modern Narcissus, a water color—whether good or bad Denis was not competent to say—which appeared to have been painted in one of Lakeland's innumerable slum alleys, other things such as ash trays and belt buckles. He looked inquiringly at Clisby, whose blond hair was blowing about his bony face in the never-weary spring wind.

"You've never met the Larrabees?" Clisby asked, his thin face relaxing into one of the most infectious smiles in Lakeland. The man's coloring was neutral, but the rest of him was not.

"No." Denis smiled back in spite of the fact that there was no particular reason.

"You'll like them."

Denis smiled again, more tentatively. "I've heard a good deal about their settlement. Lister said one day they were dangerous radicals or something similar."

"Lister is a pompous ass. . . . Oh, God, now I know I'll never be a successful manager."

Clisby pushed open the front door while Denis looked elaborately up and down Middle Street. He put his fingers to his lips and whispered, "He certainly is; now if you won't tell on me, I won't tell on you."

At the end of the short hall there was an open door, and inside the door a man and woman sat on opposite sides of a huge desk that could have been discarded in its old age by a prosperous lawyer. The room was full of odds and ends, just which odds and ends no visitor ever remembered, because there was something about the occupants of the office that usually commanded his full attention.

"Hello," said the man, rising and holding out his hand.

"Dick Larrabee, Denis Sandzen," Clisby said. "I apologize, Carol, but your husband rushed in ahead of you; Carol Larrabee, this is Denis Sandzen."

The Larrabees were both small and both dark. They were both attractive, too, but the feature visitors remembered was in both cases the eyes; not their color, which was dark brown, but their warmth. They were shrewd eyes, but honest eyes; they looked beneath the surface but they did not hide what was in their owners' minds either.

"We're glad you came," Carol Larrabee said. Her voice was low, and there was a reedy quality in it like Denis' own, pitched higher. "I want to thank you for an enormous amount of pleasure, Mr. Sandzen."

"Thanks," and try as he would Denis could think of nothing to add.

"Hungry?" Dick Larrabee asked. "I am—only don't expect very luxurious food. We're just as poor today as usual."

"What is it?" Clisby asked. "Franks again?"

"I'm afraid so," and Carol led the way through a door roughly cut into the next building and into a dining room set up in a lean-to. The tables were plain wood, the chairs, half of them backless, could have been gathered from the city dump— and some of them had been. Some of the youngsters in the room might almost have come from the same place.

Denis looked about, a little startled. Half the dozen diners were Negro, and three of the boys wore nothing at all but the briefest of brown shorts. Carol caught Denis' look, and explained.

"They're part of a dance group. They're good, too."

Besides the Negroes there were three Italians, one of whom spoke so little English that her conversation was mostly sign language, and three startling blonds, a boy of perhaps sixteen with hair that tumbled down on his forehead almost as if he were imitating Denis' darker mop, and two girls who were just as blonde and less reserved; the three talked among themselves in Polish, and when necessary translated into back-alley English.

The adults sat at one end of the table occupied by the three dancers. While Carol went to the tiny kitchen for food her husband made introductions, "Jerry, Jim and Lee, this is Denis Sandzen. He conducts the Lakeland Orchestra. You know Farrell."

"Hi," said Jerry. "Gee, maybe you'd watch us dance?"

Denis smiled. "I'd love to. When?"

"Soon's you finish your franks?"

"It's a date."

There was no very serious conversation with the food. It would have been difficult, because at one time or another everybody in the room but the Polish boy made his way to the table with a question or a comment. Nor was much conversation needed to set the pattern in Denis' mind; he had never seen a settlement house in his life, but he had seen a social worker or two, and the Larrabees resembled these only in the fact that all appeared to be mammals. Here there was a curious feeling of equality; the smaller children called the Larrabees "Mr." and "Mrs." and the older ones used first names, not as a means of establishing familiarity, but simply because it was natural.

Before he quite realized it, Denis was committed to at least three projects. He was to watch Jerry, Jim and Lee dance; he was to visit the silver-working class, and he was to see a play next night. He also was looking forward to his commitments.

"Look Den—Mr. Sandzen," Jerry said as he finished, "we'll be in the theater. You'll come?"

"Sure. And Denis is all right."

The three grinned and left. "You've made a conquest," Carol

said in her gentle voice. "Those are three terribly nice boys."

Before lunch was finished, Denis knew all he needed to know about Larrabee House. He heard how it started, with the Larrabees leaving college and renting a cottage in the middle of the Negro district. How sometimes they were hungry, but how little by little their neighbors began first to tolerate, then to trust them. How they added first the tottering corner building, and then the one next to it, and how continuously the project teetered on the edge of ruin. How they had been able to persuade perhaps a dozen people to help part time, teaching whatever the youngsters were interested in.

They were having a second cup of coffee when Clisby suddenly remarked, "You three remind me of each other."

"How?" Dick Larrabee asked.

"All of you know exactly what you want, and are going to get it, come hell or high water."

Carol's small head turned, a little like a bird scouting his feeding ground for invaders. "I hope," she said, "we are doing as much good as Mr.—may I say Denis?"

Denis frowned. "Need you ask? And frankly I don't know what you mean by 'doing good.' I don't believe much in 'doing good,' the way that's usually meant."

"Neither do I. And I resent the way they bottle up the orchestra in that hall. More than eighteen hundred people should hear it. Even so"—she stood up, ready to guide Denis to the dancers—"you do good. You make music sound as if you'd just thought it up at the moment you play it. Does that make sense?"

Clisby answered for Denis. "It's as high a compliment as you could pay a conductor. Sure it makes sense."

"And perhaps next season, or sometime soon, you could get them to let the ordinary people hear, too. Pop concerts, or something like that."

Denis merely nodded, his eyes faraway. The others exchanged glances in which there was a little spice of satisfaction.

"Look," said Carol, pulling aside a curtain, "but be quiet."

The three brown bodies were in motion, a kind of ecstatic movement that was not confined to limbs and torso, but somehow seemed to involve viscera as well. There was no music, although one of the boys was humming something Denis thought he recognized. It was warm in the room and what light there was came from the part of the street windows not covered by another old curtain; it fell grayly on three bodies shining with sweat in an effect more beautiful in its way than any lighting expert could have arranged. Denis sucked in his breath and without realizing it, caught Carol's hand in his and squeezed it hard. He held it until the boys reached the end of their dance and collapsed on the floor as gracefully as if it had been a Roman couch.

"I thought that guy was comin' " one of them panted. "Wish he coulda seen that one."

"We did see it," Denis said. "It was wonderful."

"Gee." The three jumped to their feet. "Wanta see it again?"

Denis laughed. "Where's your music?"

They returned the laugh. "Jim was hummin' only he gets outa wind, kind of."

" 'Juba Dance'?"

"See—I told y'all." Jim was triumphant. "Betty said that was it. She can't be here much, so we just do without music."

In one corner there was a piano which had stood in a downtown movie lobby, until it was discarded into the arms of the Larrabees. Denis crossed to it and sat down. "Do it again, boys," he said, and began.

They did it again, twice in fact. Then they clustered around the piano. "Gosh, you certain'y can play," Jim said admiringly.

"Play something else, just anything," Jerry broke in. "We'll make up something."

Denis played the first thing that came into his head, which was Chopin's E flat nocturne. The boys listened a moment, and drifted off. Slowly they began to circle, their masculinity quite submerged. They seemed gradually to forget the boundaries, the floor, the walls, their own bodies. Nor were they looking for something meaningful, a design for motion. They hesitated when Denis reached the cadenza at the end; then, while the other two boys sank slowly down Lee went off into a patternless, effortless whirl that subsided as the music died.

"That was wonderful," Denis said after a moment. "Tired?"

The three brown heads came up. "No. Play a fast one."

They danced something they probably never could repeat to the old A flat Polonaise, and then Denis rose. "I'll have to be going, boys," he said. "Could I come back?"

"Sure can," they said almost together. "When?"

They made a date for the second day following, and gravely shook hands on it. "Thanks, Denis," Jerry said as the party left.

The group made the other visits, and Denis explained that before long he would be going East for the summer and that he had an idea. It was nothing to talk about, not yet, but perhaps it might work. And he was grateful for having been given something he never had had before.

"Clarissa will most likely be in a snit," Clisby said as he started his car.

"Let her." Denis lowered the window next to him, and let the breeze tangle his hair. "I'd like to do something good, back there. . . ."

Clisby's thin face was quite expressionless. "Money?"

"Money—sure. I'll send them a check tonight. But maybe something else—that music is all wrong for those boys. I haven't tried to write anything since I was in school, except a cadenza or two for somebody's concerto." His voice trailed off into thought.

For a couple of blocks there was silence. Then Clisby spoke, "It was a plot, Denis. Not on the Larrabees' part—it was my idea." He glanced at Denis, who was still staring ahead and seeing nothing. "Maybe I'm overstepping, but—well—I thought it might do you as much good as you could do for Larrabee House." He hesitated again. "There is another side to things besides the Lister Hall side. Know what I mean?"

Slowly his companion returned from his imaginary journey. "Do I know? Yes, of course I do. It's a matter of time."

"It's a what?"

"It's a matter of time." Denis' look was now as direct as it had been vague before. "I've set myself one thing to do, and that's to take over the New York Symphony before I'm thirty-five. I'll do it or tear myself up in the trying."

"I believe you."

Denis appeared not to have heard. "But if I want to do this thing I mentioned, I'll make time for it. Watch me."

That I shall do, thought Clisby, turning neatly into the drive at Lister Hall.

John Dudley was a temporary bachelor, and that night he, with Denis and Clarissa, had been asked for dinner by Gloria. Denis was so wrapped up in his experience that he might have forgotten but for Clarissa; in any case he was of so little use through the rest of the afternoon that Clarissa finally gave him one of her most ladylike reproachful glances and asked him where his mind was.

He put away his thoughts and turned innocently back to the little pile of papers which represented the half-dozen programs he had determined on up to the minute. "Right here," he said stiffly. "Right with you."

"Perhaps. But I've asked you twice whether you want to try a big choral work for next season. You haven't answered yet."

"Because I'm thinking of something else. A pop concert series."

She looked disturbed, but only for an instant. "I don't think Douglas Lister wants them, Denis."

"We wouldn't get Lister Hall dirty. We could use the Municipal Auditorium—charge fifty cents and probably break even."

She thought a moment, balancing pros and cons quickly and expertly, and at the same time working out the best way to present her conclusions to Denis. One thing she would not do— she would never state them positively because that would be the surest way to rivet down her young conductor's attitude, whatever it was.

"Well . . ." She waited a few seconds, although now she knew quite well what she intended saying. "Well . . . perhaps. During the regular season, or after?"

"During. It's too damn hot later."

"How many?"

"Six—ten, I hadn't thought."

"That would mean a lot of extra money to the men. You know the union—unless perhaps you'd give up one of your rehearsals."

He was indignant. "I certainly won't!"

"Then it'll be expensive." She appeared to do some mental arithmetic. "Twenty-five hundred a concert, at an absolute minimum, not including rental and trucking the stuff down and back—thirty thousand for ten concerts might cover it if we could work the advertising out of the regular appropriation."

Denis got up and strolled absently to the window; there was actually sun outside although it brightened only the parking lot and a few elms still hopefully green after years of experience with Lakeland weather. "That's just what I get each year—until next year, when I get five more." He came back to the table. "So I'm only worth the price of ten pop concerts? Like hell I am."

"No. You get the price of ten, which is quite different."

Denis was playing now with Clarissa's silver letter opener, tapping a rapid rhythm on the polished table. "If we could get five thousand people at fifty cents we'd pay for most of it . . . Let's try, Clarissa. Will you?"

Now it was time for a delaying action. But something underlay the business, and sooner or later she would find out what it was. She said, "The last board meeting is a week from today. Shall I bring it up, or will you?" She looked at the silver clock which stood on a heavy silver tray on her desk. "Oh, dear, it's nearly six, and I'm not dressed. You've not forgotten Gloria's little dinner?"

"Oh, Lord! Thank you for the reminder." He was on his feet at once. "Got your car? Oh, I know you have. Look, Clarissa, I'll pick you up at seven sharp. At your house."

"Yes. Think over the pop thing, will you, dear?"

He did. He not only thought about it, but made up his mind to do it if he had to make up the losses himself; he told Clarissa that when he drove smartly up to 6900 Scott Road at the precise stroke of seven.

Oh, dear, she thought. I'll have to get Douglas Lister to squelch it after all. But she merely said that of course he wouldn't be expected to do anything so extravagant. He'd be giving his services and that was enough.

"And I'll get a completely different type of audience," he went on as if he had not heard. "I'll murder them, too."

They found Gloria hopping about, more rabbitlike than usual. "Oh, dear," she said, "I'd counted on the girls being back, only they aren't. So we'll have drinks here and go slumming later. Mammy's Kitchen."

Clarissa said with dignity, "Some very nice people go there on maid's night out." And looked at John Dudley severely when he snickered.

Nothing was said about pop concerts, or about anything else serious. Clarissa went one over her limit of two drinks, and the others rather further than that. Denis felt inspired to burlesque Percy Grainger playing the Grieg concerto, and Mischa Levitzki doing the Black Key etude with an orange, and finally Paderewski delivering a Chopin polonaise with more elegance than accuracy. Then Clarissa asked a question that left him stunned.

"Can you play 'Danny Deever'?" she demanded, and when he agreed to fake it, she rose regally but not quite steadily, and stood in the crook of the piano, and became Ernestine Schumann-Heink.

By the time she was half through, her garbled English and raucous lower voice had reduced the others to incoherent gasps; at the end, when her voice broke magnificently with a sound like a heavy sliding door being closed, Denis ran around the end of the piano and hugged her.

"My God, you're wonderful!" he laughed. "Take a third drink oftener, won't you?"

It was a lovely party, even after food had blotted up a few of the drinks. Mammy's was, of course, an imitation log cabin with red-checked tablecloths and gelatin salads, but the salads were good and the steaks were better, and Gloria had brought a bottle of good Bordeaux in a paper bag, which proved helpful. There was a great deal of laughter, in the midst of which John Dudley leaned across the table to Denis.

"Know that little colored boy over there?" he asked. "He's grinning at you sort of oddly."

Denis waited until one of Mammy's mammy waitresses in calico and white apron removed herself and then looked in the direction indicated. "I don't think . . . of course I do. He's named Lee something-or-other. He looks different with his clothes on."

"What?" Clarissa was thunderstruck, and the others were more than politely interested.

Denis glanced around the table, his face puzzled. Then he laughed and motioned. The boy approached slowly, first carefully disposing of his huge tray.

Denis slipped his arm around the boy. "This is Lee—what's your last name?"

"Mitchum, sir." His informality was gone, Denis noted.

"This is Lee Mitchum," Denis repeated. "I saw him dance this afternoon; in fact, I played for him and two other boys."

Lee's bright eyes ran around the table, rested on Clarissa. "Where?" she asked.

"At Larrabee House." Denis smiled. "I had a wonderful time, and Lee has a wonderful gift."

Only John Dudley seemed to retain his interest. "Has he now? And at Larrabee House?"

Lee started to speak and then froze, his eyes on Mammy's imposing stomach as she ponderously pushed it through the room. Lee was frightened, although Mammy wore a buttery smile.

"Son," she said, the voice cooler than the smile, "you hadn't ought to bother the guests."

"He wasn't bothering us," said Gloria. "Mr. Sandzen called him over; he knows him."

"Oh. 'Scuse me," but she turned back to Lee. "Now you run along," and added when he left, "Y'all's very nice, only I don't want the kid to get ideas. They gits mighty uppity, given a chance."

The utter stupidity of what he heard did not come home to Denis until Mammy was well out of earshot. "I'll be damned," he said to Dudley. "Ideas? Lee's got more than ideas; he's got gift."

Rapidly and perhaps a little bitterly he told the others the story of his luncheon and its afterpiece. As he talked, he forgot Mammy and his enthusiasm grew. "And," he ended, "I'm going back. Maybe I'll try to write some music for the boys. I haven't tried composing for years, but——"

"Now, Denis." Clarissa took command as if daring anyone to challenge her. "You've got enough to do without wasting time on Middle Street; you've got your public to think about, and a good share of that thinks the Larrabees are pretty—well—pretty radical."

Denis flared. "Am I to consider myself spanked?"

"Personally I think the whole thing's damned interesting." John Dudley was bent on rescue. "That kid—I can't express it, but he moves—I started to say like a beautiful horse, but that sounds silly."

Gloria laughed. "What is it they say? He's got 'it.' "

Then Clarissa made one of her few mistakes. She pulled in her chin and surveyed her three companions. "Perhaps, Gloria, he does have 'it,' whatever that may be. But we've all got jobs to do, and they have nothing whatever to do with a boy named Lee Mitchum."

Gloria looked at her stern face, and rose. "The food's gone and so is the wine. Let's go back to the house for a nightcap."

"I don't think so." Clarissa looked at her watch. "It's late, and if Denis or John will drop me off . . ."

John Dudley's duty was plain, and he did it. At least Gloria was happy as she climbed into Denis' car and they wheeled out of the parking place; she stretched luxuriously and a little alcoholically, and asked Denis to drive her down through Hampton Park to the lake.

"Sure," said Denis shortly, and added after a minute, "Why was Clarissa so damn testy about the Larrabees?"

This was not the way Gloria had planned the conversation. She tried another bait. She slid her left hand along the back of the seat and tickled the short hairs on Denis' neck. But this, too, failed.

"Don't Gloria. I'm serious—why should she be so kind of bullheaded?"

"I'm sure I don't know." If he wanted seriousness, he should have it. "What's more, I don't much care. What I wonder is whether she knows about us."

At least that returned his attention to herself. He said, "As indiscreet as you are sometimes, I wonder whether the whole damn town doesn't know."

Gloria concentrated on the street ahead and said nothing.

"No. I mean it, Gloria." He had stopped for Mather Street, waiting for a hole in the traffic. As the car moved again, she put her hand on Denis' arm and he glanced quickly at her, but not quickly enough. He meant to cross Mather Street into the narrow road leading past Hampton Park Manor, into Stoneman Park, and so to the lake. But in the instant that followed the touch of Gloria's hand on his arm an old and shaky Model T sedan struck his car obliquely, and the two locked together and slued sidewise into the opposite traffic line. A third car, this one driven by a chauffeur in uniform and carrying two women in its rear seat, came to rest with its bumper nuzzling the radiators of the other two. For an instant, nobody moved except a man and a woman on the sidewalk who ran into the street, their faces marked with the usual look of spectators under such circumstances—a look half of horror and half of hope for something truly gory.

Denis could not open the door on his side; he and Gloria slid out the other side and immediately the larger of the two women began berating him. She wore a turban and looked rather like Queen Mary, but her language was perilously close to the gutter. Suddenly the smaller woman plucked her sleeve and whispered something in a gentle voice.

"Then it must be his fault," she said, pointing to the driver of the Ford. "Of course it is."

The man had at last gotten out of his ancient car, carrying a tin lunch box for no reason he could have given. He was tall and stooped, with a frazzled mustache hiding his mouth and a lumpy felt hat with no band almost hiding his watery eyes. "No, ma'am, 'tain't," he said slowly in a flat drawl that could

209

only come from Vermont. "He druv plumb in front of me."

"I had stopped," Denis said. "I was trying to cross Mather Street. I don't think you have any brakes."

"Don't need none, sonny. On a Model T you can use reverse."

The smaller of the two women stepped up to Denis. "I'm an attorney," she said in a soft, unexpectedly sweet voice, pushing back a hat quite as shapeless in its way as the man's. "Want me to handle it?"

Denis looked quickly at Gloria. "Sure. You'll find my license and insurance stuff in the glove compartment." He could see a policeman approaching at a lumbering run, probably cursing the bad luck that had gotten him out of a comfortable bar down the street.

"All right," the gentle voice said. "Don't leave until the officer takes your name—I'll do the rest. By the way, we live in the same hotel. I'm Mrs. Rutherford Lodge." She leered at Denis.

The officer began taking names with furious inefficiency, and presently Denis and Gloria were free and walking down the street toward the Hampton Park Manor.

"Wait for me in the lobby," Denis said. "I'll tell the garage to pick up the car."

When he came back Gloria looked a little wan, and he suggested a nightcap. For the first time, she refused. "Just have the doorman call a cab, Denis. I'd better go home. I don't know what about the servants."

"Oh. Well, I'm sorry about the smash."

"That doesn't matter. I'm sorry I can't go upstairs." She laughed shakily. "Maybe I'm getting timid because I'm getting old."

"Oh, nonsense." Denis spoke to the doorman, and in a minute put Gloria into the cab. "Want me to ride out with you?"

She shook her head. "I'm all right. Run along."

Denis did just that, with relief. He wanted to be quiet; it seemed to him a good deal had happened that day, and that perhaps Larrabee House was the best happening for a long while. He was stretched out on the sofa with nothing on but his shorts when someone tapped at the door.

"Yes?" he called.

"Mrs. Rutherford Lodge," and he thought the voice seemed almost too sweet considering the woman's appearance.

"Just a minute," he said. "I'll put a robe on."

He let her in, and she at once gave the room a quick survey. "Alone?" she asked pointedly.

"Quite." For no reason he could fathom at the time he wished he had left the bedroom door open.

"Oh." The syllable was sugary, but it also expressed not-so-polite doubt, and about that he could do nothing. "Well," she went on. "It's all right. You weren't damaged much and you've got insurance. I told that man who hit you that we could sue, and would if he didn't shut up."

"I don't want a suit."

"Of course not. Mrs. Wallace, she's my friend and we were just coming from a D.A.R. meeting, she's also insured. It'll come up in traffic court tomorrow, and I'll fix it. You don't need to go down."

"Thanks. Lucky you were there; I don't know much about such things."

"Was lucky." Denis thought she glanced pointedly at the closed bedroom door, but she was pushing back her hat at the time and he could not be sure. Strands of her dead black hair were escaping all around her head, and her suit, the same suit she had worn in the morning, showed a spot or two from whatever the D.A.R.'s had been eating. "I'll get along. Send you a bill."

"All right. Good night, Mrs. Lodge."

At the door she paused. "Mrs. Gordon's a nice-looking woman, isn't she?"

Denis' mouth tightened. "Very," he said shortly. "It was her dinner party we'd just left."

Mrs. Lodge was in the hall now. "Really?" she said. "I thought the Gordons lived in the Heights."

He had an unreasoning desire to ask the old busybody to

search the apartment, but he did not. He only said, "They do. Good night again."

The bill came within two days, and it was for fifty dollars, which seemed quite enough to Denis, whose experience with lawyers had been nil; it was Elisabeth's lawyers who vetted his contracts, and it had never occurred to him that somebody, Elisabeth of course, had paid them. He would try to remember when he saw her.

He also wondered how much more she had paid that he knew nothing about and for what. For a moment he even wondered whether his twenty-five thousand inheritance had covered everything through his debut concert. He began to see, lying alone in his bed, that mostly he had been taking, with small thought for the giver. Terry—how long had it been since he had written him? Delphine? Claire? Elisabeth he heard from often in little dictated notes which he could answer through his secretary. He should write Terry, and he would, tomorrow. He snuggled down into his bed and wrapped his arms around his pillow, as usual. At least he was paying his way now, he thought drowsily. He would need money for the future, but he could give money too. He had told Clisby two days ago that he would give money to Larrabee House, and he had not. That, too, he would do tomorrow, and it was a good feeling to know that he at last had all the money he could reasonably use. He was just about to drop off when he sleepily remembered something else, which was a line in the note accompanying Mrs. Rutherford Lodge's bill. It said, "I shall be looking forward to renewing our acquaintance in the fall."

What, he wondered in the fuzzy instant before sleep finally overtook him, did that mean? What made the old golliwog think she would renew anything, unless perhaps she might knock again on the wall? And Gloria—she would have to be more careful in the fall. He slept.

In the morning he sent a thousand dollars to Larrabee House, and felt good about it. The programs for next season began to fall into line; it was hard to believe that next season would be 1934-35 and that he was now twenty-seven. It seemed a great age to him, even though he was beginning to realize that he was the sort the papers would call "The young American conductor" when he was in his mid-sixties. He was still feeling buoyant when, a few days later, Clarissa called him in as he was on his way home.

"Sit down, Denis," she said, but there was no clue to whether this was to be a veiled reproof or something better. Clarissa would be portentous in either situation.

"Sure." He lit a cigarette. "Good news?"

She nodded. "You get your pop concerts. I raised the money."

Denis leaped from his chair and flung his arms around her. "You're a wizard," he half shouted. "You really are."

"No." She was no longer the bearer of news, merely a woman who knew she was clever and who took pride in it. "I'm no wizard, Denis, but I want to keep you happy. You've given us a wonderful season. . . ."

"Thanks. Where'd you get the money, Clarissa? Steal it?"

She laughed. "Practically. I suppose technically I actually did steal it."

"I'll serve half the jail term. How?"

She reached across the table and took the letter opener out of Denis' hand. Slowly she began tapping it on the metal corner of the blotter in front of her. "Don't tell, Denis; I mean that literally." She put down the silver blade, rested her elbows on the table. "Little by little for years I've been putting odds and ends of money into a little secret fund; unspent parts of special funds, one or two contributions that have been in cash. If anybody knew they could string me up for embezzlement. Only I wanted a little cushion that I could use if things got really bad—and they haven't. It's been a back-breaking job, Denis, but I've made the pledges come in, and I've never had to touch my extra money."

"They'll get up very early in the morning to beat you," he interjected fervently. "Four o'clock or so."

Clarissa loved approval, next to her orchestra. She expanded under it.

"Be that as it may," she went on, "it's a little over ten thousand, and that's a big enough cushion—I hope. We can gamble on taking in twenty thousand at the box office. Although"—she looked a little weary, as if her decision had cost her more than she admitted—"although money's awfully tight and——"

"We'll do it. Clarissa, I'll never forget you for this. I can't repay you, but I'll try."

"We understand each other better than most. All I want from Denis Sandzen is another season as good as this one has been. That's all."

Denis got up suddenly. "Come on. I want to buy you a drink in the gaudiest bar in town." He caught her hands and pulled her to her feet.

"Denis! Stop it—if you upset this ink well I'll murder you."

"The hell with it. Let's be gay."

She pretended to be disturbed on the way downtown to the Slater, but Denis knew she was not.

18

The summer flew by so fast that later it seemed never to have been at all. Even so, Denis could remember several things when he really tried, and chiefly three.

The first memory was a set of three concerts in Paris, concerts arranged by Gus as usual and backed by Elisabeth as usual, but this time there was little risk. This time everybody who was at all in the know, or who knew anybody who was in the know, attended without urging. It was the first such concert of the year actually to bring in expenses at the box office, and it made Denis very proud.

A couple of days after the last concert Elisabeth and Denis

and Claire drove south in the long top-heavy Rolls Elisabeth had rented, and this brought on the other two memories.

They drove through the Rhone Valley and by way of Aix to Toulon and Nice, and up the hill to call on Grandmère.

They found her a little less forceful than Denis remembered, but wonderful. She knew, this time, Denis was coming and she had written her old friend Mme. Grandjany to clip the Parisian papers for her. She had also, for reasons best known to herself, sent notices to *L'Eclaireur de Nice*, and they had been printed. On her felt-covered table there was a neat little pile of cuttings each pasted on stiff paper, and it was obvious from their thumbed condition they had been shown more than once.

"I have, Madame," she said to Elisabeth while Claire watched almost dotingly, "a famous grandson." She indicated the cuttings beside her. "These things I show my friends. But I do not need them. I have heard him, and I know."

Claire broke in, her dark face animated. "He will be the greatest, in time."

Grandmère nodded sagely. "You are right. . . . And now, you will honor me by staying for supper?"

"You are too good," Elisabeth replied, "but we have come to ask you to join us. It will not be so good, but it will please us."

"I go out so seldom." She thought a moment, and nodded. "Yes, I shall go. I would like to see my grandson in his own surroundings." She clapped her hands, and when the same little maid appeared, she said, "I shall not dine at home. And you will please help me dress."

"She's adorable," Claire said while she was out of the room. "She's like a very old, wise doll. I love her."

Madame returned, a picture in severe black out of an Edwardian magazine. The beading on her dress, the white jabot, the tiny beaded bag, the black hat with its white bird wing—all were perfect. "I should at least have given you tea," she said, "but I thought that in your very large motor we could drive a little. I should like to show you some things."

"Perfect." Elisabeth collected her gloves and returned the lorgnette to her bag. The little procession moved out.

They drove farther up into Cimiez for Grandmère's favorite

view of the Mediterranean, and then back through the old market, littered now with the day's discarded vegetables. They drove the length of the Promenade des Anglais and on to Cagnes-sur-Mer resting on its great rock like a gull on her nest. Then Grandmère said, "It is a little late, but perhaps you would like to see the house in which I used to live?"

The car halted before a hotel, which sat behind a walled garden—the Hotel Brice.

"It has been added to," said Grandmère, "but it was large even when my husband and I lived here. When he died I took guests, paying guests."

Her bright old eyes seemed to fade for a moment, and then the light returned. She looked unbelievingly at two men who were coming out of the gate. "The window," she cried. "Lower the window!"

Denis hastily turned the handle, and she leaned out. "Monsieur Eugène," she called to the older of the two, a man who might have been as old as she. He carried a guitar and when he turned, it struck the elbow of the younger man and hummed faintly. He was so stooped that in order to look up at those in the car he bent his neck almost at right angles to his old dry body.

"Madame!" he cried. They shook hands through the window.

"Ah, Eugène, it is so long." Her smile was a little tremulous. "Do you still know the barking song, Eugène?"

"But certainly." He went down on one knee, and rested the guitar on the other. Denis had no idea where the song might have come from; perhaps Provence. But the end of every line ended with a husky bark, and it was very funny. Madame was fumbling in her purse; when the song was ended, she handed out a coin.

"For old times' sake," she said. As they drove away, she called back, "Come see me in Cimiez, Eugène; do come." After a little while she patted Denis' knee. "You will find, my dear, that when one grows old, one's friends leave. You may be glad to see the man who barks, once more."

But her mood was gone when they reached the Negresco, and she was as dignified as a tiny woman could be when they crossed the red-carpeted lobby whose ornament had surely been squeezed out of a wedding cake decorator. "You will not," she begged, "ask me to have a cocktail?"

Denis laughed. "While we freshen up, I'll ask them to bring you Vermouth. Right?"

"A very, very little. Yes."

It seemed a good thing to dress in Grandmère's honor, which they did. Both Elisabeth and Claire returned to their sitting room in white, and Denis was not able to say which was the better picture—Claire in a bouffant skirt and tight bodice and no jewelry at all, or Elisabeth with her blonde hair and her diamonds. It had been years since Denis had seen the diamonds, and once more it occurred to him that Elisabeth was one of the few women on earth who could wear three bracelets and a wide necklace and not look like a dress manufacturer's wife.

They entered the tall, cool dining room regally. Their escort included the maître d'hôtel, two captains and two waiters. Their table was by the large center window, and they were seated with ceremony, a man to each chair and the extra waiter dashing about flicking imaginary dust off the chairs with a fresh napkin.

The meal was enormously long, with all the courses and all the wines. It was good, too, since the Negresco, when it wanted to, easily lived up to first-rate French standards. Grandmère was even allowed by the maître d'hôtel to make a suggestion about the fish, she being the guest of honor. When at last the sweet disappeared and fruit and cheese were brought, it was she who most alive, the others having reached the depth of satiety where sleep is more attractive than anything else.

At last they filed out of the room, still with escort.

"Now," Grandmère said, "I should like it if all of you would drive me home. It is time I should go, but each of you I like and I should be pleased to keep you with me as long as possible."

Denis swallowed before he answered. "Of course, Grandmère. The car is outside."

They drove slowly past the Casino and through the old town,

slowly up the hill to her house. At her door she smiled at each of them and said softly, "At my age one never knows which parting is the last one."

"Grandmère!"

"But, yes, Denis. It is true. If this is the last, let me tell you I love you, and I wish you well."

The little maid opened the door. Grandmère turned again before she entered the house.

"Good night, my dears," she said softly.

They drove on to Monte Carlo over the Grand Corniche, and then quickly back through Nice, without stopping there, and to Antibes. It was full of British nobility economizing, and they left it for Cannes, which was full of the same.

"Perhaps San Rafael?" Claire suggested, and they tried that. It was dull and the food was not digestible. At last they asked the chauffeur, who said his name was Pierre, which was safe, and that brigand suggested a small inn in Vence.

"It is owned by a couple related to me, Madame," he admitted, "but the food is superb, and I can drive you to Juan-les-Pins to swim. And, Madame, this late there will be few people about."

"Very well, Pierre," Elisabeth agreed, looking again at his brigandlike face. "In a couple of hours."

L'Auberge des Fleurs was, however, exactly what the brigand said it was, and so was the food. It made a wonderful point from which to explore, it was quiet, and the old part of Vence resting partly on and partly behind its twelfth-century walls, had only one cocktail bar and almost no tourists at all. A week went by before the idea of swimming occurred to anybody, and then Elisabeth begged off.

"I'd like to write some letters," she said, "and perhaps wander about the village a little. Run along, you two."

It was eleven o'clock. "Come back at one," Claire told Pierre as he dropped them, "and we'll have luncheon at Eden Roc."

She and Denis sat for a while on the sand, she in the almost invisible suit she had bought in Cannes, and he in a great deal less, something as nearly nothing as a posing strap. After a while Denis pulled her to her feet and raced her to the placid Mediterranean. They ran in, flung themselves down, and swam out a hundred yards. They could still stand.

"Oh, dear," Claire said, "it looks so cool, and it isn't."

"Like lukewarm soup," Denis agreed.

They threshed around a few minutes, nevertheless, and gave it up as a bad job. Back on the sand they watched two children pedaling back and forth on a kind of catamaran propelled by a wooden paddlewheel and something like a bicycle chain. This was approximately as dangerous as sailing a cake of soap in a bathtub, but it kept their agonized nurse and their mother running to and fro in the heat crying, "Take care!" and "I have fear, my children." Farther out two little boats floated in a dead calm, their bright blue sails languid, and farther still a French cruiser lay at anchor under a thin, lazy feather of smoke.

"For two cents," Denis said at last, "I'd swim out and upset those children."

Claire laughed. "I'd rather upset mother. Such a silly fuss."

"Meaning that, if you had two children, you'd not act like a mother hen?"

"Yes. There's something sort of repulsive about the way French mothers hover over their kids. I like the English 'throw 'em in and let 'em swim' style better."

Denis was lazily covering Claire's feet with sand; they were good substantial feet, he noticed. "Um," he said after a while, "my French half should rebel at that, I guess."

"Your Swedish half has your French half pretty well controlled," she answered. "Most of the time, anyway."

"It's my governor. The French half provides the steam."

Claire kicked the sand off her feet, part of it into Denis' face.

"Hey, you! Stop it. Want to blind a good conductor?"

There was a thin edge of irony in her reply. "No—but being blind wouldn't stop you. Nothing would."

But it was too warm to take offense and the feeling of entire laziness, of nothing at all that really had to be done, was too pleasant. He said, "Don't make sidewise remarks. You're too attractive today."

Suddenly she turned on her side facing him, something between wonderment and mischief on her face. "Denis," she said, "this is a red-letter day. I think that's the first compliment—well—personal compliment, you ever paid me."

He laughed. "I guess we act more like brother and sister than most brothers and sisters do."

"Don't laugh. It tells too much about you—me too, maybe."

A launch was putting off from the cruiser, heading for Antibes. Denis watched it for a while, as was almost necessary inasmuch as the entire French family including nurse and newly arrived papa had gathered at the water's edge to exclaim over what appeared to be a phenomenon, a unique phenomenon.

"Oh, for God's sake," Denis said, "haven't they ever seen a launch before?" And when Claire said nothing, he turned to her and saw something that disturbed him a little in her face. "What's wrong?" he asked. "Did I do something?"

Her smile was bittersweet. "You never do anything. Anything but conduct and play piano."

"And what should I do? Walk a tight wire?"

"You couldn't go where you're going any more directly if you did," she said, and got to her feet. "There's Pierre. I could use a drink."

She was halfway to the car before he overtook her. "Imagine your needing a drink, a kid like you."

The look she gave him was withering, but there was a little pathos in it too. "My dear brother Denis," she said, "tomorrow I shall have a sign painted. It'll read 'Claire McKee is now twenty-one years old.' "

In mid-September Gloria Gordon had only just returned from New Hampshire, where she had been physically well cared for and at a loss otherwise. There had been, in her opinion, nothing whatever to do but motor, and that she had done so constantly and so thoroughly she might have written a guide to the state—if such an idea had occurred to her.

Even yet most of the people with whom she was friendly—and they were not too many—were still away. September in

Lakeland is not a good month; the summer drouth has reduced vegetation to a crisp brown substance that crumbles at one's touch, and the first fall rains are still some weeks away. Even when they arrive prematurely the effect is seldom good. They have a dull habit of hanging on and with the help of the heat, of producing mildew on shoes in closets and sneezes among the populace.

Therefore Gloria was sitting this afternoon before the huge radio-phonograph in her drawing room wishing that it would go berserk as it once had, and pick up a parcel of records and smash them on the tone arm. She hopefully watched the skillet-like device hoist the records of Brahms' first symphony as recorded by Leopold Stokowski, but it turned them and carefully deposited them again on the turntable. Why won't Denis record? she wondered, knowing the answer perfectly well—that he would not accept second billing for himself and the Lakeland Orchestra, and could not yet get precedence.

She heard a car brake squeakily in the street, and turn gingerly into the drive, and it pleased her to think that someone might possibly want to see her, someone to whom she could give tea or a drink. Still, it could be someone for the servants. It probably was.

She heard the buzzer's distant hum, and after a decorous interval, saw a maid slip into the hall and open the door. "Mrs. Rutherford Lodge," the maid said. "She wants to see you about some club."

Gloria was not one for clubs; this would probably turn out to be a bunch of old biddies, calling themselves the Lakeland Heights Improvement Group, anxious to annex a new and solvent victim. But she was bored. "All right, Leah, I'll see her."

Gloria was quite unprepared for Mrs. Rutherford Lodge, whose only concession to her errand was to substitute a dark blue dress embroidered in white fleur-de-lis for her usual muddy gray suit. The dress could have done with a thorough cleaning, too. Her black hat had, apparently, been sat on recently, although the large red rose on the brim looked fresh enough. Her badly dyed black hair was tucked under the hat after a fashion, her legs were wrapped in black lisle stockings, and her shoes were so sensible they seemed unreal. So did her voice when Gloria first heard it.

"Mrs. Gordon?" said Mrs. Lodge, sounding dulcet like a New-England-born mockingbird. "Now it's real nice to catch you home alone."

Gloria was wearing as little as possible, considering the fact that there was a manservant in the house; a white, backless sun dress and white sandals, nothing more. Under Mrs. Rutherford Lodge's stare she felt as naked as if not only her clothes, but the outer layer of her skin had been peeled off. She rose, nevertheless, and asked her caller to be seated.

"Thank you very kindly," the woman said.

"Can't I get tea for you, or a drink?" Gloria asked. She could think of nothing else to say.

A little frown appeared in Mrs. Lodge's weathered face at the word tea. But it disappeared when Gloria finished her sentence.

"Well now," she said just reluctantly enough, "maybe just a little whisky? And a very little water?"

Gloria crossed to the bellpull, thinking that such a voice really could not come out of such a dewlapped throat, and if it tried, should be choked back. "Bring the drink tray," she told the maid. "Don't bother about soda."

"Well, now," her caller began when Gloria returned to her chair, "you probably wonder why I'm here. I don't blame you . . ." She laughed, or in any case made a gurgling noise which could be taken for a laugh. "That's right, isn't it?"

"It's nice of you to call," Gloria said noncommittally.

"Yes. Well now, it's this way. Do you belong to the D.A.R.?"

"The—what?"

"The Daughters of the American Revolution, Mrs. Gordon."

"Oh. No, I don't. As a matter of fact, I doubt that I'm eligible."

"Well, now. The committee on membership, of which I am a member, is not overly curious."

What in heaven's name is she trying to say? Gloria thought. And why should I want to belong anyway? She merely looked vague, however, and said nothing.

"Well, now," Mrs. Lodge went on after an interval, "I'm an attorney, and I'm in a position to investigate. It's not expensive, really."

"It's not that, Mrs. Lodge. It's that I don't particularly like to join things. I don't know what's the good."

Mrs. Lodge pushed a few stiff-looking strands of hair under her hat, and they promptly fell out again. "Our group has a program of great value to the nation, Mrs. Gordon. We are combating"—she hissed the word—"creeping socialism."

The tray arrived, and Gloria gave her caller a stiff drink; she took one for herself, too. Then she said, "What is creeping socialism?" in her most innocent, defenseless voice.

Before she had an answer a good share of the drink disappeared into Mrs. Lodge's leathery face. Then she said in a lowered voice, "What that man in the White House is doing. I'm from Massachusetts, and there we believe in standing on our own feet."

Involuntarily Gloria glanced down at her guest's feet; they did form a substantial base, though not for all of Massachusetts. "I can't say I'm much interested," she replied at last. "Politics aren't for me."

"Well, now." And the rest of the drink disappeared. Mrs. Lodge gestured with the empty glass until her hostess took it from her and refilled it. "Your maiden name was Lawson?"

"Yes."

"I'm sure, Mrs. Gordon, we could establish a line for you. And as I said, it's just a little fee for investigation—perhaps a thousand dollars."

By now Gloria was genuinely bored. She barely knew what the organization was, she cared not at all, and she certainly did not want to combat socialism, creeping or whatever. "I'm sorry —it's not the cost, it's just that I'm not interested much in clubs. But it was nice of you to think of me."

She expected more urging, but she got none. Mrs. Lodge appeared to accept refusal gracefully, talked awhile about the room and the weather and finished her second drink more slowly. Then she got up to go, Gloria trailing her to the door. There she turned.

"Oh, by the way," she almost whispered, "how is your friend Mr. Sandzen?"

"What? Oh, Denis." What Gloria wondered, could have produced the question? "He's all right, I suppose. I haven't seen him since spring."

"Handsome young man, that. You know I live next door to him," this with a direct gaze that was shifted almost at once. "Well—good-by, and thanks for your time."

Gloria said good-by rather faintly, and went immediately to the telephone. She rang Mary Lister, and unexpectedly got her at once.

"Are you a member of the D.A.R.?" she asked after the barest preliminaries had been got through.

"What in the world?" Mary Lister thought rapidly. Was Gloria suddenly anxious to join? "Why, yes. I am. Why?"

"Do you know a Mrs. Rutherford Lodge? A very—well—peculiar-looking woman."

There was a light laugh. "I know what you mean. Yes, I do know her, or rather I see her occasionally at meetings. She's a lawyer, I think."

"That's right. Well, thanks. How are you, after the summer?"

"I'm fine. Gloria, why this about Mrs. Lodge?" She usually kept Gloria at arm's length or more, but after all a mile or two of wire in between was defense enough. And she was curious.

"Oh—nothing, really. She stopped by and asked me to join. Said she was on the membership committee. I told her I wasn't interested."

"But my dear, she's not on that committee. I'm sure she's not. How odd!"

Gloria almost blurted the business about tracing her family tree for a consideration, but a kind of animal caution halted her just in time. "Oh," she said. "I thought that was what she said."

Gloria knew that this conversation would be repeated; she had just as soon it ended, and it did very soon. But it left her puzzled and worried, and it was the reason she called Denis almost the moment he entered his apartment; he was still opening windows and checking the leaning stack of scores on his desk to make sure the maid had left them strictly alone as he had ordered. She had.

"Hello," he answered brusquely. "Who is it?"

"It's me, Denis. Gloria."

"Oh, how are you?"

"I'm fine. Hot of course."

"It's terrible. How's Harry?"

"He's fine. I've hardly seen him the last few days. We came home early because he's buying something or other."

Denis had just about run out of standard questions. "Good summer?" he asked, and was a little surprised by her answer.

"Terrible, up to now. Oh, Denis, I'm glad you're back. I've got to see you."

Of course, he thought, and not altogether with resignation. He had just come to the surface after a solid month of nothing, nothing at all, but preparation for the new season. "When? I'm sort of settling in right now."

It was about three o'clock. She did not hesitate. "Come out right now. Please do."

"My dear girl," he said, "I just this minute came in. I'm dirty—you know."

"You've got to come. I don't care if you're as black as night." Her voice was urgent, and it shook a little.

"I'll shower in two minutes, and drive on out." He looked at the small stack of letters, one from Terry on top. "I'll not even look at the mail."

"All right . . ." Her voice trailed off and he could hear the phone click as she put it down. He wondered what could have disturbed her so much. She was not easily disturbed. And then he forgot whatever it was in the pure joy of torrents of cool water and a fresh outfit. Just the same, he hurried, and it was very little more than half an hour later that he turned into the Gordon's familiar drive, and slapped his horn twice.

She met him at the door, kissed him quickly. "Come in and I'll get you a drink. You'll need it."

"What in the world, Gloria? You look like a scared——"

"Rabbit. I know—I'll tell you in a minute."

She scooted off and returned in a couple of minutes with

225

two glasses. "Let's stay inside," she said. "The sun porch is baking hot."

"All right. Let's have it."

She curled herself in the end of the sofa opposite him and her voice was low. "That Mrs. Lodge, the one who lives next to you. She came to see me." And she told him the whole story, almost word for word as it happened. Gloria had a memory as good in its way as Denis'. "You see," she ended, "she's got some dirt up her sleeve."

Flippantly, he said, "She's probably got dirt on the front of her dress too."

"No. I—it's not funny. The thousand dollars to investigate my family tree, when she must know I haven't got any. And her asking if I'd seen you, when your name hadn't even been mentioned."

Denis did not feel funny, because he suddenly recalled a remark made in the late spring—something about Mrs. Lodge's seeing him in the fall. He could not help but think that if there was to be a mess it was Gloria's fault, and then his Swedish half shamed him. Certainly she had been indiscreet. Certainly, too, he could have kept her away from the Hampton Park Manor; he could not honestly say even to himself that any woman, even as persistent a woman as Gloria, could have forced him into bed. And if it was the scene with the lamp that had started all this, then it was he who lost his temper and knocked the thing off the table. A little chill ran lightly, delicately, up his spine.

"You think it's blackmail, then?"

She nodded. "What else?"

She looked as if she might cry at any moment—and he looked into the future, and his goal looked a little less secure than it had. "Maybe we're wrong, Gloria," he said slowly. "She looks like such a ghastly old bat that you, sort of—well—sort of read the worst into everything she says."

"No. She only made one mistake, and I couldn't even prove she made that—I mean about being on the membership committee. Why would she go through all that? And why that remark about you? There's no use being naïve, Denis."

He took a deep breath, picked up his forgotten drink and finished it. Then he held out his cigarette case and gave her a light, all in order to have a moment for thought. "There's no use rushing into anything, either. Listen, Gloria, you've got to pull yourself together and not give anybody the slightest indication that you're afraid of anything."

"Anybody being Harry, of course."

He nodded. "And I'll just lie low, and wait. Anyway I'm forewarned, if she does try something. And then I'll think what to do."

Gloria seemed to feel a little better. "I'll manage Harry, all right. Only promise me you'll tell me exactly what happens."

"Of course." He got up. "I don't want to be here when Harry comes in. I'll run along."

At the door she quickly stood on tiptoe and kissed him good-by. "Don't forget to let me know."

He nodded again, and ran down the steps to his car.

Driving away was rather like driving into a fog, although the weather was actually clear. He had driven several blocks, he was starting the long, easy descent from the Heights, before his mind began working at all. This was impossible, this blackmail thing, because he had no time for such things as blackmail. He, Denis Sandzen, conductor of the Lakeland Orchestra, had several years of blazing work yet to do before he could reach the position he had determined long ago he would reach by the time he was thirty-five—the musical directorship of the New York Symphony. For this he had given up practically everything—and he was honest enough to admit practically everybody—not likely to help.

There was Elisabeth, not that he had actually forsworn her, but how close was he, really? And when he saw her, was it not usually in connection with something he was doing? There was Claire, too; he was not so stupid that he did not know Claire was 'interested,' although he could not believe her interest was exclusive. And he could not quite get the picture of her on the beach at Juan-les-Pins out of his mind, no matter how hard he tried. Oh, well. . . .

There was Terry, he almost had said "poor Terry" to himself. He had failed Terry, and there at least he could not blame himself. Nor help himself. But Terry was still the closest friend he had in life, ever had had, for that matter. He was a man of fine appearance and finer mind. He was understanding, patient, and his interests were very broad indeed. When Denis could manage it, he always stopped thinking of Terry at a certain point, which was the point at which he would be forced to admit that Terry loved him. That and its corollary: that he did not often enough return what little he could return for Terry's love. For the most part, not even letters.

Cécile? He never wrote Cécile, except Christmas cards, and for that he neither had nor needed excuse. He had been—and at this point he frowned—merely a sexual convenience for Cécile. Perhaps on the world's scale, a scale he did not pretend to understand, he owed Cécile something in return for initiation. But he really did not think so.

Delphine? He owed Delphine a great deal, even though Delphine had had repayment of a sort. She really wanted an orchestra and the pleasure of managing it, and that much he had given her. Paul de Knize? Him he owed nothing; if anything it was the other way about. Paul wanted an orchestra, and paid for it, because he personally wanted to hear it. He did not give a damn, Denis was certain, that the orchestra gave pleasure to others.

Gus? Gus understood him and took his percentage. Neither owed the other—or perhaps each owed the other. Clarissa? Nonsense; Clarissa was getting exactly what she wanted. She always would, which characteristic was something Denis could and did understand wonderfully well. They had the same drive, the same outlook, the same ruthlessness. Perhaps also the same ability, for it seemed to Denis there were touches of genius about this woman, sycophant one moment, autocrat the next, with the great purpose always behind every attitude. But was she truly close? Did he allow her to be?

Harry Gordon? Yes—he owed Harry a great deal when Harry was sober, and sometimes when he was drunk, too. Harry was a strange man with roots, ability—and unsureness. Denis had crossed Mather Street without noticing, and was driving down the incline to the garage when he was struck by a curious thought—that it was Gloria who was Harry's unsureness, that perhaps Harry understood his wife's weakness but could not quite condemn it because he loved her, and had a weakness of his own.

And that left Gloria. He was fond of Gloria; he demanded nothing from her, he got fleeting moments of satisfaction, and she made him feel like a cheat. If the fact was that he thought of her as a convenience, not even realizing that she was a slightly shopworn substitute for something that he should have wanted desperately at his age, then something *was* lacking. And suddenly he realized there was someone he was beginning to care for, a whole group of someones. Else why would he have forced himself to make time for composition this last summer? And for work that he could not hope would bring anything more than a personal pleasure? He thought of Larrabee House with warmth, and it was the first warmth that had touched him since Gloria's telephone call earlier that afternoon.

When he reached his apartment he tossed his jacket onto the sofa and at once began riffling through the stack of letters. There was one from Gus, whom he had seen a couple of days before—two contracts for guest jobs the coming season which had not been ready for signature. There were three letters from Terry—he would answer them after dinner, no matter what happened. A note from Elisabeth, reminding him that she had taken seriously his promise that she might sing at the last of the season's new pop concert series, made him smile; it was possible that Clarissa's hidden ten thousand might not make up the loss after all, and that Elisabeth might not sing.

He shuffled out a number of advertisements from neighborhood shops, and came at last to a large, plain envelope with no return address. He looked at it oddly for a moment, shrugged, opened it. His instinct had been right. It was from Mrs. Rutherford Lodge, and the letter was written on her letterhead, badly typed, and signed in a handwriting so tiny it might have required a reading glass of someone without Denis' very good vision. It read:

I am sorry to have to tell you that your accident proved much more difficult of adjustment than I had thought. I have spent a great deal of time on it this summer, and should be glad to have your check for $1,000 in return.

That was all.

It was, however, enough. Of course she had spent no time on the accident; if she had, she certainly would have included some detail, and not written what amounted to a bald demand. She would expect a telephone call from him, probably not a letter. Then she would make another casual reference to Gloria, probably look off into distance like an ancient harpy whose hair had been stirred with an egg beater, and if she got the thousand the whole proceeding would be repeated in a month. Would be repeated as often as she thought she dared repeat, and she would dare rather often.

Denis felt like a fly in a bottle. Even a young man wrapped in a cocoon of his own making could see the possibilities, and pretty tawdry they were. He was not fool enough to see this as the ruin of his life, for he was willing to admit it probably would not be that. He was simply too good at his job. Even if there were a scandal, he eventually could land on his feet elsewhere. He started to tear the letter across, and instead he hid it under the pile of scores on his desk. He might need it.

He had to move about. He got up and went into the kitchen to make himself a drink. He took a long swallow, and the whisky tasted vile. Nevertheless, he carried the glass back to his living room and finished the drink. He forced himself to cross to the window and look down on the lake and the park.

He realized he was gripping the glass fiercely, as if it were the dewlapped throat of Mrs. Rutherford Lodge.

"Goddam it," he said aloud, "I don't want to be thrown off the track. And Harry . . ."

He felt very small, as nearly humble at that moment as it was possible for him to feel. And suddenly he realized that he was thinking quite as much about Harry as about himself. The business with Blum was the beginning of a debt. It was true that it had given Harry an opportunity to get something said he evidently had wanted to say for a great while. But it was a magnificent scene, just the same. Not only because it had been useful to him, but also because it had dimly perceived general values, Denis liked it and in a way fed on it.

Now this, this frowsy, lizardlike creature was not only about to throw Denis himself off course for nobody could know how many miles; she was likely to deal Harry Gordon a blow in the one place he might be truly vulnerable. Right now the she-bat was probably sitting under her crushed old hat next door, hoping for a telltale noise.

She should have it, Denis thought grimly, but childishly. He went into the bedroom, sat down on the bed and deliberately banged it a time or two on the wall. He raised his voice, and said "I hate you, I hate you," knowing the wall was too thick for his neighbor to distinguish actual words. He moved a chair, allowing it to tap the wall gently, grinning at his own small game though not with much humor.

Then he picked up the phone and ordered dinner, and in a couple of minutes crossed the living room to the hall door, opened it quietly, closed it softly. And listened.

He thought he could hear Mrs. Rutherford Lodge's door latch click—she would be peering down the hall from under that hat. He could not imagine her without an outlandish hat. Nor did he pretend his little game had resolved anything at all, unless it was his bitterness of the moment. But when the waiter came he was hungry, and he ate with pleasure. Then he undressed and put on his robe, and wrote Terry.

19

Clarissa, next morning, found Denis unusually remote. He was sometimes deliberately remote, and she thought very little about it until luncheon, which they had at the Hampton Park Manor. Twice she had asked him how many of the ten pop concerts he wanted Dingbat to conduct, and neither time had he given the slightest hint that he heard. Instead he seemed fixed on the door of the dining room, where under a carved coat of arms which no expert could read, the headwaiter stood hopefully. The hotel had few luncheon guests, and Denis had suggested it because he thought it hardly likely that Mrs. Rutherford Lodge would bother to come all the way out from her office to eat there.

Clarissa tapped gently on her plate with her fork, and when Denis looked at her she smiled and said, "For the third time, how many of the pops do you want Ding—Walter to take?"

"Six," he answered. "I want four—the first and the last and I don't care about the others."

"That's settled. Denis, don't you feel well?"

"Of course I do."

"Then what's wrong? You're not here in Lakeland at all. Your mind's wandering all over."

I'm very much here in Lakeland, he thought. I wish I weren't. But he forced a smile, and said, "I suppose I'm just tired. I didn't sleep at all."

If the explanation was unsatisfactory, she gave no hint of it. When Denis had signed the check and they were leaving she remarked, in an offhand manner, "Don't forget Harry's coming out to the hall at four." Nor did she seem to notice the quick glance Denis gave her. "You know, I think I shall tell him about that ten thousand. He's the only member of the board who would understand."

"You know best about that," he said, nodding to the head-waiter. "Do you mind walking back to the hall alone? I've got some things to do."

"Of course not. You'll be there at four, won't you?"

"Of course. Maybe I'll take a nap."

But he took no nap. He got out Mrs. Rutherford Lodge's letter and reread it. It still carried its implied threat, and he still felt shattered by it. He rather wished Gus were in Lakeland, and for a panicky moment considered asking him to come. Or Terry. He could think of only one other person likely to be helpful, and that was Hans Mayor. But he had seen almost nothing of Hans the last years, and in any case he was in Philadelphia and not the kind of man one approached with the problem of blackmail after a long silence.

I'd better call the old bat up, he thought, and then thought better of the idea. She would have him where she could whirl him around her forefinger like a child's toy. It would have to be a letter—and if he could he must stay out of her sight until it was delivered. Denis wished he could use a typewriter, so he could make a carbon. He made three drafts before he was satisfied; the third seemed possible. He wrote:

> Dear Mrs. Lodge:
> I am astonished that you ask such a substantial fee
> for a service for which I already have paid you. I shall
> of course not send you the check you request.

"But won't I?" he asked himself grimly, as he sealed the envelope and stamped it. Before he walked down the wide hall to drop it in the mail chute he found himself pushing aside the little flap over the peephole, scouting the neighborhood. I'm acting like a criminal, he thought; still, I don't want to meet her until I have to. And that probably will be tomorrow after she gets the letter.

Back in his room he dug out the score he had found time to sketch in that summer. He read it through, and at the end he was chilled to find that he remembered nothing at all; he, Denis Sandzen, who usually could read a strange score through once and remember nearly everything essential. Finally he took the music to the piano and played it straight through and up to time. Twenty-four minutes, which was all right for a ballet. And he liked it; he had been trying to write a ballet that would express the South, one that could be danced by Negroes, one that would not rely on the old clichés—no Uncle Toms, no good ol' Massa. After a couple of weeks away from it, he was pleased, so pleased he almost called the Larrabees. But with the telephone in his hand he changed his mind. He quite simply could not face their complete trustfulness. He wondered why, too, for they certainly were living in the world as it really is; they were surrounded by situations which certainly were as difficult, and what was more, they could and did cope with them. There was Lee, whose sweetness was proverbial but whose father was a murderer, and it was Carol Larrabee who had walked alone up the cinder path leading to his door and quieted the man when the police were content to hide behind trees and cars and wait. He knew the Larrabees would help him, too, but his pride would not allow him to ask.

He looked at his watch; it was only three o'clock. He heard the telephone. Cursing mildly, he walked into his bedroom and picked up the phone.

"Denis, dear," Gloria's voice said, "has anything happened? I'm terrible worried."

He told her briefly about the letter, and had no sooner finished than he wished he had kept the business to himself.

"Oh, dear. Denis, I can hardly look at Harry. I——"

His patience and his nerves both were worn to a razor edge. "Of course you're worried. So am I. Only I said I would think a way out of it and I will. Now please just sit tight. And don't act as if you'd robbed the Lakeland National."

He thought he heard a childish sniffle. "And for God's sake stop crying."

"Don't be so hard. I—we——"

"I'm not hard. And if the very worst happens, it still isn't the end. That old hellion can't prove that we—we actually slept together."

This was a very unconvincing remark, and Denis knew it. Gloria all night in Denis' apartment would be quite enough for most minds, including Harry's. Still, he had to say something.

"Also Gloria, I've got to see Harry at four. He's stopping by the hall for something about the pop series."

"Oh. . . . Oh, Denis, I wish I could see you, just for a minute."

"Well you can't," he said more shortly than he intended. "There isn't time. And we shouldn't be seen together anyway."

At last she hung up. When he reached Clarissa's office he was not only nervous and exasperated; he was hot from having hurried. And Harry was drunk, not reeling drunk, but enough so that it was difficult to pin him down.

"So," Clarissa said firmly, "I think the gamble's worth while —and I can scrape up the money."

Harry looked at Denis waggishly. "Our girl friend's a gambler. Bet she swiped the dough, too."

Denis looked quickly at Clarissa, who frowned a "No."

"Bet she did too, Harry," said Denis. "These people from the wrong side of the tracks . . ."

" 'S it. 'S tracks does it. I know, on account I'm from the wrong side, too." He looked at Denis, but his eyes would not hold steady. "Seen Gloria yet? Poor girl missed you."

Oh, God, thought Denis. Did she tell him I was there, or didn't she? He moved his face into something he hoped was a smile. "Talked with her on the phone just before I came over," he said. "She sounded fine."

"She's not. She acts funny; got the pip maybe."

Clarissa felt the conversation slipping out of control entirely. She tried to bring it back. "Harry," she said, "how much of the auditorium ought we to use? Four thousand? Six thousand?"

" 'S this a chicken show?" Harry laughed. "Have everything there, chickens, Shriners, horses, every damn thing."

"No. Please Harry. I'm serious."

"Never more serious m'self. Six thousand, an' put the chicks in the basement."

Denis nodded. "Let's make it six—a dollar on the floor and half a dollar in the balconies."

Harry was not too drunk to figure; he rarely was. "'S good." House scale around four thousand dollars that way. "'S good."

"All right." Clarissa looked at the memorandum pad in front of her. "Then let's settle——"

"You settle." Harry got to his feet, still steady. "Got a drink, Denis? No . . . le's all go my house for a drink. C'me on." He made a wide gesture and for the first time he staggered a little.

Again Denis caught Clarissa's slight frown. "Look, Harry," he said, "I've got a date. Bottle too; sit down and I'll get it."

"No party." He said it sadly, and his handsome face fell. He looked for the moment like a small boy who just has dropped an ice-cream cone. "Okay. Bring a bottle."

Exasperated, but grateful too, Denis walked down the hall to his office and got a bottle of bourbon out of his closet. "Got three glasses?" he called down the hall, and Clarissa said she had.

"Here you are, Harry." Denis handed him a glass, poured ice water out of Clarissa's silver thermos.

He poured drinks for Clarissa and himself, and the three sat solemnly around the tables. Harry raised his glass. "To the pop-pops. Goes the weasel."

Harry had two more drinks, and by that time, having poured the last two himself, he was ready for home. "I'll take him," Clarissa said. "I can always manage better than anybody."

"Manage," Harry said thickly. "Bes' manager 'n world. Bes'."

"How about it at the house?" Denis asked softly. "Frankly, I'd rather not go, but——"

"The houseman. He's good at things like this. You help me downstairs—Harry can leave his car here."

It was not easy, getting Harry into Clarissa's car, but with the help of the watchman on the door, they managed. Denis looked quickly at the half-dozen cars in the parking lot; Harry's was not there.

"He must have come in a cab," he said, and Clarissa nodded.

"That's splendid. Now you run along."

As the car turned into the street, Denis could see Harry fall gently toward Clarissa with the look of one already asleep. Oh Lord, he thought, it's always the way. You expect a hard time and worry because you think somebody will read things into everything you say. And the somebody goes to sleep on Clarissa's shoulder like a child. Maybe—and instinctively he looked right and left as he gained the sidewalk—it'll be that way with Mrs. Lodge. But he felt that would be too much to expect.

By morning he still had not met the woman, accidentally or otherwise. And this was the morning of his first rehearsal, for which he was more than ready in every way except temperamentally. He would have liked to postpone it—this would be the first time he had ever rehearsed his orchestra when he felt less than utterly confident. They won't know, he thought, and the thought meant nothing. He would know, and it was this that made the difficulty. What, he wondered as he told the librarian what music to put on the stands, would the orchestra think if they knew that a female scarecrow had their revered young leader over a barrel? He knew many would feel glad. For he had relaxed nothing in the way of discipline, and the fact that he was also scrupulously fair made very little difference. They felt he was too young to be so sure of himself. They would have liked it if he were wrong more often, but he was almost never wrong; and when occasionally he went counter to the accepted way, they always found his position was at least logical. All this did not make for ease. The men wondered how the same young man who drove them relentlessly and refused to allow anyone to step even an inch out of line could prove so extremely charming to his audiences.

The rehearsal went badly. The men were rusty from summer jobs, some from lack of practice. The hall was stuffy, and when Denis called for a quick run-through of the Beethoven Eighth, half the men found they had the Beethoven Fourth on their stands. When the break came everyone, including Denis, was ready for it. He found Farrell Clisby in the wings.

Farrell handed Denis a paper. "You're supposed to call that number immediately," he said.

237

"Thanks." Denis took the paper and went on into his office. There he looked at it, holding it away from him as if it carried a bad odor. There was no name, merely a number: Mather 6969. It was a downtown number, from the exchange. It also was no number he knew.

For a few minutes he sat on the corner of his desk, tapping with his fingers on its shining mahogany top, not even thinking. At last he turned to the phone, picked it up. But he did not call the number.

I'm damned if I will, he thought. The old bitch should know this is no time to call. He set the instrument down carefully and poured himself some water from the carafe which sat beside the phone. She can call me at the hotel or she can write. She would, he was quite sure. She was shrewd enough not to put on heavy pressure at the moment, he was confident, and probably never a pressure heavy enough to break her victim. That was the delicate thing about blackmail, he sensed; how to make the pressure stiff enough that the victim would pay, and light enough to keep from breaking the golden eggs.

The second half of the rehearsal went better, much to Denis' astonishment. Either the men were working better, or his attention was distracted and he didn't notice. He looked often at his wrist. If he could keep rehearsing indefinitely, he might be safe, for surely she would never stalk out on the stage and—what was the phrase?—put the finger on him.

Then it was noon. Clisby was passing his office as he reached it, and on the spur of the moment Denis asked him for lunch and Clisby agreed. "Give me a minute to check this stuff with Aunt Clarissa," he said. "Lots of things I want to ask you—Europe and all that."

Before they ate, Denis and his guest walked around to the hotel so Denis might change from his rehearsal clothes. There was no message at the desk, and of course no letter; there had not been time for a letter. Denis was getting out clean things and shedding his rehearsal clothes when he heard the piano. It was the music of the new ballet Clisby was playing, and not very well.

Denis was a little annoyed. He wanted to let the score soak a while longer, so that he would be perfectly sure what he thought about it. But he had left it on the piano, and he could not blame Clisby for looking at it. He was, in fact, glad when he emerged from the bathroom to dress, and caught a glimpse of Clisby's face.

"Hey, Denis," Clisby shouted. "Please play this for me right. I can't do much with a full score like this. It's simply swell, Denis. It really is."

Denis had gotten into his shorts. "All right. Only it's hot and I'd rather do it naked, or kind of naked."

He began at the first bar, which was a deliberate quotation from Louis Moreau Gottschalk and caused Clisby to nod his head appreciatively. He played through without a pause, thumping the bass with his fist when he reached a brief solo for kettle-drums, singing once in a rather dreadful voice when an off-stage tenor was supposed to come in. At last the music died away in a brief, gay run for flute, and Clisby released his breath in a sigh.

"I know who you did it for, and they ought to knight you," he said. "It's—it's superb. Don't you do anything badly, Denis? Really?"

"It's not that good, Farrell. Honestly it isn't."

His guest looked at him a few seconds before speaking. "Maybe I'm speaking out of turn," he said finally, "but so help me God you ought to do something badly, just to keep the balance. You're too goddam good to be true."

"Don't be stupid. I tell you it's not that good." Denis had started for the bedroom and the rest of his clothes, but he turned back. "I do plenty of things badly," he said quietly. "And I cheat myself out of a lot of things other people have. Deliberately, of course."

Clisby only shook his head at his retreating host. This was truth, an admission he felt sure Denis had never put into words before, at least not in Lakeland. And Denis in his turn was surprised at himself, and a little shocked. For a moment he felt an impulse to tell the whole story of Gloria and Mrs. Rutherford Lodge to Clisby. He had all the faith in the world in Clisby—and he could never bring himself to confess to him. Never. . . . The Swedish half of him shut down flatly at the thought. To whom, then?

"Want to stop by Larrabee House?" Clisby asked as Denis emerged, tying his bow tie as he came. "How the hell do you do that?" he continued. "It's all I can do to tie one in front of a mirror."

"Question one, no. Question two, it's easy."

"All right. It was just an idea."

They drove downtown to the Slater, and had a drink in the bar before going in to lunch. They talked mostly about the Larrabees, and particularly about the chances of producing the ballet.

"First I've got to work out a scenario," said Denis. "I've only got a skimpy one, and this isn't the sort of thing the boys can improvise. Besides, they can't do it alone; there would be girls in it. More boys, too."

Clisby agreed. "Mind if I take a shot at it? The scenario, I mean."

"Of course not. Come over some night soon, and I can tell what I have in mind. You can take over from there."

They ate in silence for a couple of minutes before Clisby suddenly asked, "How many men will you need to play it? That's probably the big trouble."

"Twenty-six. It's scored pretty light."

"They've got a little orchestra at Larrabee House, but I don't think it's good enough. That's why I asked."

"Look—so far nobody knows it will be produced, Farrell. Let's not worry yet."

"It'll be produced if I have to take my life savings to do it. No—look, Denis, I think I know enough men in the orchestra I could ask. But would you mind?"

Denis gave his guest a sidelong glance. "Aren't you being subtle? You know I wouldn't mind."

"Maybe I was." Clisby was drawing lines on the tablecloth with the handle of his dessert spoon. "Probably I really meant the Board, Lister and the rest of them. Not Harry Gordon."

"You know a lot more about them than I."

"Very likely. And I think they would object. Some of them think Dick and Carol are—shh-h!—radical. That we ought to let the Negroes and Poles and Czechs and whatnot go back where they came from if they don't like what they get. You know—the Larrabees pamper them."

For a little while Denis said nothing. The check came and he paid it. As they started out of the big room he suddenly grinned at Clisby. "Ever see me in action?"

"Only with the orchestra men. I've seen you cutting them down to size."

"Think the same sort of thing would work with, say, Douglas Lister?"

His companion pulled down the corners of his mouth and at the same time puffed out his cheeks a little. The resemblance was amazing; except for his younger skin he might easily have been Douglas Lister viewing with alarm. This was something Lister did readily and for reasons as varied as that man in the White House, and the parlous state of Lakeland's youth, what with full-grown boys beginning to appear on Stoneman Beach with no top whatever to their swimming suits.

Denis laughed all the louder because underlying all their talk and all the pleasure he felt at Farrell's enthusiasm there had been the gargoyle and her possible course. As they left the hotel he said, "I'll handle it. If you can get the men to play and the union to let them, I'll promise the rest."

"Fine. I'll do my share." But Denis thought there was a little doubt in Clisby's tone, doubt that may have come from the fact that he had been born in Lakeland and knew the Lakeland attitude better by far than Denis ever could know it.

It was three o'clock when Denis got back to the hotel, and this time there was a message for him. He was to call Mather 6969, and there was no name given. When he got to his room, he called the hotel operator and asked whether she had been on when the message was received. She had.

"Didn't they leave a name?"

"No, Mr. Sandzen. She didn't."

"She? It was a woman?"

He could almost see the girl looking about to make sure no one could overhear. Then she said, "We're not supposed to guess at things like that. Only I think it was that Mrs. Lodge."

"Oh!" His voice sounded, he thought with some surprise, as if he really were astonished. "Well, I can't imagine what she wants, but if she expects me to call her she'll leave her name. Thanks a lot."

He put down the phone slowly. Then she really means business, he thought, if she'll call here and take the chance of their recognizing her voice. Knowing they would almost certainly recognize it. Or was she merely bluffing, screwing the nut just a little tighter for the pure pleasure of knowing he would squirm? All at once he wanted someone near him, knowing that there was no one he could call, not even Gloria. Harry might very well be home nursing his hangover, for that morning Clarissa said that before she left him the night before Harry had been hovering over another bottle. Why, he thought tangentially, does a man with all the money and all the looks in the world have to go on these periodic bats? He smiled tightly. All his thoughts seemed to be questions today.

He had nothing to do, or rather he wanted to do nothing he could do. According to formula, he would play a concerto in the first program, Mozart this time. He knew the concerto perfectly, but for something to do, he sat down at the piano and began playing the first movement at about half speed, the way he played a work new to him. Habit was very strong, and so was his concentration. He surprised himself by turning up a couple of spots where he was not sure. He knew the notes exactly, and he got the effect he wanted. But he was not perfectly sure how he fingered the passage, or had not been until now. He laughed at himself—Denis the perfectionist, the chap who never leaves things to chance. And here was proof that his native ability had fooled even himself.

For more than an hour he worked; it was a quarter after four when he looked at his watch and asked himself the obvious question: What am I waiting for? He answered the question. For a drink. There was no loose ice in the box, so he pried a tray out of the binding frost and held it under the hot water tap, demanding for the hundredth time why someone in this great land of progress had not produced a device that would free ice cubes mechanically. Then he forgot the problem, mixed his drink, and returned to the piano. There would probably be kinks in the ballet too, and he might as well go through that critically, all the time with Farrell's warm appreciation running round inside him. He had had a vast amount of applause in his short career, and he had not much missed the fact that few people outside his own small circle had felt close enough to him to speak the way Farrell had spoken. Applause from an audience was, he thought, quite different from the spontaneous welling of pleasure in a perceptive person like Clisby.

Farrell's nice, and he's good, Denis thought. Still, he can't ever mean what Terry means.

The buzzer startled him, but he was too tightly wrapped in his own thoughts to be nervous. He crossed to the door and opened it, and if he had found a rattlesnake coiled just outside he could hardly have been more unnerved. But he had faced too many audiences, too many orchestras some of which were hostile, not to have developed control. He started, and then said, gently, "Yes?"

Mrs. Lodge moved forward, and Denis stood quietly in her way. His heart was suddenly hammering inside him like an old-fashioned one-cylinder motor, but she could not hear it.

"We'd better have a talk," Mrs. Lodge said with incongruous sweetness. "Right now."

"Just tell me what it was you did that was worth a thousand dollars."

Again she moved, and still he stood his ground. She pushed back her hat, and mechanically tucked in a flying strand of black hair. "Not here in the hall. I'll come in."

This is foolish, Denis thought. There could be half a dozen ears plastered to half a dozen doors, listening to everything. Still he stubbornly held his position; she could not enter without a flying tackle, and she was not made for such exercise. He said again, "I'd like to know what you did. I can't ask you in—I'm expecting guests."

"Young man, I did plenty. And I'm not used to being treated

this way. My late husband, Mr. Lodge, would thrash you within an inch of your life." The pitch of her voice raised a little, and so did the volume. "Let me in!"

"I won't." But he was by no means sure he would be able to hold out much longer. "Your bill is excessive, and I won't pay it until . . ."

The elevator door groaned and opened, and a woman got out, and came, slow and stately, down the hall, her front almost as impressive as those described in weather reports. Mrs. Lodge turned sharply, and Denis wondered at the Duse-like change in her. Her frown became a smile, and she turned briefly to him and said as sweetly, "Thanks, Mr. Sandzen. I'll get in touch with you." And to the stranger, "My dear, you're early, and I'm delighted."

Denis closed the door in a daze. The second woman was familiar, but he was sure she was no one he knew. Then he remembered, and his tension slipped away temporarily in a great laugh. It was the woman who had been driving Mrs. Lodge home the night he and Gloria had had their accident. The member of the D.A.R. Probably, too, one of the few women before whom Mrs. Lodge would feel compelled to preserve appearances. For she had posed as a member of the committee on admissions. And Mrs. Lodge was not a member of the committee, for Gloria in her rabbitlike way had found that out.

It was not much, but it at least postponed things.

He heard nothing more from his neighbor that night, nor was there a telephone call or a letter next day. The rehearsal went better, too, and after it Farrell Clisby greeted him with the news that he could get together the twenty-six men needed for the ballet, and was all ready to approach the union. He did not see how that group, tough though it was and always would be, could very well object since it was obvious the performance would be a charity date, and if it was not played free by union men, it would not be played at all.

"Hadn't you better speak to Clarissa?" Denis asked. "She might resent it if you went to the union without——"

"She would," Farrell interrupted, "and I dread speaking to her."

"Why?"

Farrell hesitated. "Well—I don't honestly think she has anything against Larrabee House, only most of the people she gets money from do. They think Dick and Carol are just one step removed from Bolsheviks."

"Oh, hell . . ."

"Yes. Oh, hell. As a matter of fact they're Democrats, or were. Now they refuse to register in any party, so they can pick the best man. If there is any best man, that is."

Denis thought a minute, and finally said, "Let me ask her. Will you?"

"Well . . . I suppose so. Look, Denis, be tactful, will you?" He suddenly looked confused. "I don't mean that you're brash generally; I just mean catch her with sugar instead of with salt."

Denis could not keep from laughing. Also, the urge for friendship that had risen the day before came back stronger than ever. Farrell was weedy-looking. But he had strength of a kind, and after a period in which he hardly knew the young man existed, Denis realized all at once that he liked him. That he enjoyed him would probably express it better.

"Of course I'm brash, Farrell," he said. "Also the best friend I ever had said once I had a one-track mind. I have, too. But this time I'll try to be—well—subtle if that's what you mean."

Farrell nodded. "Better hit her now; she's in a swell humor, on account she caught the U. S. Concert Bureau charging her four hundred more for that new Austrian pianist than they asked Chicago."

Denis went immediately to Clarissa's office. Farrell was right; she was delighted with herself, and immediately told him the whole story. "What they don't know is that their Aunt Clarissa has a personal friend in practically every orchestra office in the country," she ended.

"I'd hate to try to hide anything from you," Denis agreed, and he meant it. "That's why I'm here now."

In his turn he told the whole story of his dealings with the Larrabees, part of which she already knew from the incident in

Mammy's Kitchen. He told her about the ballet ("When on earth did you find time for it?" she asked), about the orchestra, about the necessity for negotiating with the union. And there she balked.

"You shouldn't do it, Denis," she said firmly.

He could feel the slight tingle under his scar that came when he met opposition; it was the feeling he had at rehearsal when someone got out of line. This time he forced himself to disregard it. He merely said, "Why?"

Her answer was indirect. "I like the Larrabees. They're doing what they think they ought to do, and they are fighters. I like that. But Denis"—she gently reached across the desk and took the tapping letter opener out of his hand—"I imagine everybody on our board except Harry Gordon and John Dudley think they're no better than Socialists. Or worse. You've got your pop concerts. Why don't you let well enough alone, at least this season?"

He could feel real anger now, and he could not control it completely. He pushed back his chair, bit his lip nervously. Then he blurted, "Clarissa, they haven't bought every minute of me. What I do with my spare time's my own business."

"They won't look at it that way. It won't be a question of spare time, or any other kind of time. They'll say you're spending your talent on a group of, of——"

"Niggers and bohunks; go ahead."

"Well, maybe not that strong. But they'll think you're out of character, lowering the dignity of the Lakeland Orchestra. And if you do it in spite of them, they'll be nasty." She tried a sidewise appeal. "They don't understand what they have in you, Denis. They know you're terribly successful, but they don't understand you're the best there is."

The anger subsided. In spite of himself, Denis laughed. "You're pretty good yourself," he said. And then he sobered abruptly. "But I won't promise. Maybe we won't ask the union for favors; maybe I'll just pay the men out of my own pocket."

Clarissa knew when to stop as well as when to start. She looked at her watch. "Take it easy," she said. "We'll talk later. I'm due to speak to the East Lakeland Community Club in twenty minutes." She sighed. "God knows how much chicken à la king I've eaten for this orchestra."

When she left, Denis rejoined Farrell, and reported. Before he had quite finished, the telephone rang and the operator inquired gently, "Didn't you get Mr. Gordon's message asking you for cocktails this afternoon? I put it on your desk when you were still in rehearsal."

The message was there. Denis swallowed his alarm. "Should I call him?" he asked.

"No. He said if you could make it you needn't call—it's not a party."

Oh, God, he thought, I wish it were a party. He turned back to Clisby. "Let's let it ride a day or so. I mean the ballet."

Clisby nodded. He had seen that odd remoteness in Denis' face before and he knew what it meant.

20

Until he played slowly through the concerto with which he planned to open his season, according to rite, it never had occurred to Denis that there was any part, however small, of anything he knew that he had not mastered. Nor was he the victim of any doubts about his capacity now; he merely realized that he had at some point been careless, and he intended to correct the carelessness before it became a tendency. He had intended to spend the entire afternoon at the piano, restudying the concerto as if he never had seen it before.

Now the prospect of the long afternoon alone in his apartment was extremely unappetizing, as for that matter was the prospect of food alone. Clarissa had gone to her chicken à la king, and he did not know where Farrell was. On occasion he lunched with his concertmaster, but he had long gone. On impulse, he sent the watchman out for a couple of sandwiches and a couple of bottles of beer, remembering to give him money for a couple of bottles extra. He ate alone at his desk, and then he returned to the stage and pushed the piano out of the wings.

When Clarissa returned at three o'clock, she heard the faint sound of the piano and tiptoed down to listen a minute. Farrell Clisby did the same. He met the librarian as he went back to his office. "How long has he been working?" he asked, and the man shook his head.

"I don't know," he said. "He was at it when I got back at one, and he hasn't stopped once."

At four o'clock Clisby tapped at Clarissa's door. "Denis has a date at the Gordons for cocktails. Ought I remind him?"

She smiled. "Let him have half an hour more. We had—well, maybe he's working something out of himself."

Clisby went back to his room, where he was deliberately wasting the orchestra's time thinking about Denis' ballet, and how best to handle it. He would like to have talked at once with Dick and Carol Larrabee—but he dared not. And then he forgot the ballet and Larrabee House in his most pressing personal problem, which was how to pay a dentist fifteen hundred dollars for straightening his young son's teeth, when he had barely fifteen dollars left from his vacation.

At four thirty he heard a ladylike, silvery tinkle from Clarissa's office, and knew it came from Clarissa's tiny traveling clock. In a moment he heard her purposeful step in the hall, and a few seconds later the distant sound of the piano stopped, and two sets of footsteps climbed the stairs. As Denis passed his door he called, "Good going," and Denis, his face showing fatigue, said, "Thanks."

Denis was actually thinking that he was a fool. He had barely an hour to get to the Gordons, and he had no idea of what he would find when he finally arrived. Usually cocktail invitations came from Gloria; was this one merely a trap? Harry could have heard something from Mrs. Rutherford Lodge; after all, he had practically held her in the hall by force the day before, and she might have done anything after the lady of the breastworks left. Or this morning.

He slipped out of the hall alone and hurried around the park to the hotel. There was no message and no letter at the desk, which further disconcerted him. He was beginning to dread the walk down the hall from the elevator, feeling that probably the peephole of the apartment next door framed an invisible eye. In his own place at last, he quickly showered and put on slacks and a sport coat—it was no party, Harry had said, and sport clothes were quite good enough if it was to be an execution. It was about twenty minutes after five when he was ready, and before he opened his door he peered out through the peephole into an empty hall. This is absurd, he said, but he looked again to be sure.

The elevator door opened as he reached out for the call-button, and Mrs. Lodge stepped out. "Oh, Mr. Sandzen," she said with a gleam in her eye. "This is fortunate. May I have a minute."

Denis said, "Wait," to the elevator man, and "I'm sorry, but I'm late for my date now," to his frowsy neighbor. He stepped past her.

"Later tonight," she called as the door closed.

"What's the ol' bag want outa you?" the elevator man asked because he was the kind of elevator man who made conversation with his passengers.

"She handled a little accident case for me," Denis said, and he imagined his relief showed in his voice.

"Lots of people think she's a freak and kinda dumb," the man went on. "She ain't—I'd sure hate to have her on my trail." He looked around at Denis. "God she's ugly, ain't she?"

Denis agreed. He supposed that he should have kept up the forms of chivalry, but defending Mrs. Lodge against that charge was a palpable absurdity. As he started his car, he thought that his dodging game was equally absurd. It could not go on much longer.

Gloria met him at the door; often he wished she would let the servants answer the bell once in a while, but she seldom did. She said, loudly enough to be heard in the drawing room, "I thought you'd deserted us," and whispered, "Hear anything?"

He shook his head, and she had no idea whether he meant that he had heard nothing, or perhaps that he couldn't say now. Then they were in the drawing room and Harry, sober enough and the perfect, genial host, rose to shake hands.

"We never see you except with a lot of people around," he began. "Thought maybe we could have a quiet drink and just talk."

Does he mean it? Denis asked himself, or is he just playing with me—with us? He swallowed and said, "Hello, Harry. I've been working like a dog and it's nice to relax." He took his drink and settled into the corner of one of the big sofas, with his host and Gloria opposite him. And what now? he thought.

"Good vacation?" Gloria asked, and Harry laughed.

"This one doesn't have vacations," he said. "He just works in a different place."

Denis made a quick decision. "At least I worked on something different," he began. "Composing."

If Harry had anything in mind beyond a casual talk he certainly gave no hint. Denis plunged at once into the story, and he told it all and well. Once in a while Gloria said, "Oh," and when he reached the business of performance, Harry asked rather timidly, "Can you play some of it?"

Denis would have played the ballet if he had spent ten instead of four hours at the piano that day. He even sang the phrase or two for tenor, and Harry grinned delightedly. When it was over he said, "God, that's wonderful. I can't stand garbage-can modern, but that makes sense."

Denis rode his impulse further. He told about his talk with Clarissa, and Harry frowned a little.

"Trouble is, she's absolutely right," he said slowly. "But hell—it's got to be done." He thought a few seconds. "I'll bet Larrabee House is the only place in town you'd get a decent performance, too. Well, what's to do?"

"I don't know." Denis picked up his second drink. "Would it make trouble for you if I just went ahead and paid the orchestra myself?"

"And conducted it yourself?"

Denis said, "Certainly."

"Yes, it would," Harry said. "Only I can't say I'd care much."

"I'd care." For a second he glanced at Gloria, who was more quiet than ever before in his experience. "Just because you're sympathetic is no reason for me to——"

Harry interrupted. "I've got an idea. Why don't you dedicate it to Gloria, and let me arrange the production?"

"Oh, Harry!" Gloria half gasped. "But he doesn't want to."

"But I do." Denis meant it. "I'd love to. Only I don't think that would appease Brother Lister and the others."

"I don't know." Harry scratched his head. "I think that the boys are getting a little more bold. F.D.R.'s managed to hold the house together, and now they—well, they're not out of the woods by a long shot, but they think they see light between the trees."

Gloria giggled for no reason, and then proceeded to think up one. "It's funny, Douglas Lister lost in the woods, like Little Red Riding Hood."

"You're thinking about Hansel and Gretel, aren't you?" Harry looked more than fondly at his wife, and the look struck near Denis' heart, like a stiletto. What he and Gloria had done was all the worse if this man were so much her slave. Denis felt he could not bear Harry's knowing, but that if he did know he might be weak enough to shut his eyes, rather than lose Gloria. Suddenly the room seemed oppressive. Denis got up.

"Let's think about it," he said. "Maybe Clarissa will come up with something."

"No." Harry got to his feet also. "She won't, because she has to be on that side of the fence. You see, Denis, I may be the largest contributor, but I can't swing the whole thing. She's got to get two thirds of her money from Lister, et al. And she——"

"And she won't let anything stand in her way. I know that." He looked at his hostess. "Anyway, the dedication stands. That's definite."

"Thanks, Denis. I'm very proud."

He followed Harry to the door. "God it's hot," the man said, and then in a lower voice. "Give us a ring when you can, Denis.

I don't know what's wrong with Gloria—she acts peculiar. I think you're good for her."

Oh, God, thought Denis, please make him stop rubbing it in. But to Harry he said, "I will. Things have sort of stacked up on me, that's all."

His host was still standing in the door as he drove out. Denis waved, and called, "See you soon." He drove into the street without looking, and was given a rich cursing out by the driver of a taxi who managed to miss him by inches. But he drove on, oblivious, trying to think where he might have dinner alone and not be recognized. Eventually he would have to go back to the hotel and to bed, but he had no intention of seeing Mrs. Rutherford Lodge this night if he could avoid it.

He turned left on Mather Street, still without a destination, and drove the length of it, past the used car lots, the decayed and decaying castles of old Lakeland, past Blitzstein's big shop with its windows full of antiques, mostly big antiques and dark in color. He passed the Lakeland Club and momentarily regretted having refused membership; one could dine alone there without attracting attention, the trouble being that it was necessary to say 'Hello, Jim,' and 'Hello, John,' and pretend some interest in the goings on, when actually he had no interest at all. The Slater would not do; there was a restaurant in the Terminal, he remembered, and that would be as good a place as any.

The restaurant was a melange of Navajo blankets, murals spotted with Navajo hogans, and travelers showing the effects of travel, but the food was decent. He lingered over it until the waitress impatiently snapped his check down on the table and took up a position, arms folded, three feet away. In spite of himself he grinned, and was amazed when she grinned back. She looked just a little like Gloria, he thought, and quickly changed his thought to the question of what to do with himself until midnight.

First a brandy in the cocktail lounge, not that he really wanted brandy. There was a paper lying on the banquette next him; there was also a picture of himself and a story about his summer activities—that being Clisby's work. He looked through the story and wondered, as he had the year before, why the paper bothered to print it since he had done nothing that could conceivably interest the general public.

He left the brandy unfinished, and walked up a long ramp to Mather Street, and down the street slowly, as if he were killing time between trains. A stooped little Irishman whose face was a network of red veins supporting a small nose and two eyes like raisins, asked for a dime to get a sandwich, and Denis gave him a quarter. He'll drink the sandwich, Denis thought, and impulsively called him back and added a dollar to the fund.

"God bless you, young man," he said. "It's a good deed you've done this night."

Denis shrugged, and said, "Enjoy yourself." Then he joined a small group in front of an appliance shop. In its lighted window an electric refrigerator stood, its door constantly opening and shutting at the touch of a cardboard child with blonde hair and ferocious lips the color of a burlesque queen's.

"It's a pretty thing," a woman in a calico house dress said. "Wisht I had one."

"Hum," the man with her grunted. "These days you're lucky you got a shirt to your back."

"I ain't got but one," she returned.

Denis strolled on, but he was thinking something new to him. These are people, too, he thought and they're in a wholly different world. They wouldn't know me from Adam, and if they did they wouldn't care. They aren't the people Lister Hall was built for and they'll never even see the inside. What the hell do they do?

It was difficult for him to understand that to nine tenths of Lakeland he was not even a name. The idea was humbling, too. Suddenly he thought of a possible headline: "Husband Sues Orchestra Conductor." The story under the headline would probably be his one contact with the couple watching the nervous refrigerator. He might conduct the best performance the world ever had heard of Beethoven's Ninth without causing a ripple on lower Mather Street. But the other would make him famous all through what Clarissa would call the lower levels of Lakeland.

At the next corner a boy and girl were standing close together, waiting for a trolley, and for a moment Denis could not think why two young people standing under a street light should seem so familiar. Then he knew it was because they reminded him of another couple years before, when Cécile had at last kidnaped him and they were driving to the park. Then as now, the glimpse was of two people who were one—at least temporarily. The glimpse hurt; this way there was at least physical contact out of desire, even if the contact were on a corner under a street lamp. Marriage to an ideal, however great, rarely produced the desiring touch of flesh on flesh.

Denis turned left off Mather Street toward a cheap-looking movie labeled "For Adults Only," and perversely got into line behind two fourteen-year-old boys who were admitted without question. The theater had begun life as a store. The floor creaked, the ancient plush seats, secondhand in the days of Adah Isaacs Menken, had lost their stuffing through holes big enough for a man's fist to enter. And the film was so gloriously bad that it fascinated Denis: the story of a girl of good family who went to "The City" to earn money with which to pay off the family mortgage, who fell into the "clutches" of white slavers, who "drank the dregs of life," who eventually had as one of her numerous customers her own brother. Then, *allegro molto*; recognition, rejuvenation, reunion at the wonderful speed of a bad director who is soaked with a worse film and says the hell with it.

The trouble was that Denis laughed so much he very nearly was asked to leave; what the annoyed patrons near him could not know was that he was laughing more at himself than at the film. Was this the group he had imagined was waiting around the corner for pop concerts at a price it could pay? Well, he thought as he pushed his way outside through a combination of popcorn smell and body odor, I may be naïve, but at least it's worth trying. Mechanically he walked back to his car, and drove home. He hardly thought of Mrs. Rutherford Lodge on the way; when he left the elevator, however, he again felt an invisible eye on him, and he was right about it. Her door opened as he put the key in his lock. She had discarded her hat and the jacket of her gray suit, exposing the rumpled white blouse underneath. But her eyes were as sharp as ever, showing no strain from several hours of peering through the peephole.

"Good evening," she said. "Come in, please."

Denis sighed. "No. You come into my apartment."

She made herself at home on Denis' sofa while he turned on a big oscillating fan in the corner. But she said nothing, and finally Denis was forced to speak.

"Just what was it you did that was worth a thousand dollars?" he asked.

Mrs. Lodge cleared her throat, looked angrily at the cigarette she was smoking, and said in the gentle voice Denis was beginning to know too well, "Is that important, young man? You have a good deal at stake, you know."

"But you said the accident was settled—and I paid you."

"Suppose it had been a worse accident. You had a passenger, don't forget."

He felt anger in his chest, and said sharply, "I know what you're hinting at. Since when is there a thousand-dollar charge for driving one's hostess home from a dinner party she herself gave? You tell me that."

Mrs. Lodge lifted one leg over the other, brushed cigarette ash off her skirt. Slowly she said, "You were going a rather odd route to get to the Gordon house. Remember?"

"Don't be a fool . . ."

"And don't you. Let's recapitulate. You make thirty-five thousand a year, I believe it is. Your main support with the orchestra is Harry Gordon. Mr. Gordon loves his wife. He is very fond of you, I gather. You are ambitious, and the Lakeland Orchestra, I'm told, is the best possible stepping stone to one of the top Eastern orchestras. You have a manager whose name I know; he would be very—shall we say annoyed?—if you involved yourself in a scandal. And yet"—she savagely snubbed out her cigarette, and if possible her voice grew even more pleasant—"and yet, young man, you have had Mrs. Gordon here alone at least six times to my personal knowledge. And twice she has stayed the night. I ask you, is that sensible?"

"You damned old snoop!" Denis' face flamed, with fury, not embarrassment. "How would you go about proving it?"

The woman merely laughed. "Heavens—I'm not a blackmailer, my boy."

"You're a liar. A goddam liar, and you know it."

"The gentlest kind of hint would be enough, Mr. Sandzen. You know Mr. Gordon is far from stupid, except when it comes to caring for that little twerp he married."

"She's not a twerp. She's twice the woman you are."

"Avoirdupois?"

"Christ," Denis shouted, "what a reptile you turned out to be."

Both of them started when the telephone rang. Still glaring at his visitor, Denis started for the bedroom to answer.

"Take it here," Mrs. Lodge said, pointing to the instrument on the desk.

"You go to hell," he returned, banging shut the bedroom door.

It was Terry. "I wrote you," he said, without preliminaries, "and then I was afraid you'd be stupid. Forgive me, Denis——"

"I am stupid. Worse." He poured out the story of his visitor, and her demands. And hints. Terry tried to break in, and finally succeeded.

"Please, Denis. This will get you nowhere at all. Can she hear?"

"I don't know."

"Say something about you'll listen, put the phone down and find out."

Denis said, "All right then. I won't say a word, just listen." And crossed the bedroom swiftly. He jerked open the door, and Mrs. Lodge all but fell into the room. He laughed in spite of his anger. "Go sit down," he ordered with a calm that surprised him as much as it did her. Then he returned to the phone, leaving the door open.

"She was at the door, Terry."

"I thought so. She'll probably pick up the extension in the living room, so I'll hurry. Have you got the letter she wrote about the bill?"

"Yes. It's——"

"Stop it! Just make sure she doesn't steal it. Get rid of her anyhow, even if you have to promise to pay. Then call me back."

"All right. God, Terry, you don't know how wonderful it is to hear your voice."

"I'm glad. Now don't waste time; just get rid of the old bitch quick."

"Thanks, Terry. Thanks a lot."

Mrs. Lodge had not picked up the other phone; she had been busy, however. If she guessed that about the letter, Denis thought, I can't help it. Then he began again.

"I think you're a blackmailer, and probably going to land in jail. And I'm tired and don't want to talk any more."

To his astonishment, she got to her feet at once. "Mr. Sandzen," she said, "I shall expect a thousand dollars cash from you before two o'clock tomorrow afternoon. No check, and no bill over twenty dollars. Good night."

He walked ahead of her to the door. When he faced her his eye caught a little triangle of white in the V of her blouse. He glanced at his desk. The stack of scores looked subtly different. His hand was quick from long years at the keyboard. Almost before either of them knew what was happening, he had snatched the letter out of its not-quite-secure hiding place.

She turned on him, but before she could say a word Denis snapped, "A thief, too. Good night." He pushed her into the hall.

When Denis heard his visitor's door close, he sat himself weakly down in his desk chair and looked carefully at the stack of scores. It was not difficult to see why Mrs. Lodge had found her letter so easily; the thin film of dust that settled daily on everything in Lakeland, no matter how carefully it was cleaned, showed a small clean area where apparently a corner of the envelope had been exposed. He looked carefully at the scores. They had been lifted, and replaced a little carelessly, so the pile tilted considerably from the perpendicular.

Denis felt weary and drained. He would have liked to take a couple of sleeping capsules and go to bed at once. But Terry would be waiting, and probably with an idea. Denis' call went through magically; he was talking with Terry five minutes after Mrs. Lodge's departure.

"All clear?" he asked, and Denis said yes.

"Fine. Look—I did something that I would not have done if you'd still been in town. I went to a lawyer friend of mine, and put one of those phony hypothetical questions to him."

"Oh, Terry—you shouldn't."

Terry laughed. "Why not? Actually, he thought I was asking because I was in a scrape. They always think that when you insist the question is hypothetical."

"That's what I meant. You——"

"Denis, stop it. He understands things. He probably thinks I'm vulnerable, on the other side of the fence, that is. Anyway, when I said my hypothetical friend had received a letter demanding an outrageous sum for services in a case that was already settled, he picked up his ears."

"I don't see why."

"I didn't either. But he says that if she actually has done no more work on the case, and of course she hasn't, she's put her head under the hammer. He says that—by the way, you actually have the letter? You're sure?"

Denis explained what had happened, and could hear Terry's quick sigh of relief. "You shouldn't take Poe so seriously, Denis."

"I what?"

"He had a theory that the safest hiding place was the most obvious. And it isn't."

"Oh—in a story, you mean." Denis' tension was ever so little relaxed; he was a little astonished to realize that the adhesions under his scar had been paining him, but he said nothing.

"Yes. Have you got a lawyer you can trust?"

"No. The only lawyer I know, besides the old hag, is Forrest Sawyer, and he's on the Orchestra Board."

"Not him." Terry was silent a moment. "Have you got any-body you can trust who's a native? With connections, perhaps?"

"Clarissa?"

"No. I'd not chance her. Anybody else?"

Something like the feeling he had had earlier, while walking up Mather Street, returned to Denis. A feeling of being in a town, but not of it. "I'm trying to think, Terry . . . give me a minute."

"All right. I'll tell you what my friend suggested, and maybe that will suggest someone. It's this: he says to have someone, preferably a lawyer, simply telephone Mrs. What's-her-name and say that he has in his possession a letter which proves attempted extortion, and that if she says anything or does anything further, it will be turned over to the grievance committee of the Lake-land Bar Association for action. And then he hangs up—answers no further questions."

"Why can't I do it myself?"

"No. Certainly not. You want her to know that you have sup-porters, and of course the reason the man, whoever it is, must say nothing more is that presumably he knows nothing more. Unless it's someone you know well enough to trust with the whole story."

"Oh, hell. I wish I—say, maybe Clisby, Farrell Clisby."

"You mean the man who took you to Larrabee House first? He sounds ideal—can you trust him?"

Denis thought a minute. "I think so. I think I have to, as a matter of fact."

Terry reviewed the thing again, and added, "The worst part will be waiting to see what happens. But I'll take ten-to-one odds nothing does. The fact that she bothered to steal the let-ter proves that she knows the letter was a mistake. I think she misread you; she thought you were more naïve than you are."

For a moment Denis could not speak for laughing, and there was relief in the laugh. "You're a sweet guy, Terry," he got out at last. "She didn't misread me. She just didn't know I had a bright friend down South."

"Nuts. One thing more and I'll hang up and save you a few dollars on your phone bill. Don't let anything stand in the way of that ballet. Please, Denis. You need something like Larrabee House desperately. Understand?"

Denis thought again about his walk on lower Mather Street. "Thanks, pal. I'm growing up a little."

But next morning when he waylaid Farrell Clisby, he was not quite so sure of growth. He felt like a bird in the midst of drouth who sees water rushing from a hose; he badly needed what he saw, and he was afraid to plunge. He was hurrying to rehearsal, and all he could do was ask Farrell for lunch, and then worry through the next hours about how to present his case.

It was easier than he thought. He merely told Farrell the bare bones of the matter: that he had paid the bill, that the second bill was an attempt at extortion, that he had been advised by an out-of-town friend what to do.

Farrell smiled. "You've never met my lawyer brother, have you?" he asked.

"I didn't even know you had a brother—maybe he could . . ."

"Hell, no." Farrell looked at his watch. "It's twelve fifteen, let me try now."

Denis tried to say that he was grateful, but the other shrugged it off. "I'll not give the number to the operator," he said as if talking to himself. "She needn't know about it."

He picked up Denis' phone, and motioned for Denis to close the heavy door. "Yes?" he said. "Mrs. Lodge?" It was Mrs. Lodge's office girl; she put her principal on.

"Mrs. Lodge? This is Mr. Clisby." Then he repeated Terry's formula exactly. "Is that clear?" he ended.

Denis could hear a confused splutter, into which Farrell's voice cut sharply. "I asked you whether you understand what I said."

Another splutter. "Very well. Good-by."

He was laughing when he hung up. "She's got a voice like a little girl—and she's madder than billy hell. Now"—he looked hard at Denis—"may I suggest that you let me seal that letter with ribbon, wax and whatnot, and put it in the safe here in the hall?"

Denis handed it over, but Farrell put it down and went into

his own office for wax and the rest of the equipment. He was still smiling when he came back, but he had the look of a man who had come to a decision. "Please forgive me, Denis," he said quietly, "but you said something that was a straight tip-off. You said the old gal lived next you in the hotel."

"Yes."

"Well . . . oh, hell, Denis, try to keep a certain person out of your apartment." He colored. "I know it's not my business, but I'm terribly fond of you and you're so—so kind of vulnerable. Please don't think I'm snooping," he hurried on. "But, well, Clarissa said something once about . . ."

"Gloria. All right, Farrell, I don't mind your knowing. And it really wasn't fear so much for myself; not that I'm noble, but the fact is that even a scandal wouldn't wreck me. It was Harry."

Farrell pursed his lips and wisely shook his head. "I'm glad you said that. You truly are all right, Denis. Lots of people think you're just a kind of heartless music box in a handsome case; let's forget the deal now, and if Lodge is fool enough to go ahead, I'll tell my brother what I've done, and he'll take over. He's a young chap, but he's good."

Denis sucked in a deep breath. He got up and put his arm around Farrell, who seemed pleased to the point of embarrassment. "Hell. It's nothing—say, what about the ballet?"

But it was not so easy to wait, especially when that night Farrell called to say that Lodge had at once telephoned his brother's office, but had gotten no further than the telephone operator since her employer had been out. So the second Clisby had to be let in on part of the secret, and no one knew whether the bluff would succeed.

"Anyway, Bill said he'd be delighted to get something on Lodge," Farrell concluded. "Seems she's been on thin ice for a hell of a time."

"The circle widens," Denis said a little ruefully.

"Right. Only it's an iron circle, don't forget. We Clisbys stick like the well-known leech."

And Gloria. Denis called her, and found her in an odd sort of state, suspended perilously, like a pith ball on a stream of air. "Can't I come over just for a drink?" she begged, and Denis said no.

"We're out of the swamp," he insisted, "and by God we stay out. Just let me catch you in my apartment."

"But I'm lonesome."

"You'd better be lonely and safe than neither, Gloria."

He finally convinced her that there was nothing to be done but wait and that her waiting would have to be done in her own house. Then Harry called.

"I think the ballet is going to be all right," he said at once. "Provided you can take time for it out of your winter vacation."

Denis considered that. "I've got four guest jobs, Harry. I'll cancel one of them."

And Harry considered that. "I hate to have you do that. And I don't mean only the money. Every time you conduct in Boston or Philadelphia, or even St. Louis, it's good for Lakeland."

"It's little enough for me to do, God knows. I'll knock out Philadelphia; they'll take me next year."

Harry consented reluctantly, but he seemed to want to talk more. "Uh, Denis," he asked slowly, "seen Gloria since you were out?"

Off base, Denis stuttered. "It's only been a day or two."

"Yes. But she acts so damn queer. She's usually—oh, I don't know, so kind of gay. Look . . . uh, Denis, don't feel I'd mind if you dropped in pretty often. Anything she wants is fine."

Why does he have to twist the knife all the time? Denis thought. Does he guess something? And if so what in hell makes him act this way?

"I know," he said. "It's just that I'm awfully busy. You know how it is."

"Sure. Well, be seeing you."

To make things worse, the parties were beginning, the kind of parties that one had to attend, for reasons of business. The kind of parties that Lakeland seemed to run to—cocktails with elaborate canapés and a total lack of intelligent conversation; dinners with people invited, and usually seated, according to rank or notoriety; late parties after some event or other which offered liquor and a chance to discuss whatever had happened, and to tamp down this with a supper which, if hot, was chicken in a more or less disguised style, and if cold, was a collection of cheeses and cold meats which led to indigestion and morning headaches.

At least, Denis thought as he left a lecture by Bertrand Russell for a party by Mr. and Mrs. Horace Cogshill, both of whom had slept through the talk, Mrs. Lodge can't be here. Nor was she, but there was an adequate substitute who descended on Denis and Gloria just after Harry had left them alone with too elaborate casualness.

"Dear Mr. Sandzen," she began, "you won't know me of course. I'm just a poor, non-professional—musician I mean. The violin."

Gloria came in for the rescue. "Of course he does, Mrs. Clooney. She's president of Phi Mu Omega, Denis."

"Oh. Of course. Do sit down."

Mrs. Clooney sat. "Now, Mr. Sandzen," she said, rearranging a number of attachments to her gown, ribbons, buckles and such, "I have a question."

Oh, Lord, is it a guessing game? he thought. And smiled.

"It's this. Why don't you play more Bach?"

"Because there are other good composers," he said, a little more shortly than he had intended.

Apparently this acted as a goad. "None, Mr. Sandzen, as good," with heavy emphasis on the "as."

"Why not? What about Mozart?"

"Or Beethoven?" Gloria inquired with innocence.

These Mrs. Clooney brushed off as if they had been gnats. "But compared to Bach?"

"I don't mean to be pedantic, Mrs. Clooney. But there is a lot of Bach that quite frankly is dull, dreadfully dull." He looked despairingly across the room at Clarissa, who was giving the red-carpet treatment to a man who looked familiar; of course, he thought, the chap who inherited all that real estate in Columbia. His wandering attention was snatched back in an instant.

"You *simply can't* mean that," Mrs. Clooney declared. "There is not a measure of Bach that is not a precious gem."

And she looked at him rather like, he thought ruefully, a judge pronouncing judgment on a particularly repellent criminal. Perhaps one who slept with other men's wives, for example. Then a reasonably sweet revenge occurred to him.

"Look," he said, "come over to the piano and I'll show you what I mean."

Patting down her ribbons, Mrs. Clooney followed Denis and Gloria across the room; as usual when Denis headed for a piano, others began drifting in the same direction. He struck a few vicious chords to reduce his head of steam a little.

"Know this?" he said casually, beginning something that caused Clarissa to give him a quick look. It was a fugue, and it started ingeniously. But presently it ran into a tangle of imitations, ornaments and sequences, one of these last repeated five times, and ended in a soft cadence which seemed to float gently into nothing.

"Certainly," Mrs. Clooney said triumphantly, "from the Well-Tempered Clavichord."

From behind he heard a muffled snicker from John Dudley. Denis grinned disarmingly up at his victim, however. "No, Mrs. Clooney, it's right out of my head. And the fugue subject was 'Where O Where Has My Little Dog Gone.'"

There was a gasp from Mrs. Clooney, and a quickly controlled laugh from the others. "You see," Denis went on, "that was a joke. But if you want me to, I can play you dozens of pages out of Bach that are as bad or worse."

And then, before anyone could speak, he began playing again, improvising on the same tune, making a set of variations so fascinating and in the end so complicated that his audience slowly forgot Mrs. Clooney and Bach and did what he wanted them to do, which was to concentrate on himself. At last he stopped, but only for a second. Then he began the "Waldstein" sonata of Beethoven, and perhaps because he was excited and a little pleased at having exposed what was to him the worst kind of criminal, namely a musical pretender, he played it as he never had done before. There was no movement until he had finished. Then he looked up at John Dudley, and said, "I call that music."

"Poor Mrs. Clooney," Gloria said next afternoon on the phone. "I'm afraid she'll not be re-elected president of Phi Mu Omega."

"Small loss." Denis should have been in his office, and he wished Gloria had not chosen that moment to call.

"Yes. Look, Denis, I wonder if I couldn't help about . . . you know."

"Oh, Lord, Gloria. Now what?"

"Well, you remember I called and found out she really wasn't on the membership committee of the D.A.R. Maybe I could get her exposed."

He wanted to laugh, but he dared not. "My dear," he said, that's about the worst possible thing. What excuse would you give Mrs. Lister, or whoever it was you called? Please let it be. You understand?"

"But . . ."

"But you're worried. I know. Only so far it's working out and let's not disturb anything. Anything at all."

Gloria's sigh was audible, indeed almost tangible. "Oh, well," she at last said, "you probably know best. Come to dinner next Wednesday, won't you?"

At the moment Denis would have gone to Louisiana on a skating party to keep Gloria quiet. "Of course. I'd love it. And now I've really got to get back to work. We're finishing up the pop schedule."

They were and they did, the others being Clarissa and Farrell Clisby. There was more to be done, and there were rehearsals, and a chamber of commerce luncheon and several dozen things besides. Through it all he felt, as he confessed to Farrell, like a man living with cancer and trying to conduct his affairs so no one would know. For the first time in his life he was not satisfied with his rehearsals, and Clarissa found his attention wandering, and began speculations on her own; perhaps, she thought, a premature offer from the East. And yet Gus Wagner had promised there would be no shenanigans, and she trusted him.

On the afternoon of Gloria's dinner Denis burst into Clarissa's office in a flaming rage. He flung a score on the table and wheeled around. "Who in God's name wished this stupid ass on me?" he shouted. "Somebody should have known better."

"Hold your horses," Clarissa suggested. "What ass?"

Denis yanked at the score. "Harlow—it looks like Bugby—the writing's so damn fancy I can't read it."

"What's the matter?"

"Oh, God. He brought in this, this crap. He said he had an appointment. And he talked for forty-five solid minutes before I could get rid of him. About his roots as a composer, Bach and Edgar Varese and the Prophet Elijah probably. He had the effrontery to say that he certainly did not want a performance at a pop concert. He . . ."

"And?" Clarissa was determined to let Denis talk himself out.

"And when I finally got him out of the office I looked at it. Honestly, Clarissa, it's as if I tried to write a play . . . I wish you weren't such a goddam lady, I'd tell you what it really is."

She could not keep down a laugh. "All right, Denis. I'm to blame."

He said nothing, but his look was eloquent to the point of incandescence. "After all these years. You . . ."

She nodded. "Me. His people have money. It's that simple." She picked up the score. "Now I'll get you out of it. Leave it to me."

His shoulders lowered in defeat. "All right. Only you can't give me back my forty-five minutes." He got up. "I'm going to the hotel and wash off this muck," pointing to the score. "I'm crawling."

"I'm sorry, Denis. And would you mind picking me up on the way to the Gordons? I don't want to keep Jim up; he's got a cold."

"Of course. But I ought to make you walk."

She watched him leave, a little smile on her face. He was back in a couple of seconds. "Sorry I blew up," he said, and hurried down the hall.

When he left the elevator at his floor of the Hampton Park Manor the old feeling of being watched returned; he had not noticed it the last few days. Nothing happened until he turned the key in his door; then the door next his opened abruptly, and Mrs. Lodge appeared in a dressing gown that had been out of its adolescence in the administration of the first Roosevelt, a dreary affair of mouse-colored velvet, the pile mostly worn off. She held out a yellow paper.

"Here. Take this," she said.

Denis drew back. "I don't want anything of yours," he said.

The soft voice was at last laced with vitriol. "Take the damn thing anyway," she snapped and flung the paper at him, backing into her apartment and slamming the door as she did so.

For a moment Denis considered leaving the paper where it was, and then his curiosity got the better of him. He bent down slowly, picked it up and carried it into his living room. It was the carbon of the letter she had written asking for a thousand dollars; it also was Mrs. Rutherford Lodge's surrender.

I'll have news for Gloria, he thought. His chest tightened, and for a moment relief had him on the verge of tears. Then he carefully folded the yellow sheet and put it in his jacket pocket. He went slowly into his bedroom and bowed to Mr. Edward Bear. Mr. Edward Bear was sitting huddled in the top of an otherwise unoccupied candlestick. Denis raised Mr. Bear's front legs in a gesture of triumph and returned him to his place.

"We're free again, Mr. Edward Bear," he said.

21

The feeling of well-being almost lasted the year out. Behind him was the most successful opening he had had in Lakeland, and the first three of the ten pop concerts. These were not a financial success, not yet, but the audience was growing and

Clarissa had drummed up two or three businesses which were "sponsoring" one concert each, and doing it without too much of a return. "A certain type of man can't resist the chance to 'do good,'" she remarked to Denis one day. "Don't worry about the pops. We'll manage."

Even the weather was a little less than completely awful, which was a relief to everyone. Farrell worked out a scenario for the ballet, and the Larrabees found a choreographer. The art class was making a set, and Denis called a preliminary rehearsal of his twenty-six men (for which Harry Gordon paid) just to be sure the score would "sound." It did, and it gave its composer more satisfaction than anything he had done since his first great success in Lakeland; this sound not only reached the audience through him, it came out of him. He supposed the feeling was a little like that of a mother bringing a child into the world. Then he laughed at himself, wondering who the father might be, and returned to his usual single-minded course.

He was brought up short a few days before Christmas. Harry called and announced in a tense voice that all hell had broken loose, and Denis was to be called on the carpet. He added that Denis was not to get the wind up; Harry had his ideas and they would ride out the storm together. But Denis was far from happy as he walked to Lister Hall, scuffing through the first light snow of the winter like a child with a bad report card. He went directly to the board room, and found every seat around the long table occupied, something he had thought unlikely. He had learned not to expect understanding, but to receive acquiescence. This time there was an air of quickly concealed hostility, however; before it he felt defenseless.

"Good afternoon, gentlemen," he said quietly, taking his place next to Clarissa. "What is it?"

Harry's face looked drawn, as if he were holding back something that hurt. "The meeting would like to question you about —ah—about some of your outside activities."

This roused Denis, as Harry knew it would. "Why, please, am I being questioned about my outside activities? Aren't they my affair?"

The group stirred, moved pencils, resettled well-upholstered bottoms in chairs that were almost too comfortable for business; Denis suspected that Clarissa had chosen them deliberately for that reason. Finally Douglas Lister cleared his throat, and having thus served notice that he would speak, he did speak.

"The activities have nothing to do with your personal life, which is blameless so far as we know," he began pompously. "These are—uh—musical activities."

"He means," Harry broke in impatiently, "that the Board dislikes the idea of your doing the ballet at Larrabee House. Let's stop beating around the bush."

Lister flushed, but he nodded. He usually looked at his conductor as if Denis were from a different world; now he looked as if the world were unsavory as well.

"If you'll pardon me," Denis said, consciously maintaining an air of youthful innocence, "that appears to me—well—a little less than gallant."

"What?" Lister demanded, touched slightly off base.

"A little less than gallant," Denis repeated.

John Dudley's eyes betrayed him; they twinkled in his wide, round face. But his voice was quiet, almost without inflection, as he said, "You'll have to explain that to Doug."

"Surely," Denis was still being young and charming. "I wrote the ballet and dedicated it to Mrs. Gordon. It's about the South, and written to be danced by Negroes. The only place in Lakeland I can get a decent performance is at Larrabee House, and"—his voice hardened a very little—"I expect to produce it there. In honor of Mrs. Gordon."

Silence hung almost palpably about the table for what seemed to Denis a full minute. Then Lister spoke again, more pursily than usual, "Very commendable. I'm sure it's well deserved. But why at that place in the slums? Aren't there plenty of good dance teachers elsewhere in the city?"

"No." Denis' answer was flat.

"There must be."

"There aren't. Not good enough for this ballet, anyway."

"But those people are—well—I've heard rumors. And they're radicals, hardly better than Socialists. The orchestra, sir, can't afford to be mixed up with trash like that."

Four or five heads nodded, but before anyone could speak Clarissa said quietly, "Douglas, I wonder if you understand that although Denis proposes to use men from the orchestra, they are being paid by Harry Gordon. The original idea was to ask them to give their services, but it was abandoned."

"Clarissa Garfield," Lister exploded, his face purple, his hands shaking, "I don't give a damn who pays the men. I object to the conductor of the Lakeland Orchestra hanging around with trash like that."

"And I object to such a damn fool statement." Harry was on his feet, fury about him like a cloud. "What you really mean is that the Larrabees treat their people like people, isn't it? You're afraid they'll 'forget their place.' Aren't you? I say the hell with it."

"Now, now." John Dudley sprang up lightly for so round a man. "This won't get us anywhere."

"The hell it won't!" Harry was glaring around the table. "It'll get you my resignation, gentlemen, and a Merry Christmas to the lot of you."

He left the stunned group and started for the door. In a couple of seconds Denis rose.

"It has got you mine, too," he said, and followed Harry from the room.

What a queer change, Denis thought, from his beginning in Lakeland. Then Harry had seemed merely a climber who was inexplicably wrapped up in a woman of little background, a kind of device created by Clarissa to provide money for her orchestra. Now Harry was, Denis sometimes thought, the only man in all the town upon whom he could rely without reservation. And the only man he had wronged, so far as he knew.

"Harry," he called, closing the door of the directors' room after him. "Wait for me."

Harry waited, speechless with anger and perhaps also with the sense of defeat. Denis motioned toward his office, and closed the door firmly behind them. He dug down into his desk, found the bottle of bourbon he always kept there, and poured each of them a heavy drink. "Don't try to talk," he said, "until you get this down."

Harry nodded, and stood for a few minutes looking out of the window at the scattering of cars in the parking lot behind the hall. Denis sat on the edge of his desk, swinging one leg and looking at nothing. When the older man turned toward him, Denis was smiling.

"You didn't need to resign, Harry. That damn ballet has put you on a bad spot and I'm sorry."

Harry held out his glass. "There's more in this than you see," he said. "There's a lot of jealousy—the Board doesn't much like me, you know. They resented the fact that my business was almost the only one that kept on making money, lots of it, when they were crawling around Washington on their bellies begging F.D.R. to save 'the American way of life.' Which meant their goddam Blitzstein houses and their wives' diamonds."

"I know. Only that's still no explanation of the Larrabee House thing."

"Sure it is. Look, Denis, these lads imported all the Poles and Negroes and Italians themselves. They did it for cheap labor. They could keep labor costs down just so long as they could keep the hunkies and niggers and wops ignorant. Bottle 'em up in their little communities. Make them jealous of each other. . . . It's an old routine."

He took another long drink. "Ever notice how the Museum is run? Everything is calculated to scale—room enough for the people who matter, no room, no activities for the others. Why do we have eighteen hundred seats here in the hall, fill 'em twice a week? Because there are about thirty-six hundred people who are acceptable. I'd be on the outside too, if I didn't have a hell of a lot of cash. Believe me I would."

"And they're afraid of Dick and Carol?"

"Of course they are. Where else could three talented little Negro boys find a place to dance? For pennies in a pool hall, that's where."

"I don't like it." Denis' mouth set. "And by God I'll do that ballet if I have to dance it myself."

Harry's tension burst in a guffaw. "That I'd like to see," he roared. "I really would."

"I wouldn't. I'm a clumsy ox on my feet. Look, Harry, what do we do?"

"Not one damn thing. We don't call the papers, we don't talk, we just sit tight."

"Should I call Gus Wagner?"

"My hunch is that Aunt Clarissa is probably calling right now. Sure, call if you want, but tell him to keep his mouth shut."

"There isn't anybody else they can get," Denis said slowly. "Anybody good, that is."

"That's probably true. If I were you, I'd turn the afternoon concert over to Dingbat tomorrow, and the Friday night one too, if nothing's settled."

Denis picked up his telephone, asked the operator to find his assistant conductor. In a minute Walter Dattner was on the wire and Denis explained that he was ill, unable to conduct. It seemed rather to please Dattner, who was beginning to think Denis indestructible.

Through the heavy door they could hear footsteps, none of which hesitated as they passed along the hall. After a minute there were lighter steps, and then a knock. Clarissa came in, her hair a little mussed for the first time in Denis' experience. She closed the door behind her, and motioned toward the bottle. "I need it," she said wearily. "Badly."

No one spoke until she had gulped down a third of her drink. Then she said, "Well, boys, you've really tangled things. You're making Aunt Clarissa's life a hell." She looked almost dreamily at Denis. "If you tell on me I shall say you're both liars. But I'm glad you did it."

Denis suddenly bent over Clarissa and kissed her. "Thanks," he said.

"Now." She looked sharply at Harry. "Do you really mean what you said?"

He nodded.

"And you Denis, will you conduct tomorrow?"

"No. I called Dingbat. He was delighted."

Clarissa snorted. "I'll bet. And have you called Gus?"

"No—have you?"

"They forced me to call him from the directors' room. He was furious; he said we'd damn well make it up with you, or go without a conductor."

"Sounds like him," Denis remarked. "Only he can't force them into that. I think Douglas Lister would abandon the orchestra before he'd give in."

"John wouldn't. He's going to tip off the papers."

Both the men went rigid. "Why?" Harry asked.

"Remember the business of Blum and the little speech a certain newspaper man made in that same room? John's going to tip him off to the real reason for all this mess."

"And where does his paper get its advertising?" Harry asked bitterly.

"I know," Clarissa agreed. "But my editor friend also learned a lesson. They can't hang him for reporting exactly what the two of you say. He can be . . ."

"What do we say?" Denis broke in.

Clarissa smiled wearily. "I'm strictly caught on the fence, boys. You know why—and if you didn't I couldn't help it anyway. If I were you I should tell the truth."

"Even though that will make things very tough for you." It was what it seemed, a statement, not an implied question. Harry looked at her with admiration.

"I suppose so." Clarissa smiled again, still wearily. "But it might, just might, help."

At eight o'clock Denis was in his own living room, waiting for a reporter. He had talked with Gus, who first berated him for a stiff-necked young fool, and then admitted that he probably would have done the same.

"I told Clarissa to tell those stuffed shirts I'd see them in hell before they got a conductor worth the name," Gus ended. "I hope to God she did."

"She did. Also, the morning paper is coming to see me. At eight o'clock."

"You'll get nowhere. They know where their bread's buttered."

Denis explained what Clarissa had already explained to him, and Gus was slightly impressed. "Could be they'll do a strictly factual story." Denis could hear the shuffling of papers on Gus' desk, and then a kind of triumphant grunt. "Here it is. Say, how'd you like another handful of guest jobs after your vacation—hell, it's not a vacation now."

Denis refused. He explained that he intended staying in Lakeland for the ballet, come what would, that he was canceling his Philadelphia date, that he did not want to be exhibited through the late winter as the man who got fired.

"Sure. I'll keep them open anyway. Sir Tommy decided not to come over and——"

"Do as you please. I won't promise anything now."

He doesn't much mind, Denis thought after he had hung up. Either he thinks we'll win, or he's got ideas. And then it occurred to him that there might be other roads to his goal than the one he had mapped and was stubbornly sticking with, and he picked up his telephone again and ordered up a steak, which he was just finishing when the reporter arrived. He was a young man named Greene who said as soon as he had shaken hands with Denis, "Look, I don't know a damn thing about music."

"This has nothing to do with music," Denis replied.

"Fine. Snedeker tried to tell me something about you, how good you are and . . ."

"And what?"

Greene was embarrassed, but only slightly. "Well, since you ask, he said you also were pretty tough. He didn't mean to be nasty."

That was quite all right with Denis. He supposed he was tough, but he had also supposed that knowledge of it was confined to the men of his orchestra. His former orchestra, he thought wryly.

He gave Greene some brandy and a cup of coffee, and said without preamble, "There's a lot in this that I can't say. The

Board is not even unanimous against Mr. Gordon and me. But it's—displeased, most of it."

The young man's face was very attractive when he grinned. Then the flight of freckles across his cheekbones seemed to rush together, giving him an impish, very young, and yet very wise appearance that just might, Denis thought, be justified. He grinned now, and said, "Uh huh."

"The question is very simple. I have written a ballet, largely because of an experience I had one day at Larrabee House."

This interested Greene very much. "I know Dick and Carol. They're swell."

"They certainly are. Anyway, I met three young Negroes there who are close to geniuses at dancing. I played for them, and liked them, and decided I wanted to do more than just that.

"So last summer I took time from work to write the ballet. I decided to dedicate it to Mrs. Gordon, who is, naturally, a friend of mine. Then Harry Gordon got interested, and he wants to help with the money end of it—we plan to do it just after the holidays. We've been rehearsing, off and on, for quite a while.

"This afternoon I was called before the Board of Directors. I said it was my affair what I did with my spare time, such as it is. Harry Gordon backed me up. Douglas Lister, speaking for the majority of the board, said in effect that it was lowering the dignity of the orchestra for me to conduct in the slums. Harry resigned as president—I resigned as conductor. That's all there was."

Denis' visitor held out his coffee cup and his host refilled it. As he took it back he said quietly, "Oh, Mary Mother of God! It's made to order."

"What's made to order?"

"I could hang those bozos to the handiest sour-apple tree in Lakeland. Baby!"

"Meaning?"

Greene finished his brandy and got a refill on that, too. His impish look returned. "Those guys don't want what you just told me printed—and I hope you noticed that I took it down in

275

shorthand. Don't like that kind of thing very well; bad reporting. But this is one of those delicate, interlocked situations. And I doubt very much whether the other side wants to talk."

Denis still was a step behind, and his expression proved it. Greene returned his scratch paper and pencil to the pocket of his jacket, and then leaned forward, his hand on Denis' knee.

"Look," he said. "Howard Dietz talked to me before I came out. He told me about Blum, and how we burned our fingers. He said this time we'd play it flat. We quote you exactly; Gordon, too. And Lister or whoever the hell speaks for the dodoes. No comment whatever in the story. Day after tomorrow an editorial: how good you are, what a cultural loss your leaving would be, and not a word about Larrabee House or anything Lister could object to. Get it?"

"That's absolutely fair. It suits me."

"It also leaves the paper free to jump whichever way it wants," Greene commented slyly.

"That's fair, too."

Greene got up. "Will Gordon say about what you said? I'm writing the piece, but they sent another guy out to talk to him."

"Yes. He can't say anything else, because that's what happened."

"Wonderful. Now I'll talk out of turn. You know who's going to present the Board's side?"

Denis shook his head.

"Your Uncle Dudley. It's good, huh?"

"John?"

"None other. I've seen it; there's a lot behind that round baby face of his. It's a lulu."

With that Greene left almost in a lope. And Denis made a few phone calls, answered a call from Walter Dattner, who was close to splitting down the middle from trying to keep a leg in each camp, and went to bed. He was amazed to find that he had been much more nervous over much less, and went to sleep almost at once.

It was nine o'clock when Harry's interview was over, and he was more than half drunk, although his interviewer would not have thought so. Harry turned away from the door after showing the man out, his shoulders low with fatigue and something worse. It was the feeling that came to him occasionally that he was after all no real part of Lakeland, but only accepted on sufferance. The telephone rang as he reached the drawing room, and it was Denis. They compared notes briefly, found each had told the same story in almost the same words. Gloria came into the room as the conversation ended.

"Anybody I know?" she asked. She was her old self, Harry thought, whatever that was. There had been only a couple of weeks when she was anything else, and it had ended as suddenly as it began.

"Denis. About the orchestra thing."

"Oh." She sat down on the arm of his chair. "Harry . . ."

He waited a moment and she did not go on. "Harry what?" he finally asked.

"I was thinking about the ballet—you know. Does it mean we're out?"

"Excuse me, honey." He got up and returned in a moment with a drink. Then he said, "Would you care? A lot that is?"

She was a long time answering, and when she spoke it was in a voice he hardly recognized. "I haven't any right to care," she replied in a thin, almost babyish voice. "None."

"Meaning?"

For a third time there was a long pause. "You forced Denis to dedicate the ballet to me. Your money forced the orchestra crowd to be nice to me. I'm not anybody, Harry."

Oh, Lord, he thought, I thought she was so much better. And she is in some ways. He said, "What's really on your mind, Gloria? Anything I can do anything about?" He took her hand, and began separating the fingers fanwise, and squeezing them back together; suddenly she snatched her hand away and flung herself down upon him, crying wildly.

"Honey!" His voice sounded rather more grim than desperate, but he felt far from grim. He felt helpless. "Don't cry. Please don't."

She seemed not to hear, and the tears did not stop.

He shook her. "Don't, Gloria. You're hysterical, please stop."

Finally she looked up at him, tears streaking her make-up. "I—I—Harry, I've got to tell you something." She seemed a little more quiet, and he had the courage of a good deal of bourbon. His arm slipped around her and he held her tight.

"Listen to me," he said slowly. "Don't say anything, just listen. Will you?"

She nodded, twisting her small fists in her eyes to clear them of tears, like a child.

"Don't say anything. I've got something I ought to tell you. It—it's that I know about Denis. And it's all right, Baby. Honestly."

Gloria sat up instantly, her eyes wide. "You what?" she demanded.

"I know. I've known for a long time." He finished the drink beside him, a guilty look in his eyes. "I suppose I ought to play the heavy husband. The only trouble is that like most husbands, I've done the same thing myself." He put his hand over her mouth. "Shh . . . just a minute. I just want to say that I don't know what it is, but you mean enough to me, Gloria, for me to want to be honest."

She left him and stood staring out of the tall window beside his chair, staring into the dark garden, feeling his miserable eyes on her, feeling, too, rather like a worm. Finally she turned.

"I hardly know myself," she said quietly. "I think I've grown up a lot in the last few years."

"So've I, honey. Do you mind too much about me?"

Her smile was bittersweet. "How could I? You didn't love her, whoever she was. I know that. And Denis—I guess it was just that he was so beautiful."

"I didn't even have that excuse. Liquor, more than anything."

Neither spoke for a time, and then it was Harry who said, "Let's forget it. And for God's sake, never tell Denis. Drink?"

She nodded. "Just one." Her eyes followed him as he mixed the drink. In these few minutes she had fallen through the thin ice and found the water warm; her woman's instinct told her that the evening held dramatic material for a lifetime. But the only thought she had was a curious one. When Harry handed her the glass she put it haltingly into words.

"Harry," she said slowly. "You're beautiful, too."

He laughed, and there was a dash of alcoholic truth in his reply: "Sure. Distinguished—but pretty close to a hundred years older, don't forget."

They both felt purged. They also felt an anticlimax, as if they should signalize their understanding by some action which did not materialize. Neither was thinking of Denis. At last Harry slipped his arm around Gloria and said gently, "Let's go to bed."

It surprised Denis very much to discover, next morning, that he had so many friends, or at least so many interested acquaintances. Farrell Clisby was not, of course, one of the johnny-come-latelys; he explained with candor that he had kept out of the way the day before because he was afraid of what he might do, his temper being the free-swinging type. Now he wanted to know what he could do and Denis said, "Have lunch."

Before Farrell was due to arrive there had been eleven calls from people Denis barely knew; a little woman in East Lakeland who volunteered to picket Lister Hall; another in his own hotel who wanted him to know that she thought Douglas Lister was exactly right; a young man who accused him of using his race, meaning the three Negro boys, to secure sympathy for himself. But there were others more temperate, people who took the time to say that they felt he and Harry were right and God bless them both.

The Larrabees called to say that if the business of Larrabee House was embarrassing Denis, he was free to forget all about it—which he warmly refused to do. Clarissa asked him to give her a message for the orchestra, which was understandably confused, and he commissioned her to make one up and deliver it. And John Dudley telephoned, a little cryptically, Denis thought.

"Good story," he said, adding in effect that Denis was simply to sit quiet, and wait. Also to tell the afternoon paper exactly what he had told Greene the night before, something he already had done for the obvious reason that there was nothing more to say.

"You're in a difficult position, John," Denis said, "and you mustn't think I don't understand."

"I know you do. The whole thing's stupid, typical Lister. Just sit tight, and if it doesn't work out the town's the loser."

By the time Farrell arrived Denis' arm was half paralyzed from holding the telephone, and he had told the operator to put no more calls through. He was rereading Greene's piece when Farrell knocked, and he found it exactly as that young man promised. Farrell grinned when his host opened the door, newspaper in hand.

"Boy," he said, "the whole town's split wide open."

There was a flash of humor in Denis' eyes as he said, "Not the whole town. Just the right side of the tracks."

"You're learning. But call it what you will, it's the side that puts the butter on your bread. God, it's hot in here."

Denis opened a second window. "I haven't had the heat on in the living room since I came to Lakeland. I'm damned if I can see how the place gets so uncomfortable."

"I'd like to take you to lunch," Farrell said. "Any ideas?"

"Thanks. Only I'd a lot rather eat here. We'd be sure to see somebody if we went out."

Farrell was forced to agree, and Denis phoned down an order. Then Farrell talked.

"I've been keeping out of sight at the Hall. But I know Lister's been there half the morning; I heard him and Clarissa arguing, down the hall."

Denis merely shrugged.

"Dougie boy's furious at the paper. Says it misrepresented him." That aroused Denis.

"I don't believe him. Greene wrote exactly what I said, and I'll bet he wrote what the other side said the same way. He's a nice fellow, Greene."

Farrell nodded. "I know him. Fact is, he called me last night."

"Good. . . . Oh, my God, I forgot to call Gus. Excuse me."

Denis put in the call, and they talked on quietly, each saying what the other already knew for the most part, and taking a certain comfort from doing it. The call went through just as the waiter arrived; through the clatter of dishes Farrell heard the few words Denis was able to insert into the conversation, and found them singularly unrevealing. He was scratching his thin blond hair when Denis hung up.

"The man must be wound up like a clock," he said, and Denis laughed.

"He is. Lister called him, and apparently Gus told him off a hundred miles an hour."

"Good boy."

"He wanted Gus to come out and talk conductors, and Gus said he not only wouldn't do it, he'd knock any of his people off his list if they came out. He meant it, too."

"Good boy again." They began on the food and found that both their appetites were unimpaired by the excitement. Suddenly Denis looked up. "I haven't heard from Harry. I wonder why."

"I could guess. He's probably punishing the bottle."

"I doubt it. He's got a queer faculty for staying sober when you'd least expect it. I'd better phone him when we finish."

Denis seemed gradually to grow more remote, and his guest knew him well enough not to notice. Suddenly Denis came back to the present with a rush. "I've been thinking what this will do to the orchestra, and me, if by any chance the business is settled. I've been—well—in absolute command. Will this sort of trim me down?"

Farrell thought awhile before answering. "I don't think so. If you win, it'll mean that you've backed the whole goddam Board into a corner. The men will understand—they're not stupid."

"Funny. I'd never have dreamed it, but I honestly don't care much."

"Sure?"

Denis was drumming on the table absently. "Oh," he returned at last, "I don't mean what I said quite literally. I mean

281

for my own sake it's not as important as it might be." Then he told Farrell about his walk of a couple of days past, and how small he felt as a result.

"Haven't you gone overboard a little?" his guest asked. "When you decided to be the best conductor possible, you didn't really think you were—what's the phrase?—working for a mass market, did you?"

"I didn't think at all, if you must know. I felt I had to do it." Denis frowned a little, trying hard to think back to the very early days. He went on, "That's not quite it, either. The truth is that I wanted it for myself. I'm only beginning to get a perspective now."

Farrell felt sure he was witnessing a change that not many men experienced, either in themselves or in others. He would have liked to probe for causes, but his instinct said no. Sufficient that something was happening to turn a very great gift into something more than a personal expression. Whether the seed was planted by the Terry whom Denis mentioned occasionally, down South, or by Jerry who danced, or by a walk in Mather Street mattered very little.

They finished lunch, and Farrell again could feel a tension growing in his host. Of course, he thought. The concert. "I wonder," he said, "whether it wouldn't be possible to sneak in somewhere and hear Dingbat. Would you like to?"

Denis nodded. "Only I don't want to be seen. It wouldn't be fair."

"I know. We can go in the stage door, and through the basement, and slip into the projection booth. It hasn't been used for years and it's probably dirty. But we can hear. Want to?"

"Wonderful." Denis quickly got into street clothes and the two of them half ran to the hall and let themselves into the booth. The hall was full, as it always was, and even through the slots of the booth they were sure they felt a certain excitement in the audience—perhaps a hope that something scandalous would happen, or that the quarrel would have been settled and Denis walk dramatically out and deliver his curt little bow.

Instead Walter Dattner, nervous to the point of jitters, made a tentative entrance and received the barest minimum of ap-

282

plause. "You can see where the sympathy lies," Farrell whispered, and Denis smiled.

But the concert was a nightmarish experience for Denis, and he insisted on leaving at intermission. This program he had rehearsed, and from the sounds he heard, there had been no run-through that morning. The orchestra knew quite well what it should do, and did it; the difficulty was that the frightened assistant did not know, and was reduced to following the men as best he could, a circumstance that produced one mis-cue after another, and almost brought disaster toward the close of the Fourth Beethoven. When it ended Farrell quietly pulled Denis' hand from his arm. "You've almost paralyzed me," he said, "but I can't blame you."

In a tormented daze, Denis looked unseeingly at Farrell. "I didn't know I was doing that," he said. "I'm sorry."

"Let's run for it. It won't matter if a few of them see you; they're all women anyway, and we can outrun them."

"Sure. I can't stand the second half." They scooted downstairs and through the basement. Just inside the door they ran into an obstacle, and it was Harry. For a moment Denis thought he had been wrong, that Harry was drunk. But when he spoke it was in a perfectly sober voice.

"Busman's holiday?" he asked, laughing a little grimly. "I'm taking off—I can't take any more."

"Same here. Farrell and I were in the projection booth."

"I'm sorry for Dattner. He's scared out of his pants." Harry put his arm around Denis. "We're going to win this thing yet, son. Watch me."

Farrell laughed. "You'll have to forgive me. I know I ought to be sorry for the guy, only he's so long and skinny and sort of like me physically that I kept seeing myself on the podium. I'll probably dream about it tonight."

"You two boys come home with me," Harry suggested. "I'll buy you a drink. Unless you want to go to your office, Denis."

"I'm damned if I will. The next time I go into that room I'll be walking over the prostrate bodies of the directors."

Harry released Denis, giving him a little push. "What a sight that would be. Come on, I've got my car."

It was pleasant at the Gordons. They had had a couple of drinks by the time Gloria came in from the concert, full of gossip.

"Oh, Harry," she began, "the women simply ganged me. 'What does Mr. Gordon say?' and 'I think it's a shabby thing' and all sorts of remarks."

"And Madame Lister?"

"She never left her box. *He* was there."

"He heard a hell of a concert," her husband said. He explained that he had stood under the stage in the basement, and that Denis and Farrell had hidden in the projection booth. "I couldn't see, thank God. But they could."

Gloria said, "Oh well, forget it." She looked at Farrell, "It's nice to have you here. You never seem to come out."

He looked sharply at his hostess. "It's no fault of mine," he answered finally. "I don't mean this quite the way it will sound, because I know how Clarissa operates; but she likes a clear field, you know. And my job isn't with the big boys, it's with the papers and—you understand."

"Now you're here, you'll stay for dinner. It's stretchable."

They did stay. For almost the first time Denis felt entirely comfortable in the house, felt, indeed, closer to both Gloria and her husband than ever before. He was glad, and he was puzzled, too. And relieved not to feel Gloria's eyes running over him.

Next morning the editorial Greene mentioned appeared. It was exactly as he said it would be, merely an appraisal of Denis, his work with the orchestra, and a statement of what would be lost if he were to go. There was nothing evangelical about it, and not a word about the quarrel. It was, therefore, a masterpiece of fence-walking which still got over a point. Denis' telephone began all over again. Clarissa arrived to ask that he take over the concerts until the matter was settled, which of course she knew he would not do. John Dudley called, his voice actually smiling over the telephone. "I have the answer," he declared. "Next week Douglas Lister will conduct."

Greene called, too. "Just to check—want to say anything more?"

"No. Yes I do, too. You might say that I've decided to call the ballet 'New South' and that it will be given January fourth, fifth and sixth." He thought a minute. "Yes, and I'll be leaving for some guest performances right after. One with my old orchestra down South, one in Boston, one in Chicago."

"Good boy. Your old friend Greene is going to alert our correspondents. Nobody can stop us from carrying stories about you."

"Nobody?" Denis laughed. "You know better."

"No, I don't. The stories will just be quotations from the papers and a line or two about the audience."

Denis wondered, after he hung up, why people were troubling to support him, people like Greene for example. He wondered a very short time, because a bellman arrived bearing a box of flowers the size of a small coffin.

"Good God," he asked, "what's this?"

The man grinned. "Gettin' married?"

"I hadn't heard about it. Open the thing."

The card read: "With the best wishes of the East Lakeland Orchestra Auxiliary." He could remember, with effort, the president of the group because once he had been dragooned into lunching with the Auxiliary, by Clarissa, of course. He shook his head in wonder.

"Got a girl?" he asked the bellman.

"Sure."

"Well—give these to her. I'll take out a few roses."

The man grinned even more widely. "Look, Mr. Sandzen, she lives in an apartment about six feet square. Let me take them to St. Clare's Hospital. Huh?"

"Wonderful. Here's your cab fare." The man retied the huge box and disappeared, leaving Denis holding a dozen red roses in his arms.

So many people called, and so many letters arrived that Denis was a half hour late for rehearsal, this being a piano rehearsal for "New South."

"I'm sorry," he apologized to Carol Larrabee. "Things are complicated."

"Don't be sorry." Her manner always had the effect of calming Denis; he began to relax as she talked. "And I meant what I said when Dick and I called. Please, Denis, don't go through with this just because you promised. We'd all understand."

He tossed his topcoat to a chair in the corner, and motioned with his head toward the piano. "That man tune it?" he asked, and then remembering, "Look, Carol, I'm doing this because I like to do it. It's pure selfishness on my part."

"Nonsense. I admire you for it, but——"

"Stop butting. I'm going to beat that crew yet, I think. But if I don't, I'll go somewhere else. The boys here?"

"Somewhere about. Jerry!"

The three of them came tumbling into the room, lined up, produced burlesque salutes. Denis shook with laughter. "The three imps, Jerry, Jim and Lee. Where's your girl friend?"

"She says we're so naked she's shamed to show her face." Jerry's grin was all-inclusive as his clothing was not; he and the others wore only the tiniest of breechclouts, dyed in each case to match their brown skins. And when the fourth arrived she wore very little more.

They got to work at once, Denis playing and Jerry substituting for the choreographer, who worked days and could not come. They worked hard, because Farrell's scenario called for athleticism and for subtlety, and the music was simple only on its surface. At times Denis felt that the further the four got from the choreographer's ideas, the better was the effect. But he said nothing. After forty-five minutes they took a break, the dancers dropping to the floor around Denis.

"Sure am sweating," said Lee, shooting drops off his legs with his fingernail. "Bet you don't have much pity for your orchestra."

Jerry turned on him. "Shut up, you cluck. What'd I tell you?"

"Aw, Denis. I'm sorry."

"Don't be," said Denis shortly. "I can take care of myself."

"Sure can." Jim was inclined to agree with anything as a matter of principle. "You got what it takes."

The girl, whose name was, improbably, Naila, looked up. "Y'ever give piano lessons? We, I mean the House, sure need somebody can teach."

"She's good," Lee said, motioning toward Naila with his shoulder. "Not like you, of course, but she's good."

Denis had not seen Dick Larrabee come in. The others had, and it was Jerry who read Dick's mind and spoke for him. "You all better not try to get something more out of Denis. He's a busy man."

Dick chuckled. "Thanks, Jerry. You're right."

"Is he?" Denis wished he could be sure what his own motives were—whether, for example, his sudden determination to teach Naila was from stubbornness, or from genuine interest. "I'm not sure he is. Could you come to my apartment tomorrow about eleven, Naila?"

Lee's gentle voice took the sting out of the situation. "That's a real sweet idea, Denis. Only—the Hampton Park Manor?"

"I'm sorry." Another Lakeland hurdle, Denis thought, and realized in the same second that he was being unfair. It wasn't only Lakeland; it was almost everywhere. He looked at the four brown faces around him. "You know I used to conduct down South, and my skin is pretty dark. One summer I got so tanned I was almost thrown out of the Cleveland Hotel."

It was a dangerous thing to say, and he knew it. But it was true.

"I'll come here." Denis looked up at Dick Larrabee. "You won't be offended if I have a piano sent in, will you?"

Dick exploded into laughter so abruptly that it was obvious he too felt the danger of what Denis had said. "I'm not sensitive, Denis. Only they may be afraid to rent it to us. We owe everybody."

"I'll buy a good used Steinway. This afternoon. They'll deliver it where I tell them to. Now, up and at it, kids."

After rehearsal the Larrabees caught Denis on the way out. "Sit down," Carol said. "We want to talk with you."

Denis looked at his wrist. "Ride downtown with me. I've only got about half an hour before the stores close."

"You go, Carol; I've got some things to do." Dick brought Carol's coat and held it for her. "You know what we want to say."

In the car she sat facing him, one leg bent on the seat little-girl fashion. "It's this," she said in her quiet voice, "and don't interrupt me until I've finished.

"We're afraid we've sort of caught you on the rebound. We've been partly the cause of a nasty situation, and we're afraid you're angry because of that, and inclined to take your feeling out in doing things for us you—well—might not have wanted to do otherwise. Going too far, too fast." She put her hand on his arm as he started to interrupt. "No—I'm not finished. You see, it's not that we think you're insincere. It's that we don't want to take advantage of——"

"Stop it," he broke in. "I understand all right, and it may look that way. But you're wrong, Carol. Dead wrong." His mouth twisted bitterly, but the dusk was too far along for her to see. "The truth is that I never knew anything but music until— well, not too long ago. It's hard for you to believe, but it's true. I just didn't know."

"Still——"

"No. You keep still now." On impulse he told her the story he had told Farrell: his lonely dinner, the walk, the awful movie. "It's not a sudden come-to-God conversion, Carol. Only I can see a few things I used not to see."

"Then we want you to teach, and we want the piano."

"And what you get will be me, and I guess I'm difficult. Don't make the mistake of thinking I've relaxed so far as what I want to do is concerned, because I haven't. It's just that there may be more than one way of doing it. Can Naila play?"

"She's as gifted as the boys. Not in dancing—piano."

"Then I know what to do."

Carol said nothing. It was a gift she had. As if talking to himself, he went on, "I'll teach her myself until she's ready, and then let Elisabeth McKee have her." He was thinking grimly of something more as he parked the car. "And if I'm still conducting when she's good enough, she'll play with my orchestra, too." He held the door for Carol.

"Douglas Lister would absolutely shrivel," she said.

"A good shrivel would be fine for him," Denis replied, and to the salesman who came up to them, "Is that Steinway 'B' I tried a week or so back still here?"

"Yes, Mr. Sandzen."

"Fine. I want it sent to Larrabee House tomorrow morning." He took out his checkbook.

"Can do, Mr. Sandzen. Can do."

Next morning there was an official letter from the Orchestra Association containing a check for Denis' salary up to the day of his resignation. In the afternoon, there was a personal letter from Douglas Lister suggesting that perhaps Denis would lunch with him next day, together with Harry Gordon and (at which Denis laughed) John Dudley.

He called Harry, and they decided to accept. "It's going to be a lousy day," Harry complained, "weather as well as everything else."

He was right. Next day would be Christmas Eve, and Lakeland would have, if not a white Christmas at least one the color of a much-worn fleece-lined union suit. As Harry picked Denis up, the snow began, a typical Lakeland snow containing quite as much soot as frozen water. By the time they had been dropped at the Lakeland Club it was impossible to see the opposite side of the street, something that increased if possible the bonhommie inside the institution.

They entered and were assailed by half a dozen "Hi, Harrys" before they could cross the high, columned, red-carpeted hall. In the lounge they found John, carefully reading *Time* upside down. He jumped up at once, and said, "Doug's talking to his office. Something broke loose."

"Hmm," said Harry, and John looked sharply at him.

"Look, fellow," he said gently. "Do me a favor. Keep your temper, won't you?" He gave Denis the same look, and said, "That goes for you, too."

"Then make it as easy as you can," Denis said. "And don't expect any backing down, for it won't happen."

"All right. Here he comes."

Lister was, he probably thought, striding impressively across the lounge. Actually he was walking rather stiff-legged as if he were rheumatic, which he was not. The frown on his red face was not because of the meeting, however. He announced as soon as he had shaken hands that one of his foremen had thoughtlessly stumbled into a tub of molten iron, "Good man. They'll have trouble replacing him."

They headed for the bar, again through a hail of "Hi, Harrys, Hi Dougs, Hi Johns." Denis smiled at Dudley. "Doesn't anybody ever just smile when he passes?"

"Oh, no. It's considered more manly to do it this way." They dropped behind a couple of paces. "Fact is, it's even better if you can haul off and knock the wind out of your friend. Like this . . ." They were passing a familiar fat man, somebody Denis had met somewhere.

"Hi, Lucky, you old skunk," John said suddenly, and handed the other a terrific wallop on the right shoulder. "Excuse me, Lucky, I was just demonstrating something for Denis Sandzen, here."

Denis was convulsed, which was exactly what the other wanted. He was still grinning as the four seated themselves at an extraordinarily Tudor table in the extremely Tudor bar, full of talk with a slight Elizabethan flavor, all conducted at a huge volume. The drinks came, four bottles because each man had a different brand.

"Only bar in town where they trust the customer," said Harry, pouring liberally. "Let's eat here, too. Mind, Doug?"

"Certainly not." Although Lister's collar was no higher than anyone else's, it seemed to be. "Matter of fact, I always do."

The talk was about nothing much through the first drink. They had a second, and suddenly Lister blurted, "You two know why we're here, of course."

It was a statement. Denis and Harry merely nodded, thus easily making it difficult for their host. He cleared his throat, and began again. "I—uh—we thought that perhaps you—uh— we all had been a trifle hasty. That we might find it possible to—uh——"

"What Doug is trying to say is that we all probably made mistakes, and we'd like to correct them. Right, Doug?"

"Yes. That's right."

Harry was staring into his bourbon and water as if hypnotized. Just before the wait grew impossible, he said quietly, "How do we start?"

The expression on John Dudley's cherubic face was embarrassed, to put it mildly. "Douglas wondered whether it would be possible to put off the ballet until after the season ends." He was looking at nobody, twisting the jigger in front of him.

"No." Denis' voice was low, but firm.

Lister's normally red face purpled a little. "May I ask why?"

"Certainly. I shan't be here." Actually Denis had refused to make plans or accept summer dates. He had an idea, very vague but also attractive.

"Then would it be possible to find someone else to conduct?"

Harry answered. "It would not. Why would Denis want a stranger to conduct what I personally think is a little masterpiece?"

Lister was holding tight to his temper, barely under control now. "As a third suggestion, could that place get together its own orchestra, make the affair a charity enterprise, as it were."

Denis' temper was more volatile, but under unusual control. "Amateurs couldn't possibly play the score," he said quietly. "It sounds simple when it's well done, but it isn't simple. It's damn difficult."

"You see, Doug, I was right." John Dudley poured himself a third drink with the air of a condemned man having his last wish. "What's wrong isn't what Harry and Denis want to do; if you'll forgive me, it's what you and the others think about the Larrabees."

The expression on Lister's face was the prelude to a great oath, but what came out was "Pshaw!" which proved that exchanging Methodism for the Episcopal church had not entirely destroyed his early training. "I don't understand what's so attractive about those mousy little people and that ramshackle old store building."

If Denis' voice had been precooled in an ice box it could not have been more chilly. "Those little people, as you call them, are not mousy. And the ramshackle old store is all they can afford." He too poured a third drink, and signaled the waiter for

291

more ice. There was the thin edge of a smile on the waiter's brown face; he had been listening.

"I'd like to clear the air, if our host doesn't mind too much. I'd like to say that when I received that check yesterday morning, I considered it a formal acknowledgment of severance. I spent the rest of the day at Larrabee House rehearsing. I agreed to teach piano in what little free time I have. Late yesterday I bought a decent Steinway and had it sent out to the Larrabees. I will not go back on a single promise I have made, no matter what happens here."

Thick veins beat under Lister's purple temples. Nevertheless, Harry came in directly behind Denis. "Doug, I know perfectly well why I'm president of the Board. I've got more free money than most of you. If you allow this boy to resign for a stupid reason like this I withdraw at the end of the year, and I'll put every nickel I've been giving the orchestra into Larrabee House." He grinned wickedly. "I'll also issue a statement to the papers that will curl your hair, old boy. And they'll print it." He suddenly lost control. "Also, goddam it, the Lakeland Steel Company won't incinerate any foremen in scrap from my company. It's too much trouble for you to replace them." And he subsided again.

Almost as if someone had given a signal, the four raised their glasses. No one wanted to speak first, but John Dudley did. He said, "I'm convinced."

"You gentlemen want to order?" The waiter fanned out four menus.

They ordered four sandwiches, which came almost at once. The sandwiches were eaten with speed, and the moment they were consumed, Harry called the waiter.

"Ask the doorman to call my car, please," he said.

They rose, and Lister spoke for the first time in ten minutes. "I have a meeting. Please excuse me."

He walked stiffly away, ignoring a number of "Hi, Dougs." John bowed gaily to the others as soon as their host was out of sight. "You've won, boys. His lawyer told him this morning that the orchestra has absolutely no control over Denis' spare time as long as he doesn't molest little girls, rob banks, or otherwise exhibit moral turpitude." He laughed. "I think he also told him he was a stiff-necked old fool, but don't quote me."

At five o'clock that afternoon Clarissa was driven to the Hampton Park Manor through the accumulated snoot, which was the word coined by the irreverent out of snow and soot to describe winter's glory in Lakeland. She sailed through the lobby, and at the elevator met Denis just going out. Without a word she kissed him soundly, tears in her eyes.

"It's over, dear," she said. "Give me that check. I'll send the regular one on the first of the month."

Some reasonably small things can make deep dents, Denis reflected as he left Clarissa and walked up to Mather Street. He wanted to buy aspirin, having exhausted his supply in the last few days. The store was crowded with people he did not know, and he had to wait, standing in front of the telephone booths. He also had to listen to the woman in the middle booth, since she had left the door open and had a voice with a serrated edge. He paid no attention until he heard a familiar name: Lister.

"Well," said the voice, "I personally think it's a shame. I love his concerts, and I know it's Douglas Lister did it."

Apparently her friend asked how, and Denis was surprised how accurate the woman's guess was; by now he was hoping the clerk would not finish with the customer ahead of him soon. She finished her version of the dismissal with a remark that brought a smile to Denis: "And my dear, he's head of the Liberty League, too."

This was true. Lister had gone full circle; he had learned not to be afraid of fear.

"Also"—and there was a gulp which might have meant the transfer of gum from one cheek to another, or merely bad air—"also, do you know he owns those two awful old shanties Larrabee House has?"

Denis' ears must be standing straight out, he thought. She went on.

"He does so. I know." A pause. "I do know. My Murray handles them—it's one of those dummy corporation things. I *thought* you'd laugh—only it's really no laughing matter. Murray says both buildings are going to fall down one day when somebody scratches a match on them. He's *so* clever, Murray is."

That was quite enough for Denis. He bought his aspirin and hurried back to his apartment. He called Harry.

"Clarissa stopped by," he said. "It's wonderful—thanks to you."

Harry shrugged it off.

"But listen," Denis went on. "I've just heard something— overheard is the word, I guess." And he repeated the woman's statement. It was as if he had touched off a cache of fireworks.

"Oh, baby. Oh, baby! I wouldn't take a million bucks for that. Just wait . . . what was the name of the real-estate man?"

"I don't know his last name, Harry. She just called him 'my Murray.'"

"I'll know by noon tomorrow. And then watch Uncle Harry! Somebody's going to get a lovely Christmas present. Say—has Gloria caught up with you?"

"No."

"She wants you to come out tonight. We have a little private shindig Christmas, just us and she wants to have Clarissa."

"Love to."

"And lunch with me tomorrow, if you can stand that much Gordon. I'll have a story for you."

He did. They met at the Lakeland Club for a reason. After the barrage of "Hi Harrys" they found a corner table in the bar and were as secluded as if they sat in the middle of a forty-acre field. All around them Lakeland business was working on its holiday binge, and noisily.

"It's okay," Harry began, pouring drinks lavishly. "The guy's Murray Harris—I thought he would be. Good egg, too. And the corporation is called the Greater Lakeland Realty Company. And"—Harry beamed—"it owns enough whorehouses in the Larrabee House neighborhood to make a good-sized village, scaly old houses that probably were condemned ten years ago."

Dimly Denis could see what was coming. "Go on," he demanded.

"I'm going. The Greater Lakeland Realty Company is ninety-nine per cent owned by Dougie-boy, bless his little heart. So the gentleman who deplores our connection with Larrabee House collects rent from Larrabee House and a lot of the women whose kids get mixed up with Larrabee House, if they're lucky."

"Well, well."

"So just before I came here I called our benefactor. I said it was Christmas, and although I'm Jewish, I always sort of celebrate. I said I was sending the Larrabees a check for ten grand, and I thought it would be nice if they got a deed to those two ramshackle old hovels."

"And he said go to hell?"

"Um. . . . He said, 'What are you talking about?' So I said 'I'm talking about your Greater Lakeland Realty Company.' "

"This begins to smell like a devil's food cake burning. Very good."

"I'll cut it short. He laughed in my face, and I said that at the next meeting of the Orchestra Board I'd mention the fact that I'd tried to buy those buildings, and found that Dougie-boy owned them, and wouldn't sell. And he folded."

"There he is now, just coming in."

"He won't come over."

But he did. He walked straight through the room, and stopped at their table. His face was controlled; he might have been saying hello to a pair of dear friends. What he actually said was, "Your little blackmail job is working. I've just ordered a deed sent to Dick Larrabee."

"Fine. Have a drink." Harry pushed the bottle toward him.

"No, thanks. I'd like to add that it's small loss—the rent didn't pay the taxes and repairs."

"O-ho! Careful now. My research was pretty thorough. You've been getting two hundred a month, the taxes last year were a hundred sixty-three dollars and thirty-one cents, and there are no repairs."

Lister's dignity deserted him. He spat out a four-letter word beginning with 's' and turned on his heel, his face once more purple. He had nearly reached the door when he seemed to stumble, and put out his hand to steady himself on a chair. He missed the chair and fell. By the time the two doctors lunching together in the bar reached him, he was dead.

"My God," Denis cried. "Not that!"

"Easy, boy." Harry was on his feet. "He's had a heart for the last ten years. This thing isn't to blame."

A little group gathered around Harry and Denis. "What on earth?" the man next to Harry demanded. "Was he sick when he was talking to you?"

"No. He just stopped to tell us that he'd decided to give Larrabee House those two old buildings they occupy."

"Give? Douglas Lister?" But he thought better of the remark; after all, the man was dead. "That's nice," he finished. "Very nice."

22

The ballet performances were so successful, when they came, that thirty rather than three evenings might have been given. The four leading dancers could hardly have been better. The little orchestra played wonderfully, the stage looked well, and the audience was the most astonishing Lakeland ever had known. This was because everyone who possibly could buy tickets was there, white, black and all the intermediate shades. Since the Larrabees refused to have special sections of the hall reserved, one sat where one could, and there were no riots. To begin with, Denis allowed the three boys to improvise on three tunes. Then he gave the stage to Naila, who was, he felt, the best piano talent he had seen in Lakeland. And then the ballet . . . something quite new, a statement of the South as it is, which still exposed the roots dug into the past, wonderfully

296

simple on the surface and equally complex in meaning. The audience felt something leave them as they watched, perhaps an attitude inherited but not understood. But they applauded wildly, so long on the last night that Denis almost missed the train which would take him to Chicago and then South. He left Lakeland almost perfectly happy.

Terry and Delphine met him. Delphine kissed him as he half ran out of the train shed, and Terry put his arm around him and squeezed him.

"It's wonderful you came," Delphine boomed. "When I heard you'd canceled Philadelphia I was afraid you——"

"That's a long, long story," Denis interrupted. "Too long for a railroad station."

"We'll go home," said Terry. "We can have a nightcap and talk awhile."

They did, and Denis gave them the whole story of the Lakeland incident, down to the death of Douglas Lister. "Oh, dear," said Delphine at that point, "how sad."

But Terry merely looked at Denis appraisingly, and finally said, "You probably don't realize it, Denis, but you've grown ten feet taller in the time you've been away."

Denis smiled. "I'm still kind of a pygmy in some ways," he admitted.

Delphine looked from one to the other, slightly at a loss. "You mean about colored and white sitting together?"

They both roared, and Terry explained, "Of course not. So far as I know Denis didn't have that kind of prejudice." Terry glanced at his friend. "I mean he's beginning to see that what he does has got to be related to what the rest of the world does."

"But of course." Delphine got up. "I know Denis is tired and I've got to get back to Rats. I'll see you at rehearsal tomorrow." She laughed her burbling laugh. "Like old times, Denis. Wonderful."

After she had gone the talk went further back into Lakeland history, to Gloria and Mrs. Rutherford Lodge.

"The recipe worked, didn't it?" Terry asked.

"Yes. I felt like a heel to bother you, only . . ."

"Who else would you have bothered? Don't you understand at all? Don't you know I'd do anything, literally anything, for you?"

Denis got up to fish a fresh pack of cigarettes out of his bag. As he passed, he squeezed Terry's shoulder. "I understand better than I ever did," he said. "I wish I could do more about it."

"No. I wasn't thinking of that side of it. And anyway, it's just as well we're not together any more. I—the situation might not have been good for your career."

Denis started to speak. He hesitated, and after a moment went on. "I was going to say there were bigger things in the world than my career, Terry. But I think I'd have lied. I haven't changed that way, and there's no use in my pretending. I'm still a son-of-a-bitch with the men; they're still afraid of me."

"I suppose so. Maybe that's right . . . certainly your successor here could use a little son-of-a-bitchery. He's pretty lax."

"I'll find out tomorrow. That's not really what I was driving at, though. I . . . I was just wondering what I'd do if some kind of scandal had started here. Whether I'd have behaved, or whether I'd have been a bastard there, too. I hope not."

Terry had slumped down in his chair so far he was actually looking more at the ceiling than at his guest. Perhaps his position was deliberate. "I'll say one thing, and then let's forget it and go to bed," he replied. "I'd give up anything in this world rather than hurt you in any way at all. I'd even give you up." He straightened. "One more little one, and we sleep."

It was very like old times to get up in the morning and find orange juice in the icebox and a note from Terry saying he had gone to work, but would show up at rehearsal. It was more of the same to shave and dress leisurely, and walk through the Quarter to the Auditorium as he had done hundreds of times before—only now, even in the morning, the Quarter seemed more lively than it used, as if a lot of subterranean activity was now on the surface. Repeal, Denis thought, and a good thing it is.

Labate met him at the stage door. "Ai, Maestro," he bubbled, "it's wonderful." He embraced Denis, tears in his eyes.

"Maybe you come home to lunch with me, you and Mrs. St. Martin? My wife would make a pizza?"

Denis swallowed. "I'd love it, Labate. Might I bring Terry Metoyer?"

"Of course. Oh, yes, of course. Now if you excuse me I telephone quick." He trotted to the telephone sidewise, like a roly-poly pup, one eye still on Denis.

The orchestra rose, and applauded. "I can't greet each one of you now," Denis said. "Just let me say I'm glad to be back. The Mozart concerto first, please, and"—he looked over the group sternly, but with a little twist in the corners of his full mouth—"no monkey business!"

At the break there was a general shaking of hands. At least, Denis thought, they don't hate me for having beaten the hell out of them. As he said "Hello," and "How's the bassoon these days?" he wondered from the way they pressed around him whether they, too, might not have grown a good deal in understanding. Perhaps they were glad once again to play under someone who would take no monkey business, who knew exactly what he wanted and exactly what they could give—and would be satisfied with nothing under their limit.

Delphine and Terry came in together, and after the last chord they stood in the wings and applauded, and Denis brought the men to their feet, and bowed as if it were a performance. Later Terry said, "It sounded like another bunch altogether. You'd never believe it."

"Yes," agreed Labate softly. "Now we go for pizza? It is not good when it is cold."

There was pizza, of course. Labate's wide-built wife was by no means satisfied with pizza alone. There was also chicken, and wonderful artichokes in a rich oil sauce, and minestrone to begin with. . . . It was three o'clock before the luncheon was finished, and the eating was as great a labor of love as the preparation. The two stood outside their door as the guests departed, flushed and smiling. Said Labate, "Ai, Maestro, we could have some music, only me, I have no wind at this time."

The old group made this visit a sort of prelude to Mardi

Gras. There was a basement party at Delphine's shop at which Madame Aimé heard about the other grandmère in Nice and Denis saw Cécile for the first time, and found her less tense than he had ever seen her, cordial but unpossessive. Next night Denis had guests in one of the private rooms at Antoine's. And the night after the concert Paul de Knize took everyone who mattered upriver on his boat for dinner at The Oaks. There were cocktails, perfectly legal ones this time, all the way and since this was one of the very warm Januarys, dinner was served on the lower gallery while a group of men from the orchestra played Mozart divertimenti under the oaks.

"I wish Elisabeth were here," Denis said to his host.

"So do I. I see her in New York occasionally, but she hasn't come South for two or three years."

"I owe her a lot," Denis continued.

Paul de Knize looked shrewdly at Denis. "Ah, well," he half whispered, "she collects in her own way."

Denis was not quite sure he understood, but he asked no questions about Elisabeth. "How're politics, Paul?" he said after a moment.

"You can't shoot a man without making confusion. But it's all right—I was never Huey's buddy, you know. Certain things were necessary." Paul seemed a little uncomfortable. "Perhaps we might play a little Mozart? For old times' sake?"

"Of course. I'd like to." And the longer Paul pinned him to a piano, the less time there would be to walk under the oaks with Cécile; and something told him there would be a walk with Cécile, however unpossessive she had appeared at Delphine's party.

Not everyone wanted to listen, but a good many did. Paul played second piano as usual, and Terry turned pages for him. They had gone through two concertos and were about to start a third when Cécile stepped through the tall window behind the pianos. She looked lovely, Denis was forced to admit. She also looked determined, which was characteristic. "The three of you have had each other long enough," she declared. "There are other guests, you know, and I should think the host——"

"Very well." Paul closed his score with the reverence he always showed the great god, Mozart. "I didn't mean to monopolize Denis."

"But you did."

"And now," Terry broke in, "you want your turn."

"Oh, stop it, Terry. I hate that wise man from Orleans Street manner of yours."

Terry said, "Tut tut, my love," and made a very creditable exit through the window just used by Cécile.

She turned to Denis. "It's different this time," she remarked, a shade too casually.

"How?"

"I'm not chasing you, and you're not hiding from me. I rather like it."

"To be frank, Cécile, I think you're a hell of a lot nicer this way."

She laughed. "Let's walk down the alley; lots of others are."

The white lanterns Cécile loved were hanging in the live oaks, swaying gently. As they stepped through the window one of them caught fire, and flamed garishly for an instant. A man and a woman were standing underneath; she screamed, but not too loudly, and ran out of range of the falling bits of paper.

"Remind you of anything?" Cécile asked, and Denis shook his head.

"It reminds me of me, Denis." They stepped off the gallery, stopped to pick up a drink at the table under the first oaks. "I've almost written you this a half-dozen times, but I couldn't quite manage it."

They walked slowly down the magnificent alley, now a mysterious tunnel dotted with white lights which did very little to push back the dark. Denis said, "I'm afraid I'm not much of an inspiration as a correspondent. Poor Terry, I hardly ever write him."

"Damn poor Terry!" She sounded more like her old self than she had all evening. "I'm talking about us."

"I gather you are."

She gave him a quick look. "Don't you want me to?"

"I'm a little older now," he answered. "I'm not afraid of you any more."

"I know. I never could understand why you used to . . . oh, you know how you were."

Denis finished his drink, tossed the glass into the air and caught it. He said gently, "You were the first—and you smothered me. Do you understand?"

"I suppose so. I was a fool, too. An arrogant little fool."

"You've changed, too—you'd never have said that when I was here."

"And I was furiously jealous of Terry. I know better now."

Denis had whirled on her at the mention of Terry, but she gently laid her hand on his lips.

"Don't say it. Terry and I understand each other now. I even understand me."

"Well, I don't. Suppose you tell me?" He looked at her and was shocked at the utter whiteness of her face. "Cécile, what is it?"

They had reached the last pair of oaks, and were standing alone, looking across the flat fields toward the high levee. She put her hand on his arm. "I may as well tell you, because I think Terry is right. He says I was just determined that I— that I forced myself to want a man. That I really wanted something quite different."

Denis covered the tense white hand on his arm, pressed it hard. "Happier now?" he asked at last.

Softly she said, "Yes, I am."

"I'm glad." They walked back up the alley, into the party, hand in hand.

The party went back down the river on the boat, and it was late. The wide water looked like a mirror grayed by time under the moon in the west, and the low shores were mysterious in grays and black. Gaiety had drained out of the party; the moment at which one remembers business on the morrow had come. A messboy circulated slowly, filling glasses and removing empty ones, and from the stern rose the inevitable noise of part-singing out of throats too relaxed from alcohol. Terry and Denis took their glasses and went forward, past the deckhouse, where there was no one. They sat against a hatch and smoked as they listened to the swirl of the water and muffled rumble of the engines. A heron flew over them and into the moon, speaking harshly as he passed.

"I wish I didn't have to leave," Denis said at last. "Life's better down here."

"Perhaps. Visitors think it's lazier, too."

Denis thought a minute. "But it isn't. People get as much done."

"Yes." Terry put his glass down on the deck and lighted a cigarette. "You had a talk with Cécile?"

"She told me something I should have guessed—perhaps."

"Not necessarily. I think she's happier; certainly she's easier to be with."

"And you? Everything all right?" Denis squeezed Terry's knee gently.

"As right as can be, I suppose. Let's not go into that."

"Sure." Denis stretched lazily. "It's hard to believe that it can be so warm in January. When I left Lakeland the temperature was twenty-two."

"And snowing, I suppose."

Denis laughed. "What else?"

"Yes. Look Denis, let's do go into that. Part way, at least."

"What do you mean?"

But it was hard for Terry to go on. He finished his drink, and snubbed out his cigarette. Then he lighted another immediately. Finally he said, "I mean that sometimes I'm afraid our . . . friendship . . . might be dangerous to you. People might talk. . . ."

It was perhaps the one thing Terry could have said that would have angered Denis. "Might they?" he flared. "What makes you think I'd give a damn?"

"You might. When I don't hear from you for weeks on end, I can't help wondering."

"You've got me on one count. I hate myself for being such a rotten correspondent. But Terry, I really am growing up a little. Honestly. I . . . I love you in my way. If people want to misinterpret the business, they can and the hell with them. No—let me finish." He put out his hand as if to push away Terry's protest physically. "I'm beginning to value people for what they are and not for what they can give me. I really am. When I came down here I was a pretty raw specimen, and without ever lecturing me, or demanding that I read this or do that, you managed to get me ready for Lakeland. Not consciously, like a project of some kind. Just by letting me be with you. I'm just as ambitious as I was, Terry, every bit. Only now I'll never be satisfied with just myself."

"With whom? Claire?"

Denis hesitated. "I, well, I don't know that I'm ready for that. I was thinking of things like the Larrabee House mess."

"Oh?"

"You do understand?"

"Partly. Maybe more." He turned the conversation once more, and clumsily for him. "You said you were determined to teach piano, too. Any talent?"

"One big one, so far. A Negro girl named Naila Marsh. She's got facility, and—oh, I guess you'd call it instinct. Even when she's bad technically, you still know what she wants. You feel it."

Terry's mood was new to Denis. It was not that a distance had come between, perhaps just the opposite. It was more as if for the first time in Denis' experience Terry himself were directionless. He was like, Denis felt, someone who has reached the edge of familiar ground, and was uncertain of his turn. With a quick stab of intuition Denis felt something more: that it was he, himself, who was the familiar ground. But he could do no more than continue an aimless conversation.

"I don't know what her chances are," he went on, "but she'll have them, whatever they may be. When I think she's ready, I'll turn her over to Elisabeth and her Foundation."

"Good. And the three colored boys?"

"That's a tougher proposition. You know Vernon Clegg?"

"By reputation."

"He's got a new opera, very modern words, very simple-sounding music. I heard there's some dancing they could do in it."

"Know Clegg well enough?"

Denis shrugged, and of course Terry could not see the gesture. "I can play some music of his, and maybe suggest the boys to him."

"Try it—although where they go from there God knows. Probably Pullman porters."

The flat town was tucked under the levee and visible only as a blur of light that steadily grew stronger. They passed a long string of barges balanced on the nose of a tiny diesel tug pushing slowly upstream. "How's it feel being a millionaire?" someone called from the lead barge in a high, thin voice. His only answer was "I've Been Working on the Railroad" from the stern of the yacht.

Terry spoke again after a moment. "Speaking of millionaires—did you know Paul proposed to Elisabeth and got turned down?"

"Good Lord, no. Why?"

"Why not? What's Paul got that she hasn't got more of?"

The remark did not sound like Terry, and Denis let it pass. After a while the yacht veered sharply left, and docked at the foot of Canal Street. There was a brief flurry of good nights, and a few suggestions of nightcaps, and then the dock was empty.

"It's only three," Denis said, "and you're not working tomorrow. Let's stop by Tony's. I'd like to see how the place looks now that saloon-keeping is legitimate."

"Sure." Terry laughed. "There's not much difference," he said. "Even Lulabelle's still there."

Claire and her mother were in their rooms at the Hampton Park Manor dressing. They also were complaining because Lakeland, unable to make up its mind whether April were spring or winter had suddenly made it summer. Outside the late dusk vibrated with the equatorial sort of heat that seems to build up toward dark. Below them the little park was dotted with shirt-sleeved men and women in hastily disinterred summer dresses; across the park the traffic flowed lethargically past the somber façade of Lister Hall, the drivers snailing along in the hope of finding a breeze, or an excuse to stay out of hot houses and hotter apartments.

"Mind if I wear white, too?" Claire asked. "I simply can't bear the thought of anything dark on a night like this."

Elisabeth, her mouth full of pins, shook her head. When she could, she added, "We'll look like sisters—now do say I'm right."

"Oddly enough, it's almost true. You do look almost as young as I."

"Don't be silly. Oh, damn!" She began peeling off her slip. "I've got to shower again. I can't stand it."

Dressing was finished barely in time for dinner, and dinner barely in time for the season's last concert. In spite of the heat the hall was full and the concert went well—as well as the last of the pop series the Sunday before, with Elisabeth as soloist, and a soloist who had worked hard. "After all," she said to Denis afterward, "I'm surprised I can sing at all."

"Yes?" He looked quizzically at her. "You know that's not

true. You worked at getting back into shape exactly the way you work in your office. Right?"

"As if I could tell you anything about work," she replied obliquely.

Tonight there was an end-of-season party, another of what Clarissa called a typical Lakeland party. It was just that, and furthermore it had been suggested and engineered by Clarissa herself, and the victim handpicked by her as well. The victim was a lawyer with an ambitious wife and almost enough money to pay her way; it was not Clarissa's fault that more than half the guests would be unable to remember the name of their host and hostess when they were ready to leave the Hampton Park Manor after supper.

When the last chord had died and the usual backstage congratulations were finished, the part of the audience which Clarissa had felt mattered streamed across the block or two of common ground to the hotel, and assaulted the bar with reasonable decorum and absolute determination, time being limited. Denis was cornered by a parcel of women, halfway to the bar, and might have gone unrefreshed had not Farrell Clisby slipped into the group and surreptitiously handed him a drink. Denis bore the business well. It was one more thing to be done, something that was necessary and productive according to Clarissa. And release was around the corner—two or three weeks with Clarissa and Clisby would wind up the work, and leave him free for the summer. Or almost free; there would be a few jobs, the Hollywood Bowl, Ravinia in Chicago, the Stadium in New York, a parcel of them abroad. And there would be study as well, and perhaps even a little composing. All of which was not difficult, because it could be done as he chose, all but the conducting, and even that required no fresh study.

Finally supper was served and Elisabeth, on her way toward the traditional salads, linked her arm in his and, that simply, rescued him. He was filling Elisabeth's plate when Gloria came by.

"I want to ask you something," she whispered. "Not now—pretty soon."

Denis smiled and nodded. Gloria was fun now that she had

left off being a nuisance. Then Clarissa steamed past, picking up Elisabeth and leaving Denis to her assistant. The room already had begun to vibrate like a railway station with the passing of a long freight, and as a defense, he and Clisby began what appeared to be a very important conversation.

"Those two are picking you to pieces," Farrell said, inclining his head toward Elisabeth and Clarissa. "In a nice way, of course."

"Perhaps." Denis frowned down at the inevitable crab salad, and then took some because he was starving. "I think Elisabeth's pumping Clarissa about the Larrabee House business." He pursed his lips wisely. "Elisabeth can hold her own with that one, never fear."

"Someday," Clisby said parenthetically, "I'm going to persuade somebody to give one of these parties and serve hamburgers and hot dogs."

"Like hell you are."

"Yes. Speaking of those two—I think you're wrong. In fact, I damn near know you are. The mother of us all is trying to get some dough out of Mrs. McKee. Some kind of scholarship contest and the soloist to play with the orchestra, or screech, depending."

Across the room Denis saw Claire, the dark face over the white gown desperate. "Those two harpies are working on Claire," he said. "Excuse me while I do a rescue."

He hastily filled a plate and crossed the room without accident. "Excuse me," he said, "but I've got something to ask Miss McKee." He bowed. "It's nice to have seen you."

Denis hurried Claire around a pillar and through a tall window onto the terrace. "Here," he said, "eat your supper."

She laughed "Hide it somewhere. I can't possibly eat it. But thanks, sir, fo the thought."

"Then let's walk down to the lake. Nobody'll miss us."

She thought a moment. Finally she said, "I was just trying to decide whether I could get that far without working up a sweat, and I can't. We'll slip around the corner; nobody'll come, you know, because they're afraid they'll miss something. God knows what."

"This is part of the game, Clarissa says. She usually knows."

The terrace ended in a stone seat partly sheltered by a dusty palm retired from the ballroom for out-door therapy. Denis spread his handkerchief for Claire, then sat down and yawned hugely.

"Thanks for that," she said. "I'm as good as a sleeping pill."

"Oh, hush. If you'd had to conduct in that heat you'd know why I'm worn out."

"I know. I was joking." She yawned in her turn. "Frankly I'd rather conduct as athletically as you do than be nibbled to death by those ancient female ducks in there."

"I was going to hold your little hand, only now I won't. Some of them are nibblers—not all."

"They are. I even saw that Gloria Gordon give you the high sign, and please don't say I didn't."

"Claire . . ." He was honestly disturbed. "That's not fair. You certainly wouldn't call her ancient."

She stiffened. "I certainly would. If you laid all the wrinkles under that expensive make-up end to end they'd make another Panama Canal."

"Stop it." Denis got up; he was sure he had heard a step on the terrace. But by the time he reached the corner he could see no one. He went back to the bench, took Claire's hand and drew her to her feet. "You're not being fair, and it's——"

"Unbecoming to a young virgin like me. I know. Let's go back."

Gloria found Denis almost at once, and said, "All I wanted was to ask you and the McKees to come by the house afterward."

"Love to." He looked at his watch. "I can get away at midnight, and I'll drive them out."

Denis thought, for the hundredth time, how much more of a person Gloria had become—at least to him. There were only John Dudley and his wife and Clarissa, and both Harry and Gloria met the group at the door. I'd like to rename Gloria, Denis thought. The name doesn't seem right. And then something struck him with a thud when he caught the look his hostess gave Claire; it was Gloria's step I heard on the terrace, he said to himself. I'd bet a hundred dollars. As usual when he sensed a situation, he headed straight for the piano, but this time music was not enough. Behind him he heard Gloria's voice, very sweet indeed.

"Can you drink?" she asked Claire. "Or should I get you some Coca-Cola?"

Denis plunged headlong into the first piece he thought of, which happened to be the B minor Brahms rhapsody. John Dudley, as usual, drifted to the piano and leaned on it, watching Denis' hands. Denis finished, and John said, "Another lesson for your Uncle Dudley. I'd give my few remaining teeth if I could do that."

Before he started again, Denis looked over his shoulder. Gloria now had her arm about Claire; he could hear his hostess say, still sweetly, "There *is* an art to make-up—now for instance . . ." and her hands went up to Claire's eyebrows.

Denis plunged again, this time into the "Winter Wind" etude. Over its tempestuous sound he could hear Dudley's voice, just barely.

"Drowning something out?" he asked, and Denis grinned and nodded.

But after a while he ran down and turned back to the room. Claire had escaped, an odd look on her face. Denis crossed the room to her, and asked, "Have a nice talk with Gloria?"

"Damn Gloria," she replied between set teeth. But there was a look of respect in her eyes just the same.

Denis was still amused when, at three o'clock, he and his guests reached the Hampton Park Manor. "You might give me a nice good-night kiss," he said in the elevator, and Claire obediently put up her face. But when Denis touched her lips she bit him.

"Oh, dear," Elisabeth said, "that's hardly nice."

"I think this is one of the nights I hate him," Claire announced.

"Never mind," Denis said as the car stopped at the McKee's floor. "She's just furious because she got put in her place. Coca-Cola, dear?"

"You and that woman!"

The door closed and Denis took out the letter he had picked up at the desk. It was a special and it was from Terry. He let himself into his apartment and quickly got out of his tails. Then he opened the letter.

It said:

> I know this is cowardly, but by the time you read this I'll be gone. You must not think that I'm doing this because of what you can't give me; it's *that* you can't give it, and it's worth nothing from anyone else. And I can't bear the thought that perhaps something I may do or say will hurt you or your career. There's nothing in the apartment that will connect us in any way except one picture. It's in the silver frame behind the old picture of Mother, and I can't destroy it. Love, and good-by.

That was all.

Not quite believing his eyes, Denis read the note again. He sat for a long time without moving. This is how an animal feels in a slaughterhouse when he's hit by the sledge, he thought. The letter fell from his fingers with a light rustle, and the tiny sound aroused him. God, he prayed, don't let him die. Then he looked at the letter, which was not dated. The postmark was blurred; he can be dead now, Denis thought, and put out his hand for the telephone.

It would have to be Delphine, there was no one else close enough to him, not Cécile certainly. He could not face Cécile, even over the phone.

The call went through immediately. He held the telephone in one hand and pulled at his tie with the other, for it was choking him. The studs in his shirt stuck; he ripped the garment off and tossed it, forgotten, on the floor. Far down in the South he could hear a soft-voiced operator repeating Delphine's number, and the ring, and in a moment Delphine's deep voice, heavier even than usual from sleep.

"It's Denis, Delphine," he said, the words tumbling out. "How's Terry?"

"Oh, Denis—I didn't know until this afternoon. They kept it quiet. I tried to call you . . ."

"Delphine, please. How is he?"

She hesitated a second. "Not too good—he's still unconscious. They think——"

"He's alive." Denis shivered suddenly as if from cold. "But Delphine—will he, is he going to pull through?"

He could hear Rats mutter something from his bed, but he could not understand what he said. Delphine hesitated again. Then she said, "They don't know. He took sleeping pills, handfuls of them. Maybe . . . oh, Denis, I don't know."

His mind was clearing. "I'm coming down," he said. "I think I can get someone to fly me down. Please, Delphine—I'll wire you when I'm due and you'll meet me? Please?"

"Of course, my dear. If they let anybody see him I'll . . . if he's all right, that is."

"Thanks, Delphine. I'm going to hang up now, but I'll wire you."

He jiggled the phone, and called the airport. No, there was no flight. No, they didn't have anybody at this hour who could make the trip. Denis suddenly lost control. "Goddam it," he shouted, "the best friend I have is dying down there, and you yammer about the time!"

"I'm sorry," the man said. "I'll do what I can and call you back."

"I'll be packed. Hurry, for God's sake, man."

Denis almost leaped from his evening clothes into a street suit, and threw the necessary things into a small bag. He called the garage and asked them to have his car waiting, and then telephoned Farrell. For a moment Farrell did not understand, and then he came alive with a rush. "Sure," he said, "I'll explain to Clarissa and the McKees and cancel whatever you've got for the next few days. Say"—he was trying hard to be useful—"why don't you pick me up on your way to the airport? I'll drive your car back."

"You don't need to do that at this hour."

"What's time to me? Of course I will. I'll be waiting."

In fewer than ten minutes the airport called back to say a

plane would be ready at five o'clock. It was nearly four, then, and Denis could not face another minute in the apartment alone. He picked up his bag and half ran down the hall; downstairs he flung the bag into the car and drove out into Mather Street as if there were no other cars in Lakeland. Fortunately there was none at that corner.

Farrell's house was only a couple of blocks off the route, and he was waiting in the living room, a paper parcel in his hand.

"I thought you might need it," he said. "It's bourbon."

"And you're wonderful to think of it." Denis pulled out the cork and took a long drink on the spot. "You drive. . . . I, I don't feel like it."

Farrell chuckled. "Another drink like that and you can't," he remarked dryly.

"You're a terribly good egg, Farrell. It's a help just to talk with you."

"I'm glad." He was driving slowly, wondering what he could say without seeming to pry. But he needed to say nothing, for suddenly the dam burst in Denis, and he poured out the whole story. "I feel like a bastard," he ended. "I've never known what to do, and in spite of everything he's the best friend I've ever had. He's . . . he's wonderful, and he's done more for me than I can ever repay. Even possibly."

They were turning into the airport; it was not quite five, but they could hear a plane revving up on the other side of the building as they drew up at the entrance. Farrell turned off the motor, took Denis' bag.

"Look, man," he said quietly. "Don't blame yourself. That's all I can say. Even Terry knows it's none of it your fault."

Denis turned a stricken face toward Farrell. "If he knows anything, that is."

The flat land around the port was beginning to take on features in the early dawn, a tree emerged where before there had been a black velvet blur; a truck which a few minutes ago had been only a tiny high light where a lamp from the administration building flung a beam against it. Farrell looked around; they were alone.

"Look, Denis." He held out the bottle. "It may be against

the rules for people to drink and fly. Only you look awful—take another big one."

Denis' face moved in what was almost a grin. "Fine." He poured down almost a third of the bottle, shaking himself afterward like a dog coming out of surf. "Whew! You know I hate heights. It's almost sacrilegious to mention a little thing like that, only I had something happen when I was a little boy. It was months before I could look out of the window in my apartment here without being afraid."

"With all that in you, you'll sleep. Got any pills—oh, I shouldn't have said that."

"It's all right. I've got some in my traveling case. Maybe I will."

Farrell walked with him to the plane; the pilot was standing beside the door shouting orders to the mechanic inside. "You Mr. Sandzen?" he asked, and Denis nodded.

"You going to want me to bring you back?"

"No. I may have to stay some time."

"Okay by me, but you must be in a hell of a hurry to pay double price."

Fatigue and liquor were catching up with Denis. He merely said, "I am," and turned to Farrell. "I forgot Delphine—wire her. . . ." He turned to the pilot. "What time should we get there?"

"Two anyway, Maybe before, if we get a break on the wind."

"All right," Farrell promised, "I'll do better. I'll phone her when I get back to the house."

"Good. It's Uptown 9990. Thanks, Farrell."

They shook hands and Denis climbed into his seat. The single motor roared, and the plane slid out onto the runway. Denis turned in his seat; Farrell was standing alone on the concrete apron. As the pilot gunned his motor and they streaked across the field he waved once and turned away, now only a tiny dot in the frail morning light.

It was a horrible trip. It was rough, and although Denis held things down, he wished repeatedly he had not; he felt for hours as if he could no longer contain himself, as if the world below him had suddenly cut loose from its moorings and were dancing far below the little plane. It appeared directly below one moment, and was gone the next; he could neither bring himself to follow its mad movement, nor keep from looking through the window.

The pilot was proud of himself, and disgusted with his passenger. He had the common complaint of pilots who have taught themselves to push somebody else's invention through the upper air; for him those who neither appreciated his tremendous skill nor had an interest in flying were stubby little creatures, rather contemptible, and as soon as he realized that his passenger was bored as well as sick he retired into the sulks.

They came down at Nashville, Denis thought, although it might have been Memphis. He got out of the plane and walked into a shabby building where in a men's room, deserted by everything except its odors, he finished the bottle Farrell had given him. When he returned the pilot gave him a slanting look, and said, "Okay, buddy. Time to go."

Neither said anything the rest of the trip. Denis dozed, and the man busied himself with the gadgets in front of him, making as much of his activity as possible in the hope that his passenger would be impressed. It was exactly two o'clock when they saw a wide clearing in the sugar cane below, and the pilot said, "Here we are."

"Thank God!" snapped Denis. He could feel tension reaching muscle after muscle in his body, tension and fear as well. They landed with a bump, and taxied up to a rambling group of buildings. "I'm damned if I can see how you can stand bouncing around in this chicken coop," Denis added.

"Greatest feeling on earth," the pilot said as he opened the door and took Denis' check. "Feel sorry for them that don't get a kick out of it."

Delphine stood in the shade of the largest building. The sun blinded Denis, and it was a moment before he could see her; then he half ran to her. "How is he?" he called, and then dropped his bag and kissed her.

Delphine blinked back tears. "He's alive. You know how hospitals are—all they'll say is that he's conscious at times, but on the critical list."

Denis crumpled on a bench beside her, tears in his eyes. She looked down, patted his cheek. "Do you care so much?" she asked.

He looked wanly up at her. "Yes," and then something in her look stabbed him straight to the heart. "It's not what you might think, Delphine."

How very much people know beyond what you think they know, Denis thought. And how much more wonderful some of them are than you understand. She said, "I almost wish it were. I thought it was when you wouldn't have Cécile."

They were hurrying toward Delphine's car. Denis stopped abruptly, his eyes as wide as a little boy's when he comes suddenly out of sleep. "You're quite a wonderful person," was all he could think of to say. "I love you."

Delphine drove rapidly into town, and to the hospital. "I hope they'll let you see him," she declared, "but I doubt it. Anyway his mother is here."

That was something Denis had not thought of at all, though why he had not was beyond him. "How is she?" he asked. "It must have been dreadful for her."

"She seems—well—fairly good. It's not easy for her, either."

Denis barely knew Mrs. Metoyer. She had stayed once in the apartment while he was there, but usually she went to friends, and there was a period when even the cost of a train ticket was enough to keep her home. He shrank from meeting her, for Terry must have left a note for her, and it would have been like him to tell her the truth. The truth might . . . he refused to think of possibilities.

Delphine let Denis out at the hospital. "I'll see you later," she told him. "They'd never let two of us in, and anyway Paul de Knize's waiting for me at his apartment. Next season's money, you know."

"I'll call you around dinnertime," he replied, and hurried up the steps.

There was a short delay, and then he was sent to the third

floor. Mrs. Metoyer was waiting at the hall desk; she seemed glad to see him, and at the same time she appeared to have withdrawn from him. He tried to tell her how he felt, and failed. Then they were outside Terry's door.

"You mustn't stay more than a couple of minutes," she warned him. "And don't be surprised if he doesn't always make sense. He's alive, thank God."

Denis slipped into the room and met Terry's eyes, their gray now darker. But his mind was clear. "Thanks for coming, Denis," he said in a low voice.

"Of course I came." Denis sat down in a chair beside the bed and took Terry's hand. "You'll be all right, Terry. Your mother told me."

Terry spoke slowly, with effort. "I guess I miscarried, Denis. I feel all kinds of fool."

His face seemed very thin, and his hand shook a little as it lay in Denis'.

"Want to tell me what happened?" Denis asked. "Don't if you'd rather not. There's no hurry."

"I'd been at Delphine's for dinner," he said, his voice small. "I went home, and it was raining. I was standing in—in the dormer in the living room. I—it just hit me." He turned his head away. "I'm so ashamed, Denis."

"That's the end of it. We'll not mention it again."

A nun quietly opened the door and stepped into the little room. "I'm sorry," she said to Denis. "You'll have to go."

Denis got up, gave Terry's shoulder a light squeeze. "When can I come back, Sister?" he asked.

"Tomorrow morning." Her eyes wrinkled at the corners. "You look as if you needed rest, too."

"I'm fine. Just had a hard flight down."

Outside he found Mrs. Metoyer waiting; Denis thought she looked less remote, but her manner was still far from cordial. "I wish you would take me to the apartment, Denis," she said, and at once changed her mind. "Not there. Could we go someplace for tea? I—I feel sort of all gone."

Denis smiled. "Of course, if you don't mind the way I look. Even the sister was appalled."

The answering smile was faint, but there was one. "Of course I don't."

"We'll go to Le Clerq's," he suggested. "I need a drink more than I need tea."

They picked up Denis' bag, and found a taxi at the entrance. On the way neither spoke, and it was an uncomfortable silence. Denis sat with closed eyes, as if he were refusing to look at the familiar streets because of the memories they suggested. Or as if he were brutally tired—and both reasons held.

At Le Clerq's Tom was a little put to it to find tea, but he managed. Denis' double bourbon was much easier. He remembered Denis, and asked about Terry.

Before he could answer Mrs. Metoyer broke in. "He's better, and a very lucky boy."

Tom's look asked for more.

"He'd been at one of those awful, endless cocktail parties," she went on, "and he was tired. Probably a little tight, too. He went into the bathroom for some vitamin capsules, and he took a handful of nembutal capsules instead. He might not be alive, only one of his neighbors was having a party and wanted to borrow a bottle of gin. She found him."

Tom clucked. "Sure a lucky boy," he said. "A very lucky boy."

When he had left she turned wearily back to Denis. "You know better," she added.

"What do you know, Mrs. Metoyer?" Denis asked miserably.

She answered obliquely, "I hope you haven't destroyed him, Denis."

He was honestly puzzled. "Please," he said, "tell me what you mean."

She did not speak for a moment, but she did not look away. He felt as if she were trying to read what was in his mind, or perhaps what was in his spirit. The room was very quiet, the horseshoe bar almost deserted, and the only moving thing was the tiny flame in the fireplace, which burned winter and summer.

Her voice came at last, very low. "He told me everything from the first," she began. "I've always known—about him. And when the two of you met, I knew how he felt." She took a sip of the tea, poured more milk in it. "Denis, couldn't you have given him more?"

"I tried."

"What happened?"

"It didn't change anything between us," he replied slowly, "only it didn't mean to me what it meant to him. It was one morning on the beach at the lake."

Denis looked wonderingly at the sad, still lovely face opposite him. Without her there, looking just as she did look, the conversation would have been unbelievable; it was hard to imagine the intelligence and the understanding that had led to her acceptance. For that matter, Denis found it difficult to understand her acceptance of him on either plane.

"Knowing what I did," she went on, "I suppose I should have guessed. Terry loves that very old picture of me as a girl. I was looking at it this morning, and I found your picture behind mine."

"Yes," Denis said, "that was taken when——"

"You were very beautiful," she went on as if he were not speaking. "You are very beautiful."

Denis shook his head impatiently, then with a tired gesture rubbed his unshaven chin, looking out into Bourbon Street. But she can't know that this talk about the way I look bothers me, he thought; he suddenly leaned across the little table and touched her hand.

"Mrs. Metoyer," he said in a rush, "I think Terry's the finest person I've ever known, and I've hated meaning one thing to him and being another. Hated it. But I can't help it."

She drew in a deep breath and stood up. "We can go to the apartment now, Denis," she said quietly. "You can have your old room."

He picked up his bag and they walked through to Orleans Street. He had expected to feel strange, different somehow, about the apartment, but instead he felt only pleasure at returning to it. As he so often had, he sat down at the piano and played scales and arpeggios for a few minutes; then he shaved and bathed, and when he returned to the living room Mrs. Metoyer was waiting, whisky and ice on the table before her.

"I'll join you this time," she said, smiling. She mixed the drinks and gave Denis his, and for a while they talked of everything but Terry and what had happened; about Denis' work, and Lakeland, and what he hoped to do. He found himself telling her about Larrabee House and the four colored youngsters of whom he was so fond, and found her sympathetic. "There's more of that sort of thing down here than people imagine," she remarked. "One reason it makes so little impression, I suppose, is that there are so many more Negroes here, and it takes more time."

And a little later, she said, "I've not had anything except that cup of tea since this morning. Could we have dinner?"

They went to Galatoire's, after Denis called Delphine and reported. By degrees, in that curiously impersonal restaurant where the food is so surprisingly good, the conversation drifted back to Terry, and Mrs. Metoyer said with sudden bluntness, "I think this is as difficult for you as it is for me. The basic thing for me is that I think my son's life with sex is, quite simply, his own affair. And I think he is a worth-while person, and should be accepted for what he is, and not condemned for what he can't be."

Again the feeling of wonder came to Denis. "You do know, at least, that I've always accepted him without reservation?" he asked.

"Yes. But have you given him all you could?"

Humility was new to Denis, but now he was truly humble. "What shall I do, Mrs. Metoyer?" he asked. "Can I do anything at all?"

She looked down at the lobster in its nest of water cress, and picked lightly at it, trying to make a decision. At last she looked Denis straight in the eye, and said, "I'll have to tell you what he told me, I think. He—he'd not like it, but it's only fair to you——"

"Don't if you'd rather not," Denis broke in, but she went on as if he had not spoken.

"He wrote me the night he wrote that last note to you. He said he was—doing it—because, because little things told him that being even as close to you as he was might injure you with your world, and he couldn't face giving up the little he had. So . . ." She pushed away the lobster. "May I have some coffee?" she asked in a voice like a small girl's. "I'm not hungry."

Denis nodded to the waiter and ordered. When he turned back to her, her hand quickly pushed back the dark hair which still tumbled down over his forehead. "You're a lovely, puzzled boy still," she said quietly, "and there's no combination more winning. Believe me."

He shook his head. "But what can I do? Could he go abroad with me again? Or would it make things worse?"

"Be honest, Denis. Is it pity, or do you truly want him to go?"

"Of course I want him. It wouldn't be any good if I didn't."

"It would be fine, then." She seemed to be appraising him, her eyes, gray like her son's, full on him. "I think I am beginning to understand you," she said, "and to like you. Now let's go home."

They were both too tired to talk, and even the piano deserted Denis. He felt drained, as empty as a summer-resort water system when all the people have gone home. It was a little past nine when Mrs. Metoyer gave up. She looked oddly at Denis, and then said, "It's a strange request, right now. But have you any sleeping pills? I'll never get to sleep without them."

Denis got the capsules for her at once, and after she had gone, took a couple on his own. Then he went to the dormer and stood quietly there until he began to feel drowsy. There was no rain tonight, only moonlight, but the slates shone dimly, and to the right, in the Cathedral garden, the statue seemed to glow with a white and supernatural light. It came to him as he waited for sleep that the pain under the scar was draining away; now the tension slipped out of him easily, and he knew he could rest.

"I'm a lot better," Terry declared as his two visitors came into his room next morning. "I can go home tomorrow—and I hate to."

Mrs. Metoyer touched his hand. "You mustn't feel that way," she said. "Nobody really knows, except perhaps Delphine. They think you made a mistake in the dark."

Terry laughed bitterly. "That story is gray-haired, Mother," he said. "The paper carries it once a week."

"It will do," Denis broke in. "It's possible, and people certainly won't argue with you."

"It's not what they say; it's what they think," said Terry. "Anyway—I've learned my lesson. I'm glad I miscarried."

The sister came in, and as usual both her eyes and her glasses were twinkling. "It's time for your bath," she said firmly, "and you will not take it in the tub."

"Please, Sister. I can walk across the room as well as you."

She looked at Terry wisely. "They always think they can; anyway, it's orders and that's all there is to it."

While they waited in the sunroom at the end of the corridor, Mrs. Metoyer said very little. But before the sister called them, she turned to Denis. "I wish you'd go in alone. Will you?"

"Of course." Denis was puzzled.

She left him then, saying, "I'll take a little walk, and come back in half an hour."

Denis nodded, and in a couple of minutes was back with Terry. "I'm glad you're alone," he said at once. "I want to say something to you."

"Your mother's clairvoyant," Denis answered.

"Perhaps." He looked around the little white room, and blinked at the sharp morning sun pouring through the window. "Turn the blinds, Denis, won't you?" he asked, and hurried on.

"Is this awful business going to make a difference? Please tell me the truth, even if it hurts."

Denis stood over the bed shaking his head slowly and a little sadly. At last he said, "I've grown up more than you realize." He sat backward on the side chair by the bed, his arms over the back and his chin resting on them. "If you mean will I ever forget it, the answer is that I can't. But if you are trying to ask me whether—whether I'll think less of you, it's no." He took a deep breath. "I think the question is whether you'll think less of me."

Terry was not quite satisfied. "But you admit you'll not forget. Do you mean that every time you see me you'll remember this mess? I'd rather not see you if it does."

Again Denis shook his head. "You don't understand. What I'll remember is that you tried . . . you did this really out of love for me. And that I'm not worth such a price. It's a kind of warning for me, Terry." It was as difficult for him to put his thought into the proper words as it was easy for him to translate an emotion into music. "It proves that nobody can bang their way down the middle of a street without running into somebody, sooner or later. Do you understand what I mean?"

Terry's head moved against the white pillow; his light hair looked darker against its background and his face thinner. "It works the other way around, too. I had no right to do this to the two people I am closest to in the world. None at all."

"Can't we just push the thing aside? I know that sounds like the easiest way out for everybody but you, only . . ."

"For me too." Denis could almost feel one compartment of Terry's mind close, and another open. "How long can you stay?" he asked, and Denis said a couple of days more.

"And then?"

"Clean up in Lakeland, a handful of summer dates, Europe. Terry, can you go with me—abroad, I mean?" Then, because he knew what would be in Terry's mind, he rushed on, a little clumsily, "You could help me a lot, and maybe this time we could have some fun, too. I've got plans . . . only I don't want to talk about them. Not now."

"When?"

"Late in June. Two months or a little longer. Say yes."

Terry might have ignored them if there had been signs that this was an effort at repayment, but it was evident it was nothing of the kind. "I'd love it," he said.

24

The summer dates were quickly over, and the notices were superb. The reviewers were tiring of their bright remarks about Denis' athleticism on the podium, or perhaps they were merely running out of similes. Nor were there any snide remarks about his refusal to conduct invariably from memory, and nobody pretended longer that it was his looks and tailoring that captivated his audiences, just as they eventually had grown tired of hinting that Koussevitzky had to be taught his scores by someone before he could rehearse them. These were small matters; actually, Denis minded barbs like this very little; he absolutely knew what he could do and how he could do it, and what people said made little difference as long as they listened. They did listen.

He and Terry eventually reached Munich, with no dates ahead and at least a month of free time, time as free as it ever was for Denis. They went to Munich because Guy Patterson and his wife were there, and Denis had met them earlier in the year in California. The Pattersons had in addition to their two children, twenty-odd students, a stream of visiting dignitaries (all of whom were deftly juggled by Nona Patterson) and two American Steinway concert grands; Denis was brushing up on the fourth Beethoven concerto in odd moments and these would come in handy. And for a while it would be possible to close one's eyes to the incessant parades of Hitler Jugend and their elders.

On this day there had been no parades past the enormous old

house in Ludwigstrasse the Pattersons had taken for the summer —not only a huge house, but one so ugly Nona Patterson insisted the parades avoided their block because no one could bear to look at it. Today the Pattersons, all four of them, were picnicking in the mountains near Garmisch-Partenkirchen, and there were neither students nor dignitaries about. It was a bright day, but cool, and all morning Denis had been drudging at one of the pianos, with Terry playing at being an orchestra on the other. For the fourth or fifth time Denis botched his first solo passage.

Without warning he snatched the score from the rack, ripped it down the middle and flung it at the large, bronze god, probably Norse, which guarded the door. "Screw the goddam thing," he shouted. "It's so easy I can't play it."

Terry laughed, mostly with relief. "Sure it's easy," he said. "But you've been at it three straight hours and you're tired."

Denis picked up the handkerchief lying in the piano and swabbed off his face. "No—I'm thinking of something else," he replied. "Let's go get some beer at the Löwenbräukeller. It'll be cool there."

"And Hitler's little friends don't go there much."

"Thank God."

On the way out Denis picked up his brief case, and Terry laughed. "What's the idea—trying to be a true German?"

Denis looked at him inquiringly, and Terry pointed to the lederhosen they both wore, and to the brief case, without one of which no respectable male German would be seen on the street.

Denis grinned. "Not these days. There's something in it I want to show you."

Except at one table under a plane tree in a far corner, no one was talking politics, or even looked political. The two found their own table and tree and ordered, and while they waited, Denis pulled the huge, white radish out in a spiral and salted it. "I love these things," he said, "but don't let me eat too many or I'll get a bellyache."

"I couldn't stop you," Terry answered out of his experience. "I wonder why Americans can't be as sensible as Bavarians," he added.

"Why do you think Bavarians are so sensible?" Denis looked about him. "If you said 'good-looking' I'd understand better. Male and female, they're the best in the country."

Terry agreed. "I mean their clothes. Every American male has got to stick his legs in two tubes of cloth, wear a shirt and tie, cover the whole thing with a jacket—no matter what the temperature is. Why not leather shorts for business?"

"I never thought about it; you tell me."

"We haven't any guts. We're so damn afraid people will think we're 'different.'" He laughed. "It's only in the last year or two men could appear on beaches without a rag around their chests."

Denis leaned back in his chair and roared. "You're right," he admitted as the waiter set two seidels in front of them. "I'll wear shorts if you will."

"I probably won't; I'm the biggest coward of them all." Terry took a long drink and came out of the seidel with foam on his nose. He wiped it off and added, "God this stuff is wonderful! Why can't they make beer like this at home?"

"Better not let Der Führer hear you, or he'll sign you up."

"Like hell he will. Denis, what's in the brief case?"

As if to delay his answer, Denis finished his beer and held up two fingers for the waiter. Then he slowly opened the case and handed Terry a Manila folder filled with scraps of score paper, stuffed in without order. "This," he said.

He watched as Terry sorted through the papers, his face more and more like that of a puzzled small boy. The beer came, and he ignored it.

Finally he looked across at Denis. "Planning to write a symphony or an opera or something?" he asked slowly.

"Not exactly."

"Then what? These things look like ideas you'd put down: the sketchbook of the Swedish-French-American Beethoven, or something like that."

"Sample the second seidel and I'll tell you." They drank and nodded to each other, and Denis went on. "The ballet thing went to my head."

"Nonsense."

"Yes—I don't mean it made me big-headed, but I liked the feeling it gave me."

Terry said, "Yes. Go on, Ludwig."

"Oh, shut up. I really mean it; I felt as if I had done something—well—permanent. I'm not saying it properly, I suppose."

"Forgive me. I know what you mean, only it's a new approach for Denis."

"It was sort of between highbrow and lowbrow. It was musically good, pretty good anyway, but it could be liked by almost anybody." Now that he was faced with the need of putting his thought into words he floundered. But he floundered on.

"I don't think opera, the old-time sort of thing, is for Americans. I never did, especially Hitler's predecessor, Herr Wagner." Denis grinned. "Old Wotan always did remind me of a watchman at a grade crossing."

"So you want to write something the—what do they call it?—the wider public can take?"

Denis nodded eagerly in spite of his determination to be calm, and critical, too. "Exactly. Something not a musical, not grand opera, something in between." He hesitated. "To be honest, that's about as far as I've got, except for all those scraps you've got there. Because I can't write. Words, I mean."

Terry waited a long time before speaking. He finished his beer and so did Denis, and they ordered another. The seidels were huge and they were hungry; they were beginning to feel the beer a little. Denis picked up his third radish, and Terry held up a schoolteacher's finger. "Remember the stomach," he said solemnly, and Denis answered by taking a bite.

"I don't think you've thought this out," Terry said at last.

A little impatiently, Denis replied, "I said I hadn't."

"I don't mean the opera, or whatever you call it. I mean your career."

Denis frowned. "What's it got to do with my career?"

"You still want New York before you're thirty-five?"

"I certainly do."

"Ever think that getting into the theatrical racket might queer you for Carnegie Hall?"

"But I don't intend to get into the theater."

"Where will your whatever-it-is play? Grand Central Station?"

Denis was vexed and showed it. "Certainly not. In a theater, only that doesn't make me a George M. Cohan."

"Thanks be to God." Terry thought a minute before he went on. "It's the middle-aged and older people who put up the money for orchestras, my lad. The conservative people. They're buying a good safe cultural product—and how I hate the word culture!"

"Yes, Terry, but——"

"Wait a minute." He folded his arms on the table and leaned toward Denis. "They're buying prestige, most of them, rather than music. They want their man to be socially acceptable, handsome if possible, presentable at teas and dinners, impeccably dressed, *solid*."

"Hell's bells! What's that got to do with it?"

"Everything. You've got a strike or two against you. Mostly your youth; they won't see that your age has absolutely nothing to do with your ability. I'm talking a lot, Denis. One thing more and I'll stop. I don't think you realize that Gus has got a hell of a job selling a boy in his early thirties to a board of directors with an average age of fifty-five or sixty. He won't like this idea either."

"I still want New York more than anything," Denis admitted after a pause. "Tear the things up."

Terry laughed. "Now I've got to jump to the other side. They're too good to tear up."

Denis was genuinely, and completely, puzzled. "Then what the hell do you mean?" he demanded. "You say I mustn't try the what-ever-it-is one minute, and the next you say I mustn't give up the idea."

"It's not very consistent, I admit." He held up his hand. "Wait a second. I might as well finish the lecture. You're not going to write this thing in the next month, or year either. Why, Denis, you hardly ever go to a theater—there's a whole technique to learn."

"I know that."

"So I suggest that you take it slow, see a lot of light stuff over here and at home, and maybe five years from now things will be different." He grinned and after a second Denis smiled back.

They ordered Bauernwurst and kraut and various other indigestibles, and they talked most of the afternoon under the plane trees, and above the noise of the band. Finally they came to the agreement Denis had had in mind from the first: that Terry would try a book, that the work would aim at getting the feel of some part of America onto the stage, that there would be good dancing which would look nothing like the usual chorus line but instead would tell part of the story and establish part of the mood of the piece.

"What part of the country?" Denis demanded, his face flushed with the beer.

"Whew!" Terry said. "I'm a little tiddledy."

"So'm I. What part of the country?"

Terry laughed. "Some of those scraps you've got sound Southern to me."

"'S wonderful. I hoped you'd say that. We'll call it 'Louisiana.' Just one word, like that."

Solemnly they shook hands, and arm in arm they left the garden carrying the brief case between them, so each would feel respectable. But the day was not quite finished.

When they left the cab in front of the Pattersons the upstairs maid ran out to meet them. She handed Denis a cablegram, three days old, which had been forwarded from place to place doggedly, and at last had caught up.

Denis read it, and slowly passed it over to Terry.

"I'm sorry," Terry said. "Don't feel too badly, though."

"Grandmère was very old," he answered, "but she was very alive, too. It's tough—I'd counted on your meeting her before we go back."

"I'd have liked to."

Denis straightened, took a deep breath. "Your word would do for Grandmère," he said as they went in. "Though not quite in the same sense. She was solid, that one."

On the morning of April 17, 1937, Gus Wagner and Moira Dillon sat together in Gus' office, commiserating sadly. Gus had just delivered himself of a blast at the idea of any neutrality act's keeping this country out of any fracas. He had paid his respects to the Japanese in China, and to Germany and Italy in Spain, and was about to devote considerable time to Father Coughlin, Dr. Francis E. Townsend and Gerald L. K. Smith as representatives of the peculiar idiocies which afflict the lunatic fringe of a democracy, when the telephone rang. Moira answered, listened a minute, said, "Oh, dear!" and hung up.

She turned back to Gus and said, "Now if you can let the rest of the world alone, maybe we can talk business."

"What was that call?" Gus demanded, ignoring the rest of it.

"The box office in Carnegie Hall."

"Passing the time of day?" he suggested with somewhat obvious sarcasm.

"Saying that the hall's sold out for the Lakeland Orchestra tonight. Damn!"

Gus snorted. "O ye of little faith," he remarked. "It was you who insisted on all that paper."

Moira was caught, for once. "It was and I was wrong. And when have you admitted your fault like that, I ask?"

"Oh, well . . . we didn't give too much away, and now we'll have people demanding seats and what little standing room there is will be full. It won't do any harm. Matter of fact, I'm rather glad. Seen Feodor today?"

"You know where he is, just as well as I."

Gus smiled indulgently. "Of course. I read minds."

"I'll bet a buck to ten he's hanging around Carnegie Hall listening to Denis rehearse. Want to take it?"

"No, ma'am."

They were wrong, however. Feodor Solomon had been listening, but at the moment he was in Moira's office trying as hard as possible to overhear the conversation behind Gus' closed door, and fortunately failing. In a moment he knocked, and Moira opened the door.

"A talented boy, that," he said. "Very, how you say—athletic? But he knows. He's splendid."

It was an opportunity to give a lesson that Gus felt bound to seize. He looked at Solomon's huge frame and granitic face and agreed offhand. "The best," he said, "and a boy who will take advice."

"Yes?"

"Yes. He sees the people he should see. He doesn't hide all the time."

Feodor, who was as English as his first name was Russian, due to a tangle of nationalities which he never bothered to explain, set his chin and looked coldly at Gus. And as he often had done before, Gus thought that the man was so vast he almost could have played a 'cello under his chin, like a fiddle. Feodor said, "It is my business to make music, not to play lap dog."

"All right. We won't discuss it. You'll be glad to know the house is sold out for tonight."

"I am. It's a good orchestra he has; I might like to have his first horn."

"You might at that. But you can't have him."

"Who said anything like that? No, no, no."

"Rats. You know perfectly well you'd steal him in a minute. But don't let me catch you trying, Feodor. Denis is also a client of mine."

Feodor's shrug was in proportion with the rest of him; it was as if a quake had disturbed, briefly, Pike's Peak. He looked at Moira, who so far had said nothing whatever. "A charming young lady was listening. With a youngish man."

"If you'd accepted a certain invitation, you'd have known her," Moira said coolly, and to Gus, "Claire McKee, I imagine."

"Probably. Look, Moira, run over to the hall and see whether Denis can have lunch with me."

"Sure. I'll tell him you'll go out."

"Huh?"

Moira smiled. "Everybody doesn't like to eat delicatessen sandwiches and beer for lunch. I'll ask him to meet you at the club."

Gus nodded and turned back to Feodor. "You can't have the chorus," he said flatly. He had learned in the one season Feodor had been in New York that a flat statement was the only possible way to make an impression. "Too expensive."

Feodor sat down and the big chair shuddered on the verge of

collapse. "But the chorus sings for nothing. How can I do the Ninth without a chorus?"

"You can't. And the chorus has to be transported from New Haven to New York. There are other expenses, too." Gus was a little weary of explanations that should not have been necessary. He held up his hand to keep the other quiet. "Also, it's silly to open with the Beethoven Ninth. The chorus won't have had time to work it up, and the orchestra—oh hell, you ought to know."

"But I don't play piano like Sandzen. If I could play the Liszt E flat as he will tonight, it would be different. I——"

"That's a special case. The boy sort of got trade-marked, and incidentally, he really can do a performance. He can even make the Liszt sound wonderful. I've heard him."

"But a few singers? It's nothing."

Gus' voice chilled. "You heard what Moira said? About knowing the girl? Well, her mother is Elisabeth Scrivener McKee, and she's got more millions than you've got teeth. I never asked you to go around sleeping with women for business purposes. But a little common decency, just a little interest, might get you help you'll never get by sitting around playing chess with the solo 'cellist. Now you'll have to run along. I'm busy as hell."

Feodor rose from the quaking chair. "You have not my interest at heart," he said slowly. "Good day."

Gus watched him as far as the door, then said, "That's exactly what I have got at heart. Good-by."

Moira found Claire and Terry in the back row of the empty hall. Denis was sweating through the Liszt, not because it could not have been played without rehearsal, but because he was never sure it could not be played better with one more run-through. Moira motioned the two out.

"Mr. Wagner has to see Denis," she said, "so if you're waiting for him . . ." and she smiled, her empty hands turned up.

"Have lunch with us, then," Terry suggested, and Moira shook her head.

"I'd love to—only I can't. I'll tell Denis you're going on."

They slipped back into the hall and slid into their seats for

the last ten minutes of the rehearsal. They were in time to catch
Denis in one of his rare congratulatory moods. The concerto
came to its end, and he rose, his face shining, and said, "Gentlemen, I do not believe there is an orchestra in the world that
could have played a better accompaniment than that. I thank
you."

Taken off guard, the men looked at each other and then
applauded. "That's all until tonight," Denis finished, and still
flushed with pleasure, walked off stage and past Moira without
seeing her. She followed him upstairs.

Claire and Terry strolled slowly down Fifty-seventh Street toward Sixth Avenue. It was early for lunch, and they turned
north and into Central Park. They found a bench facing the
little lake, occupied only by a squirrel, and after convincing him
they had no peanuts, they were grudgingly allowed to sit down.
In a few weeks the park would begin to look dingy, and the
ducks on the lake would be too blasé for any but the better
tidbits. Now it was all fresh, including the ducks, and the air
smelled more of spring, and less of the winter's incinerator
fumes.

A plane went over, lower than it should have done. Terry
watched it, and when the noise had abated, said, "I never see a
plane without thinking how Denis hates heights."

"He told me he made a flight south," Claire said absently.

Terry looked sharply at her. "He tell you why?"

"No. But he said he hated every second of it."

Terry watched a pickup man with his spiked stick and burlap
bag, transfixing empty cigarette packs. He was round and
Italian and hummed as he stabbed the ground. He looked at
Claire in her gray tweed suit and tiny blue straw hat with relish,
almost as if she were the finest hothouse peach in a sidewalk
display, and he were hungry.

When the man had passed, Terry said, "I envy that man."

"Yes? Why?"

"Oh . . . he knows what he wants. It isn't much, but what it
is he can get, probably."

For a moment Claire thought Terry was hinting at her own
situation with Denis, if, she reflected a little bitterly, she actually

had even so much as a situation. But a glance at his preoccupied face told her she was wrong. "You may be oversimplifying it," she replied quietly. "He may have seven children, a sick wife, and owe three months' rent."

Terry's smile was a shade bitter. "There are worse things than a pack of children, illness and poverty," he said. "Much worse."

Neither spoke for a while. From the Avenue came the clashing and grinding of gears on the tall buses, and from the ground behind them the rumble of a subway train. A sparrow asked for bread, and went away undiscouraged when he got none. Terry suddenly made up his mind.

"I want to tell you some things," he said in a rush. "Perhaps I shouldn't, only I have a feeling you'll understand."

"I've had a lot of time to develop understanding," she replied, and this time it was her smile that was bitter. "Tell me."

Even before he knew what the result would be, he felt better. Confession and the soul, he thought, and plunged on without too much thought and sometimes without coherence. The bench on which they sat had been in the shade. The sun overtook it, and neither noticed; lunchtime came, and neither noticed that either. But when, at two o'clock, Terry looked at his watch and they went back up the steps and crossed to the Plaza, Claire knew the whole of his relationship with Denis, both its richness and its frustration. He looked down at her apprehensively as they turned into the hotel, and was surprised that her face showed neither sadness nor disgust—rather admiration.

They ordered a drink, and when the waiter had gone Claire took Terry's hand and said quietly, "Don't you see our situation is exactly the same? Oh," she added, prompted by the curious glance he gave her, "I don't mean for exactly the same reason. But Terry, I've been in love with Denis since I was a girl in my 'teens, and most of the time he doesn't know I exist."

"I see what you mean. And I don't know what to do about it, either."

"There's nothing to do." She spoke positively. "Nothing to do about him; I suppose I could quit being a fool."

The waiter returned with the drinks, and they ordered. When

he had gone the second time, Claire went on as if there had been no interruption. "I don't know why I feel that way, exactly."

"Yes, you do. I think you love him for exactly the same reasons I love him." He thought a moment. "You're better off, too. He can return your feeling physically, you know."

"If he ever chose to notice that I have feelings."

Terry's mouth curved into a grin, a rueful grin. "I've tried a lot of times to sort of cast up Denis' assets, and I never know whether the list would even make sense to someone else."

"Try me."

"All right. First there's looks; I've never seen a more handsome young man in my life. Then there's a sort of personal magnetism that perhaps others don't feel—audiences do, but——"

"People do individually," she said. "I've watched it work."

"Then there's ability. Nobody could doubt that. And incorruptibility. He'd never do anything cheap, no matter what the inducement might be—witness the way he's held off radio until recently, only because he thought reproduction wasn't good enough. And something I call ruthlessness. He'd fire his own father from the orchestra if he didn't think he was right."

Claire interrupted. "True, only he'd also fire himself. Gus says the big reason he gets away with treating his men the way he does is that they understand, dimly at least, that he treats himself worse."

"And last—oh, there are other little things, but I mean major things—there's something you may sense but I think very few others do. It's his capacity for growth. In understanding, I mean."

"I love lobster bisque," Claire said irrelevantly, and added, "I might disagree there. On personal grounds."

"I love lobster bisque, too. And I think you're wrong, Claire. Take the business of Larrabee House—once the boy was convinced it was a good deal, he was perfectly willing to resign his job rather than give it up."

"Yes. Or just stubborn."

Terry's laugh was almost jolly this time. "I admit he's stubborn. But there'd already been signs of what you might call an awakening down South. He really disliked having Paul de Knize play ball with Huey, and let him know it."

"It's odd," Claire said, digging into her crab salad, "that you'd mention him; de Knize, I mean. He proposed to Mother, you know. She turned him down as much on account of Huey as anything."

"I wondered. Paul talked about your mother a lot. And all of a sudden he stopped."

They were almost the last of the luncheon crowd, and the waiters were standing about with their annoyance liberally buttered with subservience. Neither of them noticed until their own waiter came for their dessert order, and Claire suddenly returned to the present, and themselves. "Oh, Lord," she said, "it's nearly half past three and Mother asked Clarissa up for an early tea."

"There's plenty of time."

"Only I have to stop at Bergdorf's. Let's hurry."

When they let themselves in, they could hear music from the drawing room. It sounded like Denis, but it was not the kind of music Claire associated with him. She looked at Terry, a questioning frown on her face.

For a moment he was tempted to explain the tune as he had explained himself, but instead he only shrugged. It was a tune whose germ he had found one day in Denis' brief case while they drank beer in the Löwenbräukeller. Terry realized that the time since had advanced "Louisiana" very little, and that it was not his fault. Denis, he knew, never discarded any activity in favor of another. When he began something new it was always added to the old list. However enormous his energy might be, there could come a day when it was not sufficient, Terry thought.

But that night as the lights lowered in Carnegie Hall and the expected coughs punctuated the growing stillness, he was forced to admit the limit was not visible, if ever it would be. He sat with Clarissa and the McKees; as Denis walked swiftly to the podium without a glance at the packed auditorium there was no suggestion of fatigue or indeed of anything except the immediate making of great music. Terry sat directly behind

Clarissa. She seemed to grow in stature out of her pride as her conductor picked up the long baton he always used, bowed shortly, and immediately began the Haydn symphony which preceded his concerto. She continued to grow through the symphony and the aging old concerto which roared and sang as if it were new, through the "Scythian" suite of Prokofiev and the final "Pictures at an Exhibition," the climax of which brought the audience to its feet cheering and applauding.

As he counted the recalls, Terry thought, I'm supposed to know something about words, but I couldn't possibly make an outsider understand what has happened. I couldn't tell the thousand and one things that went into making that kind of music sound that way, or how it was that the audience understood. Great successes, he thought, are all alike. But they're always mint new just the same.

25

Almost exactly two years later Denis was standing in his sitting room in the Adolphus Hotel in Dallas, looking down into Commerce Street and cursing, not silently. It was raining, a Texas rain, big, impersonal, wetter than rain anywhere else in the world. The room was on a corner, and across the street under the typical Texas roofed-over sidewalk around the Baker Hotel were several hundred people who would have liked very much to get home, and could not. The traffic light maintained its steady patrol, now red, now amber, now green, but only an occasional truck or taxi passed underneath it slowly; water ran from curb to curb.

Denis left the corner window for its neighbor. Now he could

see across the street a drugstore on the corner, a liquor store already brightly lighted although it was only five o'clock, and next door a bookshop, the door of which opened occasionally. In the door appeared a slender, intent young woman with a broom who appeared to be sweeping out water which sneaked under the door. He turned impatiently back into the room, and picked up the sheet of score paper he had been working with when Clarissa came in. In one corner of the sheet there was a wet ring, left there by the glass he held in his hand. The glass was empty, and he crossed to the closet, poured a heavy slug of bourbon, and filled the glass from the pitcher of ice water the boy had brought an hour ago. The liquor was good, but it did not taste good to Denis, mostly because he was angry with himself.

Clarissa had been angry when she left, too. It was the first real quarrel they had had for years—perhaps ever, Denis thought bitterly. He would not have been angry at all except for the fact that it was his fault; he was tired, dead tired, and she managed to arrive exactly in the middle of the hour he had allotted for work on "Louisiana." She brought along a telegram from Gus which read, "Just canceled all of Europe; see you tomorrow." That meant the first serious disturbance in Denis' plans for a long time, too, and it did not help matters much. He had no desire at all to play in Germany or Austria, but he did want to conduct in England and France, and if possible the Netherlands. This Gus had wiped out without bothering to explain. Denis knew the reason as well as the next; who didn't with the papers full of the doings of Englishmen rushing to and from Hitler like errand boys, of Frenchmen hiding their fears behind their own political ineptness and the Maginot Line. There was even the clown of Rome banging swords about like a small-town dramatic coach preparing a rehearsal of "Richard III." Not to mention the President's asking another appropriation for the defense of the United States every time he could get the ear of Congress. Which he did often, it being his Congress in the main.

Clarissa had come in under a full head of steam, as usual. She looked at the drink on the table first, then at the sheet of score paper. She was—how old? Sixty-five? More? Never mind, she was still any man's equal for endurance, and as forthright as ever.

"You're drinking a little early," Clarissa said, and without giving him time to reply added, "Another ballet?" nodding toward the score.

"Want a drink?" he asked, and she refused.

"I'm tired," Denis went on. "I wanted to finish what I was doing and take a walk." He waved a hand toward the window. "Not a chance."

She smiled; even that rubbed him the wrong way. "You ought to rest an hour before you eat. It's the last concert of the tour, and tomorrow you ought to sleep all day. You needn't go back on the train with the orchestra."

"Damn it, I don't intend to. Gus is coming in tomorrow."

"Gus is already here," Clarissa said quietly, and that was the match in the fireworks bin. Before she could explain anything, Denis had blasted Gus for sneaking in, Clarissa for conniving with him, and had poured himself still another drink. At last she calmed him.

"If you'll look at the date on that wire," she said tartly, "you'll see it was sent last night. The mail desk slipped up. He's not sneaking in, and I didn't connive with him, and you're acting like an undergraduate with that liquor." She reached for the glass, and he jerked it back, spilling a little on the carpet. Her lips closed in a straight line and before he could speak she was on her feet.

"Denis, I've been watching you on this tour," she said in a voice that bore a considerable rasp, "and I think you've been depending too much on bourbon. You work yourself taut as a fiddlestring, and ease out of it with a half-dozen drinks. I don't like it."

"So I'm a drunkard!" His dark face was almost white with rage; he gulped the rest of the drink and slammed the glass down on the table. "The hell with you!"

Clarissa tried hard, so hard her gray hair seemed to tremble with the effort. In a small measure she succeeded, too. "You're no more a drunkard than I," she said in a level voice. "You're

—you're eating yourself up, and trying to put back what you eat by any means at all. You can't sleep, you don't eat well, you're thin and snappish, and you keep adding things to your schedule. Like that," she finished, pointed to the sheet of score paper.

Denis blurted "No!" but she held up her hand and for some reason he stopped. Usually he would not have stopped.

"I'm going to find Gus and tell him not to——" There was a knock on the bedroom door. "That's probably Gus now." She looked coldly at Denis. "I'll take him away. You get some rest." Then she left him.

He took the drink he just had poured to an armchair beside the corner window, sat down and lighted a cigarette. His hand shook a little and automatically he thought, It's lucky I don't have to play tonight. That shamed him; he, Denis Sandzen, actually doubted his own ability and for what reason? Because of a few drinks. Or because Clarissa was right and he was over-tired. She had not said it, but fiddlestrings break on occasion. Perhaps he had been afraid of just that for months now, and as one does with distasteful things, had crammed the fear into a corner of his mind and thrown debris over it—more work, for the most part.

Like Naila Marsh, who was now in New York. He had spent days—weeks, even—forcing his board to allow her to play on a pop concert, and he was right to have done it, too. For everybody liked her and she was a success.

Like the rest of Larrabee House, to which he gave what should have been his one really free day each week. Like the guest dates he always accepted for his midwinter vacation, and the children's concerts he did not need to conduct, and "Louisiana." There was much more; just thinking of it made him weary and he closed his eyes.

When he woke it was seven o'clock and he was fighting. He could not remember what the dream was, but it had ended in a battle severe enough to waken him. For a moment he could not remember where he was; he was in a hotel, to be sure, but which hotel? St. Louis? Cleveland? Memphis? He had been in all those towns and a dozen more on this tour. Full dark had come early wherever he was—and then the rain told him the truth. He was in Dallas, in the Adolphus. He had made Clarissa angry, and Gus was somewhere about, keeping out of sight. But Denis could be sure he would be within earshot when the concert began at eight thirty. The auditorium was a long way from the hotel, and it was too big, like the auditorium in which his first orchestra had played years before. The acoustics were only fair —at rehearsal he had let the orchestra play along without him and had walked to the last row to see whether the echo he heard was as bad as it seemed. Perhaps the audience would deaden it.

Denis' head was clearing, but it ached. He picked up the telephone and ordered a sandwich, some coffee and some fruit. Then he gulped down another drink to steady him and made for the shower. As he turned the water on his telephone rang, but he did not answer. As he was forcing himself to eat it rang again.

"All right?" Clarissa asked, nothing in her voice to indicate there had been a quarrel.

"Fine," he lied. "I'll be ready at ten to eight."

He was. He rode to the auditorium, which appeared to be on the edge of a fair ground, or perhaps an amusement park, with Clarissa, who was quiet but not angry. On the way the car sloshed through puddle after puddle, and the rain drummed on the roof with an insane rhythm which set his nerves jangling.

"Anybody who comes out in this really loves music," he said to Clarissa. And almost as he spoke the rain slackened; when the car drew up before the stage entrance, it was not even drizzling, although drain pipes still were running full. Denis helped Clarissa to the curb, and stepped into a puddle over the tops of his pumps. It couldn't be helped; he could at least wipe out the shoes, and wring out his socks.

"Everything's unexpected in Texas," Clarissa remarked. "We leave the hotel in a cloudburst, and now it's a fine night."

Some people were waiting to see Denis, but Clarissa steered him expertly past the group and into his room. "There," she said. "Take off your pumps and see what you can do."

She's thinking that if I have to get a cold, it's lucky it happened on the last date of the tour, he thought, grinning in spite of himself. His head had felt stuffed up all day, and he felt hot too; he also sensed Clarissa's eyes on him appraisingly. Suddenly she said, "What size socks do you wear?" and when he answered, added, "I'll see what I can do."

It was almost a religious rite by now that he should be alone the last ten minutes before he went on, but this time she violated it. Two minutes before the half hour she rapped, and handed in a pair of black silk socks. "I took them off the head usher," she said, and disappeared. But when he went on, she was standing in the wings and as he passed he kissed her boyishly on the cheek. He did not see her eyes fill, and he could not know that she caught the slight waver in his walk, and said a short prayer of thanks because the podium, according to invariable specifications, was backed by a rail. When he made his abrupt little bow he rested his hands on the rail. And when he turned back to his orchestra he knew that although the dampness would make the going rough for the fiddles and the violas and the rest of the strings, it would be a good concert. He would, by God, make it good if it killed him.

Denis could not remember exactly what happened, no matter how hard he tried. From habit, he straightened as abruptly as he bowed. He pushed himself away from the iron railing, turning as he did so. His arms went up mechanically, and in the second it took to raise them something like an explosion was set off in his mind. After it, he had a feeling entirely new; Denis was as far from a mystic as a young man could possibly be, having neither interest nor experience beyond his own world of knowledge and hard work. Before the explosion he knew and could bring into his mind easily every note of Brahms' "Academic Festival" overture—they were all there, row on row, each with its value and its exact place. He knew also precisely how each note would sound, and what its effect would be.

Yet now, something more than that came to him. If it was possible, he lost the exact picture of the notes and gained in its place an equally exact knowledge of what all the parts of it added up to; instead of an incredible total of small things each meticulously learned, there was now something like a stream of sound in his mind. The stream was made up of the small droplets to be sure, but when they merged they lost their separate identity just as the drops of water in a river lose theirs. And just as the drops of water lose nothing but a separate identity when they merge, so the notes and the rests and the bar lines lost none of their meaning, but became part of a stream of sound which without consciously willing it, Denis was controlling. Controlling utterly.

For a wild moment he wondered whether this was drunkenness, or perhaps a kind of delirium. Then he stopped caring, because what he was doing was too exhilarating, a kind of drunkenness that came from no bottle. He felt wonderful. He wondered whether his men sensed what was happening; indeed, he wondered whether it could have happened with any other group of men, since only this group knew him well enough to know what each small movement of his body meant. He even wondered whether this* great and beautiful feeling could be communicated, or whether it was something subjective —a delicious release and rebirth for him alone. And why it should come in this particular music, which was not music of any great depth.

He rode along on the stream of tone, shaping it at the same time. Little by little still another feeling came back to him from the orchestra, and it told him that the men had sensed something new; at the same time he realized that he was not now trying to hear each separate instrument for itself, but only for its small contribution to the whole. He felt in the back of his mind that if something did go wrong, he would know it, but he no longer felt that he was consciously controlling everything and everybody, holding them tight. He was free, and he had freed his men at the same time. The complications toward the end of the overture were no longer technical problems; there was even emotion in this jocose heartiness.

He released the last chord unwillingly because he felt that this new thing might go at the same time, but before he turned to the audience he looked over the orchestra with a rapt expression in his eyes and applauded them, his hands concealed from the audience. Then he turned to the audience on a great wave of sound, and knew that it had sensed something. He had expected a more or less perfunctory response, and what he got was a sort of bewildered enthusiasm; he brought the orchestra to its feet and bowed first to them, and again to the house. Finally, he stepped back to the podium and began Schumann's "Spring" symphony.

The feeling held through the concert. At intermission he refused to talk even with Clarissa; at the end, when he had built up "Daphnis and Chloe" to a height he never had thought possible, he was suddenly empty. Maybe it is something physical after all he thought, fever or something, for he was also a little dizzy. But if it is, please God give me the same fever again, he asked humbly.

The audience begged for more at the end, and he of course refused; there could be nothing more after the last blazing climax. He returned to the stage again and again, and finally brought the demonstration to an end by signaling the men to follow him off, and ordering the stage lights dimmed. The men surrounded him in the wings for a moment, and one or two tried to speak, but their words were no more effective than his own. Denis smiled at them tiredly, and disappeared into his room. Clarissa was waiting, her discreet make-up streaked with tears. She said nothing until he spoke, and what he said was so matter-of-fact they both laughed.

"I'm drenched, Clarissa," Denis remarked, and she replied, "Here's your dry shirt; I've got your topcoat here, too."

Still grinning, Denis changed; he could hear Gus' voice on the other side of the door, where he stood guard against the mob of congratulators. "Yes," Gus said, "too wonderful to talk about. . . . Yes, incredible. . . . Madam, you've heard one of the finest concerts a conductor ever gave. . . . Yes, madam, he's changing; he'll be ready in a minute."

Denis felt as if he could not bear the usual post-concert scene, and knew at the same time he would get through. His head ached a little, and he was still giddy as he tied his white tie and pulled down the bosom of his shirt. Then he nodded to Clarissa, who opened the door.

Denis woke with a head that seemed hollow except for a billiard ball rolling around inside. But even that did not obscure the memory of what had happened the night before—nor did anything explain it. He lay quiet a moment and tried to think, but it was no good. This was one experience he never could share and never explain, although now he thought it would return. He thought, too, that in the future he would not need to analyze or to share it. This was his alone, whatever it was and however it came to him.

He put out his hand for the telephone and his head throbbed horribly; he had trouble finding the phone, and he gave his breakfast order in a shaking voice.

I can't have a hangover, he thought. Clarissa only made me one hot toddy when we got back to the hotel. His face felt hot and he started for the bath to bathe it.

On the floor just inside the door was an envelope. He bent down to take it and had to help himself back to the perpendicular by holding tight to the doorknob. He carried it to the bath and almost forgot it when he saw himself in the mirror. His hair stood up like a frightwig, which was normal at that hour. But his eyes were shot with red, and a red flush lay under the dark skin and the beard which badly needed a razor. I look awful, he thought, and staggered back to the bed.

The note was from Gus. It said: "When you finally get up I'll have a cup of coffee with you."

Finally? Denis looked at his watch, which read eleven thirty, and then automatically picked up the telephone and asked for Gus.

"Good sleep?" Gus asked laconically. "I'll be up."

Denis' breakfast arrived at the same time as Gus, and the waiter was dispatched for another cup and another pot of coffee.

"You don't look very well," Gus said. "Where's your liquor?"

"In the closet in the sitting room."

Gus poured out a little of Denis' orange juice and filled the glass with bourbon. "Clarissa might not approve, but Dr. Wagner says take it."

Denis felt a little better after he had drunk the juice. But not much. Suddenly he slapped down the glass and looked hard at

Gus. "What time were we supposed to leave for home?" he demanded.

"Nine thirty. The men have gone, and so has Clarissa." Gus smiled at the look of horror on the younger man's face. "Keep your shirt on. I've got a drawing room for you at ten tonight." After a pause, he added, "You damn near cracked up last night."

Denis seemed not to have heard. "Gus. I'll have to fly." The billiard ball rolled unexpectedly from the right to the left side of his head, and he winced. But he ploughed on, "I've got a two-week recording session coming up in three days. I——"

"Shut up." Gus poured himself a cup of coffee and carried it to an armchair. "Eat your eggs if you can."

Mechanically Denis put a forkful of eggs into his mouth, and then made a face. "Tastes awful. . . . Gus, listen. You know I can't miss that session. I've been raising hell for the company to do this and that and they've done practically everything. I can't let them down."

"You won't. I called New York early this morning. It's put off."

Denis was furious, but this time he was more cautious than he had been with Clarissa. He held his voice down. "Gus," he said, "you had absolutely no right to do that without consulting me."

Gus looked straight into Denis' eyes, leaning forward with his cup ready to slide from its saucer. "I've also called the doctor for you. He's late. He promised to be here at twelve and it's a quarter after now."

Unsteadily, Denis buttered a piece of toast and spread a thin layer of strawberry jam over it. He was balanced in a straight chair; he got up and started for his bed, and made it by a hair. "Whew!" he breathed weakly. "Close call—bring me some coffee, Gus."

As he poured the coffee, Gus said quietly, "You're dizzy as hell with fever, you can't walk straight, and you raise hell when I won't let you plunge right into a recording session. Don't be such a fool."

"Then don't treat me like a baby," Denis answered, his voice steady for the moment.

The exchange was ended by the doctor. He was a balding,

businesslike man with no bedside palaver whatever; what was worse from Denis' side of the fence was that he paid no attention at all to his objections. He said coolly that Denis was on the verge of pneumonia, but possibly would escape it. He was also close to a nervous break, and evidently had been driving himself too hard, too long. He could be moved that night, but only if someone went with him. And if his temperature went up he was to leave the train wherever he might be and go to a hospital. He needed rest more than anything else, and these little white pills would insure relaxation. Finally, he must not allow himself to get chilled.

Then the doctor repacked his small brown bag neatly, and collected his fee as efficiently as he had done everything else. He said, "You'll be all right if you rest," and left.

Neither man spoke for a moment after the door closed. Then Gus roared, and Denis joined in rather weakly.

"How'd you like that one around all the time?" he asked, and laughed again. "Here. . . ."

Gus brought a tumbler of water, shook out four of the little pills. "I'll play Florence Nightingale; take these and sleep awhile. I'll go call off my date in Houston and see you later this afternoon." Denis showed signs of balking, and Gus overrode him. "Do what the doctor said, Denis, or I'll call him back."

Denis took the pills.

He was still asleep when Gus came back, and when he finally roused himself and went to the door, he was glad to find that he could walk without so much dizziness. He slipped on a robe, and the two of them went into the sitting room, so bright with the April sun of Texas that Gus turned the blinds to make the place endurable. He was smiling.

"I've been doing a neat kind of dance," he remarked as he sat down, "and I need a drink. Want one?"

Denis nodded. "And some food—some soup and a sandwich."

Gus made the drinks and phoned room service, humming "Home on the Range" when he was not talking. Denis bore the tune well, probably out of respect for President Roosevelt, whose favorite it was supposed to be. But he was sure Gus was leading, very indirectly, up to something important.

"Nice concert, Gus," he said. "What's up?"

But Gus was not quite ready to explain. "Ah, Texas," he apostrophized. "On the map she looks like a skin tacked to a door, but she's wonderful."

"Stop it!" Denis tapped with his glass on the arm of his chair. "You're sending my temperature up."

"Okay. Texas loves you, my boy."

"Were the notices good?"

"What notices? Oh, here? Superb, and they damn well should be—but that's not what I mean. Texas wants to keep you."

"Tell me, Gus," he said. "I'm not up to puzzles this afternoon."

"Houston wants a real orchestra, and you to build it. Dallas has ideas, and wants you to develop them. Isn't it nice?"

"Any other bidders?" Denis was not sure his leg was not being yanked.

"Yes." Gus leaned forward as he usually did when he was serious. "I've had five nibbles, good ones, in the last two months. Aside from the fact that I love you like a son, that's why I don't want you to blow up. You're a good property."

That was all very well, thought Denis. But there is something more. He watched Gus' studiously bland face without speaking, and he was sure he was right. Gus was biting his lower lip, or perhaps licking it. The gesture was not nervous, but anticipatory, the gesture of a child who unexpectedly sees a freshly opened box of candy in his mother's hands. How stupid I am, thought Denis, and asked suddenly, "How's Feodor Solomon doing?"

"Huh?" Gus withdrew his drink from his mouth with faint signs of choking.

"How's Feodor doing?"

"Fine. Just fine. He's a good conductor."

"Better than good. Very fine."

"Okay. Very fine. How'd you like to live down here?"

He can be the most exasperating manager a man ever had, Denis thought, watching Gus savor his lip once again. He said, "I wouldn't. I've got no objection to Texas, but I'm tired of whipping up orchestras like cakes. You know what I want."

"Hum . . ." Gus threw his little game out of the window.

"I'd never sell you down here. But Denis, listen. I've got a real job to sell you to New York. I want you to know I'm starting serious work now." He snapped his head toward the door, where there was a rattling sound. "Took room service long enough," he added.

Denis' face brightened, his hands tensed on the arms of his chair. "How long Gus? And why is it such a job?"

Until the waiter had set up the table and gone they said nothing. Then Gus said, "A year, anyway. And it's tough for a lot of reasons, none connected with your ability. Nobody doubts that."

Even though he had food and at least a little appetite, Denis had to force down his excitement to eat at all. "Then why?" he demanded, his mouth full of food he did not taste.

"You seem a mere baby to some of them. Somebody told certain people about the Blum thing. Somebody else told somebody else you're 'radical' because of the Larrabee House fight. Another kind friend says you're arrogant and bullheaded with the men." Gus chuckled at the expression on Denis' face. "Don't look so woebegone, boy," he added. "I'll probably manage it."

"God—I hope so."

Now's the time to pin him down, Gus decided, and said, "So you see why I want you to behave. Good health. No rows. Sweetness, light, and the Lord's Prayer before every meal."

Barring Gloria, thought Denis, when haven't I behaved? And possibly Cécile; the others have been so transitory that I hardly remember names. He said to Gus, "I'm always good. You know that."

"Have it your way. It isn't true, of course." He uncrossed his legs and walked into the block of sunshine by the window. "You're also a shining target, don't forget. Every conductor in the country but two would like that job, and they're not all gentlemen by a hell of a lot."

The long trip home was broken only at St. Louis where they changed trains. It was hot in the huge old Union Station, but Gus insisted that if Denis took a walk between trains, he must at least carry a topcoat. The walk was abortive, however. The railroad people had of course alerted their passenger agent, who in turn had called the cub reporter who covered the station (among other places) for the *Post-Dispatch*. This young man was impressed by Denis' name, and innocent of all musical knowledge. But he almost pushed Denis and Gus into a stuffy, steamy restaurant and conducted an interview just the same. It was torture for Denis, and two or three times Gus was forced to jump in with both feet to avoid a clash.

Later, when the two of them were snatching a breath of air on the ramp in front of the station Denis sneezed, and blew his nose, and complained sharply.

"Put on that coat," Gus ordered. He touched Denis' forehead. "Hot—we'll go back to the waiting room. And Denis, remember what I said in Dallas? About being a good boy? I meant it."

Hunched in his topcoat, Denis sneezed again and grudgingly nodded. "All right, Gus," he said, "only that boy doesn't know Beethoven from Ferde Grofe."

"The *Post-Dispatch* is a good paper, and the story'll be all right." He looked at his watch. "Thirty minutes more—I want to get you into your berth. You sit here. I'm going to the drugstore."

Denis found that sitting down was welcome; he felt tired and a little dizzy, too, and wished with all his heart that he was in his apartment in the Hampton Park Manor. Then he saw Gus picking his way through small clots of fretful children, a little package in his hand.

"Thermometer," he explained. "Wonder if I should take you to a hospital here. . . ."

Denis stood up, as if to prove he was in control. "Oh, no," he insisted. "Not that. I'll be fine when I get home. I'm just——"

"On the verge of being a damn sick man." Gus frowned. "Well—I'll chance it."

Denis was determined not to show weakness, but determination did him no good. They had not walked fifty feet when his hand reached for Gus' arm, and by the time they were in their drawing room he was leaning heavily on the older man for support. Gus helped him out of his clothes, cursing himself meanwhile for having allowed the interview. "I didn't realize you were so weak, Denis," he said.

Denis nodded. "Just as well, perhaps. Otherwise there might

have been a story that would have made me half dead. Which I'm not." He grinned, but there was not much humor in him, and no fight at all. When he was tucked into his bed Gus produced the thermometer, and he slipped it under his tongue without protest.

"Damn these things," growled Gus as he turned the thermometer under the light. "Why do they make them so hard to read?" He kept muttering even after he had returned it to its box.

Finally Denis interrupted. "What did it say?" He looked sharply at Gus. "Don't lie to me."

Gus shrugged. "A hundred and three. God, I don't know."

"We're going home," Denis said in as strong a voice as he could manage. "Please, Gus."

"All right." And the train started and settled the matter.

At Indianapolis Denis was asleep, but muttering in a series of dreams that seemed uniformly bad. Gus wrote three telegrams and gave them to the porter. As the train started again Denis woke and demanded orange juice, but when a waiter brought it, he found he could not drink it. He tossed all night, with Gus lying, half dressed, on the sofa. It was a bad night for them both, with Denis coming to the surface every hour or so, sometimes delirious, and sometimes so weak he could only just speak. When it was time to get ready for Lakeland, Gus helped his patient into enough clothing for decency, wrapped his dressing gown and topcoat around him, and as the train halted in the oversized Lakeland terminal, Gus and the porter all but carried him off.

If Denis had had strength to produce it, there would have been a violent scene when he saw the wheel chair, flanked by Clarissa and Farrell Clisby; as it was, he merely sank down into it feebly and nodded to the little group. There was an ambulance outside, and that did set the patient off. "I'm not riding in that thing," he said in what he tried to make a firm voice. But again he lacked the strength. He said nothing more until they reached the hospital, and then he shocked Gus badly. "Thanks a lot," Denis whispered. "I'd have had a hard time without you."

Gus patted Denis' shoulder, and swallowed.

For three days Denis was delirious, waking at times only to shiver as if he were trying to shake apart the bones of his body. Finally his fever was reduced; a few days later visitors were allowed. The first was Gus.

"I've made a long visit," Gus said, his back to the window and the rare Lakeland sun. "Longest I ever made you."

"Thanks, Gus," weakly.

"You had us scared." Gus was smiling, but his face was in shadow and Denis could not see it. "I just want to tell you that I've put over everything until fall—recording, everything. No summer dates, no Europe, no nothing but rest."

The measure of Denis' strength was in the fact that he did not protest. "I'll get better fast," was all he said.

"I know you will. Clarissa and Clisby will work with you when you're able—they're both giving up their vacations. And if you get everything settled—those twenty-four radio programs, all that—then you might go to Elisabeth's place for a month or two."

Denis nodded. He was weak, but not in mind. Gus was leading up to something, and now he had reached it.

"I'm going to leave tonight," he went on, "but I've got to say something more. Don't talk—just listen." He cleared his throat, ill at ease. "I've been staying in your place. I didn't exactly snoop—only I found that you're composing again. Looks —well—theatrical."

A slow flush crept over Denis' face. "You did snoop, though."

"We're not going to argue about this. Wouldn't be fair, with you so weak. I just want to say that if you really are working on a musical I'll have something to say later. Maybe——"

"Maybe you shouldn't pry." There was more than a little of the old Denis in the tone.

"I started to say that maybe I shouldn't have mentioned it at all. Only I did." He had not moved from his station before the window, but now he crossed to the bed and rested his hand briefly on Denis' arm. "Son, I'm working hard for you. And I just want you to know that the Symphony Board wouldn't take kindly to your getting mixed up with Tin Pan Alley."

"It won't be that kind of thing," Denis said, stirring nervously in the bed.

"All right. We'll go into it later." Gus smiled. "Now I've got to run along."

"Thanks for everything," said Denis, and in spite of himself, his eyes closed. I must really be weak, he thought as the door closed behind Gus. Then he drifted off into sleep.

26

Denis arrived at Elisabeth's house late in July with a trunkful of scores and no plans excepting that sometime in the summer Terry would probably join him for more work on "Louisiana," behind Gus Wagner's back to be sure. And Claire settled things in a sentence.

"You're thin," she said, standing in the door of his old room at the back of the house as he unpacked. "We're not in Connecticut this summer; Mother wanted to rough it at Cape o'Sands. You're coming to us there."

"It's all settled?" Denis looked up. "You'd better move out of the light. I can see through you."

"You've seen me in a swimming suit. Yes—seriously, Denis, why not?"

"Where in God's name is 'Cape o'Sands'? I never heard of it."

"On Fire Island. It's a kind of poor man's seaside Tuxedo Park. Stuffy, but a gorgeous beach."

"The better to lie upon, my dear." It seemed rather pleasant to have someone order him about, at least if the someone were Claire.

"Room enough?" he asked, and Claire laughed.

"The place sleeps eighteen besides the servants, and do they hate it! You know, they're used to the Connecticut place with all, every one, of the gadgets. This is quite good for Fire Island, but . . ."

It would be quite good enough, Denis knew, and besides Elisabeth lost no servants, ever, due to the fact that she paid them better than anyone else. "As long as I have money, I shall spend it for what I please," she said firmly to the occasional reproachful friend. "Call it spoiling them if you want; it doesn't matter."

So Denis joined the group at Cape o'Sands. Elisabeth's house was enormous, if unplastered. There were three floors and a secret room on the second of the floors which one reached by pushing on a set of bookshelves in a certain way. Then the shelves obligingly retreated, and there was the room. It would sleep two, but never did because no one who deserved suffocation was likely to visit Elisabeth. Steinway's had sent out a piano, which fitted readily enough into a corner of the L-shaped living room, but was too heavy; the back leg went through into Ellen's room and until it was pulled out and the floor shored up, Ellen was mildly hysterical. And the Cape o'Sands chairman called to leave a card, and to make it quite clear that whether or not one played tennis, one paid for the privilege, and that anyone caught buying groceries any place but in the community store would be severely dealt with, and quickly, too.

Claire played tennis indifferently and Denis not at all. Claire swam beautifully, and Denis so badly that people had been known to laugh themselves into tears merely watching the process. But none of it mattered, because all either of them wanted was to be allowed to do nothing. All of Cape o'Sands was on the beach at eleven, soberly dunking, or recovering from something not quite so sober the night before. By twelve thirty, the beach was deserted except quite possibly by Claire and Denis; the Cape o'Sandians were having a pre-luncheon cocktail, or half a dozen of them, either on their verandas overlooking the Atlantic, or in one of the lesser cottages back from the front. These back cottages were occasionally landscaped a little; it seemed to be a point of honor to leave the front houses stark in their sand and dune grass.

At three o'clock the beach crowded up again, children with or without nurses being relatively more numerous, since by then a certain percentage of their parents would have fallen into a bottle or moored themselves alongside a bridge table. But at five there was a second exodus, as if a great gong had rung and there were severe penalties for laggards. Then small agglutinative masses would again gather for cocktails, and dinner would follow sooner if the servants were strict; much later if they were easygoing. Later there was bridge, or one of those games which become endemic in resorts. It was anagrams this summer.

All this left Elisabeth's household quite cool. Since she was the Mrs. McKee ("Darling, she's got millions, simply millions!") ("My dear, Johnny says she's the only person in New York who made huge sums *honestly* in the depression.") ("Well, Mary Jane, she can *afford* to be snotty."), invitations were inevitable, and Elisabeth accepted two or three. She detested bridge, and spelled too badly for anagrams, so the affairs were unsuccessful, and the later invitations were refused.

Elisabeth sailed across Great South Bay once a week and disappeared into New York for a day; sometimes more. She always came back with someone, usually one of her Foundation's protégés. One week end a young bass would fill the neighborhood with his voice, and almost drown the surf. Then it would be two boys who were determined to be the best duo-pianists alive, even if they had to play ten years in saloons to manage it. And a soprano, and a fiddler, and a boy whose strange ambition it was to make a career as an organist. He managed to make Denis' piano sound heavy and organlike, and fascinated Denis hours on end. One Friday it was Naila who arrived with Elisabeth; Denis had never looked at her as a person before, and he was as delighted with her beauty as with her talent.

"What a gorgeous skin," he said to Elisabeth when Naila went upstairs to shower. "Probably she'd resent it, but the only thing I can think of that's the same color is the very best grade of Swiss milk chocolate."

Elisabeth would not smile. She glared at Denis, and then apologized. "I'm not angry with you," she explained. "It's those ghastly women."

"What ghastly women?"

Elisabeth gestured toward the rest of Cape o'Sands, which was easy since her house was in a corner of the preserve. "Stan dropped us at the dock in Bay Shore," she said, "and we got on that awful little tub, *Excalibur* or whatever. Naila was standing against the rail, and I was sitting in a deck chair—I *hope* she didn't hear."

"Hear what, Elizabeth? You're——"

"I know. I'm still angry. The woman next to me leaned over and looked up at Naila, and said, 'I thought all your servants were white, Mrs. McKee.' I was furious!"

"I don't blame you. What did you say?"

"I was more vulgar than she. I'm so ashamed I could die." Her hand closed over Denis'. "I said, very nastily, 'They are. All twelve of them.'"

If Denis had spent thirty minutes working out the least likely thing for her to have said, he could not have approached the reality. His jaw dropped, and then he began laughing. He put down the ice tongs with which he was working toward a Martini for Elisabeth, sat down on the floor at her feet, and howled. "It's so wonderfully un-Elisabethlike," he choked, "it's gorgeous." And went into another paroxysm.

But there was no further incident. Elisabeth's house being where it was, her segment of the sacred sands was also at the end of the strip, and there were no invaders. There was a great deal of music, however, and even though the nights were chill under the wide, cool moon, Elisabeth kept her windows open in the futile hope that someone else might enjoy, or at least be annoyed by, Naila's playing. So far as she could tell, nobody even noticed.

The last week of August, Terry arrived from the South, and the Saturday night before he was due Claire and Denis took off alone for Sis Harris' in Ocean View. They had been there before, though never on a Saturday night, and they knew the requirements. "Long Pants and Shoes on Saturday Night" the sign said. Their jeans were rolled up, but they qualified as long, and each carried loafers to put on at the door. They would be allowed to go out the Cape o'Sands gate, but on the return trip it would be locked, and they would have to walk the beach.

It was dark in Bay Park, which was the scattering little settlement next Cape o'Sands, but the moon was back again and they could see enough. On the right was Great South Bay, gray-shining in the moonlight and limited by the line of lights on distant Long Island. Nothing moved excepting a low cruiser whose running lights drifted by a hundred yards out. On their left there was flat sand grotesquely ornamented with the black smudges of wind-twisted pines and holly and, a quarter of a mile away, the unseen roaring surf.

The walk was narrow, but they managed with care to walk hand in hand. "Watch out for toads," Denis warned. "They're not nice to step on."

"Always the romantic, aren't you?" Claire said, but her voice was gentle.

The remark touched a little lever inside Denis. They stepped off the walk into the sand to let a girl on a bicycle pass, and then he said, "Claire—how do you feel about me?"

"It's not a fair question," she said slowly.

"Yes. Or at least I think it is. Tell me. . . ."

Even in the faint silver-gray light he could see her small gesture of impatience. "I like you," she answered flatly. "I've always liked you, even when I was a—a child and made snide remarks."

"It's odd," he said, and his voice sounded as if he were a little disturbed and even more puzzled. "We used to be together so much, and then things opened up for me, and——"

"You needn't finish. You began eating yourself up, instead of others . . . oh, Denis, that sounded dreadful and I didn't mean to."

He squeezed her hand. "But it's true. I'm not hurt." After a moment he added, "I'm puzzled, I guess. I cracked up this last season, and I've got a worse one ahead."

"And . . ."

"I can't say any more, only there's something after that."

Claire laughed, not the sort of laugh that fills in the chinks of a conversation, but a really merry laugh. "I simply couldn't guess what that is, you know."

He tightened his grip on her hand and turned her toward him. "What do you know?" he demanded. "And how?"

"Gus Wagner thinks you're ripe for the Symphony and he's going to try to sell you to the Board this winter. Mother told me."

"Oh, God! Elisabeth?"

"You're underestimating Mother, Denis. When it's important she can keep a secret, believe me. How do you think she manages her money? By broadcasting everything?"

"I'm sorry. Only Gus was so determined that——"

"He's right. But when he starts working on the Board this fall, it'll be out in ten minutes."

They were in Sea Beach, where on the corners there were lights and people passed them occasionally. "Odd, isn't it," Denis said, "that if I were to say in front of these people 'I'm going to be the next conductor of the Symphony' they probably wouldn't know what I was talking about."

"Don't be so sure, Denis. There are all sorts of people out here—music, theater, even the columnists." And she knew that for the night her moment had passed. She was not too displeased; I'm a fool and probably a hussy, too, she thought, but he did seem to realize I was on earth for a few minutes.

Then they were in Ocean View, where half a block away the Saturday night clatter in Sis Harris' was audible. At the door it was incredible, like the sound of a Childs restaurant being destroyed by tin men from the Land of Oz.

Inside the sounds were louder if possible, but also they began to sort themselves out. A piano was being propelled through an assortment of popular tunes, sometimes two or three at the same time, by a small fellow with very short hair and even shorter shorts. Once in a while he sang, although what he sang was never more than barely audible. There were tables, but a glance made it clear that one could sit down only by sitting on someone else, since there was a dogged expression on all the sitters' faces which meant they were glued to their chairs or their section of table top. The bar closed the far end of the room, a large room. Before it people of all ages and all sexes were jammed four deep, and fringed out from this solid mass were perhaps a hundred people with freedom to move slightly. The long pants rule was disregarded—hardly any legs were hidden, male or female. But shoes were different; shoes were necessary, because glasses were forever being dropped and broken.

Denis grinned at Claire, who grinned back. There was not much use speaking under a shout. And shout Denis did. "Let's fight through to the bar," he bellowed, and Claire nodded and got behind to push if needful. They made the fourth row from the dripping bar after five minutes of hard work. There the head bartender, a dark, round-faced, scholarly looking man behind shining spectacles, discovered them; when Denis shouted, "Two bourbons and water," the information was relayed to the bar by other patrons, the money went in the same way, and presently the drinks and the change were handed back.

Claire and Denis held their station; they would want another drink presently and they had no intention of brawling for it. Claire half screamed, "Thanks, Denis," and raised her glass. Behind her two arguing boys made a sudden movement, and she lost half her drink.

"I don't care," the boy in purple shorts said, "you can't just go back to town and leave me dead broke."

"Oh, Lord, Denis," Claire shouted again, "let's give a little ground. I can't even drink here."

As they inched back a stocky gray-haired man, very like the scholarly bartender except in coloring, caught Claire familiarly by the arm. He leaned close to her ear and demanded authoritatively, "Didn't I hear you say 'Denis,' Miss?"

Claire nodded.

"Denis Sandzen?"

Oh, dear, she thought, I've got Denis into something. But it was useless to pretend, so she nodded again.

The man maneuvered himself into position between them. His head struck a level about halfway between Claire's and Denis'; he wore a tan leather coat in spite of the heat, although his scarlet sport shirt was open over his coat collar. Underneath Denis could see lederhosen worn with the insane little knitted

359

bands around the calves that answer for stockings with some Bavarians. One of these had lost its grip and was slumped around an ankle.

"I'm Josiah Morgan, the producer," the stranger said in a peculiar high tenor that pierced the racket like a stiletto. The sentence was supposed to produce a reaction in Denis, but it did not. Denis had never heard the name. It was Claire who rescued him, if the operation was a rescue.

"How's 'Girls, Girls, Girls' doing this summer?" she asked.

"Wonderful. But it only represents a stage for me, something I had to do. It's not important."

Both Denis and Claire nodded understandingly. The nods pleased Morgan, who returned the compliment. "I'm very musical," he said. "Know a lot. What you want to conduct for when you can play such piano?"

Denis had a fearful desire to say it was none of Morgan's business, but it was simpler to lift one shoulder in a movement that could mean anything.

Morgan suddenly raised his voice, in volume if not in pitch, which last would have been difficult. "Get off that stool, Goony darling. Let a real pianist play."

"Oh, God, no!" Denis caught Morgan's arm. "They don't want my kind of thing."

"Yes they do—and don't get me wrong with my 'darlings.' I'm as masculine as hell. Come on."

Once again it was easier to go along than to make a stand; an odd quiet was beginning to fall as word went 'round. Glasses still clinked and there was still a low hum, but in half a minute the whole room knew what was about to happen, and was waiting for it.

Denis looked desperately at the piano, an old upright which obviously had had too much salt air in its time. He turned to Claire, his eyebrows raised in the center. "The loudest thing you can think of," she said calmly, and he at once plunged into the "Revolutionary" etude. The action was awful; half the left-hand part barely sounded. But there was authority as well as volume, and the room grew still as he went along. When he finished there were cheers and people shouted "encore."

He suddenly remembered Godowsky's "Alt Wien," and played it softly and gently, and with much schmaltz. Again there were shouts, and this time he went back to Chopin and played the A flat polonaise as well as he ever had done; it sounded fresh, not like a spavined old war horse. And it made its effect. Toward the end, Denis was racking his brain for a tune to play with—and thought of one of his own.

It was slow and sinuous, and it breathed the South. It was part of "Louisiana," and when he had played it through once he decided not to do tricks with it after all. He got up and mechanically dropped his abrupt little bow.

"What the hell was that last?" Morgan demanded. "It's—it's haunting, that's the word. Wonderful—what is it?"

"Something I made up," Denis replied shortly.

"Can you make up that kind of tune? Good God, man. You're for me."

Claire glanced at Denis' frown, and announced curtly, before the increasing clatter could drown her out, "I want another drink."

Morgan loosed his voice again. He handed the short-haired pianist a bill. "Get four bourbon and waters, darling," he ordered, and to Denis with no pause, "You're going to do a musical for me. The hell with the long-hair stuff."

No more uncomfortable situation could have been found for Denis. His face darkened and his eyes smoldered. "Look here, Mr. Morgan," he began, "I——"

"Call me Josy. Everybody does."

Denis ignored the interruption. "I have plenty to do. I'm busy. You can't . . ."

Goony was back. He handed Morgan his bill, and delivered the drinks. "Fum, the intellectual bartender, says no dough. Gee, Denis, you certainly can wham those old white teeth."

"Thanks. So can you."

"Go away, Goony. This is business."

"Oh, shut up. I like this guy."

"Like somebody else." Josy inserted himself between Denis and Goony and sailed along as if nothing were happening. "Let's go down by the door, Denis—you too, Miss——"

"McKee," said Claire.

Morgan pushed them along, and when it was apparent at the door that shouting was still necessary, he opened it and commanded, "Go on out. Take your drinks—everybody does."

Morgan spoke to them, but never waited for an answer. He had found a man to do the book and another to do the lyrics before they reached the corner. They turned toward the beach, and within a hundred yards, the sets, costumes and lighting were arranged. Finally Denis felt bound to brake him down.

"Mr. Morgan—Josy," he interrupted loudly, "please let me talk a minute. No matter what you say or do, I won't write a musical for you now. Let's get that clear. If I ever can, I'll let you know."

"Say—I've been thinking," Josy began again. "You didn't just think up that swell tune, dear boy. That tune had been worked on; you can't kid Josy. You've got something already!"

Denis was grateful for the darkness; his face must have told a lot. A second or two passed before he controlled his voice; then he said, almost truculently, "What I said still goes."

"What did you say?" Josy asked sweetly.

Claire said quickly, knowing Denis' temper, "He said that if he ever found time to do a musical he'd get in touch with you."

This was not at all satisfactory, but Denis was as stubborn as Morgan was persistent, and when they parted at the beach the encounter was still a draw. Claire and Denis went down the steps to the sand and turned toward home; as the stubby figure at the head of the steps faded into the moonlight his high voice called, "I'll write you every week until you're ready."

Claire said, "I think he will."

All this was reported next day to Terry, who refused to excite himself.

"Look, Denis," he insisted, "can Morgan, call me Josy, force you to show him 'Louisiana'?"

"Of course not."

"Then what's the trouble? Let him write every day if he feels like it."

"I know." Claire was a little troubled. "But he could talk."

"No," and Terry laughed. "I know him slightly. I interviewed him once down home, and then took him through the Quarter. He may sound as fey as hell, but he isn't. He's too canny to talk, especially if he thinks he's got hold of a good thing."

So the two settled to work, and with Claire they swam and took long walks on the beach, successfully avoiding both anagrams and bridge. But their ease and confidence vanished a week later to the day, when the German who foamed at the mouth when speaking invaded Poland. It seemed to Denis, whose slow movement toward political awareness was nevertheless steady, that his country was now poised at the head of a chute leading down to chaos, and that the push might come from behind at any moment.

Cape o'Sands felt differently about it, felt two ways to be specific.

"Now That Man in the White House will become a dictator and drag us in whether or no," one section said, and the other wondered whether a great boom might not be just around the corner. It was barely possible for the three friends to keep from answering snippets of talk they overheard on the beach—but they did. Then Gus sent a wire asking that Denis phone him, there being no phones in the houses at Cape o'Sands.

Gus laid his cards on the table. He was convinced personally that instead of things getting worse with the Symphony, they would get better. Actually, he was closing with a sponsor for the orchestra's Sunday broadcasts. But, he said, the Board felt differently, and wanted to wait and see. He thought that another year would make little difference, and he was pulling in his outriders and would simply lie low a year.

Denis was disappointed and said so. But he was too used to trusting Gus to dream of objecting. He quickly counted up: a year's delay would still get him in under the wire. If things worked out, he would be thirty-four when the call came, and that was young enough. Even, in a curious way, he was a little relieved. Passing thirty was nothing; he had not noticed. But he had marked the day he first stood before his own orchestra in New York as the end of youth and the beginning of his mature responsibility. He could wait for that.

"He's probably right," Terry agreed when Denis reported.

"And whether he is or not, that's the way it is," remarked Claire.

In the week remaining before Terry must go home and the house must be closed the two finished what Denis called their first draft. "Louisiana" was now as far along as they could take it without help from outside; the night before the piano was to be taken to town Denis played it all the way through, with Terry sketching in everything from the solos to the ballet. There were no guests. Elisabeth lay back on a sofa, and Claire hung over the piano turning the pages of the pasted-up score, rather unnecessarily, since either Denis or Terry could have played it in the dark.

At the end all four applauded, but especially Claire and her mother. Then Elisabeth slipped downstairs to the pantry. Denis said to Claire, "What do you think, honestly?"

"Honest honestly?" she asked, and Denis and Terry both nodded.

"I think you've both done what you wanted. I love the music. And the book makes sense, even with those lyrics."

Terry laughed. "Some of them are frightful," he admitted, and Denis added, "And the music will have to be altered in production I'm sure. But you really think it's got——"

"Flavor," Claire supplied.

"That's all we need to know," and Denis played the Dresden Amen, with inappropriate variations. In the midst of it Elisabeth reappeared from the regions of food and drink with a magnum of very cold champagne and a plate of sandwiches the cook had made after dinner.

"I was terribly depressed, Hitler and everything," she explained, "and now I feel good. Let's celebrate."

A couple of glasses later Claire looked slyly at Denis and said, "Shall I wire Josy to come for dinner tomorrow night?"

"God, no!" Denis caught her throat in his strong hands and pretended to shake her. He released her suddenly and turned to Terry.

"Would it be all right if we let it soak this winter? Do nothing about it?"

"Of course. We'll get some other ideas."

After the last of the champagne was gone, they left Elisabeth and walked to the beach, Claire with an arm about each of the others. The phosphorescence had begun early, and as each long wave broke and tumbled over, its comb glowed as if it were wrapped about a moonbeam and were carrying it to shore. They watched in silence for a long time, and then Terry said, "It's a good omen. It's as good as a rainbow."

"For 'Louisiana,' perhaps," Claire said sadly. "Not for the world."

27

Denis approached the first concert of the season with a curious combination of feelings and fears, all of which grew out of the last concert of his spring tour.

That day in Texas he had learned a lesson, which was that he was not inexhaustible. He had yielded enough to spend the easiest summer of his life restoring himself; it would have been impossible for him to have loafed, but at least he undertook no extra engagements, and the work he did was on "Louisiana" with Terry, and he enjoyed it.

Now, in rebellion once again against what he had learned, he forced himself into a still tighter schedule for the new season—in addition to the regular concerts and his full share of the pops, there was now a Sunday radio concert which was sponsored. He was conducting all twenty-four of these, and the programs were not easy repetitions of music rehearsed for the regular concerts. And there was an audience. Lister Hall was filled each Sunday by people who paid nothing, and in many cases could not have paid.

The other lesson from Texas was different. Denis was not afraid of what might happen at the first concert, because he knew that if his flight into perfection that spring was merely a combination of fever and fatigue, he still was the same conductor as before and his performance would still be first-rate. But he hoped—he desperately wanted once more to feel himself riding the same stream of tone, shaping and controlling it, and communicating something more than a beautifully thought out and expertly reproduced performance. To give himself every chance, he scheduled exactly the same program, and thought about it so much that he was not far from the same state of mind when he went on. He made his bow, he turned to the men quickly, holding his breath as he did so. His arms went up, and then so did his spirit. For once again he felt as he had felt months before—that his knowledge and skill had somehow been transmuted into an emotion he, his men and his audience shared equally; that all the thousands of details had at last come together for their final purpose through him.

Now he was not ill. He even could stand a little outside the event and appraise it. He could see the men yield to the flow of the music, and he thought that behind him he felt the tightening of emotion in the audience. He did not much care if all the audience understood what was being given it; most of it might better enjoy than think, for Clarissa in her box, done up for the opening in all her diamonds, would know. So would Harry Gordon, and John Dudley, and Farrell Clisby. He hoped very much that they would not try to tell him later what it all meant, so much that when once more the incredible climax of "Daphnis and Chloe" lifted the audience to its feet, he considered slipping out alone. But of course he did not, and the only remark he remembered later was Clarissa's.

"It can happen again," she said, and shuddered briefly as if a shock had again run through her.

In the next weeks Clarissa changed a little. Not in any formal sense; she merely, Denis felt, was trying to preserve what the town now had in him. It sometimes amused Denis to see her making things as easy for him as possible, because she still did not know that things could never be made easy for him, and that he did not want them that way. Such as the business of the assistant conductor, now a more shadowy figure than ever. Denis saw him in a business way only, and Dattner hung around the edges the rest of the time like an ambulance-chasing lawyer hoping for a juicy break. Clarissa spoke one day when they were alone in his office in the late afternoon, sorting out a tall stack of scores and throwing some away.

"Why don't you give Dattner some sort of break?" she asked directly.

"I do." Denis was sitting on his haunches in the corner; he looked up at her, grinning. "He gets his pair of concerts when I'm on vacation, and part of the pops."

"Your hair's full of cobwebs," she replied tangentially.

"Wait until I catch the janitor."

"Please don't larrup him. I ordered him never to touch this corner."

"Well! You know you could use him more."

"Dattner or the janitor?" Denis dumped an armload of tattered scores into his wastebasket and returned to the corner. "Dattner can't conduct," he said coolly.

She picked up a heavy chair and carried it to him. "Please don't squat that way; you'll break your back. And he can conduct. God knows not like you, but he could save you a lot."

Denis ran his fingers through his hair and combed out the cobwebs. "Clarissa dear," he said, "don't you know I don't want to be saved?"

She laughed, and gave up. But she remembered what he said a few days later when he returned her call, this time under pressure of a new idea. He would like, if the next season were to be his last, to make it a very special season. But of course he could not tell her his reason.

"Which season will the one after this be?" he asked. "For me, that is."

"Your eighth. Why?"

"Oh. I thought it might be my tenth." He counted on his fingers. "No, of course not. It doesn't matter."

"Stop being enigmatic. What's on your mind?"

"I just felt like making it something unusual. Sort of special."

Experience prompted her. "How expensive?"

"Cheap. Look—let's do it. I want to make it a—a festival of the old and the new." His face brightened and his voice grew eager. "One half of every program from the classics, the other modern. Nothing earlier than, say, 'Petroushka.'"

"A lot of work, don't you think?"

Denis shook his head firmly. "No more than usual. Look, I'd do all nine of the Beethoven symphonies, the five piano concertos, the fiddle concerto, the four Brahms symphonies, the two piano concertos, the fiddle concerto, the double concerto —how many's that?"

"Twenty-three."

"And maybe the Brahms Requiem. That's the classic half right there and I know everything except the Requiem." He thought a few seconds. "I'd love to do more. That's the trouble; there's never enough time."

Clarissa tapped away with her letter opener. Finally she said, "Fine. Only fill in with Mozart and the rest of them. It could be too much of a good thing."

It was decided, and Denis left the office wondering whether Clarissa's odd clairvoyance had told her the real reason for a festival of any kind in that particular season. If it had, she gave no sign. And with the current season and the radio concerts and all the rest of it, Denis had no time to worry. It was a good and a rich season; it was a time for maturing. When at Christmas the "Messiah" came up he asked Elisabeth and Claire to come to Lakeland and they did; as he led the chorus—not so good a chorus as Gutenborg but again not so set in its ways —into "And the Glory of the Lord," he turned toward Clarissa's box to catch a glimpse of Elisabeth. She was applauding silently and circumspectly in memory of another time and another place. And Claire blew him a kiss.

At the end of the season there was "Traviata." Before the performance a number of people, including Nathan Snedeker, asked "Why Verdi?" And Denis invariably answered, "Because he was a great composer, one of the very great."

"Oh, now, really!" said the critic.

"Yes, really," Denis answered. "Don't you think so?"

Snedeker did not think so. Somewhere he had read that Verdi, excepting perhaps in his last operas, was a barrel-organ composer and he reproduced this statement with the smug pride of a robin laying a speckled blue egg.

Oh, Lord, Denis thought, somewhere in my past I've acquired a tendency toward temporizing; I'd love to macerate him. What he actually said was, "Like Schubert?"

"Of course not." Snedeker pulled his nose, which already was quite long enough. "Schubert was the greatest melodist who ever lived."

"Or the most copious. Listen to my 'Traviata.' You're used to hearing Verdi cut up to suit the lung capacity of a lot of half-trained singers. I'm going to give him a chance."

That was exactly what happened, and once again Elisabeth and Claire were on hand to listen, and they heard in addition to "Traviata" the first speech Denis ever had made in Lister Hall. He made it gracefully, but with trepidation; he believed it was no part of a conductor's job to harangue his audience, even when it misbehaved, and certainly this was a well-behaved audience. Every white kid glove in the house, and there were many, was mint-fresh. No one chewed gum, no one was late even, since Lakeland had learned years back that being late meant standing in Lister Hall's impressively uncomfortable foyer until the first intermission, no matter how large one's contribution to the endowment fund had been. Said Denis:

"Forgive me for stepping out of character. I want you to know that you will not hear the sort of 'Traviata' you heard when the Metropolitan Opera was here last. That was a good performance, but it was a show. Tonight there will be only music—no show." Then he looked pleasantly at the soloists, smiled at the chorus, gave the orchestra a strangely conspiratorial look. And began.

For the first, and very likely the last, time Lakeland heard the old work as pure music. Nothing was slighted; at rehearsal Denis had forced the soprano, a tiny little Frenchwoman who had never bothered to learn proper English, to start her "Sempre libera" fourteen times, until she was singing every note instead of skimming over them with pretty gestures. He also forced her to buy herself another gown. He had learned from Clarissa that she proposed to appear in a hoop skirt and spun-candy hat, which would have made her look exactly like the dolls under which middle-grade prostitutes hide their telephones.

Nor did the tenor sob unless the score called for a sob, nor did the bass-baritone slide from note to note like a child on a Christmas sled. Everything was clean and up to time, and something came out of it that brought tears to a good many eyes. At the end Denis had the impression that most of the white kid gloves had been pulled off, judging by the sound of the applause. From far back in the balcony came a whistle, and he knew who sent it to him. It was a boy from Larrabee House, too black ever to sing at the Metropolitan, and perhaps too good.

Harry Gordon was a little over the edge, but not in the sloppy stage. He sat now, pounding the arm of the sofa, reviewing events abroad, damning and redamning the man responsible for it all—"not, goddam it, because I'm a Jew. Because I'm human."

Gloria patted his clenched fist. "That's enough for now," she said quietly. "Let's relax."

Claire was watching her, speculatively. Claire remembered a remark she once had made, and was ashamed of it. Now she could admit it was made from pure jealousy, and she looked about to find a way to make it up. This curious little woman was growing, too, Claire thought, perhaps faster than any of the others in the big Blitzstein-but-not-too-Blitzstein drawing room. She saw Harry look up and smile, and heard him say, "All right. Maybe part of it's relief about Denis."

Gloria frowned. "Don't let him hear you say things like that. He burned off fifteen or twenty pounds, but——"

"But he's really all right," Claire broke in. She sat on the floor with her back against the enormous coffee table, looking up at the Gordons.

"He's all right in most ways." Harry reached for his glass a little unsteadily, and Claire handed it to him. "You know what he's kidded me into doing? No?"

"No." Claire smiled at Gloria and could find no trace of annoyance in her answering smile. "What might it be?"

Harry's delight in releasing a secret was boyish, if also a little alcoholic. "He's made me promise to insist on Hans Mayor for the month he's away—I mean Denis is away—next season. I didn't want to. Mayor's a whale of a conductor, but he's mean to the men."

In spite of herself, Claire laughed. "Meaner than Denis?" she asked.

Harry's fist came down on the sofa again. "Denis isn't mean. That's not fair."

"I know. It wasn't fair." Claire was entirely serious again. "He's——"

"Incorruptible," Gloria supplied suddenly, and both the others nodded. "Personally, I think it's a good thing. For the orchestra, I mean."

Denis appeared and dropped down beside Claire, and took her hand. "You wouldn't be talking about me, would you?" he asked.

Claire nodded. "We've agreed that having Hans next season will be good for the orchestra." She gently squeezed his hand. "Also, in case you didn't start your eavesdropping soon enough, Harry said he was celebrating the way you got through the season."

"Sharp-tongued, isn't she?" Denis asked, glancing at Gloria. His free hand stole briefly to the scar; he would not have admitted it for two orchestras of his own in New York, but the flickering little aches were there. All at once he abandoned his iron-man pose, and said almost shyly, "Tonight was tough. I was ready to pistol-whip that woman over by the piano." And he nodded toward the soprano, who looked as if she might sing at any moment even without much urging.

"Always the perfectionist," Claire said lightly. "Actually she was very good."

Denis grinned. "Yes. But she thought she had me over a barrel—you know, hanging onto the high one after 'Ah, fors' è lui.' I fooled her; I just left her hanging."

"Denis!" Clarissa bent over the two on the floor as far as her girdle would allow. "That woman wants to sing. Please play for her."

He looked up with a grin. "She doesn't want me to play. She's afraid of me. You do it."

Clarissa's idea of proper poise would allow her only a tight little smile, but she bestowed that on her conductor. "She probably will sing the 'Marseillaise'; she's been lecturing on the war and how France is to be next to go, and so forth."

"She's also probably right," Harry volunteered. "Damn it."

Denis got slowly to his feet. "It's my duty," he declaimed dramatically. "But I'm damned if I play 'Funiculi-Funicula.'"

They laughed, but the laugh faded shortly. Harry slumped down in the sofa, and caught Clarissa's eye. He patted the place beside him. "Come here," he said quietly. "We've got some planning to do."

"Yes?"

"Absolutely. They're going to have selective service all over again, and Denis is probably young enough to register."

Gloria had drifted away into her duties as hostess; only Claire was left still sitting on the floor before them.

"Would they take him?" Clarissa asked. "And anyway, it may not happen for a long time."

Harry beckoned and the houseman took his extended glass. "It'll probably happen this fall, they tell me in Washington. And then it probably would be quite a time before men were actually called up. What I mean is that he might get the fever and join up."

"If he does it won't be aviation," Clarissa said with determined lightness. She won a small smile from Harry. For a while the two listened to the soprano, who miraculously had changed from her white gown to the hoop-skirted horror Denis had banished. She had also retrieved her hat, and as she sang little gobbets of tulle and clusters of pink rosebuds shivered. She was singing "Lo Here the Gentle Lark," and Denis was forcing her to sing it in exact time. Under cover of the extremely polite applause that followed Harry retrieved his full glass, and said, "I've just got a feeling, Clarissa, that sometime next season something will happen. That's all. Just a feeling."

28

Although Harry knew nothing about it, something began to happen within the week. Not a great deal, but something which started a chain reaction extending through the summer and fall, leading to certain talks between Clarissa and Hans Mayor, between Clarissa and Gus Wagner, finally between Clarissa and Harry.

Two days after "Traviata" ended the season, Denis asked Clarissa to stop by the Hampton Park Manor for lunch. He was downtown when he called, sitting for still more pictures because he had been forced to it; he still felt it was ridiculous that anyone should cherish his picture. Since the bearded White Russian who was taking the pictures spent more time running about the studio on his points than at the camera, the sitting was delayed.

Clarissa arrived exactly at twelve o'clock, which was when she had been asked to arrive. She parked her car in a forbidden area, gave the doorman a dollar, and sailed across the lobby to the desk.

"Has Mr. Sandzen come in yet?" she asked, and was told he had not. "Then let me have a key. I'd rather wait upstairs."

The clerk would no more have thought of refusing than of appearing for his trick at the desk without his trousers, and Clarissa took the elevator upstairs. She did not need the key; the door was open and the maid was just finishing her dusting.

"Good morning," Clarissa intoned. "I'm Mrs. Garfield."

"Oh, yes, Mrs. Garfield." The maid seemed to want to say more, and finally did. "May I just take a look at the kitchen before I go?"

"Of course." Clarissa seated herself on the sofa and picked up the morning paper. She watched the woman over the top of the paper; there was something in the dumpy figure with the thick legs that stirred her memory. When she disappeared into the kitchen, Clarissa looked back at the paper, and then put it down abruptly. The maid was singing, not under her breath but almost full voice. And the song was lovely—not precisely a popular song, but not an art song either. It had a warm melody, rather a Southern melody, Clarissa thought. The maid stopped her song, and came back into the room.

"What was that you were singing?" Clarissa asked. "It was lovely."

"Something Mr. Sandzen wrote," the woman answered, and then suddenly put her hand to her mouth. "I shouldn't have looked, I guess. I'm sorry."

Clarissa was puzzled. "Did he play it for you?" she asked, and before the woman could answer, "And who are you, anyway? You look familiar."

She answered in reverse order. "I'm Mary Roland. And he didn't play it, at least for me. I—here, look, it's on the piano."

"Good God," said Clarissa. "Not Mary Roland? You sang beautifully. Years ago."

The maid nodded. She looked down at herself before she replied. "I don't look so good now. Too much booze," she said in the flat voice she might have used to order a half-dozen bananas. "Oh, well . . ."

Shaking her head, Clarissa followed her to the piano. The considerably corrected, very untidy score of "Louisiana" lay closed on the tail; Mary Roland opened it and pointed with a small, fat and by no means clean hand.

"Well, well," Clarissa said. "Imagine!" Then she turned back to the maid. "I'm sorry you've had trouble. I do remember you —oh—from twenty years back. You had the loveliest voice in town then."

But Mary was not asking for sympathy; she seemed as anxious to go as she had been to stay in the first place. "I asked for it," she said briefly. "Now I'm late, so please excuse me."

Clarissa waited until the door closed and with an almost

Russian air of conspiracy crossed to it and looked down the hall through the peephole. Only the maid was in sight; she returned quickly to the piano and began running through the score. Then she closed the book and slowly crossed to the window by Denis' desk and stared down into the little park with eyes that saw nothing, at least nothing external. She stood tapping with her left hand on the desk, and when she turned away from the window she stumbled on the wastebasket and it overturned.

The first intervention of fate was Denis' delay. The second was Mary Roland. And the third was the fact that the only paper that fell out of the basket was the latest of Josiah Morgan's letters, the latest of dozens. Clarissa read it without the smallest hesitation. "Dear Denis," it began and she thought, so he calls my boy "Denis."

"This is the thirty-second letter of the series, and please don't answer unless you're ready to proceed with the show," it read, and was signed, "Love, Josy."

He simply can't do it, she thought, dropping the letter into the basket. After all that's happened, he simply can't. The Board would never stand for it. But she was fair, according to her lights. He's written some lovely tunes, she conceded. Really beautiful. Then she heard the distant bang of the elevator door and quickly got back to the sofa and opened the paper. There was nothing in her manner to rouse suspicion when Denis stormed in.

"Get any good ones, do you think?" she asked quietly.

"How would I know? That nancy little fool spent all the time dancing around the place."

She chuckled. "But he's good."

"I'll bet he's got no chin at all under that beard. And it's going to rain."

"We'll eat here. Get me one drink, that's a good boy."

He looked keenly at her; there was a tiny false note somewhere, but what caused it he could not have said. They had their drink and ordered up food and talked programs until four o'clock. Then Clarissa went straight to her office and put in a call for Josiah Morgan. For of course she knew him, just as she knew practically everyone else in New York. Denis still was amazed when they went to the Metropolitan Opera together to find that Clarissa knew more people in the audience than he did in the entire United States of America, including its overseas possessions.

"Josy, this is Clarissa Garfield," she said abruptly when the call went through. "I want you to keep your hands off Denis Sandzen."

"Darling! How wonderful! How did you happen to call me?"

"Oh, hush. You heard me and I mean it. I want you to keep your hands off Denis. No musical comedies."

The darling phase slipped off and Morgan said quite coldly, "Whose business is this, anyway? And who talked?"

"That's more like it." Clarissa's color rose but her voice did not. "Nobody talked. I happened to get wind of something entirely by chance."

"I promise nothing whatever. Understand me, Clarissa, I can't do a damn thing until he's ready, and when he's ready I'll go ahead over your prostrate body. I won't even see your prostrate body."

Clarissa made a sound which impressed Josy as laughter, although it was less than that. "And suppose I do some talking to some of your friends?"

"What would your conductor think about that?"

Touché, thought Clarissa, but she said gently, "What if he didn't know, Josy? He needn't."

Josy was far too shrewd to miss the flaw in that, but he also wanted no leaks. Denis was, he was sure, a man of his word. But it just might be made to appear that it was Josiah Morgan who had talked, and that would never do. He made imitation laughter, and pretended to make a concession as well. "Suppose we leave it this way, Clarissa darling. Suppose I say I'll do nothing as long as he's your boy." A little nastily he added, "He won't stay in Lakeland forever. Nobody could but you."

I'd like to slit his high tenor voice box, she thought, but she gave no sign of temper. "I want your solemn promise, Josy. I'll play fair if you will."

"Done. Darling, it was wonderful to talk with you. Give my love to all the better people."

Clarissa hung up without answering. And in New York Josy sat frowning for a moment, and then looked at his watch. A quarter of five. His piercing tenor rose almost to a mooselike trumpeting: "Get me a compartment on the Lakeland Limited for tonight," he ordered, and from the outer office his girl shouted back, "What with?"

"Bribe somebody; there's always space."

Josy slept well on the train; he always did. Until he dropped off he thought of nothing, or rather nothing that had to do with his mission. He had no dreams, and when next morning he had forced himself into a taxicab with three other men he was still in a passive state. At the Slater he was lucky, as usual. And when he had sent the boy away and made ready to shave, he at last brought his mind around to Denis.

If I telephone he'll probably be busy, Josy thought, looking out over lower buildings to the gray lake, on the flat surface of which only a long ore boat moved. He'll hide, that's what he'll do. He looked at his watch: a quarter to nine. Then he quickly shaved and bribed the doorman heavily enough to get a taxi to himself. He caught Denis off guard, just as he expected.

"Darling!" he cried as Denis opened his door. He walked in uninvited and inventoried the room with one long glance. "Who was that apparition I passed in the hall? Something out of Jane Austen by a scarecrow?"

In spite of himself Denis laughed. "My next-door neighbor. She's a lawyer."

"I wouldn't trust her. Now look . . . Clarissa . . . had your breakfast?"

"One thing at a time. What about Clarissa?"

Josy shook his head. "Let's start at the other end. I forgot to eat breakfast."

"All right. Wait until I get a jacket—it'll be quicker downstairs."

The moment they were seated Josy returned to Clarissa. "She knows," he declared, emphasizing the second word heavily.

"She called me yesterday in New York. How does she know?"

Denis had no idea and said so. "What did she say?" he added.

"She wants me to lay off. Says the show would ruin you out here." He paused long enough to order. "What she meant was that it would ruin you for her purposes. And she's probably wrong."

Even while he was saying, "She might be right," Denis was examining himself. He thought, Not so long ago this would just have made me furious. Perhaps—perhaps I'm learning.

"Oh, nonsense. Why would it ruin you here? And what if it did?"

"First answer: because the orchestra board would probably think something like 'Louisiana' undignified for a symphony conductor. Second answer: I expect to keep on being the best symphony conductor I can."

Josy seemed to be vacantly staring out of the window. "That church with the green helmet is positively weird," he said absently, and turned sharply back to his host. "Do I have to mollify your goddam board to get that music?"

"Of course not." Denis thought a moment. "I may not always be here," he added.

Josy was very far from a fool. He knew Denis had been years in Lakeland and that he hated it. Hated the town, that is. He knew his manager was Gus Wagner, who strangely combined honesty with a bright eye for the main chance. And he knew that Feodor Solomon was not secure with the Symphony in New York; Josy was not lying when he claimed to be musical, even though he took music through his pores rather than through his mind. Absently, he remarked, "Why would they put a German helmet on a church?"

Denis merely looked at his guest, whose agate-bright blue eyes remained fixed a few seconds longer on the offending church, and then returned sharply to Denis.

"When are you expecting to go to New York?" he demanded. "Next season?"

Most of Denis' intuition went into his music; he was not ready for the question. He said, "No."

378

"Then the season after—nineteen forty-one and forty-two. Look"—and he swept dishes and silver aside and leaned across the table—"let's make a deal. Let's take next winter to work out the musical—I call it that because you don't have a name for the kind of thing it is." He raised a hand to keep Denis from breaking in, and the waiter at once approached, and was shooed away. "I'll get someone to work with you this summer . . . a play doctor chap, sort of. Then . . ."

Denis at last stopped him. "You'll do nothing of the sort. I've got a heavy season to prepare, and I've promised to do a special kind of cantata for Larrabee House when they open their new building, and I had a tough time a year ago and spent a lot of time in bed. I'll be damned if I'll take on anything more. I'm going to have a little rest, and nothing you can say will change my mind." He finished with a sharp blow to the table that landed in his butter plate; wiping his hand with his napkin considerably weakened the force of his speech.

"Still—well, I guess you mean it." Josy's round, busy eyes filmed over for a moment, and then brightened. "We'll manage it during your season."

Denis snapped, "No we won't. What little free time I have will go to Larrabee House. That's absolutely out."

"Hard to get along with, aren't you?"

"No. I'll make you a proposition. If you'll let me alone, Josy, I'll work on the thing next January on my vacation. Not a day sooner. All right?"

The stocky little man seemed to light up, like a neon sign turned on at dusk. His voice rose. "Darling," he said, "of course. Now you're being your*self!*" And he did not notice the heads turning toward him, as he bounced a little in his chair from joy.

That night Denis wrote two letters, alone in his office in Lister Hall. Not even Clarissa was about, only the watchman in his glass cage at the motor entrance. Denis smiled wryly as he switched on the light and the dark and somehow elegant furniture came to life; he might take over his ambition season after next, but he would have no such office as this. As a matter of plain fact, he would have no office at all in Carnegie Hall, because the band he was determined to make the best in the world was only a renter. It had no home of its own. It had only a schedule, and a brutal one: always three concerts a week and many weeks four.

The first letter was to Claire, the second to Terry. He explained what he had promised, and why. The letter to Terry was easy to write, because their relationship had been stable for a long time, now. But Claire was different, and he did not know exactly how different. Except in the summer, he saw her rarely and thought of her often. But again, he did not quite know how he thought about her. She had always been a friend, his best woman friend after Elisabeth. He knew that he had somehow failed her. Selfishly failed, too, because the thing that had filled the space Claire might have filled was a part of himself; sometimes when he was alone and not too pleased with himself he could admit that his relationship with himself was almost a form of incest. He had always put his ambition back into whatever void existed in him—and he still did. But perhaps not so much the last year or two.

He read Claire's letter over when he finished. He did not write very well, but perhaps, he thought, this letter was warmer. Perhaps, after he was established in New York, he could take out his ambition, lift it out bodily, and there would be room for Claire. Denis sealed the letter, still not comfortable, and dropped it along with Terry's into the post box on Mather Street. Then he went back to his apartment and worked at the piano until eleven, worked with a kind of daemonic possession that would have got him tossed out of the building if he had not been Denis Sandzen. But it was the relief his mind needed, and as he worked, he was thankful that if he had made a prison for himself, it was a prison of music. He had no idea of being philosophical, but it occurred to him as he forced himself to play the last movement of the Schumann concerto very slowly and with enormous care, that what came to him out of the rich indefiniteness of music was something very definite indeed; that perhaps this feeling of inner rightness never could be produced by either an art or a science which worked with things having a prescribed meaning of their own.

Josy had bribed himself onto the Lakeland Limited again, through the mediation of the transportation desk at the Slater. He was in a bedroom this time, and noted with malice that two other bedrooms were vacant—bought by the Pullman conductor for resale, and there was no resale. This discovery made Josy so happy that he went back to the club car and ordered himself a nightcap.

The train was somewhere in the small chimney of Pennsylvania which reaches up to Lake Erie when Josy noticed that he was on his third nightcap, and a little the worse for it. But he was very happy, and when the girl across the aisle smiled at him, he smiled back, and when she glanced meaningfully at the empty chair beside her, he accepted the invitation and moved across. He bought another drink.

The girl's name was Buzard, Tessie Buzard, although when the name appeared on theater programs under the heading "Ladies of the Ensemble" the Tessie became Teresa. And when certain members of her circle spoke of her, they failed to accent the last syllable. She looked a little familiar to Josy, and he was just about to say so when she opened her large, free-floating mouth and said in a voice too small for it, "You've seen me before. I was in 'Girls, Girls, Girls.'"

"Of course." Josy had not only seen her; he had helped pick her out of several hundred applicants. "Why aren't you on the road with the show?"

"I got married." She was the buddy type; now she leaned over Josy and added, "And I changed to a blonde."

"So you did."

"Aw—you didn't remember that. Anyway, the marriage didn't last. So the hell with Kokomo, and back to Broadway."

Josy could hardly have explained why Tessie was so amusing, unless it might have been the liquor he was drinking that did it. But she was. He glanced at her again, his eyes sparkling. She was the perfect showgirl type, legs a little too flanky and a little too long, breasts a little too large, face a little too standard, clothes a shade more emphatic than necessary. But the face would take make-up wonderfully, and in proper undress and seen in perspective on the stage, Tessie would be a knockout.

Definitely. He ordered still another drink, which made five for him and he had no idea how many for Tessie, who showed no effect whatever.

"You look like you'd just eaten a canary," Tessie said suddenly. "It's not coming into money, because you've got pots."

Josy was really not money-proud, but still it always gave him pleasure to be known as a man of substance who could stage a flop (several flops in a row, even) and never feel it. He answered softly, for him, "I'm happy. Something good."

The train was chuffing busily out of Erie, toward the citizens of which city Josy felt a rosy, warm glow. These were not peasants, as so many of his confreres insisted. These were people who sometimes came to New York and bought theater tickets. Bless them.

And Tessie was thinking, So I've got a nice little nest egg; so what's wrong with another job? So maybe another guy from Kokomo, or Wichita? She focused her slightly blurred personality on Josy and beamed, "New show, I bet. Maybe a place for little me?"

"Not quite yet. It'll be a long time." Even two days later when things had happened, Josy could not invent a good reason for having spilled the whole story to Tessie, though he tried. It was of course Tessie, because he talked with no one else about Denis—he was sure of that. Actually, he had very little memory of Tessie, which was a blessing because Josy usually drank very little and he had a frightening head next morning and went nowhere and saw no one all day. This, too, was a severe strain, because seeing people was the backbone of his life.

There can be peculiar props to virtue. When the blow fell, Josy shuddered a shudder that would have been visible in the dollar-eighty seats, and at last remembered the final moments with Tessie clearly. Around Buffalo, or in any case around midnight when the train was standing still and walking was easier, Tessie had gone through the train with him. At the door of his room she stopped.

"Got a li'le bo'le?" she asked in curiously contracted English. "Nightcap?"

"Going t'bed," he announced, and he remembered that he said it firmly. He was pretty sure he added, "Don' get me wrong. Psychiatrist says I've got the malest reactions any man he knows."

And he was pretty sure she added, "Horsefeathers."

It was Tessie who upset the cart. It came about this way, although Josy never bothered to figure things; he was too busy bailing himself out to do research.

Tessie had no reservation, and hotel space was hard come by even then. So when the train docked at Grand Central she euchred a cab out of the clutches of two salesmen and set out for Christopher Street, the end which almost but not quite reaches the North River. Over a storeroom Tessie's one close friend shared an apartment with a friend of his. Her friend's name was Clarence Hopkins, but he was known in every Times Square drugstore as Goldie, even when his hair was brown as it was this spring. Goldie's friend was a very tall and thin and vigorous chap who had started out to be a ballet dancer and had wound up working for what he monotonously called the Agglomerated Press, whenever he mentioned the organization, which was often. When at nine o'clock Tessie arrived and yoo-hooed at their door, they were still in bed.

"Who the hell is it?" Goldie called, and a distant voice said, "Tessie. Let my hangover in, damn it."

This was done, without much enthusiasm. "Where the hell is your husband?" Goldie demanded, a bath towel very imperfectly concealing what was probably the best body of any working chorus man in New York.

"I should know." Tessie was lugging in her two bags. "We split."

"Got any dough?"

"Loaded. I settled for cash."

"Hooray!" Goldie raised his voice. "Donny! We eat—Tessie's loaded." He turned back to Tessie. "You go make coffee while I cover the body beautiful."

At breakfast, what there was of it, Tessie continued her story. "And," she said portentously, "you'll never guess who I got drunk with last night."

"Oh, God," Donny groaned. "Guessing games, yet."

"Josy Morgan. So help me. And I bet I get something out of it—maybe even a few lines."

Then she spilled everything, which might have meant nothing, only when Donny went on duty late that afternoon he rode up in the elevator with the Agglomerated Press' Broadway man who was short, very short of copy at this tag end of the season. And Donny passed on what he had heard. "First symphony conductor ever wrote a musical," he finished.

Probably it was that line that finally bound things up. The Agglomerated, along with every other news organization in America, doted on first times. It made very little difference whether a man was the first to swallow a live goldfish or the first to discover a sure cure for the common cold. The Broadway man tried to check the story, and failed. Josy had dragged himself out to somebody's cocktail party in spite of his agony, and his man had no idea when he would get back. Josy's office was closed. And the man took a chance.

It was the "first symphony conductor to write a musical" line that lifted the item out of the theater notes and into the news columns of the morning papers all over a jittery country prowled by soon-to-be America Firsters and Ex-Liberty Leaguers. Denis was well known, and so was Josy, so the item was even amplified in a good many papers, and on the first page quite often.

Denis heard about it at eleven o'clock on the night after Josy's visit. It was Greene who called, and there was a certain sound of hurt in his voice.

"How come," he asked, "you don't tell your old friends first?"

Then Denis lost his temper. He rawhided Josy, the Agglomerated, the theater. He demanded that Greene kill the story. And when he finally ran down, Greene asked gently, "But is it true?"

"Yes," Denis admitted sadly, and explained everything that had happened. "You see why I can't have this published," he finished. And there were reasons beyond the obvious one which he did not mention.

Greene thought a few seconds and then said, "Look, Denis,

you're hooked. I'm perfectly willing to print this piece and follow it with a denial from you. But the damage is done anyway; even if I could get the wire service to put out a denial for you, it would be too late for the rest of the country. They'd have to talk to you, and clear through New York, and meantime paper after paper would have been put to bed. You're hooked."

It was Denis' turn to pause; when at last he answered he made history—for himself. Because he did not this time hide behind anyone, not Clarissa and not Harry Gordon. Not even Gus Wagner, whose business it was to shelter clients whenever they needed a windbreak.

"Publish the story as you read it to me," he said, "and I won't deny it. But I want to hedge a little, Greene. Let me say that I have had a conference with Morgan about producing a kind of—of folk opera I'm working on. But we are still just talking. Will you do that?"

"You bet I will."

Then Denis called Clarissa and Harry. He told them what he had done, and each accepted it in his own way. Clarissa suffered a stab of guilt; this was her fault in a way, though it was still more Josy's. And Harry's offer of support came through a haze of hurt that surprised Denis. He had played some of his tunes at the Gordons, and vaguely they knew what was up, and that it was a long way off. At least Denis thought they did. But now Harry acted as if something had been concealed from him and Gloria, something that should have been worked out with them long ago.

Denis went to bed unhappy. He was hurt, too, and unsure. Presently he got up and took two sleeping capsules and slid at once into that curious black dark the capsules brought him. He was still asleep when Gus called him at eight the next morning, having as usual read his morning paper at breakfast.

Gus roared along, saying things Denis hoped he did not mean, things that made him feel he never could feel quite so close to Gus again. Denis was a fool, a conniver, a troublemaker, and worse, he was breaking his word. After the Dallas breakdown he had promised, Gus reminded him, not to take on too much. What did he think he was made of, anyway?

Vanadium steel? Vanadium being a word Gus had fallen in love with years before from Henry Ford's advertising. And what would his Board say?

There was a good deal more before Denis could break in and give his side of the story. After all, he had held Josy off for months and had only promised him to work on "Louisiana" in January, which was nine months off. There had been no time to tell anybody, not even Harry or Clarissa. He was hiding nothing.

Gus cooled down a bit. "What did you tell the local paper?" he demanded, and Denis repeated what he had asked Greene to print.

"That may save things," Gus said, "that 'folk opera' line."

"Well," said Denis, "it's not a folk opera, really. I don't know what it is. I just happened to——"

"I don't care how it came about. You stick to the phrase. And be vague about Morgan. He's pure theater and he could be the kiss of death for you."

When Gus finally hung up, Denis called Claire. She had seen no paper and Denis was all of ten minutes explaining exactly what had happened; when he finished, Claire said, "Why the little skunk!" and that broke the tension. They both laughed, and Claire promised to explain to Elisabeth.

Things became progressively more tangled. Josy called Denis, and Denis called Terry and into the midst of all the telephoning steamed Clarissa, her face a little flushed and her jaw set. Denis motioned her to a chair and finished with Terry. Then he turned to his visitor, half expecting a tongue-lashing.

"I've come to apologize," Clarissa said in a steady voice, the kind of voice one prepares for the delivery of a distasteful message. "I think this is my fault."

"It's nobody's fault," Denis insisted.

"Yes." And she explained it all, from Mary Roland's song in the kitchen straight through to her call to Josiah Morgan. The story left Denis staring.

Finally he caught up with his voice and said, "But Clarissa dear. You shouldn't——"

"I know. All I can say is that I told you years ago that nothing whatever would stand in the way of my orchestra, and it won't."

"My God, you're amazing!" he said softly. "And Harry?"

"He's all right now. I told him what I just said to you. He was hurt, but he isn't any more." She hesitated, not because she did not know what she wanted to say, but to be sure she put it to him properly. "You know, Denis, you've still got enemies on the board——"

"I know. There's Steel, and Coke, and Oil and——"

"That's enough. They may make a fuss."

"I know that, too. Shall I resign?"

"For something that's my fault? Of course not."

"Then . . . ?"

She crossed to the piano and began pressing out slow chords as she sometimes did when she wanted to think. After a minute she turned back to him. "Tell me honestly. Next season is your last for me, isn't it?"

Putting it so bluntly jarred him, but he nodded. "Between us, this is. Please."

"I was sure so. And you want Hans Mayor to follow you?"

"Yes. If he will."

"I think he will. I think he's weary of teaching; anyway, I hope so." She came back to the sofa. "This is what we'll do. We'll beat everybody to the gun. We'll announce in tomorrow's paper that you've just refused two offers for next season. That instead of leaving you'll conduct a special all-season festival of old and new music. We'll just ignore this—and if the board wants to call a special meeting Harry and I'll have to handle it." She shook her head and made a wry face. "Sometimes I wonder why I have to spend so much time on such silly things. But of course I know."

She's exactly like me, Denis thought. A really one-track person. He wondered about her husband, and whether he had ever been allowed even a small compartment of her mind, not to mention her love. Her scar, he thought, isn't on the belly, like mine. It's on her mind.

The rest of the day was even more strenuous. Farrell Clisby stopped in to report that Greene had been called in by Oil and pumped, that Steel had had Harry on the carpet, something Farrell knew because when he himself called Harry at his office, the operator told him her boss was talking to Steel. Farrell also mentioned something that rather amazed Denis, whose naïveté in business almost balanced his sophistication in music. This was that Steel and Oil and the rest of them were no longer depending so much on Harry. War orders were repairing the deficits of the 'thirties.

"You mean that Harry no longer has the board where he wants it?" Denis asked, and Farrell said, "Exactly."

The afternoon paper called; Denis said he had the sketches for a "folk opera," and carefully refrained from adding that in his opinion there really was no such thing. He also said that because of the character of the work, done for all the people and not merely for the few, he felt a production in the theater was better than one in a more formal house. The more he talked the more natural the pose seemed, and he ended by being quite enthusiastic.

Two men called from New York. One was dripping culture like a squeezed sponge; he was running an experimental theater in Greenwich Village and he felt that a commercial producer such as Josy Morgan was definitely not the thing for such a work as he was sure Denis had done. Denis replied that he felt just the opposite. The other call was from the Shuberts, who felt that anything by the conductor of a symphony orchestra was a pretty long chance, but wanted to talk. Denis said it was too late to talk.

Terry called back from the Deep South, and the two managed to laugh a good deal at the way a prospective disaster seemed to be turning into an asset. And Terry would be able to take January off.

There was even a call from Larrabee House, specifically from Carol Larrabee, who asked Denis to tea, and was asked to come to Denis' apartment instead. "I can't leave the damn phone, Carol," he explained. She came early, and made the tea herself in Denis' kitchen while he dealt with one final call and left word with the operator to hold all the rest.

"I have an ax to grind," Carol said when she carried in the tray.

"So?" Denis dug out a package of little cakes, and took in the plate of sandwiches the hotel kitchen sent up.

"Do you remember that you played a good deal of 'Louisiana' for me, and Terry told me the idea?"

"Ummm . . . I'm really hungry—I forgot lunch."

"You shouldn't. Ulcers."

Denis slumped back in his chair. "I like to have you here," he said, ignoring her remark. "You—you're relaxing."

"Look, Denis. I've been thinking a great deal about the—whatever you call it. How difficult would it be to rewrite it for an all-Negro cast?"

Denis jerked forward as if he had sat on a hot coal. "My God, Carol, what an idea!"

"But will it work?"

"Yes." He thought a minute or two, and finally put down his plate and began pacing the room. "The truth is that the Negroes in the thing have been running away with it all the time, and I didn't understand why. The whole idea is conflict between the old and the new. That's just as good with Negroes." He bent over Carol and kissed her soundly. "I love you," he said. "You're wonderful."

Then he picked up the phone. "I might as well bankrupt myself with the telephone as any other way," he explained, and put in another call for Terry, and another for Josy. While they were going through he kept throwing ideas at Carol, who caught them deftly and threw away the bad ones, something she had learned to do years before when Larrabee House was only an idea in a cottage kitchen.

Terry took fire instantly. "I'll begin working tonight," he promised. "Watch me—now I *do* have some good ideas."

But Josy was less eager, and anyway, he had expected a thorough chewing out, and was thrown off base when Denis did not so much as mention his sin. After he had got used to his surprise, he said, but gently, since Denis could still tear him to bits, "Look fellow, I've never worked with colored people. All my lines are out the other way. It'd be terribly difficult to get the right cast."

Denis refused to slow down. "All right, if that's the way it is. I'm getting a call every ten minutes and I'll release you whenever you say."

"Darling!" Josy's voice came through the receiver like a rapier. "Baby! Who said anything about not doing it? Don't be *silly*."

"Then get to work. There's more than a year before it can possibly go into rehearsal. But"—and Denis almost shouted the "but"—"you keep your damn mouth shut this time. So help me God, if a word of this leaks out I'll never sign an agreement with you even if I've got to throw 'Louisiana' out of the window."

"Darling, I'll never peep again. I . . . got drunk on the train. I'm sorry."

"All right—this time."

"And I'm wiring a friend of mine to hire a boy right now."

"You're what?"

"A boy to stand under your window. Just in case."

Denis could not keep from laughing. "You're terribly, sort of disarming, Josy," he said at last. "See you in a couple of weeks."

He turned back to Carol. "My dear," he said, "I promise you the gross on the third evening. And anything else I can do for you."

Carol's small round face blossomed into a gnomish grin. "Make it a regular benefit. We've got friends in New York, and——"

"Settled. Whenever you say." Denis laughed. "It just occurred to me that we're counting a lot of unhatched chickens."

29

Hatching chickens proved to be an experience for which Denis was rather badly equipped by nature. Nine months later he left Lakeland for his midwinter vacation so buoyed up by the adulation of his audience that nothing seemed impossible. As always, he went to Elisabeth's house and called Josy from there even before he telephoned Gus; he wanted his schedule settled so he could present Gus a fait accompli, and anyway he would see Gus that night.

But Josy worked by no schedule. Indeed, he seemed never to have heard of such a thing. "I'll be right up," he said at once, and Denis explained that after all, he had other people to see and could not possibly make the rest of the day free.

"All right," Josy said, "I'll come after dinner."

That was wrong; Gus was coming for dinner.

"Hell," said Josy, "we've only got a month and I had the devil's own time prying Gary Schwab away from Irving's new play. We simply can't wait, darling."

"We simply have to," snapped Denis, "and anyway, Terry won't get here before tomorrow morning. If the Southern railroad's running true to form, it will be afternoon."

Josy said it didn't matter. But he had to wait just the same. "I'll be there at the crack of dawn," he declared finally. "By eleven anyway."

"The sun rises late in New York," Denis remarked, and Josy laughed.

"I can't, simply *can't* function before eleven," he said. "Even then I'm still seeing double."

Gus was harder to handle, but it was managed. He made only

one demand, which was that Denis and Terry give him a run-through of 'Louisiana,' and soon.

"It had better be good," he said, "and by good I don't mean just an old rag that will go on Broadway. I'm going to make you conductor of the Symphony, and I'm goddamed if some cheap little——"

Denis interrupted, in a temper. "I'd just as soon you'd leave your criticism until later. What the hell makes you think I'd do some cheap little something?"

"I didn't mean——"

"You said it. After all, I do know music, and whatever else 'Louisiana' is, it isn't cheap."

"I apologize. But Denis my lad, you may know music from here to Halifax and back. What you don't know is Broadway and what those buzzards can do to a good idea. It was all Gershwin could do——"

Again Denis cut in. "I'd just as soon you left him out of this, too. 'Porgy and Bess' has good ideas, but he never made up his mind whether he was Verdi, Wagner or Irving Berlin. Whatever our thing turns out to be it won't be——"

"Excuse me, Denis," Gus broke in. "What's that, Moira?"

There was an interval of excited consultation, and then Gus came back on the wire. "I've got what I want," he said eagerly. "Just the right break. Who knows you're here?"

"Nobody except Josy Morgan. Why?"

"Wonderful! Call him right back and say you won't do anything if he says a word."

"Gus!" Denis was as confused as a cat in a dog show. "I'm just human, you know. What's up?"

So excited he could hardly explain himself, Gus roared on. "Feodor's sick. He can't conduct tomorrow night. I want you to step in—you know, brilliant young conductor races to rescue of colleague and all that crap."

"Well—but I'm going to be busy."

"Look, you dizzy boy. I can use this for a trigger. Feodor knows he's got to go. The Board knows I want you. That story didn't do you any good—even with old man Trilling. But you come in, conduct a bang-up concert, get raves, Uncle Gus calls a special meeting, Denis is announced as the next musical director of the Symphony, cheers all around. It's perfect."

"But——"

"No buts. Only there's one thing. If it leaks out you're already here, it might look like a put-up job."

Denis laughed; this was beginning to seem more funny than important.

"Stop laughing," Gus ordered. "I'm thinking. You can't just happen to be here. No drama."

In his turn, Denis was a little exasperated. "For God's sake, Gus. I *am* here. Can't you accept a simple fact?"

"Not when I don't want to. You're not going to be here. Maybe I could get some reporters to meet your train—I can feed them some guff about your great experiment, your so-called folk opera. Busy working in Lakeland. Telephone conversation with me. Drops everything, the noble lad, and takes the train for New York." Gus stopped for breath. "By the grace of God, there isn't a good conductor in town. That's a break."

"I just don't know what you're getting around to, Gus," Denis said almost plaintively, even though he was catching Gus' enthusiasm. If Gus thought this was the big break, then probably it was just that. And by now Gus had decided on a program.

"You're going to pack a bag and ride up to Albany tonight. Take some sleeping pills, because you're going to bed early and sleep like a baby—you've got one hell of a day tomorrow. I'll get you a bedroom back on the Lakeland Limited. It goes through Albany around five-thirty——"

Denis let out a hurt cry. "Not that hour!"

"Yes. That hour. You can nap on the way down, too. And I'll be at Grand Central with whatever reporters I can snag. I'll bring Moira for the sound effects; maybe Claire and Elisabeth. Anyway, it's got to look kosher and that's that. You can say a few words to the reporters, if any, and then we rush you away for breakfast, and rush you to the hall for rehearsal. You conduct tomorrow night with huge success. Peace, it's wonderful!"

"I hope. Gus, I've done just about everything you've asked.

I'll do this, too. But once I take over the Symphony, *if* I take over, I'm not going to be pushed around. Hear me?"

Gus roared. "Okay. So I don't push you. Hell, there isn't anyplace to push you to, then." He suddenly sobered up. "You call Josy Morgan right now and say that if he tells a living soul you're here you'll take your folk opera, whatever that is, away from him. Hear me?"

"I hear you."

"Fine. I'll get your space and make reservations and send the stuff up to you right after lunch. And"—he grew conspiratorial—"you might register as Axel Johnson or something in Albany. Some slick reporter might catch your name and—well, you never can tell."

After he hung up, Denis began to see the funny side of things. He searched the house and finally found Claire. When he told her she was at first a little outraged, and then disgusted. She was having a late breakfast, her gay cherry-colored robe a bright accent in the pale grays and blues of the breakfast room. She poured Denis a cup of coffee and then said, "Must you do this circus kind of thing? Do you want that job so badly you'll stand on your head for it?"

Denis poured cream into his coffee. "I tried to get out of it, Claire. Gus—well, he's worried about 'Louisiana.' He wants to have something dramatic to push the thing through before there's too much chance for talk. He's probably right. You know as well as I that he usually is."

Claire was not convinced, and not converted. Moodily she finished her toast and got up; her flaring robe swung back and revealed the fact that she wore nothing under it. Something like a chill raced up Denis' spine. "Claire——" he began, but she broke in.

"It seems a little too contrived for a simple person like me," she said. "I'm going to tell Gus so tonight at dinner. Too bad you won't be here."

"I'm sorry. I've promised, though."

She shrugged. "So I gather."

"But Claire, I told him that after I get to New York I won't be pushed around, and I mean it."

"Is there anything more that you want, after New York?"

"No."

"Sure?"

"Yes. What would it be?"

Claire seemed to be thinking hard, gently biting her lower lip as they walked slowly upstairs. "I don't know," she said in a low voice. "But somehow I can't see all that drive just turned off, like a light."

Denis put his arm around her and then suddenly pulled her to him and kissed her hard. She returned the kiss, and then pushed him away. "No," she said, "that's not an answer. Not now anyway."

She was watching him, her look queerly impersonal as if she might be watching an animal in a cage. She saw a change in his face, and it was not a protest against her rebuff. Her mouth twisted a little, and bitterly. "What is it now?" she asked.

It was some measure of his change that he knew, inside himself, that what he was thinking was wrong, was out of key. But he had disciplined himself too long to change in a moment. He already had turned away when he said, "Oh, Lord, I've forgotten to call Josy back."

Claire made no reply, but as she walked down the hall to her room she snapped off a rhododendron leaf from the greens on a hall table, and began methodically tearing it into small pieces.

A few hours later Stan carried Denis' bag down to the car and drove him to Grand Central. Denis was still protesting but not quite so vehemently; the trip seemed mad, as it had before, but it also seemed a step toward the thing he wanted. If he had troubled to analyze his feeling at that moment, he would have admitted honestly that the excitement of the game, his game and Gus', far outweighed his annoyance at the small deceit the two of them had prepared.

In spite of having gone to bed in Albany at ten o'clock the night before, Denis was a little sleepy when the Lakeland Limited drew into Grand Central. He was not too sleepy to give the platform a quick glance from the car window as the porter was handing off the luggage, however, or to be pleased with the delegation Gus had rounded up.

Claire had not come, but Elisabeth had. Gus and Moira were on hand, too, and with them were three men, obviously newspapermen. A passenger agent fluttered around, and there were six or eight of those people who inevitably smell out celebrities and collect to pick their bones, if any. It was quite a respectable showing, considering everything; Denis straightened himself, affixed just the right smile to his face, and strode onto the platform.

"Golly," Gus exclaimed as he rushed up to Denis and shook his hand, "I'm certainly glad you could make it."

"So am I." Denis kissed Elisabeth and Moira and the newspapermen were introduced. They began mumbling questions, giving every indication of being where they were without much knowledge of why they had been sent. Moira took care of that.

"Imagine," she said, her eyes twinkling, "imagine our being so lucky. Poor Feodor Solomon very sick, no conductor near, and suddenly we've got the best conductor of them all to take over. And he'll——"

"What else'll you do here, besides conduct?" one of the men demanded.

Dare I? thought Denis. He dared.

"The Symphony comes first, of course. But since I'm here, I may do something about my folk opera. If there's time, that is."

The phrase clicked with another of the men. "What's it called?" he asked, and Denis told him.

"Who's going to do it?"

Denis laughed with appropriate modesty. "I don't know that anybody will. It's just—that is, I hope it will be good enough."

The third man wanted to enter the lists. "What's a folk opera, anyway?"

Denis laughed again. "That's a hell of a good question," he answered. "I call it a folk opera because there isn't any name for what it is, really." Then he explained what he was trying to do, until Gus broke in.

"I hope you fellows will excuse us, but there's a rehearsal at ten, and this man's got to have something to eat and get ready. Thanks a lot for coming down."

The men were glad enough to leave, especially since they had more of a story than they had expected. The little cavalcade broke up in the lobby and Elisabeth led the way to the car. Stan looked sharply at Denis.

"Hard trip, Mr. Sandzen?" he asked.

"I'm worn out, Stan. Barely able to stand up."

"Gus, you and Moira come out for breakfast," Elisabeth ordered. "No—the office will manage," she added as Moira began a protest. "After all, I have an office too, and I know."

In the car, Gus patted Denis' knee. "Well handled, son," he said. "You're beginning to catch on. I mean the crack about the Symphony first and so on."

"No credit to me," said Denis. "I meant that."

Gus grunted. "Would you mean it if the board said give up 'Louisiana' or no Symphony?"

"The board would have no right to dictate."

"And there, ladies and gentlemen, you have the crux of the whole business." Gus was slightly oracular. "The board has no right to dictate what you do. Granted. But it's got a perfect right to refuse to engage one Denis Sandzen." He smiled, and smugly. "That's precisely what makes my job so hard."

"He means it, too," Moira said gently.

An hour later Gus was on hand for the rehearsal. Just before it began he walked onto the stage and explained to the men what they already knew; there is no limit to the speed of the musical grapevine, and the Symphony's was one of the best. The big orchestra room buzzed as the men gathered, and the locker room was equally hot in both senses of the word. As always, it smelled of white shirts used a little long, and worn black patents which lived in the bottom of the steel lockers from concert to concert. As the men hung up their street clothes and got into sweaters or whatever rehearsal costume they favored there was no surprise that Feodor was ill; only wonder as to whether the whole thing had been arranged, and even money that young Sandzen would get the "call."

"I hope he does," the young first trumpet said. "He's good."

"Yess," agreed a middle-aged Austrian escaped from Vienna to the inside line, third chair, first violins. "Yess, he iss good. Aber younk for such a job. So very younk."

The trumpet pushed back his hair, and the older man noticed that it was cut like Denis' and behaved like Denis' also. He smiled secretly.

The program Feodor had chosen was a familiar one: all-Brahms. Before intermission there was the "Academic Festival" overture and the Fourth symphony. Denis was happy about the overture, for good reason. After intermission Vladimir Horozovsky was playing the second piano concerto, something that delighted Denis beyond measure. People said Horozovsky was a tremendous technician and no musician. Being a very fine pianist with no ambition to make a career as a soloist, and therefore no ambition that Horozovsky could interfere with, Denis not only thought Vladimir the greatest living pianist, but said so whenever he could. It often provoked an argument.

Horozovsky came in as Gus left the stage. He looked carefully around, then said, "Ah, Denis. How lucky I am!" He saw Gus approaching. "Too bad about poor Feodor; too bad," he added.

He shook hands all around, and said that he was perfectly willing to skip rehearsal. "Nothing could go wrong," he said and meant it.

But Denis shook his head. "We'll rehearse, just for my pleasure, Vladimir," he said. "Then I'll have the fun twice." He turned to Van Cleef. "Ask them to get the piano on." His arm went around the older man's shoulders. "Remember the Deep South? I'll never forget what you did for me."

Van said in an exaggerated whisper, "Gus Wagner thinks you're his boy. But you aren't. Van gave you your start."

In a moment the piano was in place, and Denis went on. For a few seconds he leaned on the piano, the familiar small pain under the scar flickering as it always did when he was under tension. Then he rapped with his baton.

"Gentlemen," he said, "this is a great pleasure for me, and I shall make it as painless for you as possible. We'll go straight through the concerto and take a break. Afterward, we'll do a thing or two to the overture and symphony."

The men applauded, and applauded again when Horozovsky's slight self appeared. Denis added, "If you've got any tricky markings on your parts, forget them. Mr. Horozovsky plays as Brahms wrote." And the men laughed; it was not meant as a dig at their regular conductor, but it was a fact that Feodor habitually rewrote whatever did not please him in whatever music he played.

The concerto was pure pleasure. The feeling was not that of rehearsal, but as if a hundred and ten men were gathered in some very great home not yet sold to meet taxes, making music for their own selves. When it was finished everybody applauded everybody else; the first trumpet pushed back his hair and shouted, "Encore."

Much to everybody's surprise, Vladimir sat down again and with a wink at Denis, played something so unexpected it was almost as if he had pulled a rattlesnake out of the Steinway—his version of John Philip Sousa's "Stars and Stripes Forever." It was like nothing heard before on earth; a musical joke, perhaps, but also a brass band suddenly born on the stage of Carnegie Hall. When he reached the famous descending passage dear to all trombonists, it seemed as if the piano might collapse under his fingers, and somebody among the double basses cried "Yip-ee!" from sheer nervous pressure.

The pianist, as if what he was doing were nothing more than a page of beginners' exercises, looked up and grinned. The piece ended with a crash, and the men cheered.

Nothing could have made a rehearsal better; everything was easy, and the session ended in a love feast. Just the same, nobody doubted but what their guest conductor knew exactly how to get what he wanted, and had no more intention of putting up with nonsense than of standing on his head that night on the stage.

In the locker room the young first trumpet looked quizzically at the Viennese from the fiddle section. "So he's a young man, huh?" he jibed.

399

Said the Viennese, "Younk he iss, ja. But great he iss also." His head disappeared in his locker, and he was still muttering. "Ach, such Brahms," he was saying. "Echt Brahms!"

The audience that night expected something remarkable. The afternoon papers had carried stories, longer stories than Gus had dared hope for, about the change of conductors. And Denis was now a "name," just as Horozovsky was. The Thursday night audience had not quite filled the hall for some years; now it overran it, and all the standing room was sold, and people were turned away.

The truth was that it could hardly have heard anything less than remarkable, barring sudden insanity on the part of Denis, or a mass attack of locomotor ataxia on the part of the orchestra. Things had dropped into the proper groove that morning, and they stayed there. Most of the people had small idea why things went so well, or even how well they went. They merely sensed something, as they might have done standing on the edge of the Grand Canyon, or in front of the Winged Victory. Indeed, it would have been almost enough for certain of the women just to see Denis turn after the concerto, applaud Horozovsky as if he honestly meant it, which he did, and then blush when the pianist suddenly pulled his conductor's head down and kissed him on both cheeks. The recalls went on until Denis sent a man out to close the piano, and finally asked the electrician to dim the stage lights slowly.

Elisabeth and Claire and Terry were waiting in Denis' little room when he and Vladimir reached it, just ahead of the crowd surging up the iron stair. There were tears in Elisabeth's eyes as she said, "I can't wait, Denis."

Horozovsky looked from one to the other a little puzzled. But Denis knew very well what Elisabeth meant.

30

Next morning Gus asked Denis to meet him before lunch. Elisabeth went to her office early, because a special meeting of the Symphony Board would take up most of her afternoon. That left Claire and Terry alone in the big house, alone and queerly ill at ease. At least Claire seemed uncomfortable, as if she were considering something rather distasteful about which she could not make a decision. She wandered about, hoping Terry would give up working on "Louisiana" and leave his room, something he did about noon. Claire pounced, having made up her mind.

"Let's take a walk," she suggested. "It's not too cold for your Southern blood."

"Fine." Terry got his overcoat and helped Claire into a short mink jacket. She looked very young, much younger than she was, in an absurd little black hat, and a skimpy black dress under the mink. They crossed the Avenue into the park, sparkling like a jeweled mosaic under the silver-gilt January sun. "Feels good," Terry said as they turned north toward the reservoir.

Claire looked at him keenly; he was keyed up with anxiety about "Louisiana," and at the same time he was as always—as nearly always—in complete control of himself. "How are the de Knizes?" she asked absently, and then, before he could answer, she rushed on.

"Frankly I don't care in the least how they are, especially since Mother decided not to marry Paul. I want to tell you something. It's got to be you, too."

Terry was as clairvoyant as the next one. "About Denis, of course?"

"Yes. I'm not going to marry him."

He was set back on his heels, and hard. Mechanically he said, "Has he asked you, Claire?"

"Not yet. He will."

They walked along in silence now, overtaking a red-faced nurse pushing a red-faced baby buried in a cocoon of fluffy blue blanket. At last Terry agreed, slowly, "Probably he will. I think he loves you in his way." Claire suddenly laughed, not bitterly, but out of genuine amusement. She seemed surprised that she could laugh, and stopped as abruptly as she had begun, and looked up at Terry almost apologetically.

"It was what you said that set me off," she explained. "About Denis' loving me in his way. That's exactly it."

"Forgive me if I'm saying too much." Terry touched Claire's arm gently. "But I thought all these years you were simply waiting for him to come to his senses. Weren't you?"

"Yes—up to the summer at Cape o'Sands. That's where I began to think, seriously. Mind if I try to explain? I've thought it all out, but I've never said it to anybody."

"Believe me," Terry said earnestly, "I couldn't be more flattered. Oh," he added hastily, "I don't mean that the superficial way it sounds. I honestly am flattered, because you know how I've felt all these years."

She nodded. "Exactly. Well—look at it this way. I've known Denis always, or almost always. I think I first realized how I felt the day he made his New York debut, going to Carnegie Hall in the top-heavy old Rolls we had then. I was nasty, because I was—I hate to admit it—jealous of Mother. I hated her for a while, and suspected all sorts of adolescent things. This isn't very nice, Terry, but in my addled mind I thought that a woman in early middle age could hardly resist a young chap as beautiful as Denis, and"—she frowned up at Terry and finished the sentence in a rush——"I thought she was helping him because she wanted him. Or was having him. I'm ashamed to say it, but it's true."

Terry caught Claire's hand and squeezed it. "In my way I

402

thought as much and worse—not about Elisabeth, of course."

"Yes." She took a deep breath; they had reached the reservoir and were standing against the wire fence, watching the wandering sea gulls that cruise its surface in small gray groups, like scouting parties. "Well, I was wrong. And that was when the jealousies began. I hated his work. I was jealous of you, and Cécile, and Gloria Gordon, and even Clarissa. I worried about —this sounds dreadfully silly—Moira and Gus, too. I was proposed to several times a year, and I hardly saw the boys I went with at all; they all were measured against Denis, and none was ever good enough. What I never saw until that summer at Cape o'Sands was that I was just as bad as Denis."

Terry broke in. "I don't see what you mean; it's totally different."

"No, it wasn't. I made just as much a career out of getting Denis as he made out of getting the Symphony. I sacrificed everybody and everything along the line. Nobody but me knows the story—I could have been a useful person, Terry, but I had a secret career. I used people just as unconsciously as Denis." She laughed bitterly, and plunged on. "That's ridiculous—most of the time Denis *did* use people unconsciously, but I almost never did. I used to egg Mother on to ask Denis to let her sing, and then make it necessary for her to take me along. I even forced her to work, so she'd do a good job, and might be asked again. And Terry . . ." He looked down and saw that she was blushing, and that for the moment her face was beautiful instead of merely interesting and intelligent and charming. "The whole thing was pure waste. Every year or so Denis would wake up to the fact that I was alive, and maybe he'd kiss me, or hug me. And I'd remember and think I was making progress. Oh—I honestly hate myself."

"Why, my dear?"

"Because, don't you see, I had no right to expect anything from Denis. He had a right to his life and anybody but a blind little monkey like me would have seen it. You do understand? Listen, Terry—if you have thought sometimes that Denis was too ambitious and too ruthless—what about me? I've been worse than he ever was."

They were halfway around the reservoir. From the bridle path below a light voice called, "Hello, Claire!" and Claire waved back. They watched the girl, immaculate in derby and black riding habit, canter on into a group of bare trees.

"I always thought that riding in Central Park was about the silliest thing ever," Claire remarked absently. "Somebody brings a horse to the Ninetieth Street entrance, you get on and ride two or three times around the reservoir, and you hand the horse back." She looked up at Terry again. "But it's really purposeful and important when you compare it with what I've been up to for ten years or more. Isn't it?"

"I don't think so. Sometimes one can't help the way one feels. Listen, Claire, there's no reason for me to be shy with you. You know my story—I even went further than you. Remember the sleeping capsules?"

She spoke, again absently, "We'd better try for a cab; we're late for lunch." She pressed her finger tips against her forehead as if she were massaging away a headache. "Yes. I remember. But at least, Terry, you've had a really fine friendship. I could have had, but I wasn't satisfied with that. Oh, hell . . ."

They crossed the east drive, and by some miracle there was an empty cab at the corner. Terry patted her hand as the car started. "I just thought of something," he said quietly. "Perhaps it wouldn't be too much if we'd been thrown bodily to the lions. You know? When you weigh two great disappointments against the pleasure—more than pleasure—Denis has given thousands upon thousands of people."

Her smile was free of tension. "The trouble with you is that you're genuinely good, Terry."

"No . . ."

"Yes. I never thought of that scar of his as a symbol, but I can now. It's as if he were ripped right down the belly by ambition, and we're those little pains, the adhesions he feels underneath, sometimes."

Gus had asked Denis to be in his office at four that afternoon, and Denis was there. The office was two doors down the hall from the board room, and Gus wanted his conductor handy, whatever the result of the meeting might be. Gus had left Carnegie Hall the night before walking on a cloud, as had more than three thousand others. Nobody could resist what he had heard, he felt sure; so sure that he had not done as much mingling as he might have done otherwise. And now he was a little less well prepared for what was happening in the meeting than he could have been.

Denis had picked up the *Sun* and was reading about himself. He felt good, and smiled a little at the last paragraph of the review, which said clearly enough that here was another conductor ready, when and if the Symphony felt it needed one. Then he walked across the room to the window and looked unseeingly at the wedge of park visible between the buildings on Central Park South. He was deep in plans for his first New York season, so absorbed he did not hear the office door open.

"There you are," said Gus in what for him was a very small voice. Denis whirled around; one look told him the bad news.

"They . . ." he began.

"They balked. Hard." Gus rested a hand on Denis' shoulder. "If you want it, you'll have to backwater."

"Louisiana?"

Gus nodded. "That and your age and—hell, you know all those rumors. Anti-Semitism, a bastard with the men, quarrels with the Lakeland Board. All that."

"But if they understood about 'Louisiana,' they'd take me?"

Gus smiled, a wry smile and a small one. He was thinking back through the years of Denis' single-minded progress, and what this last minute failure might mean to him, if it really had to be failure. And also what it might mean to himself; far more than he ever had let Denis know, this progress had been a satisfaction and a fulfillment to him. He had handled dozens of conductors, old, middle-aged, young, and not one had had what Denis had. He remembered the day Denis ordered him and Clarissa out of the hall in Columbia. And the anxious watch after Dallas. Many other things.

"Would they?" Denis asked again, and Gus started.

"Probably." The telephone rang, and he picked up the instrument ready to shout down whoever was on the wire. Then his face changed. "They do?" he said. "All right."

"The board wants me again. They asked for a little time to talk—alone."

Denis' dark face grew suddenly eager. "Take me with you," he begged. "Please, Gus."

"Just tell me that you'll give up that musical. Otherwise it won't work."

But Denis looked straight into his manager's tired eyes and said, "I won't give it up. I'll do guest jobs until something else opens up, anything. But I won't give up something I know is good. I——"

"You said nothing would . . ." Gus began, but Denis broke in again.

"I know I did." He was about to go on when Moira appeared in the doorway.

"Hurry, Gus," she said. "They're waiting." She gave Denis a troubled nod.

Gus turned away. "All right, goddam it. I guess the guillotine's ready."

Neither of them noticed Denis, walking softly along behind them. At the door of the board room he said, his voice very low, "I'm going in, Gus. You can't stop me."

"Kid, you've got guts," Moira said. "They're . . ."

As if he had not heard, Gus pushed open the door, and the three of them filed in. Around the long table were fifteen men and one woman—Elisabeth. Denis thought Elisabeth looked almost frightened, but she raised her hand nervously, and said "Hello, Denis."

Trilling bowed, but his face was more severe than usual. He frowned and said, "What's this? You weren't asked."

Denis noticed many things in the second or two before he answered: he noticed that the board room was by no means as luxurious as the one in Lakeland; that Trilling's British manner had rubbed thin; that there were a few who seemed sympathetic, or at least interested rather than annoyed; that somebody's cigarette had fallen from an ash tray and was about to fire a piece of paper.

"Yes, Mr. Trilling. You're quite right," Denis said after the stir had quieted a little. "But I wanted to tell you some things and I have no right to ask Gus Wagner to do it for me."

Elisabeth spoke, and this time in the manner Denis imagined she would use in her office. "I think we should hear him," she said, and whether out of chivalry or curiosity a few heads nodded in agreement.

Trilling looked uncertainly around the table. "We've had our discussion," he said slowly.

"Let him talk," a huge man with no hair at all rumbled. "We're not unanimous, you know."

Denis swallowed; he was frightened, and he could feel his belly tighten and the little pains take hold. He rested his hands on the back of Gus' vacant chair, conscious that Gus and Moira were flanking him like bodyguards. He swallowed again, and began.

"I made my debut, my real debut, April 17, 1929, with the Symphony." He smiled. "Some of you heard me, even though the orchestra was merely engaged for the occasion. That day I said to myself that I was going to be conductor of the Symphony before I was thirty-five. There has not been a day since that I have not worked for that ambition. Not one."

His hands tightened on the chair back; to relieve his tension he pushed back his hair and tried hard to smile. "Now," he went on, "I'm told that if I will give up a project I have begun, you will overlook false charges of anti-Semitism, the things they say about my being too hard on my orchestra—all that. And I can have the orchestra. I don't want it under those conditions."

Sixteen bodies shifted in sixteen chairs; someone muttered, "Then that's that," but nobody paid attention, and Denis quickly went on.

"I think the people who employ me ought to take me as I am, and trust me enough that they would not think me likely to do anything beneath the dignity of this orchestra. And I am not the same person I was a few years back. My music is no longer just for me.

"Things get about, and I'm sure some of you have heard about a disagreement in Lakeland—a ballet I wrote for a settle-

407

ment house, and the quarrel that followed. I won that round, and the reason I'm glad for it is that it proved some things for me. I did not lower the dignity of my orchestra. And I learned that every talent I have belongs to everyone I can reach. I should have known that before—but I'm a very single-minded man.

"My folk opera, which is a bad name for it, may never be done, because it may never be good enough. It will be sung and danced by Negroes. It will be played in a theater, because it is far too intimate for the Metropolitan. If I'm lucky it will be the first of a new sort of musical play—I don't know what to call it. And if it's good enough, gentlemen, hundreds of thousands of people will hear something beautiful. If it fails, I will still be exactly the same person you have heard conduct, but for one thing."

Denis paused a moment; he caught Elisabeth's eye, and her glance gave him courage.

He went on, his voice raised a little. "The thing is this: I know now what I can do, and I shall never again do it for myself alone."

He turned abruptly and walked out of the room. Behind him he heard a sudden rush of voices, and one voice in particular which called, "A question, Mr. Sandzen."

He closed the door behind him without answering, and went directly home. Elisabeth arrived an hour later, and went straight to Denis and kissed him.

"You were magnificent," she said then.

Denis' eyebrows cocked. "I was truthful, anyway. What happened?"

Elisabeth dropped her sable stole on a sofa and crossed to a window. A bus ground past, the noise of its gears muffled by the thick walls of the house. The room seemed more quiet for the dull noise outside. Without turning, Elisabeth said, "What you said helped. We were six for and ten against when you came in, and now we're eight and eight." Slowly she turned to face Denis. Gus usually casts the deciding vote in a tie. But this time he refused."

"I see. That was probably right."

"Yes. Denis, ring for tea, won't you?" He touched the little mother-of-pearl button beside the fireplace and neither spoke until Ellen had come and gone. Then Elisabeth went on. "Denis, dear—Trilling wants to talk with you. He'll ask you to give up 'Louisiana.' Promise me you won't."

"I promise." He sat down on the sofa beside her. "Only one thing disturbs me," he added. "I still don't know whether it's the old me or the new me that is holding out."

"The man who never changed?"

"Exactly—but just the same, I believed what I said."

Ellen was back very quickly; she put down the tray and said, "Mr. Trilling is here for Mr. Denis."

Elisabeth shook her head wearily, her eyes closed. "Ask him to come up," she said. "I'll give him a cup of tea and get out of the way."

This she did. For an hour, the two men talked, Trilling stiffly, as if he were yielding too much even by calling on Denis, and Denis strangely gentle for one used to command—and all the more convincing for his quiet. Neither converted the other, and finally Trilling said, "Sandzen, look at it from a practical position. This is the toughest conducting post in the country. I know you're young and strong and determined. But you ought not to dissipate your energies that way."

For a moment Denis' gaze concentrated on his empty cup. Then he looked up at Trilling.

"You don't understand, Mr. Trilling. The Symphony is still first. The only thing on God's earth that would make me give up 'Louisiana' would be if it interfered with the orchestra. I know me. I know it won't."

The older man was a little shaken, Denis felt, but still not convinced. Not quite. He sat nervously nibbling at his lower lip, his eyes troubled. Denis thought, he really takes the business of dignity seriously. He really feels it.

Finally Trilling rose. "We're meeting again at luncheon tomorrow—I suppose Elisabeth told you."

"No."

"I may as well say that we're evenly divided." His honesty forced him to go on. "Nobody doubts your ability. Person-

409

ally, I thought what you said this afternoon very affecting. It's——"

"It's just that they think I'm stubborn, sir. And I am. You see, Mr. Trilling—I know what I can do."

Trilling gave Denis a sharp, quick glance. "You'll hear something after our luncheon," he said as he left.

"Denis," said Terry next morning, "you can't work on 'Louisiana' today. I don't care what you promised Josy."

Denis looked coolly at Terry. "I can, and I will. I've done everything I can about the Symphony, and so has Gus." He shrugged into his jacket. "We're due at Josy's at eleven, and we'd better get along."

When they arrived Josy looked keenly at his composer. Bluntly, he asked "How about the Symphony?"

"Disagreed; I'll know this afternoon."

A good half of Josy's success lay in being able to push important things out of the way when necessary, something in which he resembled Denis quite a lot. "I'll tell my man you're expecting a call; otherwise he'd not let us know. We're incommunicado, you understand."

Denis nodded. "What do we do first?" he asked, and without waiting for an answer, "I think we'd better play through what Terry and I have done."

Gary Schwab was a small, twinkling man, gray-haired over a youngish face and laconic almost to the length of complete disinterest. Or at least he seemed that way until one knew he was using his attitude as a fence behind which to marshall his ideas and his plans. Josy was—Josy. Terry was a little diffident, until Schwab said quietly, "Don't be shy. You are the only one of us who knows the most important thing."

Terry's questioning look made words unnecessary.

"You really know the Negro, Terry," Schwab went on. "We'd be lost without you."

The run-through was finished at half past one, and Josy's man brought in sandwiches, fruit and coffee. At a quarter after two he called Denis to the telephone. Denis closed the door after him, but Josy's hand stole toward the extension phone on the tail of the piano. Schwab grinned, slapped the hand down sharply without speaking. The three sat silently; Terry's empty cup rattled in its saucer as he put it down. . . .

The door opened. Without a word Denis walked across the room to the piano and sat down. He played the Doxology, or rather he started it.

Terry streaked across the room, and caught at Denis' arm. "You won?" he demanded.

Denis nodded, and stood up. "I've got to go now," he said. "Reporters and photographers and so on. I'll be back about noon tomorrow."

Schwab shook his head wonderingly. "Cool customer, aren't you?" he asked, and as Josy began a protest, added, "Don't be a fool, man. What else can he do?"

Nearly a week had gone by, and in the remaining three weeks of the vacation there was now almost twice as much to be done—people to be seen, calls to be made, interviews to be got through, business details settled. But from eleven in the morning until dinnertime the four of them hid in Josy's apartment and struggled. Actually it was more like groping. "Louisiana" fitted no pattern whatever. It had a primary conflict, which was the battle of the new Negro against the background from which he sprang. It had a story, too, in which a boy and a girl, one from a family willing to continue the old pattern, the other from a group not so complaisant, first must adjust one to the other, and then face the rest of the world. The white world.

The music had to help tell the story. There was to be dancing, and it had to tell more of the story. The dialogue had to be true, but also understandable to a Northern audience; more, to any audience, anywhere. That meant dealing with basic things honestly, and was no more like putting together an old-style musical than it was like writing a church service. The four of them were swimming in the dark.

But they made progress, and toward the end of the three weeks, when they were all needing haircuts and their throats were raw from too much smoking, they knew that they had something very good. Then Josy said, particularly for Terry's and Denis' benefit, "Darlings, this is wonderful. But you know we'll have to do it all over in rehearsal." He patted Denis on the back. "How are you at writing six bars of music to cover somebody's exit—in thirty minutes or less?"

Denis looked around the big living room, half buried under drifts of discarded score paper, torn sheets of dialogue, plates of sandwiches half finished, ash trays running over. "If I can stand this, I can stand the other," he said in a weary voice. He grinned at Terry. "I didn't know what I was dragging you into."

Terry was trying to retie a four-in-hand without a mirror, his face like a lopsided gargoyle. "It's fun," he said briefly. "I like it."

Josy turned back to Denis. "Look," he demanded for the tenth time. "Can't we open in September? It's better, believe me. I know——"

"You do know. You know the answer, too." Denis understood his busy friend better now, and was not annoyed, as he might have been earlier. "For the dozenth time, no. We'll open at least a week after my first concert with the Symphony. Preferably two." He looked hard at Josy. "I'm surprised," he went on, "that anybody as single-minded as you doesn't understand. That orchestra is what I've been after all my life, practically."

Gary raised his head, which he had laid gently on the arm of the handiest sofa, almost as if it did not belong to him. "I've got a headache," he declared, "and I don't feel like struggling. Only I'd like to call your attention to the fact that we still don't know what to call it."

" 'Don' know what to call him, but he's mighty lak a rose,' " sang Josy. "We might have a contest."

"We've got to call it something when we sell tickets," Terry remarked. "It would be damn hard to run a contest when nobody's heard it."

"It's a play with music and dance," said Josy. "That's good enough. After we do this one, people will compare the imitations with it. 'A production such as Josiah Morgan's "Louisiana."'"

"Nice to know you did the whole thing, Josy," Gary remarked.

They all laughed, and rather gladly separated. Three solid weeks of the same company is, as Denis remarked to Terry on the way home, quite a dose. "But I admire that pair," he added. "They know their business."

They rode in silence for a few blocks, the taxi chains kicking up fountains of January slush, dirty brown and nasty. Finally Denis cleared his throat tentatively.

"Terry," he said, "if Claire's at home, would you mind giving us a few minutes alone? I—I've got something to say to her."

Oh, God, thought Terry, here it comes. "Sure," he answered. "I need some fresh clothes anyway."

Going into Elisabeth's house was like leaving this world for a better. Lights were on, and there was a fire in the drawing room—but no Claire. Denis found her in her mother's small sitting room, her feet on the fender and her favorite cherry-red robe tucked around her. "Gosh, you look comfortable," he said.

"I am. Pull up a chair."

Denis dragged Elisabeth's beloved wing chair to the fire. "Want a drink?" he asked, and Claire nodded.

"There's a tray in the corner," she said.

Denis put together two bourbons with water. "You make a wonderful picture," he said as he worked. "Your robe matches the red in the chintz."

Claire put down her book, and took her drink. "All finished that can be finished now?" she asked, and Denis nodded. "Then here's to 'Louisiana,' whatever it may be."

They drank, and Denis put down his glass on the brick hearth. He took Claire's hand, and suddenly plunged. "We've known each other a long time," he began. "I guess you know how I feel by now."

"Relieved that you've done what you can to the musical, I suspect."

413

Denis looked sharply at Claire. "Why did you say that?" he demanded.

"My dear," she answered, "I know you very well."

He decided to ignore her answer. "Claire, dear—could you, would you marry me?"

For what seemed minutes she did not reply. Quietly she released her hand and bent down. She picked up Denis' drink and gave it to him. "Drink all of it," she commanded, "and then listen to me."

Without a word he emptied the glass.

"Better make another," Claire suggested, and again he obeyed without question. When he was once again seated, she began to speak.

"For years, Denis—I think ever since the night Mother and I drove you to Carnegie Hall for your debut—I've thought I was in love with you. Part of the time I was."

"Part of the time?"

"That's what I said." She smiled a little bitterly. "Don't think I'm as cold-blooded as I sound. This is the only way I can bring myself to tell the truth. The truth isn't very nice from my side of the fence, either.

"Look, Denis, I've just come to realize that we're a lot alike —our worst sides are alike. For more than ten years I worked at getting you, and you worked at getting what you wanted, and I've only realized in the last year or so what it all means."

Denis broke in. "I think I've always loved you, Claire. Truly."

"No—you've always known what you wanted, and the first thing wasn't I. You know it wasn't."

"But——"

"No buts. It's true, isn't it? I could wait. You told me that, in effect. . . . God," she cried suddenly, "what a mess of a love scene this is!"

Denis flushed, his dark face glowing angrily. "Maybe so," he said, "but that's not all my fault."

Claire left her chair and stood before the fire, for a few seconds lost in a thought of her own. At last she said, "No, it isn't. It's the fault of your ambition and my stubbornness, Denis. And circumstance. The fact is I'm ashamed of having done

414

some of the things I did. But now I know we could never marry, never in this world."

"I've got everything I want except you," Denis blurted, and then flushed again. "I'm sorry—that didn't sound the way I meant it."

There were tears in Claire's eyes, but her lips were smiling. "It was exactly what you meant," she declared. "Precisely and to the last syllable. But you're wrong."

He said nothing, but his look asked the question.

"There'll be something else. What good would it do either of us to marry, and then find that I got only a part of you, and you could give me only spare time. If any?" She finished the second drink. "No. I'm cured. I won't do it."

Neither of them heard Elisabeth come into the room. "I'm sorry," she said behind them. "I didn't mean to eavesdrop."

Claire blinked her tears away and turned. "It doesn't matter. Denis just asked me to marry him, and I said no."

Then Elisabeth came over to the two of them. She put an arm about Claire, and gently smoothed Denis' dark hair. "I love you both dearly," she said slowly. "I'm glad Denis asked, and I'm glad you said no, Claire." Her voice was very soft and very gentle, and her presence was a relief to each of them. "I'm not stupid, my dears," Elisabeth went on. "It's been very hard not to take a hand sometimes. I think you're more alike than either of you realizes. Just be friends."

Denis flung himself out of his chair and half ran from the room. Claire's head dropped to her mother's shoulder, and Elisabeth's arm tightened around her. It was almost their first moment of complete understanding.

"You're very brave, darling," Elisabeth said softly.

The only thing Denis could think of to do was to shower, but when he stumbled into the bath through which his room connected with Terry's, he found Terry scrubbing himself to the accompaniment of some scraps of music from "Louisiana," sung by himself and not very well. He waved to Denis through the glass door of the shower, and Denis waved back. Then Denis wrapped a towel around his middle and went back to his room to wait. He stood at the window, staring down into the tiny formal garden behind the house; a long black cat was barely visible on the wall, in the light from the servant's dining room on the ground floor. In a moment Terry called, "Come on in."

Denis showered and was drying himself when Terry returned, wrapped in the shabby brown robe he had worn almost since the day Denis met him first. For want of something better, Denis said, "I'm going to get you a new robe next Christmas. That thing is threadbare."

"Don't bother. I still like it." Then he looked keenly at Denis. "What's up?" he demanded.

Denis hung up his towel and reached for a box of talc. "Nothing," he said. "I'm sort of deflated, I guess."

But he followed Terry into his room, not anxious to say anything, yet pathetically anxious not to be alone. "I've been so keyed up that being free for even a few hours———"

"I think I know," Terry broke in. "You'd better tell me yourself, though."

Denis was shrugging into his own robe, his back to Terry. He suddenly froze, one arm in and one out of the robe. He turned abruptly to his friend. "It's Claire, Terry. I . . . she———"

"Said no."

Without answering, Denis walked back to the window. The cat was still there, and now a few great flakes of snow were drifting down through the shaft of light, into the winter-bare little garden. He heard Terry's slippers slur over the thick carpet, felt Terry's arm about his shoulders. Neither spoke for a little while, and then Terry drew Denis away from the window. "Sit down," he said, pointing to the shabby leather chair Elisabeth had kept through the years because Denis liked it. Terry brought up a side chair and straddled it, his arms on the back. "I think you ought to know that Claire and I talked about you —the two of you, that is. It wasn't just chatter; she needed to talk."

Denis looked up, but did not speak. And Terry, having started bravely, found it difficult to go on. Finally he said, "You've built yourself a—well—character is the word, and you're stuck with it. At least for now."

Denis ran his hand through his hair, which at once fell back to his forehead. "You too?" he asked in a voice full of hurt. "I thought you'd understand."

"I do understand, just as you did, bless you, years ago." He got up suddenly, and disappeared into his room. When he came back he carried a bottle of bourbon and a couple of glasses.

Denis smiled thinly. "I've already had two—I'll be drunk."

"It might be good for you." Terry poured two drinks and added water from the carafe on the bed table. "Here."

Denis took the drink, holding it in both hands to steady it. "There isn't much use to talk, I guess," he began. "You're very likely right." He gulped half the drink, and it seemed to wash away whatever obstruction there had been to honesty. The words poured out.

"You're not probably right. You are right. I can see myself better now, and maybe I don't like what I see very well." He stopped Terry's interruption with a gesture. "I wanted the Symphony and I got it. I beat the hell out of two orchestras to make them what I wanted. I wanted you on my terms, and I got you. I wanted to do the ballet and I did. And I wanted to do 'Louisiana,' and we're doing it. Now that I look at it, I have used just about everybody from Ernst Wetterstrom out in Gutenborg through to Josy. I feel like a son-of-a-bitch, if you want to know."

"Stop it!" Terry's hand shot out and clamped over Denis' mouth. "Listen. You have done that, perhaps, but the test is whether it was for a good reason or not. Perhaps—oh, hell, no perhaps—you are selfish, Denis. I admit it. But the result has been valuable to thousands of people. Compared to old Richard Wagner you're white as a lily, and yet most people would say what Wagner left behind was more than a balance for what he did."

There was a fallacy in it somewhere, but Denis could not put his finger on it. He was not convinced, however, and shook his head. "I know I can conduct. Play piano, too. But I hope I never have to swear that I did everything for the sake of art. I didn't. Partly that, but mostly for me. That's the truth."

How very typical, thought Terry grimly. When he looks at

himself frankly, he looks square. No dodging. He said, "You're too hard on yourself."

"No harder than I've been toward a lot of musicians I could name." He tried to light a cigarette and his hand shook so that Terry held the match for him. "I guess time means nothing to me; honestly, Terry, I thought that Claire was waiting for me. I wasn't ready, and time went on."

"Yes. Don't mind if I sound brutal. I don't mean to be. But ten years or so of not thinking about a girl isn't the best foundation for a marriage. Especially when the girl has been trying to sort of bring you around all the time."

Denis snubbed out his cigarette mechanically, as if he heard nothing. Then Terry's meaning struck him and he looked up. "It's true? That Claire really was—well—out to get me?"

"It's true. She told me, and it's only fair that——"

Denis broke in again. "It helps not to have damaged her so much. But it's not the whole answer."

"I wonder if there ever is a whole answer to anything emotional. You and me, for example." After a little pause, he went on. "There's something I think I'd better tell you. I resigned from the paper before I came to New York. I had to."

"What?" Denis frowned. "Why should you have to?"

Terry poured himself another drink, but when he offered the bottle to Denis, it was refused. He put it carefully down on the chest of drawers and crossed the room to the carafe for a little water. Denis watched him with something of the old ache inside him; with the feeling that out of the worst possible situation something good had come, but that it still was not enough. Terry tightened the cord of his robe, and it broke. He laughed. "I guess you'd better give me that present after all; the thing's falling to pieces."

Denis smiled a little thinly, but also he repeated his question.

"I told Mother the truth, and I'll tell you. Nobody else."

"I'm glad you will. I—oh, you understand."

Terry nodded. "I was in Tony's one night, pretty tight. I was with Emmons, and he was still more tight." His face twisted into rather a poor imitation of a grin, and he said parenthetically, "I know this is going to sound like something out of a novel about a young boy growing up . . ."

"We're all growing," Denis interrupted, not very originally.

"Yes. Well, Emmons went home after a while, and then I left. I walked down Bourbon, and I knew everybody and everything—which places were right, which were clip joints, which were strictly for tourists. I knew every corner, and every gallery and every inch of iron lace.

"When I turned into Orleans I knew who lived in every house, and whether they were whores, carpenters, painters who didn't paint, everything. It was raining a little, and I almost knew each raindrop individually. And when I got to the apartment—it was empty. It always is empty. So I walked across to —to that window and stood there looking out at the wet slates, and into the Cathedral garden at the statue. I knew it wasn't stone, really—just plaster or painted concrete, or something. All at once I knew I couldn't stay any longer. It . . ."

Denis smiled. "I understand, Terry. There's plenty for you to do here."

"Probably. Denis, I wanted to tell you before, only there was so much to do and I didn't want to upset you."

"That's typical." He took a deep breath. "For once, Terry, I'd like to say something before it's too late."

"You needn't say a word, Denis. I——"

"Yes. We've known each other—it seems like forever. And I don't think I ever told you what it's meant to me. Do you realize that you're the one person in the whole world that has never made a demand on me? I think you're the one really good person in the world—in my world, anyway." He held up his hand. "No, Terry. One thing more. Do you realize that once you even tried to die for me?"

"You don't need——"

"I do need, now. I had to say it." He suddenly reached for the bottle. "For once I'm going to get tight just because I want to." There was something very young in the defiance with which he poured himself a heavy drink and pitched it down undiluted. He shivered, and added, "If you're going to stay in

New York, why don't we share an apartment? Like old times?"

Abruptly Terry got up. This time it was he who stared down into the garden, into which the snow was blowing hard now. The little bronze replica of Michelangelo's David which stood in the end of the garden already had a cap of snow on his head. After a while he turned back to the room.

"No, Denis," he said quietly. "I couldn't. It wouldn't be fair to either of us."

"It would be fair to me."

"No. And for me it would be wrong. I know. Do I have to explain?"

Denis shook his head. "I'd like it—only I know now I can't have everything I'd like. I said once before that I was growing up, and I'm still growing. I wish . . ." and then he stopped with something very like a blush on his face.

"What do you wish?" Terry asked.

"I wish," Denis began again slowly, "that we could make some kind of arrangement so that I could have your help all the time. But it's too much to ask."

"Nothing is too much. You mean as a sort of personal representative, something like that?"

Denis nodded.

"Why is that too much? Of course I'll do it. And don't forget that if 'Louisiana' works out——"

"We'll do another. There's a lot to do." He looked at the clock on the chest, and his manner changed. "Up and at 'em," he added. "We've got six minutes to dress for dinner."

He was a little unsteady as he pushed himself out of his chair. "That last one was a jolt," he declared. "But I'm all right. . . . Maybe after dinner the rest of you could give me a bridge lesson."

"Perhaps," Terry said as he disappeared into his room. He thought that probably in Denis' case the harder the blow, the farther the rebound. And he thought it with a curious kind of pride. This was a toughness that was not altogether integrity, and yet was related. It would be unbearable in one whose gift did not justify it. But Denis' gift did.

31

Leaving Lakeland was not difficult, but leaving Clarissa and the Gordons was. The end came on May Day, at a dinner where bright-eyed, chunky Hans Mayor was the guest of honor, and Denis in the odd position of an elder statesman, retiring in favor of a man who had been his teacher only a dozen years before. There were speeches, mercifully short and happily few. But it was Denis whose duty it was to do the graceful thing, and it was Terry who told him what to say.

Outside the air-conditioned dining room Lakeland already was drying up for the summer. The trees carried leaves, and would for months, but the leaves had lost their elasticity and their green was being overlaid with gray. It was hot and dripping, and men walked slowly to their bus or trolley in the mornings, so as to arrive at business with something like a fresh shirt to their backs. And at night people strolled in pairs and larger unorganized groups, dreading the need to return to their homes.

But at the dinner it was so cool people sneezed until they grew accustomed to the chill, and the waiters brought dishes quickly to escape the broiling kitchens, and lingered longer than usual over the diners, so as to delay their return as much as they could. After dessert those who dared stood along the walls and listened.

After coffee Harry Gordon presented Denis a scroll, and there were several talks. Then Denis rose.

"I have tried all day to think of some appropriate farewell, and have failed," he said. "When I came to Lakeland I found a fine orchestra, in the hands of a splendid manager and a board headed by a man I have grown to love. It is good to leave the orchestra, a better orchestra I hope, in these same capable hands. It is even better to know that I shall be succeeded by the man who should, perhaps, have preceded me. It was Hans Mayor who taught me the things I should know, and when I have learned all he knows I shall be a great conductor, as he is to-day."

And Denis bowed to Hans, honest tears in his eyes, and sat down.

Many times in the summer that followed he wished someone, Terry or someone else, could have made life as simple as his farewell had been. He would see the Gordons and Clarissa often, and even Farrell was in and out of New York occasionally. But now none of these, not even Gus, was able to relieve him of all the thousands of details that must be handled through the long New York summer.

No man, not even a young and tough man such as Denis, could stand up to the Symphony schedule alone. So the guests had to be decided upon—and he insisted that the decision should be his. And each guest wanted to do something sure fire, something that would make an impression out of proportion to the week, or two weeks, of his tenure. And Denis was hardly modest; he, too, wanted his share of the sure things. Four days a week he worked like a galley slave with Terry's help, and three he studied. There were a few week ends out of town, but not too many. These went for the most part to Elisabeth and Claire, with Claire back in the old groove, the perfect friend and no more.

"Louisiana" went into rehearsal in late August, and by that time most of the Symphony work was out of the way. Hour after hour Denis and Terry sat with Josy and Gary Schwab in the theater, fighting like scorpions over small things that nobody dreamed could be important, not even Josy. Whether the male lead should stand facing the ensemble when he sang his first song, or should ignore it and concentrate on the girl opposite him. Whether the ballet in the first act was so long it became a set piece of its own, and forgot its storytelling mission.

Whether the girl who was supposedly lost in the first act should reappear with her chin up, or should look down fearfully. Whether the tune called "Louisiana" should be reprised three or four times, and how the hell could one get those more-than-willing Negroes to have the supple grace of Jerry, Jim and Lee from Larrabee House—a little older, now, and much more stagewise, but still the ones who instinctively knew what Denis was writing the music about. It was Lee, the sweet one of the three whose father was a murderer, who managed it.

"Look you," he said after an hour wasted, "jus' do it like you would if there were no whites around." He smiled, and said, "Excuse me, Denis." And it went better.

As Josy had predicted, there was music to be written almost on scraps of paper toweling; for one thing, a dance was needed for the last act, and again Lee helped. "Why don't you use part of the ballet you did for us out in Lakeland?" he asked—and the music fitted.

But there were smaller things far more annoying. Shag, who was the male lead, found he could not possibly make it from one side of the stage to the other, behind the scenes, in the time the music gave him—so three more measures had to be written in. And Shag's mother, who represented the older generation accustomed to yield under pressure, was perfect in every way except that she was a night-club singer who had shouted away her top tones, which made it necessary for Denis to change the melody of her three songs so she might keep a civil larynx in her throat. There were dozens of little changes, and when the company entrained for Boston, Denis at first refused to go.

"It's impossible," he said coldly to Josy. "Let's forget the whole thing."

"And all those people I got two hundred grand out of? What about them?"

"Give them back what's left."

Josy laughed. "You're new at this sort of thing. You'll be surprised." He turned to Terry. "It's your job to see that Denis checks into the Ritz tomorrow morning." And Terry nodded.

Denis did check in. And for a week still more changes were made, after the curtain and before morning rehearsal. The reviews helped—they said the idea was new and dangerous, and that there was work to be done, but that the show had an indescribable something about it that held the audience. This was true and did not trouble Denis; it was Josy's time to worry.

"I wish, darling," he said to Terry, "they'd lay off the 'new and dangerous' line. The customers won't like it."

Still, there were more than enough customers for two weeks, and when the company jumped to Philadelphia for the final seven days before New York, a few fingers had been uncrossed. "Louisiana" opened in Philadelphia on a Thursday night, which was the same night Denis led his first concert as conductor of the orchestra for which he had given all of himself for nearly all his adult life. Almost all of himself. It was a great night, and it proved to Denis that whatever happened in other fields, this was what he could do best and always would do.

He had wanted to give up his trademark for once, insisting that the public was bored with his always playing as his own soloist on opening night. Gus, recovered entirely from the shock of last January, had flatly refused to consider the change.

"Nobody but you could do it," he declared, "and you're going to. You're going to give them absolutely everything there is in you, and anything else you can find lying around."

Denis grinned. "All right," he capitulated. "The fourth Beethoven, then."

"Good boy." Gus scratched his head. "Don't forget that the damned Board wasn't unanimous when they gave you the call."

"All I ever wanted was the job, Gus," Denis said. "I'm not afraid from here on."

And now, waiting alone in his room, Denis was still not afraid —not even tired, in spite of commuting back and forth from Boston for rehearsals. He quietly forced everything from his mind but the first page of the "Egmont" overture; nothing existed for him but the orchestra and the music, and perhaps even the orchestra was forgotten. It was a superb group, and he did not need to worry about it.

Gus tapped on the door, and Denis touched his arm as he

passed him. "For luck," he said, although he did not mean it. There was no luck in this, for Denis.

He did not see the little group in the wings; he hardly saw the audience or heard the burst of applause as he quickly crossed to the podium, long baton in his right hand, and made his curt little bow. His arm went up—and the feeling he first had had in Dallas came back to him. There was absolutely nothing in his mind but the music as it poured out; that and a sense of oneness with the hundred and ten men before him. When the overture ended, he bowed first to the orchestra as always, turned to the audience, left the stage. He was still so absorbed in what had happened that if Gus had not turned him around and urged him back toward the stage, he might not have returned at all.

Then the piano was pushed out, and the same thing happened for different reasons. After he had finished he returned to bow many times. He could see Elisabeth and Claire with Terry; Trilling; a few others. Mostly the audience remained merely clay which he could mold, but responsive clay. When at the end "Daphnis and Chloe" had risen to its last miraculous height, he could hear the sudden exhalation of three thousand people which preceded the shouts and the applause. At last he returned to the conductor's room, now full of people. His exaltation suddenly disappeared; he thought, Damn, they've got in and I can't change my shirt. He thought, too, that this was part of what he had worked for and he had no regrets for the past, and no fear for the future.

Elisabeth had asked a good many people for supper, and even that Denis did not mind. He was too busy to mind anything, answering congratulations that sounded all alike with half sentences which also sounded all alike. Nothing seemed to reach him, although no one would have guessed, until at midnight he had a call from Josy. He took the call in Elisabeth's small sitting room, thinking as he ran up the stair that incredible as it might have seemed to those in the drawing room, he actually had not thought of "Louisiana" for six whole hours.

Josy was in agony. Everything had gone wrong. The lighting

425

schedule was confused, and Shag was blacked out at the beginning of his best song. Lee slipped and turned his ankle and barely was able to finish the first act. Part of the last act set went astray someplace between Boston and Philadelphia and a cabin had to be improvised at the last possible moment. Even the orchestra had had an off night, not to mention the conductor, who could not have missed more cues if he had been stony drunk. Lastly, a few reviewers and a parcel of those people willing to make a hundred-and-eighty-mile round trip to get the jump on their friends had gone to Philadelphia for the opening. And had caught the last train back to New York audibly arguing whether the show would ever be brought to Broadway.

"I've got a concert this afternoon," Denis snapped, "but I'll get the five thirty and take a look myself. Maybe Terry can leave earlier."

"All right, Baby, but cross your fingers again."

The company was shattered, but very game. They had worked all day, and by any normal schedule should have gone to bed at dinnertime. Instead, they snatched a hurried meal in the neighborhood coffeepots, and were back in costume on time. They faced a distinctly cool audience this time, after the morning reviews had taken "Louisiana" to pieces. But they worked for and at it. They did everything their tired brains could dream up to make things go. They did go, at least some better.

Later Josy turned his tired smile on Denis. "It's because the gang honestly wants the idea to go over, I think," he remarked. "Before they were just doing a job; now it's becoming a kind of crusade."

All day Saturday it was the same story, plus a matinee to play. That morning Denis caught an early train for New York, and had breakfast on the way; he went directly to rehearsal from Pennsylvania Station and worked until a quarter after twelve, when he popped into a cab, and caught the twelve thirty back to Philadelphia and the matinee. It went better still, but something that should have been there was absent, and slowly Josy was being convinced of the fact. The production sounded well prepared rather than spontaneous, Denis thought; either it should be still more routine until what happened seemed inevitable because it actually was inevitable, or something must be changed.

After the matinee he disappeared with Terry into the Bellevue-Stratford bar.

"Let's stand at the bar," Terry said. "I've been sitting all afternoon and my rear's tired."

Denis agreed, and they edged their way between the customers, a good many of whom were in uniform even then. Terry felt a nudge in his lower ribs, and turned to see whose fault it was. He saw a pharmacist's mate first class in the tightest uniform possible; without a zipper the blouse could never have been entered, or once on, could never have been shed.

"Hey," the boy said, "isn't that Denis Sandzen?"

Denis overheard and frowned impatiently, but Terry nodded.

"I saw his show," said the pharmacist's mate, "and I've heard him conduct, too. He's great."

This was too much for Terry, who asked the boy's name.

"Glen Rhodes," he replied. And Terry introduced him to Denis. Glen was not overpowered.

"I play pretty good piano myself," he announced. "Only I enlisted. Mrs. McKee didn't like it much."

So this is one of Elisabeth's protégés, Denis thought. He confessed his own connection with her, and bought another drink. They had three drinks, and with each the newcomer relaxed more.

"Gosh," Rhodes declared, "it's wonderful to talk shop. All the guys on the ship care about's food and Nellie Lutcher—not that she's not good of her kind."

With the fourth drink, Rhodes received the courage to do what he had wanted to do from the first. Somewhat too elaborately he set his rye and water on the bar, and turned full on Denis.

" 'S none of my business," he began, "but I've got a criticism of your show. The music's wonderful, and so's the idea. But the orchestra sounds too, well, sophisti . . . s'phisticated for Negroes down in Louisiana. It's too—well—too symphonic."

The light dawned. Denis beamed on his critic. "Wonderful," he almost shouted. "You're absolutely right. What about the tunes?"

Rhodes replied solemnly, "They're perfect—no, they really are. But they're dressed up too much for my taste."

Denis turned to Terry. "Score paper—where do you suppose I can get some? Quite a lot."

"There's a big bundle around the theater somewhere, unless Josy's thrown it out. I'll go see."

The sailor looked eager about something, and yet he seemed shy about saying more. Finally, after Terry had gone, he spoke. "You know, Denis, I'm a little tight right now, but after I get some food I can help. You'll have a hell of a lot of copying to do, and I'm damn good at it."

Denis smiled. "You're a terribly good egg, Rhodes. But you've probably got a date or something."

"No. I was just looking around the bar to see what might turn up."

"Fine. Come up to my rooms, and we'll order some food. Then we'll get to work."

Terry was back with a bundle of score paper in twenty minutes. "Found it in the trash can, but it's clean," he said.

The three of them ate a quick supper, and ordered in two card tables, pens, ink, erasers. Then they stripped down to their shorts and got to work.

Denis took the original score, page by page, and simplified, rewrote, eliminated needless inner voices. "I'm trying to make it sound as if Louis Moreau Gottschalk wrote it," he explained. "Kind of—oh, naïve."

"That's right," Rhodes agreed, taking a page from Denis and rapidly transferring the revision to a clean sheet.

Then Denis said to Terry without looking up, "Why don't you call Gus and tell him I'll be back in New York in plenty of time for the concert tomorrow? And tell Josy what we're doing?"

"Lucky I've got wide vision," Rhodes muttered, his dark eyes shining with enthusiasm, his close-cropped black hair bristling stiffly above his slender face.

"Why?" asked Terry from his station at the phone.

"I'm having the time of my life, and I want to see everything there is." His pen scratched hard for a minute. "Say—you suppose I could come see you fellows once in a while? I'm being transferred to the Brooklyn Navy Yard in a week or two."

"Would you play for me?" Denis asked.

"Sure would." Then the possibilities of the remark struck him. "You mean that? I'd cut off a finger—well, not a finger; something—for the chance."

"When you know Denis better," Terry interposed quietly, "you'll know that he never asks for something he doesn't want. And he usually gets it."

"I'm your boy." He glanced admiringly at Denis. "When you work, you work, don't you?"

"Um," said Denis, and that was the last sound for another hour. Rhodes could not keep up, for he not only had to copy Denis' changes, but also the rest of the score. When Denis ran ahead a few pages he stopped revising and copied too. Between telephone sessions with Josy, who was at first horrified and then delighted with the goings on, Terry mixed drinks, copied in the lyrics and did odd jobs generally. None of the three had even a vague idea of the time when Josy's trumpet became audible just outside the door.

"Let me in, damn it," he ordered. "I'm in this show, too."

Denis looked up. "Let him in, if he's alone. I don't want any orchestra director snooping around."

Terry peeked around the edge of the door, and opened up. Josy surveyed the scene, asked a couple of questions, and left. At the door he turned back. "You fellows had better knock off; it's after midnight."

"Not me," said Rhodes. "I've got a week-end pass and I'm sticking."

Josy shrugged. "Who's going to copy out the parts?"

Denis would not for the world have admitted that he had not thought that far ahead. He frowned, and said the first thing that came into his head: "We're going to ask the librarian of the Philadelphia Orchestra to line up a crew in the morning. Our dearly beloved orchestra leader can hover over that."

Josy shrugged again. "Okay, darling. Just so it's done." And he closed the door.

The hours passed and nobody much noticed. A short while before dawn Rhodes yawned and remarked almost to himself, "If I could get to the ship, I'd steal a box of benzedrine," and the three took time out to grin at each other. At six Terry went out for coffee, room service being still asleep. At eight breakfast came up, and the waiter nervously set up the table and vanished, being unused to such industry at such an hour. By ten o'clock Denis had made the last change, and again turned to on the copying. By ten o'clock, also, a small crew was at work in a room at the Academy of Music, copying out the parts for the orchestra. And by eleven Denis was shaved and showered and respectable-looking, even though his hands shook and his eyes looked like locomotive headlights seen through heavy smoke. His arm slipped around the sailor's bare shoulder.

"Look, Glen," he said, "there's no way I can thank you for this. You were the outside ear—you know, the only one of us who was able to hear clearly. I couldn't hear the music for the notes."

"Hell. It's nothing. But I got a favor to ask."

"Granted."

"If I call my commanding officer will you tell him what's up and ask him to extend the pass to midnight Monday?"

"Can you reach him?"

"Sure. I know him very well, accent on the very."

It was done. Then Denis looked at Terry with a wide, very tired grin. "There's no show tonight, of course. Get the orchestra ready at eight, and I'll take the first rehearsal. I can get back around six thirty and have dinner with you two."

"You'll kill yourself, Denis," Terry replied. "Remember Dallas."

Glen looked from one to the other of his new friends. "Sure," he said, "it's brutal. Damn brutal. But those parts will have mistakes, and who but Denis knows what's right?"

"Besides, I can sleep a little on the train. You two had better go to bed, too."

Glen laughed. "I'll ask the hotel for a radio, and leave a call.

I'm going to hear your concert on the air." He looked shyly at Denis, already at the door. "You don't mind if I use your bed?"

"My God, no. Don't be foolish."

As Denis closed the door the sailor began shaking his right hand. "Cramped as hell," he remarked to Terry. "Still hold a glass, though."

"Louisiana" opened the following Friday in New York with the usual first-night set in attendance at what rumor had it would be an extremely expensive wake. They had come in whatever clothes they thought most likely to attract attention, even including the newspaper reviewers, who seemed even more studiously than usual to have dressed in what, presumably, they would call working clothes. That is to say, the *Times* wore a dinner jacket; the *Herald Tribune* wore a dark blue business suit; the *New Yorker* might as well have been naked, concealed as it was behind a mustache and a squint, and so on through the list.

At curtain time Josy, who was by now too tired to care what happened, lurked in the too-narrow lobby behind the orchestra seats, greeting innumerable friends who licked their chops and were more or less obviously patronizing, depending on their native instincts. The gentleman who had put up the biggest chunk of the money, which happened to be seventy-five thousand dollars, wore his dinner jacket as if he rather wished he could turn it into a cloak of invisibility. And the others most directly concerned were in a straight line across the middle section of the orchestra: Elisabeth, Claire, Denis, Terry, Gary Schwab, Gus, Moira (with a paradise feather lashed to her head), and of all people a young sailor wearing the device of a pharmacist's mate on his arm. There was considerable speculation about the sailor until Josy explained to someone on the grapevine that he was a pianist supported by Elisabeth's Foundation and had just been transferred to the Brooklyn Navy Yard.

And finally, there were Those People, the people who had rather not see a show at all than to miss an opening, even if they already had made a trip out of town to see it before it had been pruned for Broadway. At least half of them had "connections," and gave not a damn about the production they were to see. They could find out what to say in intermission, and if opinion was too divided then, they could get the word from the morning paper—not that they paid much attention to the reviewers except when talking directly with them, which was seldom. The other half of Those People were the little people who stuck like small slugs to a bare foot. God only knew why they were there, or why most of them had already sat through two other openings this same week.

The very bright ones had whipped open their programs, seen there were two intermissions, and at once knew "Louisiana" was not a "musical." That was about all they learned before the curtain rose and "Louisiana" began. Afterward they learned a great deal, with celerity.

They saw and heard a very simple story about the impact of "now" on "then" in terms of a Negro family living in the Deep South where more of the life could be lived out of doors than inside houses and cabins. Only the brighter people were able to understand by the first intermission that the story was moving forward quite as much through its setting, and dance, and movement and music, as through the dialogue. Or to understand what it was about the tunes, and the way the tunes were presented, which sounded so exactly right; indeed, why the melodies themselves had the feel of something one had known—and had forgotten. They seemed to be born into the minds of the listeners. They could be whistled, and they also could be remembered.

Elisabeth's party dashed quickly up the street and into the Astor in the first intermission, partly for a drink, but mostly to avoid hearing comment. Even so, Denis heard a tall thin man whose face looked as if it had been worn for a shoe say, nasally, "They've certainly worked on it the last week."

In the second intermission, after a lot of sincere applause, Denis overheard this same man say, still nasally, and as if bored beyond endurance with his own idea, "Buzzy—buy everything you can lay your hands on. This turkey's a goddam peacock!"

At the end there were all sorts of shouts for all sorts of people; even the little people were delighted. "Louisiana" had literally everything, and the phonograph company for which Denis had recorded in Lakeland had already telephoned to Bridgeport to increase tenfold the token edition it had pressed, chiefly because an album of the show tunes was useful to butter up Denis, now that he was musical director of the New York Symphony.

When Denis and Terry went backstage with Gary Schwab they took Glen Rhodes with them. And when the last bow came around and people shouted something that could have been "Awful!" but actually was "Author," Denis stepped forward.

"Thank you," he said. "This is a new venture for Mr. Metoyer and myself. We both love you for your enthusiasm —and we wish you would tell us what to call 'Louisiana.' We still don't know."

There was applause, and under cover of it Denis walked quickly to the wings and returned pulling the puzzling young man in the uniform so tight that one could almost see the nipples on his chest. The applause dropped away sharply.

"I'd like you to meet Pharmacist's Mate first class Glen Rhodes," Denis went on. "I'd also like to thank him for the suggestion that made my share of this evening successful. And for working like a dog to help us."

The asbestos went down with a large share of the audience still applauding.

After the congratulations Elisabeth scooped up Terry, Jim, Lee, Ethel Winters, a dozen more of the cast, and marshalled her party. "We ought," she said to Denis, "to sit in Childs or somewhere and wait for the reviews. But we'll go home."

They went in Elisabeth's car and in a small fleet of Carey limousines Stanley had ordered when Elisabeth signaled him as she went back stage. They arrived happily entangled, and trooped up to the great drawing room like children visiting an amusement park for the first time. There was a buffet in the dining room and more champagne than anyone in the group, Josy not excepted, ever had seen in one place before. Jerry, Jim and Lee looked at the bar, and then at Denis.

"Remember the Larrabee House ballet?" Lee asked, "I mean well enough to play it?"

"Sure," said Denis.

"We'd like to dance it before we fill up. Okay?"

Claire, who had overheard, cleared a wide space from the hall through to the piano. The hubbub stopped abruptly, and Denis seated himself before the keyboard; through the archway he could see the boys strip off their shirts. Lee waved, and he began.

Barefoot, and bare to the waist, the three drifted into the room. After a moment their audience forgot it was in Elisabeth's house. Denis saw the bare and dusty old storeroom at Larrabee House, and Terry Metoyer the hard-pounded ground of a Louisiana back yard relieved by a round bed of tumbling red flowers, outlined by a circle of white shells. What the others saw had no connection with the McKee house, or Broadway, or New York itself. Everyone was far away, so far away that it seemed a long time after the three boys finished in their pathetic little huddle on the floor before anyone moved.

"Jesus!" Ethel Winters cried huskily. "Come here you sweet boys so I can kiss you!"

Claire had been leaning on the left side of the piano. She leaned forward and said to Denis, "Don't let me cry. I might, you know."

Without taking his eyes off the three half-naked boys Denis reached for her hand and squeezed it gently.

Then suddenly the party rose in pitch. Glen played and Elisabeth sang and Ethel sang and Josy did Dwight Fiske imitations, and nobody paid much attention to anything but food and drink. One by one the dinner jackets came off; when Denis and Glen began playing the title song from "Louisiana" in dance time, four hands, Claire and Terry Metoyer danced, and Ethel Winters caught up Lee and did something that might possibly be called a dance of their own. When Stanley appeared in the hall bearing a great stack of morning papers, half the group had already forgotten what had brought it together. But it remembered then and there was silence.

There was silence for perhaps thirty seconds, while Josy whipped open the *Times*, and Gary Schwab the *Tribune*; they turned automatically to the proper page. Then Josy trumpeted.

"We're in, darlings!" he shouted. "We'll be running ten years from now—it says so right here!"

In the bedlam papers were torn from Stanley's arms, and the sections which told about the numbers who had registered for the defense of the country, the Japanese advance into Indo-China, the Axis moving into the Balkans, were dropped to the floor from where the servants quickly retrieved them. Everybody kissed everybody else, and it was like New Year's Eve except-ing that nobody sang "Auld Lang Syne." Moira, who had by now detached her feather and lent it to Lee who was being an Indian, shouted through the din to Gus, "At least nobody calls it a folk opera, and that's good."

Gus cupped his hands around Moira's closest ear. "Look at that boy," he shouted back, moving his head in Denis' direction. "He's dog tired, and he doesn't know it."

A half hour later Ethel Winters turned her substantial voice on the cast. "We're going home," she called in her night-club voice. "We've got a show to do tonight."

Slowly the room emptied. This was a new group and a new life to Elisabeth and Claire, but neither showed it as they told their guests good night. Presently there was no one left but the two McKees and Denis and Terry—and Glen.

"I asked Glen to stay," Terry explained.

"Yes," said Glen. "It's nice to know your boss real well in the Navy."

And finally only Denis and Claire were left in the great room. She looked at Denis and her eyes were bright. "Sober enough for another nightcap?" she asked, and he nodded.

She filled two glasses and handed one to him. "To the Iron Man," she said, and drank.

Denis' smile was weary, but it was genuine. "That's not me," he said, "so I can drink, too."

They walked upstairs together; from the third floor they could hear Terry's laugh, cut off as a door closed.

"I guess I leave you here," Denis said. Then he quickly slipped his arm around her and bent over her lips. For a

435

moment she was stiff in his arms, and then he felt her go slack and her lips soften under his. Neither moved until, her hands on his chest, she gently pushed him away.

"Sorry, Claire," he said humbly.

There was a little smile on her lips, but her eyes were wet. "Sorry?" she whispered. "For what?"

Then she ran quickly down the hall and Denis, his heart pounding, heard another door close.